CHASING HAPPY

JENNI M ROSE

This book is dedicated to:

My husband and constant companion, who barely raises an eyebrow when I google things like how to make a time machine out of a microwave.

My kids, who know their mom is the one in the waiting room of whatever activity they have going on, nose against the laptop, picking away at writing a book.

My sister, my best friend, for always having my back.

My writing partner, Daniella, for telling me when it's good and when it sucks, and always keeping it real.

PROLOGUE

There was a saying about bad things being from the wrong side of the tracks.

The Railroad District was so bad it was like being across the tracks from the wrong side of the tracks. Decades ago, after the trains stopped running through Littlehope, the Railroad District became a ghost town.

The few homes or apartment buildings left in the district stood abandoned, no one wanting to buy them. Companies went out of business or moved to a better part of town. Everything had fallen into disrepair. So much so, even the local motorcycle gang, The Scorpions, had their clubhouse somewhere else. Pimps, dealers, and hookers were the only ones who did business or lived there and every cop within a fifty-mile radius knew it.

It hadn't changed in the few weeks since Butch Hardy had been there last.

Still run down and still depressing as hell.

They drove past newspaper covered storefronts and burned out shells of buildings on their way to pick up a slippery scumbag that was running heroin and girls out of a flophouse in the railroad district.

"How's the Kinsley case coming?" Jim asked.

Butch looked at the deputy driving and let out a frustrated breath. "Same."

He hated that answer but if anyone could understand his frustration it would be Jim. Butch had known Jim for years and respected the hell out of him. As a Deputy for the county, Jim always tried talking him into switching departments but he wouldn't leave the police department.

Jim kept quiet for a minute. "There are some we never get, Butchy. Some slip through our fingers and some we never even come close to catching. It'll eat you alive if you let it. Some cases you just have to leave at the office if you want to survive. This might be one of them, kid."

Butch nodded, knowing the older investigator was right. His wife, Erin, hinted at the same thing but she'd never tell him to let it go. She knew him better than that.

They and a dozen other cruisers convened around the corner from their suspected target and formed two small lines. They filed around either side of the small house, the windows all boarded up. A television blared through the walls, loud male laughter and the distinct sounds of a woman having sex wafted around them. Butch, as instructed, went in with Jim at the front, ready to clear each room.

They breached the door with a loud bang, the sound out of place in the quiet day, as were the screams and shouts that followed. He entered, gun drawn, scanning the dilapidated kitchen for threats. Two sheriffs rushed past him, removing two screaming hookers while he and Jim moved to the next room.

Breaching the room created chaos. There were at least ten sheriffs, a handful of women and two large men all in one room. The men shouted and Butch wasn't sure if they were shouting at the women or the police. He assisted in cuffing and removing both men, neither of which were small or willing.

"Happy!" one woman wailed as Jim cuffed her and dragged her out of the room. "Happy!"

Butch spotted an unopened door and stepped around a coffee

table littered with booze, cigarette butts, and heroin. Needles, all used, scattered across its surface.

"Lot of sharps over here. Be careful," Butch warned the others.

Hand on the doorknob, he turned his head.

To take stock of everyone else in the room, to look at the table again he wasn't sure. That's when he saw her, on the floor, crouched next to the coffee table. She stared up at him as if awaiting his next move. She looked to be about four and her eyes, even from a short distance were unlike anything he'd ever seen, the right eye as clear as the Caribbean ocean, the left half the same clear blue but the entire bottom half was black as night.

"Jim," Butch called, firm yet quiet as to not startle the child. Her eyes shifted away from him for a split second but came right back. When he caught Jim's body out of the corner of his eye he spoke. "I've got a door here I haven't checked but ran into a little situation. Have someone come get this room?"

Jim, brows drawn, peered around the coffee table and got a glimpse of her. She was so small, in just the right position he could have missed seeing her entirely.

"You got it," Jim answered.

When the other investigator took his place, Butch stepped toward the child. Her eyes tracked him but she didn't move a muscle otherwise. He could tell she'd been in that spot for some time. A newspaper sat in front of her and she had a pencil in her hand. There were a few stray pens on the coffee table next to her, mixed in with small pouches of heroin and needles.

"Hey there," Butch murmured, squatting a few feet away from her. "I'm Detective Hardy. What's your name?"

She watched him for a few seconds before answering. "Where are you taking my mom?"

Butch shook his head in disgust. He and his wife Erin had been trying to get pregnant for a few years. Sometimes, it struck the wrong chord with him that people who would love and care for a baby weren't able to have them, but people like this child's mother could.

"She'll have to go down to the sheriff's office. So will you."

She tilted her head then, her mismatched eyes widening, pupils dilating slightly. For a moment, Butch wondered if she might be having a seizure or if she'd gotten into the drugs around her, but when he reached out to her she focused and pulled out of his reach.

"Okay," she answered, as though the moment hadn't happened.

～

BUTCH SAT at his desk processing paperwork for the sheriff's raid, and waiting on child protective services. The little brown haired girl was sitting in a chair across from him swinging her skinny little legs back and forth. She hadn't said a word on the ride to the station despite being asked multiple questions.

Besides being found in a crack house, she was rail thin and filthy, but she was also observant, watching everyone and everything around her. She had a habit of closing her tiny hands into fists and scratching her palms, over and over.

"You hungry, kid?" He asked.

She shrugged and continued to look around the room, always watching her surroundings.

"Want to tell me your name yet?"

She never looked at him but he noticed her head stopped moving. She'd stopped scanning the room and was staring at one of the far walls. He looked as well but all he saw was the same old bulletin board.

"What is it? What do you see over there?"

She slid off the chair and walked to the wall, Butch right behind her. The kid climbed onto a chair to get a closer look, then ripped a page off the board, staring intensely at it for a second before turning her face to him.

"I know her."

She thrust the paper at him but he didn't have to look at it to know what it was. He'd put up that flyer of Elaine Kinsley himself.

Elaine was six years old, had red hair and blue eyes. When she'd gone missing two months ago, one of her front teeth had been missing. She stared back at him from the flyer, smiling and happy, looking so innocent.

He sighed, remembering the wounded sound Elizabeth Kinsley made when she realized her baby girl wouldn't be coming home from school. He'd sworn to them he would bring Elaine home and he'd meant every word. He dedicated every spare second he had to the Kinsley case and finding that little girl.

The rest of the department understood his drive to bring the child home. Most pitched in where they could, but the fact was, Elaine's case had gone cold. As lead detective the brunt of the work, after the initial searched failed, fell on him.

"You know her?" He repeated, numb.

"She plays outside with me when we live near the grass."

"The grass?"

"She lives by the grass. I don't have any grass and she lets me come over and play."

There was no way Elaine Kinsley, blue blooded daughter of a prominent lawyer and his country club wife, lived anywhere near the child standing in front of him.

"I don't think so, kid," he told her taking the flyer from her to put it back up. "This little girl is missing."

Lured from the playground at school while the teachers had their backs turned.

"Lainey's not missing," she told him with a shrug. "I know where she is."

Butch's breath caught in his throat. No one knew Elaine's parents called her Lainey. None of the media had that information. It wasn't on any of the flyers. There was no reason for this child to know that detail.

"How do you know her name?" Butch asked, his voice hoarse.

The little waif shrugged. "She told me."

"And she lives where?"

"At the grass."

Butch held his patience in check, reminding himself that this kid was just that. A kid. Not to mention she'd been through her own type of ordeal today. He added on top of that her living conditions for who knows how long and he knew she needed his patience.

"If we ask your mom, would she know where the grass is?" He asked, wanting to choke on the word mom.

She nodded her agreement.

He should have waited for CPS to come and approve speaking with the mother regarding the child, but he didn't. If what the kid said was true, Elaine was alive somewhere. Somewhere in town, no less. He would get her and he would do it today.

Butch settled the kid back at his desk and stormed into the holding area. It stank of stale cigarette smoke and vomit.

"Who's kid is this out here?" He barked.

A dozen sets of glazed eyes watched him but only one sat up straighter, her wrists still cuffed to a bar on the wall. She was a junkie, track marks climbing each of her arms, dressed in a ripped, stained half shirt, and a skirt that couldn't have been more than a few inches of fabric in total.

"I need to see my baby!" She shrieked. "Where's Happy?"

Happy? The poor, sad little urchin's name was Happy?

The woman wailed, begging to see her child

"I'll let you see her if you tell me where it is she's talking about," Butch told her unsure if he meant it or not. "She said you were living somewhere that had no grass but she played with a little girl nearby. Where's that?"

Happy's mother tugged on her cuffs again and sent pleading eyes his way.

"Let me see her and I'll tell you anything you want."

"Tell me where she's talking about."

She huffed and looked away.

"Tell me about the grass. Where the other little girl played," Butch demanded.

The woman turned to glare at him. "There's no other little girl. Happy didn't play with anyone. She's nuts, okay?"

"Tell me." Butch knew she could be telling the truth. He could be pinning his hopes on the word of some junkie's liar daughter, but what else did he have? He kept reminding himself that the kid called Elaine, Lainey. How would she know?

"And you'll let me see her?" The mother asked.

Butch nodded.

"Fine," she sighed. "I was staying at the motel on Beech Street. I saw Happy playing across the street a coupla times, talking to herself like always." She swung her eyes back up at him and sneered. "Lotsa tall grass there."

~

BACK IN THE RAILROAD DISTRICT, Butch was driving his unmarked with the unlikely named Happy in the backseat. She seemed to get more agitated as they got closer to the motel on Beech. Her little foot was shaking back and forth and she was scratching her palm non-stop.

Beech Street was a complete wasteland. He tried to imagine how anyone could raise a child in that kind of neighborhood. Drugs, gangsters, hookers and more seemed to be the status quos, but it made him wonder how many other children lived in this area.

He heard Happy's stomach growl from all the way in the front seat and he kicked himself for never making sure the kid got something to eat.

"You hungry, Happy?" He asked.

She met his gaze in the rear-view mirror. "It's okay."

It was okay that she was hungry or she was okay?

"You want me to stop and get you something to eat?"

"No," she told him, her voice firm.

"We're almost there, okay?"

After another block, he pulled up to the motel in question and let Happy out of the backseat. She pointed at the motel.

"That's where we lived." She then swung her gaze across the street. "That's where Lainey lives."

Butch followed her gaze. He felt his stomach drop and all the hope leave his body. No one was living at that house. It was an old two story home, nothing but a burned-out shell with boarded up windows and doors just like every other building in the district. The grass hadn't been green in a decade, almost more a wheat field.

"Honey, I don't think anyone's living there."

As though she didn't hear him, Happy crossed the street toward the house. She didn't even look before she stepped into the street. Out of pure instinct, Butch trotted after her and grabbed her hand as she crossed.

When she looked up at him he reminded her, "Always look both ways before you cross the road."

She let him hold her hand as she walked right into the grass.

"Lainey," she called. "Are you here?"

She scanned the yard and called out a few more times.

Butch tugged her hand, ready to tell her it was time to head back when she let out a little squeak.

"There you are," she smiled.

Butch looked around and saw no one. He glanced at Happy who obviously thought she was looking at something. He wondered how much damage the drugs had done to her brain or maybe she was nuts, like her mother said.

"C'mon Happy. Time to go," he told her, disappointed.

"No," she pulled his hand with hers. "She's here."

Butch looked around again. "Happy, honey. There's no one here but us."

"This man's been looking for you. I told him you've been here in the grass," the little girl told no one. "Tell her." He felt her tug on his hand.

"Happy," he started

"Tell her," she insisted.

"There's no one here!" He growled. "There's nothing here."

"Lainey's here." Her left eye bore into him, the top crystal blue and the bottom black. "Tell her. About the paper."

Butch pinched the bridge of his nose and pointed his face to the

8

sky. What the hell was he doing here? Talking to thin air with some crazy, junkie's kid? He'd lost it. Gone off the rails somewhere.

"She misses her parents but can't find them."

"Well, they've been looking for her nonstop," he shouted, angry at her for wasting his time. "I don't have time for you to jerk me around, kid. We're going back to the station."

"She wants to know who's taking care of Gizmo."

Butch felt himself still. Gizmo was Elaine Kinsley's kitten. Her very well loved and pampered kitten.

"She wants to know if her mom is mad because she didn't make her bed that day."

"What?" Butch whispered.

"She said it was an accident. She didn't mean to go with that man but she couldn't hear what he said, so she leaned closer and then he grabbed her arm." Happy looked up at him, her face pale, sweat leaving trails of dirt down the sides of her temples. "She said it was black for a while and then she woke up here."

Butch looked around, desperate, but still saw nothing.

How could Happy know about Lainey's cat or her unmade bed? How could she know about the man that snatched Lainey?

"Where is she, Happy?" He asked. "I don't see anything."

"Are they mad?" Happy asked.

"Is who mad?"

"Her parents," she explained. "She's afraid they're mad."

"No," he breathed. "They just want her back. They're not mad." He turned himself from Happy and spoke to the air. "They love you so much Elaine. They aren't mad. They just miss you like crazy. Gizmo misses you too, I just saw him last week. Your mother was having a fit because he got outside and was sleeping on her porch swing." He rubbed his face again and muttered, "What am I doing?"

"This way." Happy picked her way through the grass and pulled him along behind her. They trudged around the side of the abandoned house, gray with age and boarded up tighter than a drum. She pulled him past the back door, into the back yard and across what used to be a stone pathway. He could feel the hard concrete of it beneath his feet even if he couldn't see it. When they approached an overgrown laurel hedge, Happy stopped.

"In there," she whispered as she slowly raised her hand and pointed.

Butch scanned the area before letting Happy's hand go and drawing his weapon. He slowly approached the thick overgrown hedge, filled with vines, so choked it was impossible to see what was on the other side. As he got closer, he noticed a small break in the plant and something dingy hiding inside. Using his sleeve to push the plant back he realized it was an appliance of some kind, a refrigerator or possibly freezer. He put his gun away and approached again, finding the top hinge of the chest freezer and breaking the seal.

He knew then, before lifting the lid, there was something dead inside. The smell permeated the air around him as he pressed on and looked inside, seeing what was clearly Elaine Kinsley's personalized LL Bean backpack. The rest of the freezer's contents were human remains, decomposed and rotting. Dropping the lid, he covered his mouth and turned back to Happy.

"Holy shit," he breathed, blinking the tears out of his eyes.

If someone had asked him that morning if he believed in ghosts or spirits or psychics, he would have answered with an unequivocal, absolutely not. Yet there was no other way to explain what he saw after he found Lainey's remains.

Happy stood there, where he'd left her, holding Elaine Kinsley's hand. The missing girl was vague, not there, but clear as a bell and wearing the same clothes she'd been wearing the day she went missing. She and Happy looked at each other before Elaine turned to smile at him. She said something he couldn't hear and before he could blink she disappeared and Happy was on the ground.

He ran to her, finding her freezing cold, pale, and bleeding from her nose.

"Happy!" He called.

Her eyes blinked open, for a second and then closed again.

"She's gone," the little girl mumbled. "Saw her Gramma and left."

"Stay with me, Happy."

Butch groped for something to press against her bleeding nose but came up empty. In the end, he used the tail of his shirt, her head resting on his lap while he groped for his radio to call in the discovery of Elaine's body and an ambulance for Happy.

Happy's mother had been wrong. She wasn't nuts.

She was some kind of psychic.

1

———

Rosie Knight never thought she'd find joy cleaning toilet bowls. Sure, it wasn't a joyous occasion, and it didn't exactly put a smile on her face, but she found a certain soothing appeal to the whole thing. She had a nice routine when cleaning a bathroom and found the repetition and reward of it relaxing.

Most days at least. Today, however, was not one of those happy, peaceful days. Today was one of those days where her boss's harpy grandmother followed her from room to room criticizing the job she was doing.

"Oh, that spray smells terrible, Dear."

"That glass cleaner leaves streaks. We'll have to talk to Wendy about changing brands."

"You should use a different vacuum when you're cleaning Berber."

The litany of critiques was never ending. Not unkind, just never ending. Headphones helped. Rosie found herself, on days such as this, wearing her headphones often.

She'd been lucky to find this job. Being an unskilled worker complicated things enough. Add in being an introvert and job prospects seem nonexistent. But nighttime housekeeping with hours she liked to keep, not interacting with customers and half decent money sounded too good to be true. But it hadn't been. It had been real, and she'd somehow gotten the job.

Except her perfect job came with her boss's pushy grandma.

Most weeks she worked overtime and for the first time, she experienced having enough money to spare. It felt good to be secure and comfortable providing for herself. She'd been on her own since she was sixteen, and some of those seven years had not been easy.

Living in a cute little Florida beach town, with a steady income made life seem almost simple.

Most days.

"I don't think the cleaner you're using on the bathroom counter is doing enough disinfecting." Mrs. Murphy made another note on the obnoxious clip board she was constantly carrying around.

"You should go see what Marta's using," Rosie mumbled. It was nearing midnight, she and Mrs. Murphy in the law offices of the Jacob's Beach Professional Building. Marta, one of the other maids, was on the sixth floor working on the accounting firm.

"That girl doesn't' speak any English!" Mrs. Murphy complained.

"I know," Rosie laughed. "You guys would get along great."

"Funny," the older woman chuckled. "Listen, Rosie-,"

Rosie stood up from the toilet and gave it one last flush, interrupting the woman.

"No," she told her when the noise died down. When the woman opened her mouth to speak again, Rosie repeated herself. "No. Absolutely not. Not gonna happen."

With a huff, Mrs. Murphy wandered out of the room, passing through the wall as if it wasn't there.

Nearly done for the night, Rosie and Marta had one more office to clean together. If only she could get through the rest of her shift without another Grandma Murphy sighting.

She wondered what the chances were that would happen.

~

THE NEXT EVENING, she went into the Murphy Maid's office down-town to double check her schedule, gather supplies and catch a ride to the office they were cleaning that night.

She'd just grabbed her schedule from the main office and was heading out when she bumped into Lisa, the office manager.

Rosie took an immediate step back. Then contemplated taking another. When Lisa was near, Rosie's instincts screamed at her to stay back, and as much as she hated them sometimes, Rosie had learned to trust her instincts.

Then there was the dream she'd had.

"I see you've got your schedule," Lisa said.

She said it in a normal, business like tone. There was nothing Rosie could pinpoint or voice that didn't make her sound crazy. Nothing that could explain the way she felt around Lisa.

There was just something off.

"I did, thank you," Rosie replied, her lips stiff. She let out a breath when Lisa walked away.

"Hey girl!" Wendy popped out of her office. "How's it going?"

"Good. How's it going with you?"

"Well." She drew the word out. Rosie knew, from experience, her boss had something up her sleeve.

"Oh God, what now?" Rosie covered her eyes.

"Hey!" Wendy protested. "It's not bad."

"Last time you said that, we drove a hundred miles to some convention that didn't have anything to do with housekeeping."

Wendy rolled her eyes. "Okay, so that was my fault, but this isn't that. Besides, that trip turned out great. You found that little shop that makes the eco-friendly cleaners. It's my best seller."

"Okay, what is it now?" Rosie asked.

"I've got a few really great business clients that want their homes done too. I was thinking you could move to days and clean while they're at the office and I can hire some other night maids."

"Wendy-"

"I know, we've talked about this. You like the night shift. You don't drive. You don't really want to have to interact with a lot of people." Rosie nodded because she had, many times over, repeated her love of the night shift to Wendy.

"But, just hear me out. You're the best I've got."

"No," Rosie argued.

"Yes," Wendy laughed. "You don't argue when your boss tells you you're their best employee. You're great at the job, you're thorough, you're meticulous. But that's not all I want you for."

"Oh crap. There's more?" Rosie put her hands on the sides of her face, faking a scream.

"Jeez, you make it out like I'm putting you in front of the firing squad," Wendy joked. "Come into my office and we'll talk more about it."

Rosie looked around, catching a glimpse of Marta moving around the storage room.

"I really don't have time right now." She took a step back. "Marta and I are headed downtown. Maybe later?"

Wendy consulted her watch. "Tonight's your short night, right?"

"Yeah." Rosie held in a wince. Of course, Wendy would remember that. "We're done around ten."

"I'll go downtown and we'll meet when you're done."

Rosie laughed. "Wendy, I'm in my scrubs."

"I know you have a change of clothes in your bag. You always do."

Her face heated.

"C'mon," Wendy laughed. "What's the big deal?"

The big deal was that Rosie hated being in public. Too many people, too many conversations all going on at once and too many people noticing her. Her hair stood out, such a distinct silver white, people couldn't help but stare. If they happened to catch her eyes, they never looked away.

That was saying nothing about spirits that lingered in certain places or followed people around. Nothing about auras that weaved their way into her personal space.

Avoiding crowded places had just become a habit. One she enjoyed.

"No big deal," she lied, knowing she couldn't say no forever. "Just tell me where and I'll be there."

∼

"I THINK NOW'S the time, dear," Grandma Murphy repeated for the hundredth time.

Rosie's head was throbbing, the woman's repeated requests and the consequent music blaring through her headphones catching up with her.

"Wendy's such a smart girl. It's so important she know everything. How can she reach her full potential if she doesn't know the truth?"

"It's none of my business."

"It's time to make it your business," the spirit argued.

Rosie scrubbed and scrubbed. She just wanted to be home and alone, so she did her job and tried to ignore everything around her. She emptied trashcans, which in an office building you wouldn't think would be gross but that just wasn't true. She couldn't count the number of used condoms she'd seen in office trash cans.

Trash, counters, windows, mirrors, toilets. She did them all. Meticulously.

"Miss Rosa!" The shout came from behind her and Rosie jumped a mile, holding her heart in her chest.

Grandma Murphy was nowhere to be seen.

"I'm sorry, Miss Rosa, I finished downstairs." Marta was standing in the doorway looking like a deer in the headlights.

"Oh my God, Marta, you scared the crap out of me!" When the initial shock wore off, Rosie laughed. "Let's lock up. You can head back without me."

"I will drive you," Marta said.

"Not tonight," she explained.

Marta smiled like she knew a secret, "Ah, you meeting someone."

"Yeah, I'm meeting someone."

"You have a boyfriend," Marta assumed.

Rosie wanted to laugh. Having anyone in her life was the last thing she wanted, let alone a boyfriend.

She'd learned long ago that nothing lasted. Not family, not friends, not anything. Money and health came and went. Homes and cars, stability could be wiped out with the wind.

Family and friends? Well, they went even faster.

2

─────────

Rosie walked the three blocks to a bar that was jam packed with twenty-somethings, all with drinks in their hands. She'd never gotten into the bar scene but she could see where it would be fun. She watched through the glass as girls her age laughed and flirted, all of them having animated conversations and enjoying themselves.

When she opened the door, she got blasted with a wave of noise, her skin prickling with awareness of the people around her. Their auras melded together, swirling around her and creating a buzz inside her head that made her temples pound. The can lights were so bright her eyes burned and she wondered how she'd ever be able to carry on a conversation.

"Hey! There you are." Wendy appeared and pulled her into the bar.

"I grabbed a table. I thought I'd see when you got here. Sorry."

Rosie let herself be pulled to a high-top table, Wendy sitting across from her. "You look great. How do you always look so great?"

"I clean toilets for a living," Rosie replied, narrowing her eyes at Wendy. "I'm sure I don't even come close to great. Are you trying to butter me up?"

Wendy waved the comment away. "Have you ever been here?"

"No," she replied. Wendy had to have known without asking.

"I think now's a great time to just lay the cards out on the table." Rosie looked to the seat next to her and held in an eye-roll.

Grandma Murphy.

The woman was relentless.

A group of women behind them burst out laughing, the noise deafening and joyous. All Rosie felt was seething jealousy. When she turned to look she realized it was a bachelorette party, and although they were all smiling, someone in that group was not happy. Rosie's head swam with spite and hate, an angry red aura cloud surrounding her.

"Rosie?" Wendy asked. "You okay? All of a sudden you don't look so good. You're sweating and pale."

The care and concern coming from Wendy was nearly enough to overpower the group behind her but the red just kept creeping in.

"It's okay," Rosie told her.

The waiter appeared at the table then, a man in a shirt and tie smiling and saying all the right things. A muted grey energy surrounded his body, his sadness creeping up the back of Rosie's neck, like bugs trapped under her skin. Even after he walked away, she noticed a black spot emanating from his midsection.

She knew what it meant.

He was sick. She wondered if he knew.

"Oh, Rosie, you're bleeding." Wendy jumped up and moved to her side of the table.

She'd known it was a possibility. It wasn't the first time being in a large crowd affected her and it wouldn't be the last. Quickly grabbing her napkin and pressing it to her nose she waved Wendy away.

"It's okay. I'm alright. Sit down."

"C'mon. It's not okay. We're leaving."

"No, I'm fine. It's just a bloody nose."

Eventually, her boss sat opposite her, but looked like she might jump up and drag her out of the bar at any moment.

"What the hell is going on?" Wendy asked.

"You're the one who invited me here. What's going on with you? What did you want to talk about?"

"Yeah, right," Wendy scowled. "Like I'd ever let it go that easily."

When piqued, Wendy was rabidly determined. Rosie had always intended to keep her home in Jacob's Beach private, but when Wendy found out she'd been walking home at night, she insisted on seeing it to make sure it was a safe walk. She'd even weaseled her way into the camper to take a peek around. Then she'd driven Rosie to a used bike shop and helped her pick out the cutest bike they had.

As Rosie was contemplating telling Wendy what was going on, she felt a shift in the air around her. The sad, sick energy detached itself from her neck and dissipated. The angry red, jealous haze receded and the static buzz in her mind quieted.

She sat up and looked around.

Everything was just as it was before but her personal space wasn't being invaded by auras. She felt...safe.

It was disconcerting.

"Oh, good. Max is here. He can give us a ride to your place. I want you to go home and get some rest."

Wendy started gathering her things while Rosie sat there stunned. She'd never felt such peace inside herself unless she was completely alone. She'd tried, years ago, to manage having other people's feelings and emotions surround her, inside of her, trying to control seeing people and colors that weren't there, that no one else could see. Worse, seeing things that hadn't happened yet that she wasn't able to explain. She'd never gotten the hang of it. Peace was something she'd never achieved on her own.

"There's my generous big sister that promised to buy me a drink."

Rosie lifted her head to see two men standing at their table and quickly looked away. One was a broad blond, her muted senses barely reading anything but the royal blue color of loyalty that surrounded him. The other was shorter but still tall in his own right and was clearly Wendy's brother, the same shade of brown hair on his head with matching caramel eyes. A shiny emerald green aura emanated from his body.

"We're leaving," Wendy told them. "I need you to bring us out to Rosie's place. I had a few glasses of wine and I can't drive."

"What's the big rush?" the tall one asked.

When Rosie looked to Wendy, she found her boss indicating that she, Rosie, was the big rush.

"I told you, I'm fine." And, in the last few minutes, it had strangely become true. She was fine. The noise had disappeared.

Wendy's brother bent to get a closer look at her face, smiling as he inspected the napkin pressed to her nose.

"Still bleeding?" he asked.

She didn't think so, but the chances of her moving the napkin were slim to none. She wasn't looking for friends or a boyfriend by any means, but she wasn't into complete humiliation either.

"It's fine," she answered.

He looked at her for a second longer, still smiling.

"Seems okay." He shrugged and found his way to the seat next to her.

The taller guy sat across from them.

"Are you sure you're okay? You didn't look good for a few seconds there," Wendy asked.

"Stop babying her. If she says she's okay, she's okay."

Rosie could see his hands through the veil of her white hair as he fiddled with a coaster. They were working hands, dirt caked under his fingernails and calluses on the insides of his knuckles.

"You didn't see her, Max," Wendy argued.

They were talking about her like she wasn't even there. Rosie's embarrassment climbed to new heights.

"Do you need, like, medical help?" Rosie looked up at the tall guy who'd offered his help. His head reared back when she caught him in her sights. "Whoa. That's freaky as hell. Is that real?"

"The blood?" she asked.

He leaned forward, inspecting her closely. "No, the eyes. That's crazy. Are those contacts?"

"Don't mind him, he's a clod," the man standing behind him said on a sigh.

Rosie shifted her eyes to look at him. He was a huge lumberjack of a man, with a big Santa belly and a beard to match. No one paid him any attention, and Rosie knew it was because they couldn't see him.

"I hoped his mother would have taught him some tact, but I think he's got more of his father in him. My fault. Comes from my side of the family. He's a good kid, means well."

Dallas looked over his shoulder following her gaze but when he looked back, she was looking at him again.

"Not contacts. Just my eyes."

"Jesus, Dallas, could you be any more rude?" Wendy slapped him on the arm. "By the way, Rosie, this is Dallas and my brother Max. Guys, this is my friend Rosie."

"I've been wondering when we would finally meet the elusive Rosie," Max laughed. "All we ever hear is Rosie this and Rosie that. I thought for sure Wendy would have made you an honorary Murphy by now."

"He was always a sweet boy," Grandma Murphy cooed. "Happy and kind, just the way children are supposed to be. He's a lot like my Harold was."

Rosie took a deep breath. She needed to shut the spirits out, but she'd never quite mastered it. Actually, she'd never even come close. She'd learned a lot about her seeing spirits in her life, including the most important thing. Never touch them, for a number of reasons that included being unconscious and experiencing death just to name a few.

"She didn't tell us about the eyes," Dallas pointed out with a laugh and then brought a hand up to wave around his head. "Or all the hair."

"I'm going to go clean up in the ladies' room. Excuse me," Rosie muttered before beating a hasty retreat.

The walk to the bathroom wasn't long, but she found the closer she got, the louder things became in her head. The auras came back gradually, the itching under her skin persistent. The bathroom was full of women, all chatting and laughing. The energy was loud, but not unmanageable. She waited for a turn at the mirror and checked her nose. The bleeding had indeed stopped, and she wiped at the blood staining her upper lip.

"I love that color," the woman next to her told said in the mirror. She was in her mid-twenties and very attractive, her dark blonde hair in a cute bob. "What shade is it?"

Rosie inspected herself in the mirror and looked away. "It's just the color my hair is."

"Seriously. I would kill for that color."

"Yeah," she feigned agreement and walked away, at least satisfied she wasn't covered in blood.

The fact was, her hair used to be brown. The memory of getting her first French braid and staring at herself in the mirror afterwards, her dark hair clean and shiny, fixed to perfection had stayed with her for more years than she'd ever imagined it would.

Seven years ago, everything had changed.

Though it had been a gradual change, taking about a month, she'd gone from brown to white, her eyelashes and brows changing too.

It had been just one of many changes that happened in those few months. Being the least stress inducing, she'd never given it much thought. She'd been too busy trying to survive everything else.

She made her way back to the table, that sense of calm settling over her, the silence unsettling.

"Well, she's the best I've got. I can't imagine finding better."

"And here she is."

"Blood free?" Max asked.

Rosie looked at him and blushed, which was the most ridiculous reaction to the question he'd asked.

Playing it off, she answered, "Blood free and completely mortified, thank you all very much."

Dallas laughed, seemingly the type of person who took most things in stride.

"Where are you from, Rosie Knight, Wendy's BFF?"

All three of them watched her, waiting for her answer.

"Originally? Massachusetts."

"What brought you to Florida?"

She shrugged. "No snow?"

"I think I'd like snow," Wendy mused. "I can picture living in a house, looking out at a front yard covered in snow."

"Yeah, then imagine shoveling the walkway and trudging down the sidewalk on glare ice while it's below zero. Trust me, this is better."

"Is your family back there? In Massachusetts?" Dallas continued.

"Yeah." The lie fell off her tongue easily. She'd found that the second you tell people you don't have any family, they immediately peg you as a charity case. The sympathy rolls off them in waves. She'd taken to just telling people her family lived elsewhere. "Guess they like the cold," she said.

"They must like to come visit here, though."

"We'll see. I haven't been here long, so there hasn't been much time."

"You heading back home for the holidays?"

She tilted her head and tried to read is aura, to figure out what his intentions were, but found nothing other than idle curiosity.

"What's with the third degree?" She asked with a small smile.

He chuckled. "I already know everything about these two." He waved his hand at Wendy and Max. "And I'm a cop, so I'm curious by nature."

Rosie kept her expression steady, smile firmly fixed in place. She wouldn't let the fact that he was a cop trip her up.

"Ah," she said. "My parents are traveling for the holidays and won't be around," she lied again. "I'll be here."

"Traveling to visit other family?"

"No." She drew out the word. "Just traveling."

"Okay, okay," Wendy laughed. "That's enough Inspector Gadget. I actually wanted to talk shop with Rosie while we were here but then you two crashed our party."

"You know," Rosie stood and slung her bag over her shoulder. "I actually have to get back home. So maybe we can catch up tomorrow."

"I hope tomorrow you're going to tell my poor granddaughter what the hell is going on!" Mrs. Murphy scolded from behind Wendy.

"How do you think you're getting home?" Wendy asked with a laugh.

Rosie smiled. She really did like her boss. She might even consider her a friend if she were living a different life. If she was someone that could let people in. What was that saying? Fool me once, shame on you. Fool me twice, shame on me? Rosie had been fooled too many times. Fooled into trusting people and caring about them only to have them all betray her in the end. Unfortunately, no matter how caring or fun Wendy was, Rosie just didn't have it in her to let anyone else in.

Rosie waved off Wendy's concern. "I'm just gonna walk. It's a nice night and I could use the fresh air."

Even Dallas argued then. "That's crazy. Me or Max can give you a ride."

Max went so far as to stand up as if to join her.

She held up both hands, almost warding them all off.

"Please. No. You guys stay. Have a good time."

"I really don't mind," Max told her quietly, his emerald aura sparkling.

"I do. Mind," she clarified. "I'm okay. I've got it."

Wendy rolled her eyes but accepted that Rosie had made up her mind. "We'll talk tomorrow."

"Sounds good."

"Tell Gizmo I said hi."

Rosie waved and said a quick good bye before disappearing in the crowd.

❧

"Who's Gizmo?" Max asked his sister.

"Her cat," Wendy said.

3

The lady might as well have been singing Henry the VIII over and over again. Three days had passed since seeing Wendy at the bar and Rosie hadn't seen her boss since. Their schedules just hadn't allowed it, although she could admit part of it might have been on purpose.

It was Saturday, one of her days off, and she'd slept in. Full nights of sleep were rare, so she took advantage. She'd picked up her camper a little, not that it had been messy. She changed the sheets, folded some laundry, and put away dishes to pass the time. She sat outside on her makeshift patio, which consisted of a few stray Adirondack chairs and some string lights hanging around the door of the camper.

She'd fallen in love with the trailer the second she'd seen it. A few miles from town, it was well away from the hustle of downtown and the beach's tourism but close enough she could easily get to town on the bus. Surrounded by woods and trees, there wasn't a single soul around. It was on the small side, but it suited she and Gizmo just fine.

Currently, they were both sitting on the patio, she in a chair with

Gizmo on her lap. She sat, enjoying not just the quiet of her surroundings but the quiet in her mind.

A few years ago, there'd been an incident. One that changed not just her hair color but her abilities as well. Auras that used to look like hints of color floating around a person were suddenly Technicolor and huge like clouds. They moved and undulated, creeping into her personal space. Spirits that used to appear once in a while became her regular companions, and her girlish dreams, the ones of youth and hope, died. Often, her sleep was like a movie reel, playing things that already happened but sometimes it showed what had yet to be.

The quiet didn't help with her dreams, but it did with the rest.

Most of the time.

"Don't you care about her? Don't you care that her entire future is at stake?"

They'd been over this numerous times.

"It's not my place, Mrs. Murphy," she sighed, running her fingers through Gizmo's fur. He responded by purring loudly and rubbing his head into her chest.

"Not your place. She thinks you're her friend," the old woman harrumphed. "Some friend."

"I'm her employee."

"You're her friend, dear, whether you like it or not."

"She's my boss. Simple as that. Why don't you tell her?" She turned her head to smile at the woman.

"Oh, you think you're funny, don't you?" Her gray hair, expertly coifed in a bun, her pink skirt set pressed to perfection, Rosie wondered if that was how she was buried.

She knew it was. She didn't know how she knew, she just did.

"I didn't choose you, you know. If someone had given me the choice of all the people on earth that could hear my afterlife pleas, I would have chosen someone who cared to hear them. What good are you? Half the time you aren't even listening to me!"

"I didn't choose this either, you know," Rosie told her quietly. "This isn't exactly what I wanted to be when I grew up."

Honestly, she couldn't remember ever wishing to be anything when she grew up. No dreams of becoming a teacher or a pilot. She'd always taken life as it came, never having the luxury of wishes. Besides, wishes never made things come true. They just made you hurt more when they didn't.

"I'll just keep bothering you until you do it. It's imperative. She's too trusting. She'll never know if you don't tell her." The woman's head popped up. "Such a sweet boy."

Then she disappeared.

Rosie turned her head and saw Wendy's small electric car creeping up the driveway. She watched from behind her sunglasses wondering what Wendy was up to. Then it dawned on her, they'd never had the conversation Wendy wanted to have.

The little car stopped, and when the door opened, Wendy's brother, Max, unfolded himself from the seat. He was taller than she remembered, and she didn't know if it was because she was sitting or he'd gotten out of a tiny car. Handsome, in that boy-next-door model way, he was easy to look at. His brown hair was cropped close to his head on the sides but longer on top, his caramel eyes crinkled when he smiled.

"Hey," he greeted as if he hadn't just shown up at her house with no warning.

Her brows drew down. "Hey. What brings you out this way?"

Before he could shut the car door, a big dog jumped out and danced around his feet, wagging its tail, its tongue lolling out the side of its mouth. Gizmo opened one eye and immediately dismissed the dog as a threat.

"My sister." He shrugged. "She sent me to fetch you."

"Fetch me?" She narrowed her eyes behind her sunglasses.

"Pick you up and bring you to her place," he corrected. "Sorry."

His dog sniffed the ground and trotted off toward the woods. Max casually walked over and sat in a chair, an end table between them.

"Is this where you walked to the other night? Hell of a hike in the middle of the night." He was leaning back in his chair as if he didn't have a care in the world.

"I rode my bike." She pointed to the adorable powder blue rig with a basket on the front. "It's not a bad ride."

"Dark as hell, though. I live not far from here, actually," he told her. "You have any flashing lights on that thing?"

"You sound like your sister," she said. "She's always bugging me about checking the tire pressure and my brakes."

He chuckled. "Wendy's a mother hen."

"Yes, she is."

Gizmo stood on her lap and stretched, then jumped to Max's as though he did it all the time. Max laughed again and scratched the cat behind his ears.

"Is this the famous Gizmo?"

"I didn't realize he was famous."

"The other night," he clarified. "Wendy told you to say hi to Gizmo. Where'd you come up with the name? Big Gremlins fan?"

"An old friend of mine named him."

He nodded and continued stroking the cat. "He's a pretty cool guy, huh?"

Rosie wasn't sure if he was talking to her or Gizmo.

"What is it you were sent to fetch me for? What does Wendy have up her sleeve now?"

"She's elbow deep in some big dinner she's concocting for you. Didn't have time to come steal you herself so she sent me." He shrugged. "That's what big sisters do. Boss their little brothers around."

She'd almost had a baby brother once, years ago. She'd almost been a big sister. Even at seven, she'd been excited about the prospect of having a family.

"Strange," she mused. "I wonder how she knew I didn't already have big plans for my Saturday night."

"It does seem presumptuous, doesn't it?" he agreed. "I'm happy to tell her you're busy." He looked around at the peaceful woods surrounding them. "Maybe I'll just call her and we can hang out here."

"Now you're assuming I don't have big plans."

He hummed his agreement but didn't say anything, just sat there petting Gizmo. Rosie turned her attention to Max's dog for a few minutes. It had come out of the woods, hot on the heels of a toad that was lazily hopping through a clearing. She looked from the dog to Max and then back again. She'd never encountered an animal spirit guide before. She wondered if Max ever felt the dog's presence around him.

"What's out there?" Max's voice broke in quietly.

She turned her head back to him. "Huh?"

"You're staring in that direction. I just wondered what you were looking at."

"Oh, just a toad. In that clearing." She pointed her finger to show him.

"How the hell?" His ringing cell phone interrupted his question. "Wendy, I'm sure."

She tuned out their conversation, not wanting to intrude. Her attention back on the dog as she idly wondered what its name was and how old it had been when it died. Why was it still with Max, and how long it had been there? She leaned forward and rested her chin on her hand, watching the dog lose interest in the toad and roll in dirt.

"Rosie," Max's voice was loud.

"Huh?" She turned to look at him.

"Sorry, I said your name a couple times."

"Spaced out, I guess. What did Wendy say?"

"She told us to move our asses and get to her place before she ruins dinner."

She stood. "Let me get my bag."

"Want me to put the cat inside?"

Rosie pushed her sunglasses to rest on top of her head and made a few smooching noises. The cat jumped off Max's lap and went inside, Rosie right behind him. She threw a few things inside her bag and stepped out.

"I don't suppose there's any room to put my bike," she said after locking up.

31

He looked from the bike to the car. "I don't think so, but, don't worry about it. Like I said, I don't live far from here. I'll swing you home whenever you're ready."

~

ROSIE WAS quiet on the three-mile drive to his sister's house. She turned her attention to the passing scenery, and he did his best to act cool, fearing he might startle her with any sudden moves. While Rosie didn't appear to be the type of girl who was shy or afraid to speak her mind, she had an air of uneasiness that gave her the 'flight risk" vibe. Like, if she got spooked she'd be gone before he could blink.

Don't ask too many questions, he told himself. Definitely no questions about living in the middle of nowhere all alone with no car.

When he'd stopped by his sister's place earlier in the afternoon to deliver a bag of fresh produce, she'd begged him to run out to Rosie's place to pick her up. Wendy said she'd tried to call, but Rosie hadn't answered the phone. He'd half-heartedly told her he needed to get back to the farm but Wendy had patiently listened and told him to do it, anyway.

He'd tried to pinpoint what it was about her that intrigued him so much. Was it the way she'd laughed at Dallas's interrogation or the blush that stained her cheeks when she'd come back from the bathroom? He liked the way she'd just owned it and admitted her embarrassment. But there had been a look that crossed her face, some shadow that entered her eyes when she raised her hands and held them off from giving her a ride. It had just come across as bleak and he'd felt an ache in his chest for her.

Yesterday, he'd found himself on his hands and knees, tilling next year's herb garden when he stared at the sky and compared the color to Rosie's eyes. Yesterday's sky was too blue, her eyes more crystal-like but he'd keep watching to see if he found a color that compared. He couldn't stop thinking about the bottom half of her eye, completely black and mesmerizing, and her long, whitish silver hair, wavy and all over the place. Without knowing her, he could tell Rosie wasn't a woman that primped in front of the mirror, trying to be perfect, but somehow, she just was.

The girl was wearing combat boots for heaven's sake. You don't get much more low-maintenance than that. Flannel shirt, skinny jeans, she might have been the poster child for casual. He was a jeans and t-shirt guy himself. Running a garden made work boots and jeans his go-to style every day of the week.

"You're quiet," she said as they pulled onto his sister's street.

"Just following your lead," he explained.

She didn't answer, just looked back out the window. When they got to Wendy's condo, he opened the door, letting himself right in.

"Hey," he called out. "We're here."

"Come on in!" Wendy's shout came from around the corner.

He sat himself at the island while Rosie made her way to Wendy almost warily.

"What in the world is all this?" she whispered to his sister.

Wendy's face was beaming with pride, but Rosie's was a cross between shock and horror. He hoped like hell this wasn't about to blow up in his sister's face.

"Well," Wendy said in that long drawn out way of hers. "You never told me you were from Massachusetts before, that stuff wasn't on your resume. So, I thought I'd make you dinner featuring? You guessed it, food from Massachusetts." At Rosie's bewildered expression, Wendy forged on with a smile. "Boston baked beans, something called a Boston boiled dinner, which is just corned beef and cabbage. That takes a long time, so I got us pastrami and coleslaw, plus I made cranberry sauce and homemade clam chowder."

Rosie just stood, staring between Wendy, the pots bubbling on the stove and the table set for three.

"You..." She stammered.

Wendy laughed again, but Max wasn't feeling the humor. Rosie looked like she was ready to make a beeline for the door.

"I made you dinner. Come on, let's eat."

"Why?" Rosie whispered.

"To see you happy." Wendy shrugged. "Are you?"

"Am I what?"

"Happy?"

~

BUTCH HAD THOUGHT *she was just a little kid. He'd seemed surprised when she told him she was almost seven. After three weeks in three different foster homes, he'd shown up asking if she'd want to go home with him to live with him and his wife.*

She hadn't told him she missed her mom, and he'd never asked. Happy didn't really want a new family, she just wanted her old one back. At least with her mom, she knew what to expect. The last few weeks, there'd been so many people wanting different things all the time. In one house, she was always supposed to take her dirty dishes to the sink. In another, she wasn't allowed to touch the real dishes, let alone eat off them. In another, they ate frozen meals that came with their own plates. In one, she was supposed to shower in the morning and another at night. One of the houses had six other kids and some of them were mean. Really mean. When she had been staying there, she'd been too afraid to sleep at night.

"Come on, Happy." Butch knelt down so he was looking right at her. "You'd have your own room. There are no other kids, just me and Erin. The school is right down the block. You could ride a bike."

"I don't know how to ride a bike," she told him.

Butch coughed into his hand and looked away for a second before turning back to her. "I'll teach you, kid."

"I don't have a bike anyways."

"We'll get you one," he promised.

She took a deep breath. "What happens when my mom gets out of jail?"

"We'll cross that bridge when we come to it. But, until then, if you want, you can come live with us."

"What if you decide you don't like me? Will you send me back?"

Butch held her skinny shoulders. "We'll never send you back, Happy. You'll always have a home with us. I promise."

"Why?"

"We just want to see you happy."

~

"ROSIE?" The voice broke in and Rosie shook off the memory.

"I'm sorry." She held up a hand and looked around. "Of course I'm happy. This is too much, Wendy. You're too much."

She pushed Butch and Erin Hardy as far away as possible and concentrated on the here and now.

Wendy let out a breath and held her chest. "You scared me for a second."

"I'm sorry." Rosie forced a laugh. "This is just too much. I can't believe you did all this."

She sat at the table and tried to let the camaraderie of the funky dinner and friendly people ease her mind. Things were mostly quiet in her world, save the one obnoxious elderly spirit that nagged the ever-loving shit out of her.

Through pastrami, coleslaw and beans the woman harped on her. Through chowder and cranberry sauce, she nagged.

"I can't believe you did all this," Rosie told Wendy.

"I can't either. Why would she bother with someone who so obviously doesn't care about her?"

"I didn't mind," Wendy said at the same time, muddling both comments. "It was actually kind of fun."

"Do you have any idea how hard she worked to build her company? Her reputation?"

"I think shucking the clams was the hardest."

"I told her to buy frozen," Max said.

"Years of work and you'll let it all go down the drain. For what?"

"I think living up north would be fun. What kind of food do people think of when you say Florida?"

"Seafood," Rosie answered.

"Blue crab," Wendy ventured.

"Oranges," Rosie added.

"I love oranges," Max admitted. "Grapefruit too."

"Alligator." Wendy and Max both looked at her skeptically. "What? You've both lived here your whole lives. Don't tell me you haven't tried alligator."

"Never," Wendy laughed. "There's a line, and that's over it."

"Yeah, I'm with her," Max chuckled.

Rosie shrugged. "Tastes like chicken."

"Tastes like deceit. Betrayal. Humiliation. Financial ruin."

She mentally rolled her eyes as Wendy and Max laughed.

"Let me clean up. You did all the cooking." She stood and began collecting plates.

"No." Wendy waved her away. "No. I invited you, I'll deal with cleanup later. For now, we have coffee and Boston Cream Pie."

"Coffee and lies, is more like it," Grandma grouched.

Rosie sat quietly while Wendy brought pie and coffee to the table.

"You okay?" Max asked, his voice low.

She turned and found his green aura pulsing with pink. Pink could represent love, but it also denoted sincerity and friendship.

"Yeah, why?" she asked.

He quirked his mouth in a way that drew her attention. She had to pull her eyes away.

"You have this thing," he waved in the general direction of her forehead, "going on here that screams stress."

"Stress," Grandma Murphy repeated indignantly. "It's guilt, honey. Don't let that pretty face fool you."

"I'm fine, thanks." She took another deep breath and tried to let some of the bad energy go.

"You say that a lot, you know," he remarked. "That you're fine."

"Fine and dandy, letting her best friend go on living a lie. How do you live with yourself? How do you sleep at night?"

"Pie!" Wendy sang as she set the pastry down.

"No wonder you're all alone. Is this how you cared for your family? Did you leave them all to fail while you went on like nothing was wrong?"

When she held out her mug, her hand shook too much for

Wendy to get any coffee in it. Without a word, Max reached out and put his hand over hers, steadying her.

"What's that? Is your conscience getting to you?"

"I've never made a cream pie before," Wendy and her grandmother spoke at the same time.

"What a waste, making a pie for her," Grandma said as Rosie wiped the sweat off her upper lip, her hand still shaking.

"Remember the pie Mom and Dad tried to make a few years ago?" Max asked Wendy.

"What a disaster. Remember smiling through the whole thing, even though it was so awful we could barely swallow it?"

"Disaster. That's what you're leading her to."

"I've never made a pie before," she told them, her voice wobbling. "Is it a lot of work?"

Again, the women spoke at the same time.

"The crust is the most work, but I was surprised how much went into the pastry cream."

"Not as much work as building a company and losing it all because of one selfish employee."

That was it, Rosie decided. She couldn't do it anymore. The old hag was right. As much as she tried to distance herself from Wendy and say she was only her boss, that wasn't quite the truth. She cared for Wendy, even if she didn't have any plans to let the woman into her life. She cared enough that Wendy deserved to hear the truth.

"Tell her, Rosie. Tell her the truth."

Rosie looked at Max and Wendy, hating to break the mood but having to tell the truth. Even knowing telling the truth never gained her anything in life. If anything, it had been the opposite, the truth taking everything from her. Over and over again, the truth had done nothing but destroy her, but Wendy deserved more.

"Lisa's been stealing from you," she blurted.

4

She'd had the dream after her second night at Murphy Maids, the day she met Lisa, Wendy's office manager.

In the dream, she walked down the hall at work, talking to Wendy when Lisa stepped out of her office, dressed in black and white horizontal stripes, wearing a black mask like a thief. Lisa asked a few questions about one account and then disappeared back into her office. Rosie woke, knowing there was something going on with Lisa. Oftentimes, her dreams were indecipherable or took weeks to work out, but it didn't take a rocket scientist to come to the conclusion that Lisa was stealing somehow.

That had been months ago.

It was like she'd turned the volume off, Max and Wendy sitting there, just staring at her.

"Thank you, dear," Grandma Murphy sighed.

"Wait? What?" Max asked, his handsome face contorted in confusion.

Wendy was staring at her. "She what?"

"I think..." Rosie rubbed her face, trying to articulate what she wanted to say.

"You know," Mrs. Murphy corrected. "You and I both know."

"Lisa's been stealing money from the business."

"How?" Wendy asked, sounding dazed. "When?" After a second, she added. "How do you know? How did I miss it? I check the books all the time."

All their attention was on her, and Rosie tried not to avert her eyes in shame.

"A while ago, I had to go back and check an invoice I'd left at the Leland and Brown office. Their office manager asked me some random question about the check number they wrote or something, so when I got back to the office I checked their file for the invoice. But when I checked, it wasn't there."

"What do you mean, it wasn't there?" Max asked. "Like, it wasn't in the file?"

"There was no record of the invoice at all. The only reason I had the invoice number was because their office manager gave me a copy of it. She thought I'd be able to tell her the check number and she could fix her records. But I couldn't find the invoice."

"What does that have to do with Lisa?" Wendy asked. "She goes over the books with me step by step, every month."

"You did tell me last month something wasn't adding up. That you thought with more clients, you'd be making more money."

"Yeah, but I assumed it was more supplies being used and more staff eating up the money." They both looked back at her.

"I've dropped one invoice a week off at Leland and Brown, but in the file, it looks like we only bill them biweekly."

"Maybe she filed them somewhere else." Wendy sounded hopeful. "Maybe we just don't understand her filing system."

It got worse. Embarrassed, Rosie hesitated to tell Wendy how sure she was that Lisa had been stealing, because she hated for them to see what an awful person she was. She didn't want to hurt Wendy. She'd never wish her business to fail or for her to get caught up in something like this, but more than any of that, she was always looking out for herself. She'd learned that getting involved backfired on a person, every time. Telling the truth had only ever hurt her. It had come back to bite her every time.

"The office manager for Leland Brown made me copies of their checks eventually, when I told her I couldn't find the invoices. She found her check numbers, but I couldn't find the invoices. She was really nice about the whole thing."

"How long ago was this?" Max asked.

Rosie took a deep breath, knowing how this was going to play out. "A month."

Wendy reared back as though she'd been slapped. "Why didn't you come to me sooner?"

She didn't have an explanation that would appease her boss, her reasons completely self-serving. She held up her hands in a gesture that screamed, I don't know. "I didn't think it was my business."

"It was my business! How could you not tell me?"

"I'm sorry."

"But what about the money?" Max asked. "Where's the money going? If there are no invoices to Leland Brown in our records, what happens to the checks when they pay?"

She had to do this. She just had to tell them the truth and get the hell out of there.

"She deposits them into her own bank account."

Wendy lost it then, standing from the table, knocking the mugs over and sending coffee cascading across the table. Max tried to steady her. Rosie stood and took a step away.

"I can't believe it," Wendy ranted. "I can't believe she did this to me. I trusted her. And the bank isn't supposed to..." She turned her narrowed eyes to Rosie. "I trusted you. I can't believe you didn't tell me. All this time." She threw her hands out. "I'm so stupid. I thought we were friends."

Max grabbed her arm then. "Don't," he told her. "Don't say things you're going to regret. Let's get to the bottom of this thing with Lisa first, then you can figure everything else out. I'll take you over to the office and we'll go over things with a fine-tooth comb."

"I wouldn't even know where to start." Wendy angrily swiped a tear that leaked out of the corner of her eye.

"We'll figure it out," Max told her confidently.

"You should start by checking the schedules for the last few months and making sure all the invoices for all the jobs are there."

"I think you've helped enough, Rosie." Wendy was furious, and she had every right to be.

Knowing she didn't belong there anymore, Rosie dismissed herself from the table and made a hasty exit, and neither of them tried to stop her. When she was outside, she walked around the corner of Wendy's building and waited. Five minutes later, she watched as Max led Wendy to her car and they drove away.

"I'm sorry that turned out the way it did, dear." Mrs. Murphy sounded sad. "She needed to know. I'm sure she'll come around."

Rosie shrugged. "Doesn't matter." She pushed herself from the shadow she was hiding in and headed back to Wendy's door.

"What are you doing?" Grandma Murphy asked.

"Cleaning up the mess Wendy made cooking dinner. Seems like the least I can do, doesn't it?"

"This wasn't your fault, Rosie," the older woman told her as she searched for Wendy's spare key. She found it hidden under a plant.

She shrugged again as she unlocked the door. "It doesn't really matter whose fault it is, does it?" she asked. "I tried to tell you. The truth's never done me any favors. I don't see why it would change now."

She let herself into Wendy's apartment, which she realized was a complete violation. But Wendy had gone out of her way to do something nice for her and she'd ruined it. The least she could do was clean up some of the physical mess she'd made.

~

IT ALWAYS SURPRISED Rosie how dark it could be at night. The dark you experience when you're in your home with your eyes closed isn't the same as the all-encompassing dark of night.

Rosie had spent two hours scrubbing dishes and countertops in Wendy's condo. She'd made sure all the dishes were washed and put away. The leftovers were in Tupperware and in the fridge. The tablecloth Wendy had spilled coffee on was hand-washed and drying in the bathroom. The floors were swept and there was no trace of the ill-fated dinner other than the smell that lingered in the air.

She'd taken the seven forty-five bus the two miles to her stop and was walking the remaining mile to the camper. Mrs. Murphy had disappeared shortly after she'd started cleaning, Rosie assumed to watch over Wendy and Max at the office.

What would she do now? Would she have to get a new job? Would she have to move to a new town? Get a new name? That seemed extreme, though it wasn't completely far-fetched.

It was the betrayed look on Wendy's face that haunted her. The look that screamed 'I thought I knew you better than this.' Was this what she'd become? Someone who lived every second of her life for self-preservation? Someone who couldn't be trusted to protect anyone but herself? She shook her head in the darkness. That was what she'd learned. How did you unlearn lessons that had been drilled into you over and over again?

She didn't even know why she was thinking along those lines. Why would she change? Because she wanted to be friends with Wendy and Max? Friends betrayed you. Friends left you. Friends died. What was the point? When she looked back on her life, she couldn't count one single person that had stayed with her. Not her mother, not Butch. Certainly not Erin. She'd changed schools too many times to make real friends, and frankly, she'd been too weird. Kids didn't want to hang out with other kids that talked about ghosts and death all the time, and parents didn't want those kids around either.

She was happy to see the string of lights outside of her camper and trudged her way inside. She didn't bother turning any lights on, just got ready for bed in the dark. She used some wipes to take off the little makeup she wore and changed into a t-shirt and pajama shorts. Nine o'clock was too early for her to go to sleep but being in her own space was calming and she didn't mind just lying there for a while.

She considered what she would do when it was time for her to go to work in a few days. Would she just show up and work her shift as if nothing had happened? As if she hadn't betrayed the one person that had tried to be nice to her. Would she skip out and quit? Try to find a new job in this town? She liked Jacob's Beach, more than anywhere else she'd been in the last few years. Where would she go if she left? How would she get there? What, of her meager possessions, would she be able to bring?

She tossed and turned, trying to ignore the rising tension she felt at the prospect of starting over somewhere new. Maybe, wherever it was, she'd learn to keep her head down and stay out of other people's business. It would have never worked here, she realized. She'd never had a chance. How could she have given Wendy the cold shoulder she would have needed to keep her distance? How could she have acted indifferent toward her? Wendy made being nice too easy, and she wasn't someone that was going to mind her own business. She was going to pry and want to know everything.

Late that night, Rosie fell into a fitful sleep full of dreams that echoed her past. Snippets of her time with Butch and Erin, the looks Erin used to shoot Butch when she talked about the dead. She saw Lainey Kinsley, playing in the grassy yard across the street. Memories flashed of a time with her mom, after the incarceration, dim and terrifying. The dark of the closet, the smell of burning flesh and the haunting sight of her mother's crazed eyes looming above her. But this time, instead of choking the life out of her, her mother spoke.

"She's coming for you, Happy." Her eyes lit up with the kind of glee that only comes with madness. "Better hang on, because she's coming."

Her eyes popped open, and it was all gone. The memories and dreams vanished, and she was back in her sunny little trailer. Gizmo was meowing loudly at the door, ready to make his morning excursion around the woods. She threw the covers back and stood, her hair falling forward across her face. She pushed it back, keeping her forearm above her eyes to block the morning sun, and opened the door to let the cat out.

"Good morning."

She jumped at the sound of a man's voice, letting out a startled scream.

Max stood quickly, holding out his hands. "Sorry. I'm sorry. I thought you saw me."

Without a word she turned to go back into the camper.

"Uh," he said uncertainly. "Are you gonna come back out?"

She sighed, her heart still racing. "Yeah, just give me a sec."

Closing the door behind her, she took a few deep breaths. He'd scared the crap out of her! What was he doing here? Suddenly, she remembered the events of the previous night, and going back out there seemed like a terrible idea. What if he'd come to tell her she was fired?

"You know," she turned and yelled through the door, "I think, on second thought, I'm just gonna stay in here."

"You wanna talk through the door?"

His voice seemed closer, like he was standing on the other side of the door.

"What's there to talk about?" she asked.

"Seriously?" He rapped on the door. "I'll just stay out here until you come out."

"He gets his persistence from me." Grandma Murphy appeared behind her, inside the camper.

"Oh, Jesus," Rosie muttered. "I'll be right out."

She threw a bra and sweatshirt on, then put her hair up. Grabbing her sunglasses, she slid them on and opened the door to face the music.

Max was still standing there, just a few steps from the door, waiting for her while looking casually handsome in the mid-morning sun, his brown hair damp. His eyes, golden in the sun, still smiled at her, even after everything that happened the night before.

"How mad is she?" Rosie asked. Might as well rip the band aid off.

"On a scale of one to ten?" He made a face and flipped his hand over a few times. "I'd give it a six or seven."

"Did she send you to fire me?" She couldn't hold his gaze then.

She crossed her arms over her chest and looked down at her bare feet.

"What? Rosie, No." He sounded genuinely shocked. "No one's firing you. Wendy's not going to fire you."

She wanted to ask why Wendy wouldn't fire her but didn't dare. Seemed too self-loathing, even for her.

"Why'd you come, then?" she asked.

He shrugged. "I felt bad about what happened last night. And even though Wendy's pissed right now, she'd be more pissed if something happened to you and no one bothered to check in with you. I wanted to make sure you got home okay. I told you I'd bring you home, and I didn't. I've been stewing about it all night."

"All good," she assured him, taking a step back. "Thanks for checking." Behind him Gizmo came flying out of the woods like he was being chased by the devil. His meow like something out of a horror movie.

"What in the-" Max mumbled, watching as the cat flew into trailer.

What he didn't see was his big dopey dog, loping after Gizmo like it was having the time of its afterlife.

"Listen, Max. I appreciate you checking in on me. I got home fine," she brushed him off. "I'll see you around."

She turned and took a step back into the camper, but Max grabbed her arm to stop her.

"Wait, that's it?" He laughed.

She turned to face him and he let her go. "Did you want something else?"

He stepped toward her, a move that put him in her personal space as he stood in front of her.

"I brought you coffee." He motioned with his head to the Adirondack chairs. It was hard to look away from his face. She wasn't sure if it was the way he was looking at her or how close he was standing throwing her for a loop. When she looked, she saw there was a coffee cup at each of the chairs. "Come have coffee with me for a minute before I have to go to work." He took a step back and motioned for her to go ahead of him.

She did, and they both settled into the same chairs they'd sat in just yesterday. Before everything went to shit.

"Why didn't you tell her?" Max asked.

She sighed, knowing the conversation was inevitable. "Honestly?"

"No lie to me," he joked.

Rosie shrugged. "I didn't think it was my business."

"Why wouldn't it be your business? You guys are friends."

She shrugged again, sure that trying to distinguish between boss and friends was misplaced.

"Wouldn't you want to know if someone was coming here and stealing from you when you weren't around?"

"Listen," she told him. "I get it. I screwed up. I was trying to keep our relationship professional, and when I wasn't paying attention, we became friends. I didn't mean for that to happen." She let out a sigh and dropped her head to the back of the chair. "I didn't mean for any of this to happen."

"It's probably hard for you to understand, but Wendy's worked so hard to get where she is. She's had a few bad relationships, plus this thing with Lisa now and you. Trust is a real issue with her."

Rosie was still stuck on the first part. "Why would it be hard for me to understand how hard she's worked?"

"I just mean," his words faltered.

"What?"

"She's built a business from the ground up. She's worked really hard. That's all."

"That's not what you were going to say," she accused.

He sighed.

She knew what he was trying to tell her. "What you're saying is I wouldn't understand hard work. I get it."

"No." He waved her off. "I'm sure you know how to work hard. I'm just trying to tell you,"

"That Wendy worked harder," she clarified.

He didn't answer.

"Guess you've got me pegged." She stood quickly without looking at him. "It was nice of you to check up on me, but I can take care of myself."

"Rosie," he started to say.

"Thanks for the coffee." Without looking at him again she went into the camper and shut the door, leaving the still steaming cup on the arm of her chair.

It was a few minutes before she heard Max start his truck and go away.

Didn't know what hard work was? She wasn't sure if she wanted to laugh or cry. She'd put on such a good show, Max had no idea who or what she was. He literally had no clue she was just some junkie's crazy kid, born and bred on the streets. She'd started a new life from nothing, not even a set of her own clothes. She bet he had no idea how much hard work that took.

It took her a second to ask herself why she'd want him to see her for who she really was anyway, or why she cared that he'd gotten her all wrong. She was just some kid no one missed. Happy Bancroft was nobody. It would do everyone good to keep it that way.

5

The days at work after her blowout with Wendy were strange. Lisa was gone, but Wendy hadn't explained why, which had all the maids gossiping. She'd heard everything from Wendy and Lisa had been having a secret love affair to Lisa found new job and moved. She'd spied a few men in suits, in and out of Lisa's office and assumed they'd been hired to look into things.

Rosie followed her schedule and stayed out of Wendy's way. Things went smoothly until the day they ran into each other in the hall. Rosie was leaving the storage room at the same time Wendy came out of her office. She'd looked surprised at first but then the anger surfaced and she'd stormed off. After that, Rosie made sure to stock everything she needed before she went home in the morning.

At the end of the week she worked her usual night shift and was riding her bike home, the roads dark but not dangerous. Rosie felt comfortable being on her own. She rounded a corner and standing in front of her was a woman, directly in the path of her bike. Middle-aged with dark hair was all she made out before the woman appeared closer, moving in the blink of an eye. Rosie swerved her bike, even dumped it on purpose to avoid the woman but it was impossible.

Before she could do anything to stop it she slid directly into the woman.

When her bike passed through her, Rosie knew she was in trouble. The woman was dead, a spirit, and Rosie's body was on a collision course with it.

There wasn't time to prepare for being under water. Her lungs burned, there was no air. She was going to die. She felt the grit of sand and pebbles forced down the back of her shirt and neck as she was pressed into the ground. Above, through a shallow layer of water she saw the tallest of trees surrounding her, sunlight filtering through them. She groped with her fingernails, clawing desperately at the hands that held her down by the neck, choking and drowning her. She was going to die. The eyes staring down at her were filled with anger and she could hear his muffled screaming. She kicked her feet, one last surge of energy but his grip never loosened and it wasn't enough. Her fingers still tried to move his hands, but she was too weak. She'd never go willingly, never let him know she gave up. So she kept grabbing at him and kicking her feet. She thrashed as long as she could until her lungs couldn't burn anymore. Until the edges of her world became fuzzy and black. When it came, things were quieter and the water that lapped in her ears was soothing. She let it lull her into the nothingness.

~

DALLAS HUNTER LOVED BEING A COP. He was a puzzle guy, loved to solve problems and get to the bottom of mysteries. He'd never imaged he'd become a police officer. Heck, when he was a kid he was in trouble more often than not but sometimes the cards fell and you got dealt a hand you weren't expecting. At twenty-six, he was the second youngest of all his siblings and just about the most blue collar of them all. A small town cop wasn't exactly what his parent's had dreamt for him but they seemed happy, nonetheless.

He'd grown up in Jacob's Beach and wanted to make sure it stayed the same great town he knew and loved. That's why he took his job so seriously and mentored kids that didn't have good role models. It was why he volunteered at the rec center and coached a basketball team, to make sure every kid had the support to learn who they wanted to be.

He didn't even mind working a night shift once or twice a week. It gave him a chance to see who was out too late and which neighborhoods needed more patrolling. He was driving on the outskirts of town by Max's place, when he spotted something in the road ahead of him. At first, it looked like some kind of white animal but the closer he got, the more his headlights illuminated the scene.

"Oh, shit," he muttered into the dark of his car. He grabbed his radio. "This is twenty-oh-fourteen."

"Go ahead, fourteen," A voice echoed back to him.

He spoke quickly. "I'm out on old highway thirteen by the Murphy Farm and I've got a woman down in the road. I'll be investigating. Requesting an ambulance at this time."

"Ten four, oh-fourteen."

He swung the door open and hurried over.

"Shit. Shit," he swore again when he got close enough to confirm it was Wendy's friend Rosie.

When he'd been close enough, her white hair tipped him off. He knelt and surveyed the scene. There was nothing in the road he could see that would have made her crash but her jeans look like they'd torn clean through at her calf and there was blood on her arm. He didn't dare move her head in case she had a neck injury.

"Rosie," he called her name, trying to get her to come back around. "Rosie. Can you hear me?"

There was blood in her hair and he tried to assess where it came from.

"Come on, Rosie," he said loudly. "Open your eyes. It's Dallas. Remember me?"

She shifted at the sound of his voice and let out a soft moan.

"Don't move, okay," he told her. "An ambulance is on its way."

"I'm okay," she croaked as she lifted her hand to hold her head. "Ow."

"Yeah, ow," he agreed. "Let's let a professional take a look." He grabbed her hand and held it. "I'm going to stay right here with you, okay. I'm not going anywhere."

She turned to face him.

"Don't move around," he told her. "Just in case you have a neck or spine injury."

Rosie looked up at him with eyes so unique and intense. There was a big patch of road rash on her cheek and her nose was bleeding like crazy.

He smiled at her, making sure he didn't freak her out by reacting to her injuries.

"Your nose is bleeding, again. I'm going to get a complex if this keeps happening when we see each other."

She let out a little grunt and brought her free hand to her nose and pinched.

"It happens," she told him simply. "Can I sit up now?"

"No. We're waiting for the ambulance." He could see the red lights approaching. "They're almost here. Want to tell me what happened?"

"Something in the road," she said quietly. "Possum maybe. I'm not sure."

An ambulance pulled up and two EMTs jumped out, ready to work.

"What do we have, Hunter?" One of them asked as he jumped out of the rig, his partner right behind him, already unloading equipment from the back.

"She crashed her bike. I found her here unconscious in the middle of the road."

"Conscious now though." The EMT smiled down at Rosie. "We're gonna take good care of you, okay honey."

"Rosie," Dallas corrected. "Her name's Rosie and she's a friend of mine."

"Hi Rosie," the other EMT said. "I'm just putting a neck brace on." He knelt and got to work.

"Is it possible to die of embarrassment?" Rosie asked, her eyes closed.

He looked at the EMTs and they shared a smile.

"We haven't seen it yet," the first one chuckled.

"Uh, boss. You might want to take a look at this." The one who'd been putting the neck brace on was staring at Rosie.

Dallas watched him pull Rosie's hair aside and gesture to her neck. He'd only ever seen that type of injury in a text book but he knew, without a doubt what the bloody, oozing scratches on Rosie's neck were. They were a classic defensive wound, found most often on victims of choking, after they tried to pry the hands around their neck, off.

"What the fuck is that, Rosie," he asked, dropping to his knees next to her. "Did someone hurt you?"

"Hunter," one of the EMTs warned.

"What is it?" she asked, her forehead crinkled.

"Nothing, honey. Let's get you on the backboard and see if we can't get you cleaned up," the EMT smiled down at her then looked to Dallas. "You mind moving?"

They got her strapped in while he went back to his cruiser. It took a moment to process the scene, her bike on the ground and the long skid mark left in her wake. Must have been one hell of a ride, he thought. It took him a few minutes to start writing his report and draw a diagram of the accident scene.

"Hunter," The EMT trotted toward him.

"What's up?" He met him a few steps away.

"She's insisting on not going to the hospital. Wants to sign whatever waiver she has to."

"Shit," he muttered. Why were some people so goddamn stubborn? The chick was just held dead on the side of the road.

"The pretty ones are always nuts," the medic commented.

"True," he agreed, though he felt no interest in Rosie like that. She was beautiful sure. Nice face, amazing eyes, sexy hair, curvy body, they all made a nice package, but one look at her screamed complicated, and he wasn't interested. Plus, she was Wendy's friend, and he drew a line at one-night stands he'd end up having to see all the time. Been there, done that, not worth it.

When he got to the back of the ambulance, she was sitting up and signing something attached to a clipboard.

"Let them take you to the hospital, Rosie. You might have a concussion."

"I'm sure I do," she told him. "Thank you. All of you. I'm so sorry and I'm so embarrassed, but it's not anything I can't fix up myself."

"She already signed the forms. She's free to go."

The EMT helped her down from the ambulance and walked her to her bike. He talked to her for a minute before walking away and packing up his rig. Dallas hurried to where she was inspecting her now scratched bike.

"Let's put it in the back of the cruiser and I'll drive you home."

"I'm okay." She tried to send him a smile but couldn't quite pull it off, the stark white bandages on her face already turning red. The ambulance doors closed and they pulled away.

"Don't be an idiot. You're hurt and bleeding, and if you say no again, it's just gonna piss me off. I'm putting your bike in the car and I'm bringing you home. Tell me no again and I'll come back when my shift is done and wake you up every hour to check for a concussion."

She watched him for a few seconds. Without asking, he picked up her bag, grabbed the bike out of her hands, and wheeled it to his cruiser. It wasn't overly difficult to pop it in the trunk and tie it shut. He went around and opened the passenger door for her, and she eased herself down slowly into the seat without a word.

She was hurting, for sure.

"Which way?" he asked when he settled in his seat.

She pointed in the direction the cruiser was already facing. He drove not more than a half mile before she directed him down a hidden, narrow dirt road.

"Down here," she pointed.

He took another turn at her direction, and then another. All of them dirt roads, and all of them dark and spooky as hell.

"This one." She pointed to a small mailbox with a shiny, reflective star attached to it.

He turned in the driveway and was surprised to find it was near a quarter-mile long. When he pulled into the small clearing, he saw an old camper, with some string lights and a few chairs outside.

"This is the middle of nowhere," he complained as they got out. "What the hell are you doing living way out here by yourself?"

She shrugged as she took the bike from him after he lifted it out of the trunk.

"I don't mind it. It's quiet," she told him, as if it were the most simple thing in the world. She limped her bike to the side of the camper and propped it up.

"Let's get you inside and cleaned up."

She waved him off. "I'll take care of it. Ice and ibuprofen."

He let out a humorless laugh. "Let me at least see you in, Rosie. Give me some peace of mind after thinking you were dead in the middle of the goddamn road."

~

IT'S NOT A BAD IDEA, she thought as she struggled to stay standing. In case she died or something, which seemed highly possible. She didn't feel like she was bleeding internally or like her neck was broken, but she definitely felt like she'd been hit by a bus or possibly wrecked her bike and oh yeah, experienced a horrifically violent death.

She pushed the incident from her mind and swore to deal with it later. For now, she just had to survive the night.

"Whatever," she told him.

She remembered his aura, even if it was barely a wisp now. He had no bad energies running through him, nothing that screamed serial killer. She felt safe enough with him in the camper for a few minutes, so she took her keys out and unlocked the trailer.

The first step hurt like a bitch, and she made some kind of wounded animal noise.

"You okay?" Dallas asked.

"Just hurts," she forced out. "I'm good."

The camper felt even smaller with another person in it. It was meant for the kitchen table to turn into a bed but at some point her landlord had just built the table in permanently. The bathroom was in the middle of the trailer and that was where she needed to get too. She needed a washcloth and some meds.

"You got any ice in here?" he asked pointing to her tiny fridge/freezer combo.

"A couple frozen water bottles." She shut herself in the bathroom, peeled off the seeping bandages and saw her face in the mirror. Her right cheek was covered in road rash, and there was a huge gash on her forehead. The bloody nose had stained her face with streaks of blood.

"Holy mother-of-pearl," she muttered.

She set to cleaning herself up and washed the blood out of her hair and off her face. The scratches on her neck stood out, and she studiously avoided thinking about them while cleaning and re-bandaging everything else. After she stripped her shirt off, she found her forearm oozing with blood. After that was her pants which was a struggle, the small room combined with the pounding in her head didn't make a great combination.

After a particularly loud bang, Dallas knocked on the door. "You okay."

"Yeah," she said through gritted teeth. "There's a pair of sweatpants on the shelf right behind you. They're gray. Can you toss them on the floor by the door? I'll grab them when I'm done cleaning up."

"Sure you don't need a hand? I swear, I won't look. Totally professional."

She cracked a smile, even if he couldn't see it. "Thanks friend. I'm all set."

She tugged her ruined jeans off and winced. Her calf was raw, like pulp and full of sand. She washed it out as best she could and wrapped a hand towel around it. She'd have to go to a drugstore and get bandages tomorrow. She thought about it for a second and decided maybe the day after would be better.

She pulled the sweatpants through the crack of the door, put them on, and stepped out to find Dallas sitting on the edge of the tiny, built-in couch.

"It doesn't look much better," he told her.

"Thanks." She shook out a few ibuprofen and swallowed them, then pressed a frozen water bottle on her cheek. She pressed another to her neck.

"Want to tell me who the hell strangled you?" he asked, his face neutral.

He was a cop. She shouldn't have been surprised he wouldn't hesitate to ask.

"It's not what you think," she answered.

"That's it?" His laugh had no trace of humor as he stood from the couch. "That's the best you've got?"

She limped away, toward the back of the camper where the bed fit from wall-to-wall. She gingerly sat and wiggled to the head of the bed, wedged between the corner of two walls, Dallas right behind her.

"Yeah," she sighed. "It's all I've got right now. Thanks for seeing me home. It was a nice thing to do for someone you've only met once."

"Yeah, well, you're a friend of Wendy's, so that's good enough for me."

She didn't tell him Wendy hated her guts.

The room fell silent for a few seconds. "Thanks," she said again, hoping he'd get the hint.

"Oh, you think I'm leaving," he said. "Yeah, no. I'll be here, waking you up every hour on the hour."

She wanted to argue, but she didn't have the energy. "Suit yourself," she said, closing her eyes.

6

The day after the accident had been tough. Dallas, as promised, had woken Rosie up numerous times, never pressing for more details about the scratches on her throat. When she woke in the morning, he made coffee and sat with her outside, even bringing her a blanket.

"I'll call Wendy and make sure she comes out to check on you later."

"I wish you wouldn't," she told him, searching for his aura. It struck her that it was nearly gone, nothing more than a wisp of smoky color around him. "I'm not exactly her favorite person right now, and she's got a lot on her plate."

"You guys have a fight or something?"

Turns out, Dallas wasn't the clod she or his grandfather thought he was. Dallas was insightful and easy to talk to. He listened intently and had a way of asking questions that didn't seem invasive.

"Or something," she agreed with a nod.

"Well, I'm sure she isn't so pissed she wouldn't come if she knew what happened."

Rosie knew that, it just wasn't what she wanted. "Just do me a favor and keep this to yourself. I don't want her running out here because she feels sorry for me. I can take care of myself."

Eventually he'd agreed and had gone on his way, though he'd also stopped by twice during the week to check on her, even bringing her a bunch of bandages from the drugstore. He never stayed long enough to get out of his car, just long enough to remind her he was around.

～

ROSIE NOTICED in the days after the accident, things around her felt strange. There were times the back of her neck itched, like someone was watching her or there was another presence with her. When she was outside, it was almost as if the sounds in the woods were turned off, nature muted entirely. No leaves rustled in the trees, no critters moved on the ground.

She went back to work after one day off and even trying to hide the evidence of her accident was no use.

"Ouch, Miss Rosa. That hurt," Marta commented at the end of their shift.

"It's okay. Thanks." She smiled at the other woman.

"You try putting honey on it," the older woman told her, her accent melodic. "Heal fast."

Gross. "Thanks. I'll do that."

Thankfully, her bike had only sustained minor damage during her fall, and she could still ride to and from the bus stop. On her way home that night, she was following her usual route home, being more careful than the last time. She didn't need to worry, because the brown-haired woman appeared in the woods and not in the road.

Rosie pulled over and laid her bike on its side. The woman was standing in a copse of trees about fifty feet off the road, and although it was dark outside, her spirit glowed. She raised her hand and held it out to Rosie.

Yeah, not happening.

"Can I help you with something?" she called to the woman, keeping her distance.

Rosie saw her lips moving, but all that reached her was a warm wind that rustled through the trees, the words lost.

"I can't understand you," she told the woman. "I'm sorry."

Rosie made no mention of the woman's horrific death. She couldn't see that again. She couldn't feel that again.

The woman opened her mouth and let out an angry scream. The wind howled through the surrounding trees and she held a hand up to block the swirling wind. When it passed, the woman was gone.

Uneasy, Rosie made her way home and fixed herself a snack, not quite ready to sleep. All her life people had been telling her she had a gift. She'd asked once if they knew where she could return it. There were times she didn't want spirits wandering into her home or her head uninvited, times when she didn't want their thoughts muddling her own so much she couldn't even think. Her gift had brought nothing but destruction to her life.

She tossed and turned that morning before falling into a dream about the woman in the woods, except this time, she followed when the woman beckoned. She followed through the thick wood and through a small clear stream. Past an outcropping of rocks, covered with bright green moss, and down a steep embankment littered with roots and debris. She skirted what looked like a big clearing, possibly a farm, keeping to the wood line before following the woman down a small dirt path that led to a lake peppered with small tree filled islands. The spirit waded into the water and, without thought, Rosie followed. First rocks under her feet, then sand, soft between her toes. It was a compulsion to follow the spirit, she had to know where the woman was going.

It wasn't until the water hit her chest that Rosie woke. A shocked squeak escaped her lips when she realized where she was. She turned around, searching for the woman but she wasn't there.

Rosie's heart raced. How far into the water would she have gone? How far from home was she?

Intense dreams were a regular occurrence. Scary dreams,

prophetic dreams, confusing dreams were always on the menu but never something that effected her reality so acutely.

At the very least, it made her leery of sleeping for the rest of the week.

～

"I KNOW," Max told his sister again. "Wendy! I've got it."

He was proud of her. She'd shown how much backbone she had since Rosie dropped the bomb at dinner. Wendy had been working nonstop making sure her business would succeed. She'd hired forensic accountants, fired Lisa, and adopted a new filing system that had enough checks and balances she'd know the minute something wasn't right. She'd called the police and was pressing charges against Lisa and suing to get her money back, which the accountants had totaled to over thirty thousand dollars.

He'd mentioned to her more than once that if Rosie had said nothing, she'd have never known, but Wendy wasn't hearing it. She was hurt and angry that someone she trusted had been hiding something from her. He suspected that she'd get over it soon enough and in the meantime he knew Rosie was still showing up for work, if not avoiding Wendy while she was there. Wendy had at least mentioned that much.

"Are you listening?" Wendy's voice sounded in his ear.

"I hear you," he said as he rounded a corner. The roads were wet with rain and the heat was blasting to ward off fog on his windshield. "I'm on my way back to the house, like I told you. Later on, I'm coming to your office so I can help you move equipment around. I've got it. I promise."

"Okay. I just need to make sure you're coming. I can't move the stuff from storage by myself and you're cheap labor."

He rounded a corner and his brow crinkled. There was no mistaking Rosie, her white hair was difficult to miss, but what the hell was she doing? It was freezing, not a day for a walk and certainly not dressed the way she was.

"I gotta go, Wend. I'll see you later." He hung up without hearing her response and pulled up behind Rosie. Jumping out of the pickup he jogged to her, calling her name.

"Rosie."

Her feet were bare and filthy and there was a big brown spot marring her leg. She was walking away from him, almost staggering and she had what looked like a scarf tied around her wrist.

"Rosie," he called again, catching up with her. "What the hell are you doing out here?"

She stopped then but didn't turn around, just looked around, searching.

A chill ran up his spine. She hadn't heard him. She was acting like he wasn't even there.

"Rosie!" He said louder this time, grabbing her arm. When he turned her to face him, her cheek was the first thing he noticed, angry scabs ran from her eye to her jaw.

"Rosie." He touched the uninjured side of her face to get her full attention.

Her head swung around, still searching, those mysterious eyes blind. Her pupils were so big he could barely see any of the blue he'd tried so hard to match.

"There," she whispered and slipped away from his grasp. She hurried off, into the woods, heedless of her bare feet or the branches slapping against her.

There was no way he was letting this happen, he thought to himself. Not a goddamn chance. He reached her in a few long strides and without hesitation grabbed her around the waist, stopping her forward motion. She struggled, reaching for something that wasn't there, her feet moving as though she could walk on air. The crazy part was, he knew she wasn't awake. In her mind, she was somewhere different. Knowing it and experiencing it were two different things.

"I've got you," he murmured as he turned them back toward his truck. "Come on, Rosie. Come back to me."

Her feet were still moving, but she wasn't struggling against him as much.

61

"What the hell were you doing out here?" He asked, knowing she couldn't hear him.

When he finally slogged them out of the wet undergrowth, he put Rosie down enough that her feet touched the ground. Max shifted her so she was facing him and her body shook, though he wasn't sure if it was from the experience or the cold.

"Rosie?" He asked. "You with me?"

He heard her swallow, her hands fisting against his chest. "Yeah. I think so." Her voice was shaky.

"Good. That's good." He reached down and without asking, scooped her up into his arms. He thought she might have protested, but he ignored it. "I'm putting you in my truck."

He slid her in, and she huddled against the seat, holding her knees to her chest. He jogged around to the driver's side and got in, then jammed the truck in gear and took off for his house.

"How're you doing, Rosie?" He asked, looking in her direction.

"I-I-I-I'm oh-oh-okay," she stuttered through her clacking teeth.

Was there ever a time she didn't say she was okay or fine?

"Just hang on, okay. We're almost there. Before you know it, you'll be under ten blankets and sweating."

He'd never taken the corner to his driveway so fast and he pulled right up to the front porch. He carried her up the walk and through the front door. The living room was to his left, and he laid her on the couch, pulling the blanket off the armrest and covering her with it.

"I'll be right back," he told her.

Taking the stairs two at a time, he pulled the down comforter and pillow off his bed then charged back to the living room. He laid the comforter on top of the blanket already covering her and squeezed the pillow behind her head.

"Coffee." The thought struck him, she should drink something warm. "Tea." He looked at her in question.

Her eyes were half lidded but her pupils were back to normal, the black half of her left eye darker than ever.

She shook her head. "I'm sorry," she told him. "I feel so stupid."

He sat on the edge of the couch by her feet. "You scared the crap out of me. What the hell happened to your face?"

She turned, hiding what he'd already seen, making him feel like shit for asking.

"Sorry," he apologized. "I'm not trying to be rude. Did you have an accident or something?"

"Last week," she nodded. "Fell off my bike."

"Some fall," he commented. "Do you sleep walk a lot?" He changed the subject.

"Not usually no, just this week." She shivered and then let out a huge yawn, wincing and pressing a hand to her cheek. "I ended up chest deep in a lake or something."

Max sat up straighter. "You what?"

"It's salt water." She yawned again. "Must be an inlet."

"You sleep walked...into water?"

"Mmhmm," she mumbled her eyes sliding closed.

Max ran his hands through his hair. He'd already felt like crap about blowing her off this past week but between the door she'd slammed in his face and the Wendy situation, he figured it was easier to check in with her when things cooled down. Maybe when she and Wendy made up, or he figured out what he'd said to piss her off so much.

Well, he knew what he said. He'd said something about her not understanding how hard Wendy worked and she'd shut him down. Closed up and locked him out, end of story. Obviously, that was the wrong call. He and Wendy had come from an upper middle-class family and had never struggled financially, but it didn't negate how hard he and Wendy had worked for what they had. Their parents had paid for their educations but they had both started businesses on their own. That was the point he'd been trying to make about Wendy working to make her business run when he'd made the comment about her not understanding.

He'd always thought as he got older, he'd learn more about women. That they'd be magically easier to understand, but they just got more confusing and complicated.

He watched Rosie sleep, contemplating the angry scab on her cheek before pulling out his cell phone.

"Hey," Wendy said when she answered. "Don't tell me you aren't coming."

Max hesitated. Driving into town to move office and cleaning supplies seemed unimportant when compared to staying with Rosie while she slept on the couch.

"Silence? That's your answer?" she screeched.

"No, it's not that," he told her. "I ran into Rosie."

He was greeted with silence. This had been a touchy subject with Wendy.

"And?"

"And I found her wandering down the side of the road, disoriented. She's pretty beat up, says she fell off her bike last week."

"What do you mean, disoriented?" She at least sounded concerned.

"She said she was sleep walking."

"Sleep walking?" Wendy sounded doubtful

"I believe her. She said the last time it happened she woke up chest deep in what I can only assume is Smith's Cove. She's asleep on my couch right now."

"What?" Wendy breathed. She interrupted before he could say another word. "Keep her there. I'm on my way."

He didn't think keeping her there would be a problem, she was out like a light, head back and sleeping deeply. He took the quiet moment to watch her and give himself some small peace of mind that she was okay. Her hair was messy, half out of its pony tail and his gaze homed in on her neck and the handful of vertical white lines, like healed cuts.

What the hell had she been doing this week?

7

Rosie knew, without a shadow of a doubt, where she was. It was hard to forget somewhere you hated with such a passion. The Coleman State Psychiatric Hospital was right at the top of her list.

"I knew you'd be back."

A young man in his early teens, thin and waif-like, wearing hospital issued blue johnny stood next to her.

"Leo. You're still here?"

"Here. There." He gave a careless shrug. "I don't have anywhere else."

She looked around and was struck with memories, reminding her why she hated the place so much. Endless cinderblock walls, long hallways, and faceless orderlies that loved to man handle overmedicated kids.

Leo stepped away and looked out a window.

She remembered the window well. She knew if she looked through the grate she'd see an overgrown garden with a broken fountain. She'd spent endless weeks looking out that window imagining the flowers that could grow there. Like a coloring book she'd add different flowers in every corner, planting a new garden every day.

"She's coming for you," Leo said, turning back to look at her.

She was reminded of the dream she had where her mother said the same thing.

"Who is she?"

He gave her another shrug.

"Someone else already gave me that message," she told him.

"They don't care. You need to hear it again."

"Is it the woman in the woods? The one in the water?"

"No. Someone else. She needs you."

"That's enough Mr. Lincoln." The stern warning sent a chill down Rosie's spine.

Nurse Willet. The meanest of all the nurses to ever walk the halls. A most hateful woman who enjoyed inflicting pain on her charges at the hospital.

She appeared at Leo's side in the blink of an eye.

"Time for your meds kids." Her smile was straight out of a serial killer's handbook, menacing and full of hellish promise. It stretched across her face, farther and farther until it ripped her skin from ear to ear and exposed the meat of her jawbone.

Rosie took two steps back.

"You're not going to leave me here again, are you?" Leo asked, his lips turned down. "Last time you left me here I died."

"I didn't leave you here," Rosie argued weakly, taking another step away. But the truth was, she had left him there and he'd died.

"I didn't have a choice," she corrected.

"She's coming for you," Leo reminded her taking a few steps to follow her.

Rosie backed farther away but for every one of her steps, Leo and Nurse Willet advanced.

"She'll use you all up," Nurse Willet laughed, her jaw nearly unhinging. "You'll be here with us before you know it."

"You're all ready," Leo pointed at her body.

She looked down to see herself dressed in the same blue johnny she'd worn when she'd been a patient at Coleman. Panic hit her hard, sending her into a frenzy, tearing it from her body. She grabbed the front with both hands but it wouldn't come undone, no matter how she tugged and pulled.

Leo looked sad but Nurse Willet laughed, her face a macabre nightmare of bone and flesh.

Claustrophobic and full of panic Rosie pulled as hard as she could and let out a guttural scream.

~

ROSIE WOKE UP SCREAMING, jackknifing off the bed as bright sunlight streamed across her face. She was warm and dry but had no idea where she was, her scream dying in her throat. A quick look around reminded her she was at Max's house. A tall, antique dresser was against the wall by the door, a pile of guy stuff on top, jeans strewn over what was probably a chair in the corner of the room and boots littered the floor.

It took her a second to bring it all back into focus. Her crazy sleep-walking episodes, the woman haunting her from the woods, and Max dragging her to his truck.

Not Coleman.

Heavy footfalls echoed from behind the closed door headed her way in a hurry. The door flew open with a creak and Wendy stood at the door.

"Are you okay?" She quickly glanced around the room.

"Yeah," she replied breathless and feeling silly.

"You scared the crap out of me. You were screaming."

Rosie took stock before answering. "I'm okay. Just a dream." An all too real dream that took her places she never wanted to see again.

Wendy nodded. "Must have been one hell of a nightmare. I feel like whenever I have a nightmare and need to scream I can't." Wendy came and sat on the bed and kept talking, pretending the last few weeks hadn't happened. As if Rosie hadn't betrayed her trust.

"I'm just like, running through the woods with an ax murdered behind me but instead of screaming I'm whimpering."

"I've had those too," Rosie admitted, feeling out of place and guilty as hell.

She started to throw the covers off when the other woman stopped her. "Can we talk?" When she nodded, Wendy took a deep breath and looked down at her hands. "I'm still mad."

"I'm still sorry," Rosie answered without hesitation. "I wish I would have told you sooner. I didn't know how and it wasn't until after I told you, I realized I was too late."

"How could you keep that from me? I thought we were friends." Wendy had on her puppy dog eyes, exuding sadness.

Rosie shook her head thinking it might be time for some honesty. "I didn't want to be your friend."

"Ouch," Wendy muttered, her face turning down.

"I wanted you to just be my boss and keep it professional. That's what I told myself every time I felt guilty, that we weren't friends and I should keep my mouth shut. But when I wasn't looking, we became friends. I don't know how it happened." Rosie felt a very real sense of desperation, totally blindsided by the feeling of connection she felt with Wendy. She'd spent so long actively avoiding relationships and friendships she hadn't even realized she was in one.

"I kept bugging you," Wendy admitted. "I kept talking to you until you finally talked back one day. I knew you were trying to keep your life private."

She nodded pitifully in agreement. "I should have told you sooner. I just didn't realize."

Wendy held her gaze, making their conversation so much more personal. "What's so bad about having friends, Rosie?"

Rosie held out her hand and grabbed Wendy's in her own. "It's not you. I suck at the friend thing and I screw it up every time so I stopped doing it."

Wendy was quiet. "So, we're not friends." It wasn't a question.

"It's too late now! I just figured out I had a friend in the same second I lost her. See how that works for me?"

Rosie felt a Wendy squeeze her hand. "You didn't lose me. I was mad. Still am, but Max called and said you needed me so here I am. That's what friends do."

She thought about Max. "He must think I'm nuts."

Wendy looked thoughtful for a second. "Actually, he looks worried. I had to send him out to do some work this morning because his pacing was driving me nuts." She dropped her voice to a whisper. "I think he likes you."

Rosie threw her a deadpan expression.

"What?" Wendy asked. "He does. I know him. He's feeling the feelings for you."

"That's exactly what I don't need," Rosie told her. When he'd been at her camper a few weeks ago, he was sweet and adorable in a sexy way but she didn't want to feel any feelings, as Wendy put it. It would make it worse if he felt feelings too.

"Well, you didn't want or need me either, but here I am. This is all going to turn out just fine, you'll see. Now, will you tell me what the hell happened to you? I wrestled you into pajamas last night so I know how banged up you are."

She sighed. "I fell off my bike last week. I'm fine, though. It's not a big deal."

"Your leg looks like it's been through a meat grinder. And your poor face, Rosie. That must have been a heck of a fall."

"It was more of a slide," she admitted, avoiding all thoughts of where that slide led her.

There was a knock at the open door and Max stood there. "Did we kiss and make up in here?"

"Shut up," Wendy told him without heat. "Rosie was just telling me about falling off her bike."

"Slide," Rosie corrected again. "It was more of a slide. I was riding home one night and there was something in the road. When I tried to swerve around it, I slid, that's all."

Max came in and sat next to his sister on the bed.

"Thank you, for letting me stay here."

"You must have been crazy tired," he told her. "You've been asleep since yesterday afternoon."

She looked around the room, searching for a clock and climbing out of bed. "Are you kidding me? I had to work last night!"

"Slow your roll, Ace, the boss gave you a few days off," Wendy said, her eyebrows raised. "You want to tell us what happened yesterday?"

"I don't want a few days off," she said, ignoring the question and sliding her feet to the floor. Looking down she realized she was in black sweatpants that hung off her body and a big man sized t-shirt. Max's big dog was lying on the floor at her feet. "Where are my clothes?"

"Wendy washed them," Max said. "Yours were dirty. You know, from walking through the woods half dressed."

She held a hand to her forehead, not needing the reminder. Though her senses were quiet, she felt a little out of control and off balance. Auras remained wisps instead of clouds and other than the dog, her companions from the other side were quiet.

She felt the quiet all the way down to her bones. Often, she picked up thoughts from Wendy, like maybe she wanted to go the carwash or she wanted a pair of shoes she passed by, but today Rosie felt nothing.

There was just quiet.

"I need to get home."

"Come eat breakfast," Wendy started.

"I've got to let Gizmo out," Rosie continued. "And get cleaned up. I'm so sorry about all this."

"I'll give you a ride," Max said, watchful and quiet. He seemed almost somber as he walked out of the room, closing the door behind him.

Rosie felt it important to point out to Wendy, "Definitely not feeling the feelings."

Wendy laughed. "Oh my God, you're so blind. He's like, in a whirlwind of the feelings. He's feeling so many feelings he can barely even see straight."

He was? She had about zero experience with men and feelings so it was possible what Wendy said was true. If it was true, how wise was it for her to let him give her a ride home? If she did let him give her a ride home did that equate to leading him on? She barely knew him, besides thinking he was good looking and sweet. And kind of a white knight, if she thought about him carrying her into his house yesterday.

"It's just a ride, Rosie," Wendy laughed. "You look like you're trying to solve the world's problems."

She didn't dare admit she wanted to get involved with a guy even less than she wanted a friend.

"Let me grab your clothes from the laundry and then Max can give you a ride home. I have to go into the office but I'll swing by to check in on you." She ran out of the room but was back in seconds. "Are you sure you're okay?

"Yeah," she assured Wendy. "I'm fine. Just remembered something I needed to do at home," she lied.

Wendy looked concerned. "Is it something you need help with? I'm sure Max or I can help with anything if you're hurting."

"Wendy, I have a few scrapes. It's no big deal."

"Come on." Out of nowhere Wendy grabbed her hand and pulled her out of the room.

"Wait," Rosie pulled against her. "I have to make the bed."

Wendy waved it off. "Max is a big boy. He can make his own damn bed."

Wendy pulled her down a set of stairs. They looked original to the old farmhouse but updated, a warm, neutral tan color covered the wall above woodwork that had been painted white. At the bottom of the stairs they found Max in the living room, sitting on the couch, his head in his hands.

"She's ready to go home when you are," Wendy chirped.

Suddenly, Rosie felt like she was being thrown to the wolves. Why was Wendy so pushy all of a sudden and why was she shoving Rosie out the door?

Max looked up, exhaustion written all over his face, and she was immediately flushed with guilt.

"Rosie might need a hand with a few things out at her place. I have to head into the office but you said you had a light after-noon," Wendy told her brother.

"Okay." He smiled and though it didn't seem forced, it was dim. It wasn't the same smile he'd sent her when they'd met a few weeks ago.

And why would it be? He'd picked her up wandering down the road like a lunatic. She wanted to slap herself. Why did she care?

Wendy waved from the front door as Max showed Rosie to his truck. They walked down the front steps off a wide porch and onto a gravel driveway. She held her hand up to shield her eyes from the sun and looked around.

"You live on a farm," she breathed, shocked.

"I do," he answered, a smile in his voice.

She pointed to a small fenced in area she could see a corner of where there was hay strewn around. "Does something live in there?"

She looked back at him to find his lips stretched wide, his real smile gracing his face.

"Yeah," he laughed. "Something lives in there."

She began to walk in that direction, wanting to see what it was.

"Slow down there," he grabbed her arm. "You aren't exactly dressed for farm exploration."

She looked down at herself, back in her shorts and wearing a borrowed sweatshirt and a pair of Max's slippers.

"Oh," she muttered, disappointed. "Yeah. Okay."

She turned around and headed back to his truck but was distracted when she caught a glimpse of the fields behind the garage area.

"Oh," she was awestruck. "You grow things too."

"I do," he answered again.

She wanted to go look. She wanted to see everything but didn't dare ask. He was right, she wasn't dressed for it and it wasn't her place. Maybe he didn't want her traipsing all over his farm.

His farm for crying out loud.

Suddenly his aura made complete sense. He was a cultivator. Someone who grew and cared for things, everything from animals to people to relationships would fall under that heading for someone like him. He would feel fulfilled surrounded by people and things he could tend to. He was someone who loved nature and loved to nurture.

Interesting, she thought.

"Rosie," he said quietly, getting her attention.

"Sorry," she said quickly, studiously not looking at the barn with the animals or the obviously well-tended fields. "I'm ready."

They got in the truck and he quickly pointed them toward the road.

"Do you like farms?" He asked, looking over at her.

She told herself it was no big deal sharing a memory with him, the context wouldn't matter but the content did.

"I went to this petting zoo when I was a kid. My," There was a slight hesitation. "uncle took me. There was this duck and I swear to you, it followed me around the whole time I was there. I fell in love with it. It let me pick it up. It ate out of my hands. I wanted to take it home with me so bad." She glanced at him. "They don't let you do that, by the way. Take home their animals. I was devastated."

Max laughed. "Yeah, they kinda make their money on keeping the friendly animals."

"I didn't know you were a farmer."

"I fell into it," he admitted with a shrug. "It just happened to be something I love doing."

"Where are we going?" Rosie sat up as Max took a road that didn't lead to her house.

"Smith's Cove," he told her quietly. "I need you to show me."

"Show you what?" She asked, looking around again.

"Where you went into the water."

She looked at him, panic quickly setting in. "Are you kidding?"

"Do I look like I'm kidding?" He turned his head and she saw that same exhausted, tense look she'd seen back at his house.

"There's nothing to show you, Max. If you've been there before then there's nothing to see."

"I know," his voice was quiet. "But I need you to show me. I need to see it."

73

"Why?" For some reason her bodily instinct was to look for the door handle, as if she might jump out while they were moving.

"I don't know," he said, exasperated. "I can't stop thinking about it." He held the steering wheel with one hand but couldn't keep his other hand from waving around. "I keep imagining you sleep walking like yesterday and heading straight into that water. I keep wondering what happens if you don't wake up or what you aren't telling us and it's driving me crazy. I need to see Smith's Cove and I need to see you there. I need you to show me so I can understand."

He was pulling up to the public parking area, which consisted of about three parking spaces.

"There's nothing to show you, I swear."

His intense need was completely lost on her but being back at the cove terrified her.

"Please, don't make me do this," she begged, remembering nothing more than blindly following the woman from the woods and waking up in the water.

He looked at her then. "I'm not asking you to do anything. Just show me where. That's all."

It was the remnant of his aura that made her get out of the car. His bright and pure emerald green smoke was a grayish black, surrounding him like smoke. Just a thin haze around his head, barely enough that she could see, telling her he was drowning in confusion, genuinely and deeply concerned.

Getting out of the truck, she wrapped her arms around herself and took some slow steps to where the gravel beach began. She pointed toward the shore so Max could see her point of entry.

The cove itself could have been mistaken for a pond it was so well insulated. Surrounded by tall trees and woods it seemed more like something you would find on a mountain camping trip than something on the outskirts of a tourist beach town. Large rocky outcroppings formed a few peninsulas into the water and what small beach area there might have been was peppered with tall grasses.

She held herself tighter as she looked at the water and couldn't help but remember her collision with the woman on the road.

Incredibly strong hands, squeezing her throat and pressing her further into the abyss. Angry eyes, hateful and vile searing into her while the life bled out of her and all the while, the muffled sound of water filled her ears.

Eventually, the water became peaceful. Clear blue and sparkling in the sunlight, lapping back and forth so hypnotically. It was easy to feel at peace under the water.

"There's no peace here."

The water was in her ears and the disembodied voice came directly into her thoughts.

"Help me," the voice came again.

She knew it could only be the woman from the woods. This was her spot.

Eyes wide, Rosie looked to the water but didn't see the woman. She was about to turn around to scan the wood line around her when hands grabbed her by the shoulders. Instinctively, she screamed and tried to defend herself, swinging her arms wildly. The hands gentled and tried to soothe her but she fought. It was then she realized she still heard the water, deafening, the rest of the world silent.

Like she was being held underwater.

8

M ax.
She knew it was Max and stopped fighting. His hands settled around her wrists and he gently pulled her to him. She could feel the vibration of his voice rumble through his chest against her cheek. She closed her eyes but heard nothing.

"There's no peace here," the voice said again so loud Rosie's head felt like it might explode. "Help me. Please."

"Stop it," Rosie muttered to herself. "Stop it."

"Help me. Help Jack." The voice was insistent. Loud and adamant. Demanding.

Rosie still heard nothing of the outside world. Just the woman and the water.

"Help me."

"I can't." Rosie squeezed her eyes closed and pressed her face to Max's chest, her hands covering her ears. "Please, stop."

"Help me. Help Jack. Help me." The voice got louder and louder, giving her no time to recover. There wasn't a moment to gather her wits or regain her strength. The spirit bombarded her with not just her voice but her desperate energy as well. Rosie could feel it pressing in on her. "Help me."

"I can't!" Rosie pulled away from Max and screamed, her breath heaving. "I can't help you! Leave me alone!" She turned herself around, scanning for the spirit in the surrounding area.

Max grabbed her shoulder, but she startled and shook him off. When she turned, he was holding his hands up in a gesture of surrender. His lips were moving, but she still only heard that damn water, rushing through her brain.

"I can't hear you," she told him loudly, panicked.

He was watching her carefully, his brows drawn down and his mouth a straight, serious line. He tried to say something else, but she couldn't hear him. When she heaved a frustrated breath, he grabbed her hand and pulled her quickly to his truck. He opened the door for her and even helped her in before getting in and taking off. The further from the cove they got, the more the rushing water eased.

"Rosie?" The voice was like a whisper.

"Is that you?" she asked him.

He reached across the bench seat, grabbed her hand and squeezed. "Yeah. That's me." His voice was a little louder now. He sent her a small smile, like this chaotic whirlwind hadn't just happened.

That was all he said as he drove to her camper, still hanging on to her hand. She wanted to mind but couldn't bring herself to. His hand was big and warm, comforting while still sending an excited current up her arm.

By the time they reached her place, the water in her head was gone. Max's dog was waiting at her door, Gizmo rolling in the dirt at its feet.

"Looks like Gizmo is out," Max said idly.

She never kept Gizmo out when she left home. She must have let him out when she left yesterday.

Rosie got out of the truck, Max right behind her. She went to unlock her door and found it was already open, leaving her even more off kilter. That was something she never did. For a few different reasons, she kept cash in her camper and was always careful to lock up. She looked inside, just in case someone had come in overnight, but found the coast clear. She grabbed Gizmo's food and water and put them outside, threw on a pair of her own yoga pants and joined Max who was sitting in the outdoor chair looking like he'd been blindsided.

Blindsided by her crazy ass.

She sat in the chair next to him but didn't say anything and just waited for him.

"Are you okay?" he asked after a few minutes.

He wouldn't look at her. That stung, but she didn't expect anything less.

"I'm okay," she assured him. "You don't have to stay."

He glared at her. "You think I'm what? Just going to ditch you here alone after that?"

"You're not ditching me. I'm a big girl. I can take care of myself."

He let out an annoyed breath. "Will you quit it with all that shit already. I'm not buying it."

"Buying what? That I can take care of myself?"

"No." He ran his fingers through his hair in frustration, leaving those top ends standing nearly straight up. "We all get it, you live out here alone, you can take care of yourself. We all know. But Jesus, Rosie..."

"What, Max? It's all true."

"I'm not saying it's not, but give us a chance to at least try to be here for you so you don't always have to do it alone. Give me a chance."

She turned away from him. She'd given people chances before. She'd relied on people and let them all in. Never, in all her life, had that led to something good.

"What's out there?" She turned to find him staring at her. "What's out there at Smith's Cove?"

The truth seemed like a terrible thing to tell him. Did he really want to know something so morbid? Would he even believe her if she told him?

"Rosie?" he prompted.

She shrugged, blowing his question off. "I don't know. The wind must have been really loud in my ears."

She didn't dare look at him after telling such a blatant lie. She could feel his eyes boring into her, condemning her for lying.

"The wind," he repeated, angry and disbelieving. If he knew her, really knew her, he wouldn't be surprised. He'd know she was going to lie. It would be a given.

Her entire life was one carefully crafted lie on top of another.

Then again, there wasn't anyone that really knew her anymore, was there?

She turned her face away from him, keeping him on the edge of her periphery. "Must have been."

They sat in painful silence until Gizmo finished his food and jumped in Max's lap. His purring filled the air, and she couldn't help but watch out the corner of her eye as he stroked the cat's back.

Max was a nice guy. She couldn't figure out what it was about him that calmed her or why she enjoyed just sitting quietly with him. It wasn't like her to take comfort in others, especially when she'd spent so much time making sure she could do those things for herself. Not being able to get much of a read on him was strange. She would think the unknown would make her more uncomfortable, but it did the opposite. Something about Max's presence soothed her in a way she'd never experienced. Odd that it had nothing to do with knowing what he was thinking or his aura, it was just something about him.

"Are you working tonight?" he asked quietly.

"Not until eight."

"Did you want to get changed and come back to the farm with me?"

She looked to him in surprise, only to find his head turned away, like she had done to him.

"Why?"

It was the first thought that came to her mind. Why would he want her with him, especially after the last twenty-four hours? Was it to keep an eye on her and make sure she wasn't insane?

He spared her a glance. "You seemed interested when we were there. I thought I could show you around if you wanted. If you had time."

She shook her head. "I'm not crazy. You don't have to watch me."

"I'm not watching you." He sounded offended. "I just thought...never mind."

She was being a jerk. He was trying to do something nice, his aura projecting no ulterior motives, just that steady emerald green with the grayish haze.

"Give me fifteen minutes to get cleaned up." She stood and went into the camper and grabbed a pair of jeans and a sweater.

She quickly showered and changed, then considered what she was doing. She'd never had any problems making friends. It was keeping them that was the problem. When she was younger, she didn't know she wasn't supposed to make friends with spirits. She'd never kept her distance, and in the end, they'd all moved on and she'd been left behind, confused. She'd made a few friends at the different schools she attended, but between always being the new kid and being weird, none of the friendships stuck.

She thought about Butch and Erin Hardy and immediately shut it down. That had been her biggest fall to date, the biggest loss she'd ever experienced. After things with her mother had gone from bad to worse she'd put her trust in the Hardys. They'd begged her to. She'd been young and naïve, so she'd listened. When they'd turned their backs on her, it had cut deeper than any knife could. When things with her mother eventually went from worse to deadly, there'd been no one to turn to.

She threw her hair up and opened the door.

"You can come in. I'll just get my boots on."

Max ducked his head and stepped in. He stood in the middle of her tiny living space and looked around, eyeing her book and movie collection with interest.

She made few smooching noises at Gizmo, who answered with a meow before flicking his tail at Max's dog and jumping in the camper. She made sure to lock the door before heading to the truck.

"How long do you think we'll be?" she asked offhand. "Should I bring my bike?"

"I'll drive you to work later." He made it sound like it should have been obvious.

"I still have to get home at the end of my shift. I ride my bike home from the bus stop."

He rubbed his face, like he was stressed. "That's crazy," he muttered. "I'll just come pick you up."

She crossed her arms. "I get out at three in the morning. You're not coming to pick me up in the middle of the night."

"Why don't you ask Wendy to let you use one of the company cars? I'm sure she won't mind."

"I'm not taking a company car. I can get to work just like everyone else."

"Yeah, well, everyone else doesn't ride a bike in the middle of the night down deserted streets."

She could see his point but didn't need his intervention.

"Can we just put my bike in the truck?" she asked. "So, if I need it, I have it."

Her bike ended up in the back of the truck as he drove them the short distance back to his house, which really was lovely. A big, old-fashioned farmhouse with a big front porch that had a swing.

She could feel her excitement building at the prospect of Max showing her his farm, dying to see the animals in the barn.

"Come on," he laughed when they got out of the truck.

"I'm sorry." She winced at how embarrassingly giddy she must look.

"Don't be sorry. Some days, I feel the same way when I get to work out here. That's why I keep doing it."

He held the door of the small barn open for her. The smells of hay, manure, and grain greeted her. Not in an overpowering, dirty way, but just enough to know it was, in fact, a working farm.

"This is where I keep my special ladies," he told her, winking.

They walked through a hallway with gated stalls on either side. As they approached, she heard high pitched crying.

"That's Ginny. I haven't been to see her yet this morning. She's upset."

When they came to the gate, Rosie saw a herd of tiny little goats. Some were black and white, and some were white and brown, but one was a reddish-brown color, almost like a deer. The little thing was howling so loudly, it sounded like a baby crying.

"Go on," Max told her, gathering a bucket and a few other things. "You can get in there with them. Be careful though, they nibble. Other than that, they might just love you to death."

Rosie climbed over, and they immediately surrounded her. Some tried to nibble her sweater, and one went for her knee. One insistently scratched its head on her shin, which made her giggle.

"That's Luna." Max hopped in beside her, began doling out handfuls of grain and started ticking off their names. "Bella, Ariana, Lily, Minerva, Hermione, Nymphadora."

"Don't call her Nymphadora," Rosie corrected. "Tonks." She squealed out a laugh as one of the goats put its front feet on her thighs.

"Lily, no," Max scolded.

But Rosie continued to laugh as she scratched the animal. "I think I'm in love."

9

Max watched Rosie engross herself in his farm, though he didn't think she knew she was doing it. She was always conscious of keeping herself at a distance, doing things like evading questions or flat out ignoring them, but she had completely let her guard down. The only downside was she was opening herself up to a flock of chickens and not him.

She sat on an overturned bucket and watched the birds as they pecked around her feet. One of his hens, Florence, was perched on Rosie's knee.

He was much more comfortable with this Rosie than the Rosie of a few hours ago. The memory of what happened at Smith's Cove sent a chill up his spine. Not just the instant change in Rosie's demeanor while they'd been there, or the sheer panic on her face, but there was something in the air down there. An intangible sense that something else was there.

He didn't know anything about the supernatural any more than the next average Joe, but he knew down to his bones, they hadn't been alone at Smith's Cove. Something had been watching them. He also knew, with absolute certainty, whatever it was, Rosie could see or feel it.

He hadn't been expecting that. He'd thought they would go down there and she'd show him the spot where she went in the water. He thought maybe if he knew where she went in or her path from the camper, he might feel better. The more you knew, kind of thing. Holy hell, he was not expecting any of this.

"Please tell me I can keep her," Rosie interrupted his thoughts. She was smiling and laughing like everything on the farm was her dream come true. Those eyes that could hold so much mystery were clear and bright with happiness. It took him aback a bit to realize how far up her guard was all the time. This was the first time he'd seen her enjoy herself without the walls.

"Sorry. She's my favorite."

Her face took on a shocked expression. "Parents aren't supposed to pick favorites." Then she looked at the other chickens on the ground. "You all should go on strike until he takes it back."

She'd laughed her way through the goats, his three cows, and the chickens. The sheep had been a different story. One of his ewes had always been skittish, but today, when Rosie had stood at the side of the pasture, something had changed. She'd made a few shooing noises and waved her hands in the air, and strangely, the sheep had perked up and trotted off.

"You ready to see the crops?" he asked. They'd been touring the barn for nearly an hour, Rosie making sure to stop and see every inch of every pen. She even asked him to show her the inside of the chicken coop.

"Are you sure you don't mind?"

She'd asked him that a bunch of times already, like she was an inconvenience.

"I keep telling you I'm sure."

"I just don't want to wear out my welcome."

"I think you're safe there," he said. "You're always welcome here, Rosie." He held out his hand and waved for her to join him. "Come on."

So, he gave her the tour of the crop fields. She seemed surprised they could grow anything in the winter, but then he remembered she was from up north. He showed her the plants and explained the irrigation system and the building of organic soils.

She was especially fascinated with the kohlrabi and swore she'd never seen one before. He let her pick one from the ground, and they went back to the house so she could taste it. He washed and peeled, while she stood on the other side of the kitchen counter.

He handed her a slice, and she didn't hesitate to pop it in her mouth. "It tastes kind of like broccoli. I like it."

He got them a few glasses of water and they sat, sharing the kohlrabi.

"Can I ask you something?"

She lowered her glass to the counter. "Sure."

"Something I've been thinking about."

"Okay."

Max spun his glass in his hands. "Why didn't you call anyone when you had your accident? You could have called me or Wendy. We would have been happy to help."

"I wasn't in a position to call anyone, Max."

"It drives me crazy thinking about you crashing your bike in the middle of the night, plus the image of you up to your neck in water. What did you do, just get up and limp home?"

"Dallas gave me a ride."

Max's back went stiff. "Dallas?"

"Yeah. There was a whole thing with the police and an ambulance." She still would barely look at him. "It was fine."

At least she hadn't been alone, he told himself. There were worse people to have around in an emergency than Dallas.

"You need to get a ride home at night. That stretch of road isn't safe to ride your bike." The words ground out of him as he pictured Dallas showing up to save the day.

"It wasn't a big deal." She waved him off, setting his temper flaring. "Just an animal in the road. I'm sure it won't happen again."

"You're a terrible liar, did you know that?"

He was starting to see Rosie for what she really was. A liar, to be sure, but a bad one. She lied to protect herself, from what, he didn't know, but every time she did it, she looked away. Like she couldn't stand the thought of looking in his eyes while telling the lie. It pissed him off nearly as much as he found it endearing.

"I'm not sure which part you're lying about, that it was an animal in the road or that it wasn't a big deal, but I know you're lying." He stood and turned his back on her, rooting through the refrigerator. "You hungry?" he asked, changing the subject.

"I wouldn't want to impose."

He looked over his shoulder at her cold expression. Yeah, she'd shut down a little, her arms crossed over her chest.

"You're not a vegetarian or anything, are you?" He ignored her attitude and pulled some things from the shelf and placed them on the counter in front of her.

"No."

"You can go in the living room if you want. I'll fix us a couple plates."

"You're going to wait on me?" She thawed a bit, and her eyes warmed with humor. "Even though you think I'm a liar."

He leaned toward her, crowding her just a little, the counter still between them.

"I'd wait on you anytime, Rosie."

Her eyes widened a fraction, and she mumbled something, barely able to look away from him, then hurried out of the room.

He was willing to tiptoe around her a bit and wait for her to spill her secrets, but he wasn't about to pretend he didn't know what she was doing.

She was on the couch, watching How I Met Your Mother when he handed her the dish he'd made and sat down.

"Do you watch this?" she asked.

"There are two big days in any love story. The day you meet the girl of your dreams and the day you marry her."

Her fork stopped midway between her plate and her mouth.

"Ted said that," Max mentioned casually, but sent her a small smile as he put his feet on the coffee table and turned his attention to the TV.

They didn't talk for a while, just ate companionably while watching reruns. When she finished, she put her plate on top of his and extended her small boots to rest on the coffee table along with his.

She laughed at everything Lily said on the show, and he laughed when she did, enjoying seeing her lighthearted.

There was something intensely intriguing about Rosie. It wasn't just her striking looks. Those held merits all their own, but it wasn't what kept bringing him back to her. It wasn't what sent him to her camper after the fight she'd had with Wendy or what made his arms want to wrap around her every time he was around her. She was like a magnet.

Even he could admit, the first time he'd seen her in the bar, it had probably been like Dallas said, all that white hair was eye-catching. Though after being around her a few times, especially today, seeing her fresh out of the shower with no makeup, he knew it was natural, and she wasn't trying to catch anyone's attention. The second his eyes met hers in the bar, he'd felt a pull to her, like somewhere, his subconscious was calling her name.

He'd had girlfriends before, plenty of them. He'd felt a true affection for all of them, but he'd never felt the lure he did with Rosie. He'd never felt so compelled to be physically near someone.

Getting the chance to see her enjoy herself and just talk to her had been an eye opener. She was complicated, but she wasn't as prickly as he first thought. She was mysterious. She was hiding something. He could smell a secret from a mile away, and Rosie was keeping something, but he was patient and he got the feeling that waiting for her would pay off in the end.

~

"I TOLD YOU, you didn't have to go in tonight," Wendy complained in Rosie's ear.

Max had grudgingly dropped her off so she could catch the bus and head to work, but when she got there, one of the other maids had instructed her to call Wendy immediately.

"And I told you I was coming in," Rosie told her.

"But you didn't have to. I gave you the night off."

"I don't need the night off."

"I need you in the office, then."

Rosie's head reared back. "Why?"

"I was going to give you the night off to butter you up before I called you into my office for a meeting. Wait there, I'll be right over."

"I have work to do."

"No, you don't. I called in some other girls to cover for you."

Rosie gritted her teeth. "But-"

"You don't need anyone to cover for you. I got it," Wendy continued. "Just wait in the lobby. I'll be there in a minute."

Annoyed, Rosie went to the supply closet and helped the other maids prep for the night. She helped them load their cars and made sure they had everything they needed. When they left and she was alone in the office, only then did she go wait for Wendy. She was surprised to find her already in the lobby.

"Oh, sorry. I was helping them get stocked and packed up."

"I know," Wendy shrugged with a knowing smile. "I figured you would."

Rosie walked nervously to the lobby couch and sat opposite Wendy. "Why do you need to meet with me?"

"Because we need to talk about what happened."

"I can't say I'm sorry enough."

"No, it's not that," Wendy assured her. "But with Lisa gone, there are some responsibilities I wanted to put you in charge of."

"I'm not sure that's a good idea."

"Why not? All the other maids respect you. You've put in your time cleaning and know how it's supposed to be done. You always do a good job and push the other girls to do the job right. You keep to an amazingly tight schedule. You're efficient and well-liked. Seems to me like you're the perfect person to take on a little more work here."

"Why would you trust me with something like this? Wendy, that's crazy."

"No, it's not," Wendy assured her. "I have trust issues, okay. I've spent my whole adult life with crappy cheating boyfriends and now, this thing with Lisa. I won't trust you with my money. I won't make that mistake with anyone else again. But, I trust you to keep my schedule moving. I trust you to keep the service running smooth like you always do. It's small, but it's a start for me."

"But-"

"You kept something important from me. I haven't forgotten. You don't have to remind me. But, I get it. I don't like it and I don't agree with it, but I get it. You and I are on the same wavelength now, though, aren't we? We're friends. Right?"

"Yes." Rosie had to give her that much.

"Are you going to screw me over?"

"No."

"Are you going to work hard, like you always do?"

"You know I am."

"I do. I know you'll be great in this position."

"What position? Wendy,"

"I want you to be what we're going to call Head of Housekeeping. It means the other maids will report to you with day-to-day stuff, and you'll report it back to me."

Rosie rubbed her hands on her face, careful not to pull at her scabs.

"I feel like this is too sudden."

Wendy laughed. "I've been trying to get you to come in and talk about this for weeks."

"That was before."

"Before I found out my trusted office manager was stealing from me and you knew all along?"

"I didn't know all along," Rosie argued. "I only knew for a few weeks." That vision of Lisa dressed as the Hamburglar popped into her mind.

"I know," Wendy said. "I checked those invoices you told me about.

The bottom line is, I wanted to put you in this position and we had a bump in the road. That's all."

Rosie took a deep breath. "What would it mean for my schedule?"

Wendy smiled like the cat that ate the canary. "You'd be doing more work in the office, but I do have a few jobs you'd be able to take on to fit in. No more late nights, though. You wouldn't be on the night shift."

"I want the night shift."

"I know you do, but you'd still be working alone, which you like, but they'd just be higher-end, home cleans, not offices that need to be cleaned when they're closed. And you get a bump up in pay."

Rosie didn't say anything while she sat considering her options. Who turns down what's essentially a promotion with better hours and more money?

"How's Max?" Wendy still had a smile on her face.

"How should I know?" Rosie groused, feeling cornered.

"Oh, I don't know. It's not like you spent all day with him or anything." Rosie sent her a scowl. "Feeling the feelings," Wendy sang.

"Shut up," Rosie growled.

10

Two mornings later, Rosie woke up, let Gizmo out, and found a note taped to the door of her camper.

Rosie,
Stopped by but missed you.
Come by the farm before you head to work – Florence misses you.
Wanted to show you something.
~Max

She showered and dressed, picking out her favorite purple tights, long black t-shirt and grey cardigan. Without stopping to question why, she took care to braid her hair and wrapped it in a bun, then fixed her makeup. She threw on her flowered combat boots, grabbed her bag, and hopped on her bike.

The previous morning, she'd woken up in her bed, thankfully, but her vision had been clouded. Like she was opening her eyes underwater.

She had to do something about this spirit. The constant barrage of dreams and sleepwalking on top of the ghostly visits were taking their toll. She was tired and edgy, wondering what might happen next. Though she wasn't ready to follow the spirit, afraid of where she might be led, she was ready to take control of the situation. She'd planned to head downtown, as it was her day off, and go to The Third Eye.

The Third Eye was a store she'd walked past a few times but had never actually gone into, though one day, she'd been walking by when someone who worked there actually ran out of the store and chased her down the street.

"Hey!" the man had shouted. "Stop!"

She'd turned her head around to look at him but didn't stop.

"There's something following you! I can help!"

There was always something following her, she'd thought at the time.

Now, though, was a different story. She couldn't risk drowning in her sleep just because she was too stubborn to ask for help. At least the people in that type of shop believed in the kind of stuff that happened to her. No one would call her a liar when she told them what she could see.

And therein lay another of her problems. Max's dog was the only spirit besides that damn woman she could see. Mrs. Murphy was gone. The little boy that sometimes followed Marta was gone. The man with Dallas was gone. There were no spirits on the bus or the street. The auras were mostly gone, except in the people she knew fairly well, and even then, they were transparent and hard to read. It was as though the senses she'd relied on her entire life were gone. It was not an easy transition to try to make.

She rode to Max's without incident and parked her bike by his truck, near the garage. Peeking around, she didn't see him in the yard, so she went up the porch steps and knocked on the front door. After a minute, when no one answered, she made her way to the barn. She knocked and peeked her head in.

"Max?" she called.

She was met with the desperate sound of goats crying for her attention, but no Max. Eventually, she made her way to the chicken coop. When she got there, Florence, a gray and white hen with the cutest little pouf of feathers under her beak, squatted down at her feet, as if to say "You may pick me up now." Rosie obliged and carried the bird while she checked the cow pasture for Max.

She was making her way to the sheep when he ended up finding her.

"Hey, stranger." He smiled a total megawatt smile that made her step falter a little.

She smiled back. "There you are. Florence and I weren't sure where to look if we didn't find you soon."

He shook his head and stepped closer, scratching the chicken under the beak. "I've been watching for you. I was hoping you'd come by."

"Well, I got your note." She shrugged. "I was heading to town today anyway."

"So, you would have stopped by?" he asked.

She shook her head. "Probably not. But I was riding by, kind of."

"Kind of," he agreed. "Come on." He motioned with his hand for her to follow him.

After a few steps, he slowed so they could walk side by side. The air was cool, but not nearly as cold as it would be in up north, and she was still awestruck by how beautiful it was on Max's farm. The green pastures, abutting the forest that was still so full and lush with foliage, made such a gorgeous picture. The garden patches, long neat rows of thriving plants running through the center of everything, behind the bright white of Max's house and the deep red of the barn made such an intensely beautiful scene. She looked to Max. The farmer was pretty beautiful too.

"So, what is it you wanted to show me?" she asked.

"First." He held his hand out and pointed to his left. "Time to put the princess back in her run."

Rosie made a sad face at Florence, and nuzzled her head. He opened the little chicken door, and she put the bird back.

"Okay," Rosie told him. "Where to?"

"The sheep."

"I was headed there when I ran into you."

He nodded. "I've been working in the field most of the morning."

"Oh."

They got to the little barn where Max's sheep were kept, and he opened the gate, motioning for her to go first. He walked her to a giant wooden crate that looked like it was constructed out of pallets.

She sucked in a breath when she saw what was in the makeshift playpen and looked up quickly. Max was watching her with that huge smile on his face, hands in his pockets. She looked back at the fuzzy lump lying on a bed of straw.

"It's so tiny," she whispered, not wanting to disturb it.

"Only a few days old."

"Where's its mother?"

"She was the runt of a triplet birth. The mother abandoned her."

Rosie knew the feeling well. "What will happen to her?"

"We'll bottle feed her for a while and raise her here if she makes it."

"You can do that?" she asked before she leaned down to rub her hand along the tiny sheep's soft wool.

"We can." His voice was soft. "Want to feed her?"

"Can I?"

"Sure. I'll get her milk all set up if you want to pick her up."

"Oh my God," Rosie breathed. She leaned in and gently scooped the little sheep up. It made a few squeaking noises before trying to nuzzle up her body and into her neck.

"She's trying to eat," Max told her as he came back holding a bottle.

There was no way Rosie was going to pass up the chance to bottle-feed a baby lamb. She sat on the floor and let Max show her how to hold everything. She just sat there, smiling, unable to help herself.

"This is amazing," she told him.

"Yeah," he agreed. "It is."

She looked up and found him watching her, thoughtful. His green aura had pink streaks pulsing through it, like a gymnast's ribbons streaming through the air, and she tilted her head to watch them.

"What do you see, Rosie?"

Her eyes snapped to meet his. "Nothing."

"You were looking behind me. Above me. What did you see?"

She looked back down at the suckling lamb.

"I'll believe you," he told her quietly, his voice even and sure. "Whatever you tell me, I won't laugh and I'll believe you."

She shook her head. "I wasn't looking at anything."

"I know when we went to the cove the other day, there was something out there with us. I could feel it. I could see it in your eyes. I know it was there even if I don't know what it was, and I know you can see it, Rosie."

"I don't know what you're talking about."

He took a deep breath and let it out on a sigh. "Yeah, you do, but it's okay. I'll be here when you're ready."

She looked at him through her eyelashes. "What if I'm never ready?"

"You will be."

The sound of air being sucked into the bottle surrounded them and the restless lamb began to squirm.

"I think she's ready to go in the pasture with the big girls. Hopefully one of them will take to her," Max said as he stood.

He took the lamb and walked it to the gate, Rosie standing and following.

"Is that likely?"

"Maybe." He smiled as the little lamb inspected the pasture on wobbly legs. The other ewes watched from a distance.

"Should we stay?" Rosie ventured. "Make sure she's okay?"

"Nah. She's more likely to go exploring if we aren't here."

Rosie didn't want to leave. She wanted to stay in that barn, insulated from the world and enjoy the quiet that came from being around Max.

He walked the fence line and watched the lamb from afar.

"You have to work tonight?" he asked as he stopped and rested a foot on the bottom rung of the fence and leaned his forearms on the top. He looked like a real farmer. He could have been a cowboy if he had a big hat and an oversized belt buckle.

She leaned on the fence next to him and tried not to look at the thick layer of blonde hair on his forearms. He was tan underneath from long hours in the sun.

"No work tonight," she said, her hands resting next to his on the fence as the sheep inspected each other. "Wendy changed my schedule around a little, so I've got the night off."

"She changed your schedule? I thought you liked working nights."

"I do," she told him as one of the ewes, the skittish one, approached the lamb. "But she gave me a few things to do in the office, so I have to be there more during regular hours."

"On top of all the cleaning jobs?" He sounded surprised.

"No, she's got me doing some cleaning in private homes. It's not my favorite, but it'll do."

"What is your favorite?" he asked. "If you could do anything you wanted, I guess."

She thought for a second. "I don't know." She'd never really thought about, it had never been an option for her. She hadn't even graduated high school so a prosperous future seemed dim. She consciously chose not to dwell on the fact that she had little in the way of a future. It became depressing if she did. So, she told herself, when she got restless or bored, she'd move on and find a new place to live. She'd enjoy the routine of packing her things and finding somewhere else to move and building a new life. "I'm just exploring life for right now." It was the only answer she knew how to give. It was the only way to explain drifting through life to someone who had it together.

Max was established in his life, and she very much envied that. Not necessarily the farm or the business he'd built, but his drive and passion. Listening to him explain every little detail of soil components, it had become obvious he loved what he did. How could he not? He lived in this great place and cultivated things with his own hands.

"Wendy says you're the best she's got."

She rolled her eyes. "Yeah, I can clean a toilet like a real champ."

He chuckled. "I think she meant you were thorough and reliable."

"So, I can clean the toilet really well and on time?"

His brows rose. "A joke. I like it."

The skittish brown ewe was standing stock still near the sheep barn, letting the little lamb nuzzle her wool.

"She looks like she might like the little one," she mentioned to Max.

"Might be," he agreed.

She leaned back, still holding onto the railing. "Thanks for this. It's definitely an experience I'll remember."

"We'll have to feed her a couple times a day so you can come by anytime."

"I might take you up on that," she warned. "I might just take it home."

"Well, I know where you live in case she goes missing."

Rosie walked back toward the house and her bike, Max quickly falling in step beside her.

"Want me to give you a ride to town?"

She waved off his offer. "Nah. I've got my bike. I won't be long anyway, so it's not a big deal."

"Where are you headed?" He didn't seem intensely interested, more just making conversation.

"A shop on Middle Street I haven't been in. I thought it looked cool, but I haven't been by when it's open."

"Want to have lunch before you go?"

She stopped walking. They were almost to the back porch, and she looked up at the door where Max's dog sat, wagging its tail.

"No, I'll just get going."

"You're sure you don't want a ride?"

She laughed at his persistence. "I'm fine."

"You ever think about getting a car?"

"God, no." She straddled her bike. "I don't know how to drive. What would I do with a car?"

He looked flat-out confused. "Wait. You don't know how to drive?"

"No. I never learned."

"That's...weird." He sounded like he was testing the word out. "How do you ever get anywhere?"

She walked. Rode a bike. Took the bus. Hitchhiked when times had been desperate.

"How did you get around before you drove?" She was trying to make a point, that you find a way when you need to.

"My parents drove me everywhere, or I had Wendy to bug for a ride."

"It's the same for me. I do what I can when I can."

"You want to try for lunch tomorrow?"

She watched him carefully, his caramel eyes steady as he waited for her answer. She shielded her eyes from the sun that shone from behind him, trying to gauge his intent. He was showing interest in her, but she wasn't sure how to handle it. As Wendy would say, she was "feeling the feelings," even if she didn't want to.

Maybe it was that his calming energy that attracted her. He had a gentleness that made him easy to be around. Strange, as she hadn't felt it for years, but there was also temptation to tell him her secret when he asked. He gave off the vibe that he would listen and try to understand what she was saying.

Nerves danced across her skin as she imagined the possibility of being in a relationship with a caring man that might just accept who she really was. Someone who might understand and not judge her.

Fear reared its ugly head, her mind conjuring Butch's face the last time she'd seen him. The look of regret on his face had haunted her for years, one that screamed *I wish I'd never laid eyes on you. I wish I'd never listened to you. I wish I'd never let you into my home – into my life*. It had all been right there for her to see, before he'd turned his back on her and walked out the door. She'd put all her trust in him like he'd asked, and that was what she'd gotten in return. There was no way she'd put her heart on the line like that again.

She shook her head, certain she knew what she was doing. "I can't."

He grabbed her handlebars before she could take off. "The day after?"

She looked him in the eye then, making sure he could see her resolve. "It's a bad idea, Max. I'll see you around."

She jerked the bike out of his grasp and rode away without looking back.

11

———

The Third Eye wasn't at all what Rosie thought it would be. She was expecting a kitschy, witchcraft kind of vibe, but it had more of a relaxing bookstore feel to it. Bookcases lined the walls, dusty tomes and crystals dotting the shelves. There was a glass case that held more crystals where the cash register sat, with a wall full of dried herbs behind it. It was more low-key than witchy.

"I was wondering when you'd be back."

Rosie turned to find the man that had chased her on the street coming out of the back of the store. He was tall and thin, probably around thirty years old. He had blonde hair, a hipster beard, and was wearing a pair of trendy black glasses

"I'm not sure I know what I'm doing here," she admitted.

"I think I do." He held out his hand for her to shake. "I'm Jay."

She hesitated for a fraction of a second before stretching her hand to his. "Rosie."

He held her for a second longer than necessary.

"We have a private room for Reiki." He motioned to a door across the room. "Would you feel more comfortable talking in there?"

"Talking about what?"

He smiled at her, like he knew something she didn't. "About why you're here, of course."

She looked around but didn't see any other customers or employees. "Seems like we're alone enough out here."

"For now," he agreed. When she just continued watching him, he looked her up and down. "You're completely blocked, you know."

She felt blocked. She didn't say it out loud, not knowing if he was for real.

Jay walked a few steps to the coffee machine and poured himself a cup. He held it out in offering, to which she accepted, then invited her to sit at the small reading alcove.

"Do you know what's got you so backed up?"

She sat but looked away from him, watching cars drive past, unsure of how to start.

"I'm not here to judge. I'm here to help."

When she turned, he was watching her intensely. "What can you see?"

"In general, or in you?"

"In general. What can you do?"

"I get a sense of energy sometimes, but only if it's strong." He tilted his head. "Hence why I tried to tell you that day there was something following you."

"Someone. My boss's grandmother."

He sat up straighter. "You can see her?"

"Not now, but back then, she followed me everywhere. Bugged the crap out of me."

"Can you actually see her, or you just know it her energy?"

"No, no, I can see her. Ugly pink skirt set and all. She was a pain in the ass."

"Was? Where'd she go?"

Bolstered by the fact Jay hadn't laughed once when she'd told him what she could see, and that he had his own gifts, she answered. "I don't know. I don't see much of anything anymore."

"They're still here," he told her. "I can feel them clinging to you. Not bad energies, though."

"I can't see them." For something she'd wanted gone for so long, she felt like a part of her was missing without them. "I don't know why."

"Like I said, you're completely blocked. Your chakras are totally out of whack. Something's got you off-kilter."

"I used to see auras, but that's gone, too, for the most part."

"That's interesting," he murmured. "Have you always seen auras?"

"Yeah, from when I was little. I got used to knowing people before I ever really knew them."

"You relied on that," he concluded easily. "Knowing someone before knowing them."

"I did. It's nerve wracking without it."

"I can imagine. I haven't had my gifts my whole life, but I'd hate to be without them now."

"I've always wanted them to go away. The auras, the sprits, the other stuff. Now that they're gone..." She shrugged, not finishing the thought.

"There's more?" He shook his head slightly. "That's incredible."

"It's not incredible. Awful," she said. "Debilitating at times. Invasive, overwhelming. Any of those work."

His brow drew in confusion. "You still struggle with it?"

She nodded, mimicking his expression. "You don't?"

Jay shook his head. "I've worked really hard to study what I see. To make sense of it. That helped."

She shrugged. "I never knew where to start. The spirits, the dreams. It's a lot."

"Maybe I can give you a place to start if you tell me about it."

She looked away not even knowing how to begin.

"Okay." He drew the word out. "How about you tell me the first time you remember something being different."

That was easy. "I was really little. Three, maybe."

"Jesus," he muttered.

"There was this man my mom brought home. He was surrounded by all black, almost like a cloud, but not puffy like that. More like..." She struggled to find the right words. "...static. I remember wondering why he didn't take a bath, because he was surrounded by dirt."

"But it wasn't dirt," Jay finished.

She shook her head, agreeing with him. "I tried to put my hand through it, to touch it. It was so dark inside, and it moved when he moved, I was totally captivated. So curious."

"Did you touch it?"

She shook her head again. "No."

His head tilted to the side, and she knew he was reading her in some way. "Why didn't you touch it?"

"I just didn't." Her answer came quick and defensive.

"That's a lie," he told her quietly. "Why didn't you touch it?" His eyes were grave when they met hers. "It's important."

"It's really not."

"Why didn't you touch the aura?"

"Why does it matter? You wanted me to tell you about the first time. I did."

He sat back, disappointment marring his face. "This is why you're blocked, why you can't overcome whatever is happening to you."

"Because I can't remember why I didn't do something when I was three?"

"No, because you're lying about it. Not just lying to me, but lying to yourself."

"I'm not lying to myself." She huffed out a breath and crossed her arms. It took her about one second to realize how ridiculous she was acting. "He knocked me down. That's why I didn't touch it. Before I could, he hit me upside the head and knocked me down."

Jay said nothing.

"Back then, I loved the colors. I would steal crayons from places my mom took me so I could mix the colors together and match them to an aura I'd seen. Of course, I didn't know what they were until later. It took me a long time to match the colors to the moods."

"What color was your mom's aura? Can you remember?"

She watched him carefully, trying to figure out his motive.

"She had a few," Rosie told him without really answering.

"Did she know? What you could see?"

"I tried to tell her. Mostly, she thought I was crazy."

Jay leaned forward and put his elbows on the table. "The static you saw. Was that particular to that one man, or is that how it appears?"

"I think the static was him. They used to be like thin clouds, I could see through them, but they were soft. Like, when you exhale on a cold day."

"They used to be, before they stopped?"

"They changed a while back, went from thin clouds to something else."

"What changed for you that made the auras change?" When she didn't answer right away, he continued. "I've found, most people that experience a change in their abilities also experience an event that triggers it." When she just watched him, he continued. "Mine came after I got hit by a car. I was sixteen and barely lived. I woke up in the hospital, and everyone had colors pulsing from their bodies. They all thought I was dealing with a concussion and sent me to ophthalmologists and neurologists, but I was fine. I finally stopped telling them about it and researched it myself. I see chakras. Sometimes I get a quick blast of a word or picture." He shrugged again. "I can't help it. Instead of fighting it, I educated myself and eventually opened the shop. I do readings, but sometimes I do cleansings for people."

"What are the cleansings like? Do you think that's something that might work for me?"

He shrugged. "I've never worked with a medium. I don't know how much I can cleanse, because I don't know how much of the energy I see is you and how much is them."

"There's no them right now," she admitted. "Just a dog and woman."

"Both ghosts?"

She took a deep breath, never having talked this much about the subject before. "The dog is a spirit guide, I think. I'm friends with its owner, and it's always hanging around."

"That's interesting," Jay commented.

For the first time, Rosie felt like she could talk with someone about her abilities. When she was a child, Butch had pressed her, but she hadn't been able to communicate what was going on or why it happened. Being able to talk with someone that didn't judge and maybe even understood was liberating.

"You just blasted me with a wave of relief. From here." He smiled, holding a hand up to his throat, his blue eyes sparkling. "What's going on?"

"I've never been able to talk about it before like this. Most people think I'm crazy."

He nodded like he understood.

"You don't give anyone much of a chance, do you?"

He wasn't too far off. "A lifetime of rejection will do that to you."

"I imagine it would," he agreed. "Back to the dog."

She shrugged. "He's never talked about it. We aren't really close, we just met a few weeks ago, but it hangs out around his house. If he stops by my place, it runs around my yard."

"And you still see it."

She nodded.

"What about the auras? You stopped seeing those, too?"

"Only in strangers. Like I can't see yours, but I can see the people I already know."

"So, you aren't reading new information, just the old stuff."

"I can see changes in their auras when they happen, so it isn't residual, but they aren't what they were a few weeks ago. They're like wisps or strands of color now."

"What were they before?"

"They were bright. Big and bold and thick like fog."

"So, what changed?"

She took a deep breath and scrubbed her face, wincing when she rubbed her remaining scabs.

"I had a run-in with the other spirit."

"The woman?" She nodded. "What kind of run-in?"

Rosie winced. "The kind where my entire body passed through hers."

He leaned way back in his chair and watched her carefully. "Through her."

Rosie nodded.

"What happened when you did that?"

Now, Rosie shook her head and held up her hands. "I can't talk about it."

"That bad?"

"It was bad." Her voice was a whisper. "Really, really bad." The more she thought about it, which she'd studiously avoided doing, the more she felt her eyes sting.

The bell attached to the door of the store chimed happily when it opened. Jay jumped up and walked away to greet his customer. Rosie surreptitiously looked away and wiped the tears from her eyes.

While he showed someone to the case of crystals, she grabbed her bag and slung it over her shoulder. When she looked up, Dallas was sauntering down the sidewalk.

Her first instinct was to hide so he wouldn't see her, but she never got the chance.

He caught sight of her and stopped in his tracks. Through the plate glass, he smiled and waved at her to come outside.

"Friend of yours?" Jay asked.

"Not really," Rosie answered.

"You sure?"

"Not really," she repeated.

"Well, we can pick up where we left of tomorrow if that works for you," he said with a smile. "If we have time, you can tell me about your not really friend."

"Maybe." She shook his outstretched hand. "Thank you."

"Anytime, Happy."

She stilled, her eyes flying to his face.

"Just the word," he told her. "Big, bright, bold, every time we touch." She quickly pulled her hand away and he laughed. "Well you can't undo it now."

Rosie fled the store and met Dallas on the sidewalk.

"Getting your mumbo jumbo freakster on in there?" he asked. The look on his face was pure mischief, and she laughed.

"Maybe."

"Cool." He squinted down at her. "How's the face?"

"Scabby."

"Told you not to ride out there at night. It's dangerous." He turned and pointed at her bike. "Want a ride back to your place?"

"Sure," she answered. Knowing Dallas, he probably wouldn't listen if she told him no, anyway.

"I'm headed out to Max's anyway." He grabbed the handlebars of her bike and began steering toward a pickup truck. "Unless you want me to just drop you off with him." He sent her a wink.

"What's that mean?" she asked as she climbed in his truck and he took off toward her place.

"Nothing," he said evasively. "Just heard you and Max are circling each other."

She let out a loud laugh. "You make us sound like the Sharks and the Jets."

"Who the hell are they?"

"Never mind." She shook her head. "We aren't circling each other."

"Oh." He looked over at her. "When was the last time you talked to him?"

She crossed her arms over her chest. "This morning."

It was his turn to laugh. "Uh-huh. Definitely keeping your distance." She didn't respond. "I'm just kidding, Rosie. Max is my best friend, you could do a lot worse."

"We aren't circling each other. Max and I are friends." That was questionable with the way the morning had ended.

After a few more ribbing jests, Dallas pulled up to her camper and helped get her bike out of the back.

"You all good?" he asked.

"Thanks for the ride. You know..." She smiled at him. "When you aren't being an ass, you're actually a nice guy."

His face fell. "Don't tell anyone that."

12

All evening, Rosie thought about the things she and Jay talked about. Though she'd always had the ability to see spirits and auras, they had intensified later in life, as had her knack for knowing things about people without them telling her. She hadn't said it to him, but, much like Jay's gifts being triggered by an accident, hers were also the result of a traumatic incident

As a child, her mother had been charged with possession of a controlled substance, prostitution, neglect, and endangering the welfare of a child. It struck her as strange that her mother had been sent to jail for neglecting her, and then the state sent her to a foster care system that did the same thing. Home after home, some rejecting her after a few days, some she'd run from herself. Not until Butch and Erin Hardy offered to take her in did she finally think she'd found a stable home.

Years later, when her mother was released from jail, Rosie had been sent to live with her again. Things had been okay at first, and after a tentative getting to know each other period, they tried to learn how to live together again.

When she'd talked about the things she saw, her mother screamed about the devil controlling her mind. There'd been a series of punishments that involved being locked in a closet and having her mother's red-hot crucifix branded to her chest.

Still, Rosie refused to lie and tell her mother what she wanted to hear.

One night, her mother had raged and come at her with fists flying. Rosie could still smell the candles her mother burned as the rain tapped on the windows. She could still feel the carpet pile shifting under her neck as her mother pressed her down and she fought wildly for her life. The weight on her stomach as her mother straddled her, hands around her daughter's throat, squeezing until the screams died and there was nothing but a black abyss.

Rosie had woken the following day, strapped to a hospital bed, and like Jay, could see things she didn't want to see. Auras surrounded her, billowing from everyone that came in her room. Every time someone came in her room Rosie was blasted with a laundry list of patient care needs, family schedules, and money woes. She somehow knew her doctor was planning to play a round of golf after work, and that his daughter's bedroom was painted a sunny yellow. She knew their mother's names and where they born and how they liked their coffee.

Whatever her mother had done to her, whatever she'd seen on the other side, had changed her for good.

She was looking forward to talking with Jay again and felt almost hopeful about clearing up whatever was blocking her energy.

Rosie had taken to tying her wrist to the bed frame, in hopes of preventing her from sleepwalking. The first few times it hadn't worked, but she'd started using more complicated knots, and it seemed to do the trick. She went to bed eager to wake up and start the new day.

∼

SHE WAS STANDING in the middle of Butch Hardy's precinct.

She remembered the blue and cream-colored tiles on the wall.

It was empty, which she'd never seen before, the lights low, their persistent buzz absent. She took the few steps to Butch's desk. As usual, it was littered with coffee mugs and empty antacid tubes. There was a picture of Butch, Erin, and little Michael.

There had never been a picture taken with her and Michael. She'd only met him a handful of times. Erin was well and tired of the ghost show, and Happy was long gone by the time he was born.

"Who brought me here?" she asked the empty room.

"I did," came a woman's voice from the darkness.

Rosie stained to see into the void. "Where are you?"

Rosie took a step back when a woman stepped out of the shadows.

A few years older than Rosie, the woman was dressed in jeans and a sweater. Familiar clear blue eyes stared back at her, as though she was looking in a mirror. Even the woman's hair was the same shade Rosie's had been before it had changed.

"You're me," Rosie breathed, taking another step back.

She shook her head. "You're Happy. I'm Toby."

"Rosie," she corrected automatically.

"Doesn't matter. You shouldn't be here."

"You brought me here, didn't you?" Rosie asked. "Who are you?"

Toby casually walked to Butch's desk and ran her fingers across the surface. "You sat here once."

Rosie thought back to the day her mother had been arrested. She'd sat right where the other woman was sitting.

"I did. I liked it here," she admitted.

"I imagine it felt safe here, far more than where you'd been." She looked up at Rosie through her lashes. "You were lucky to get away from her when you did."

"Who? My mom?"

"She would have tried to ruin you."

"She did ruin me, just later than she would have liked."

The woman shook her head, a small smile on her lips. "No. You're better off than you think, Happy. I'll be coming for you soon."

Rosie tilted her head, confusion etching a line across her forehead. "You're the one coming for me?"

"Not now." Toby smiled. "He needs you first. I'll come later. Close your eyes."

Rosie did, the idea of not trusting her never entered Rosie's mind. It was a dream, after all.

"You have to go now," the stranger said.

Rosie opened her eyes and stood in Max's living room. He was sleeping on the couch, his feet propped on the coffee table, the TV on quietly in the background.

Rosie was startled when Max's dog friend barked loudly at the door.

"You have to go now," Toby repeated.

"Go where?"

"You can't be late."

Rosie clenched her fists. "Where am I supposed to go?"

"Don't be late."

Before she could respond, there was a rumble, like an earthquake beneath her feet. She turned to see a ball of flames coming at her. The heat was incredible, and her skin blistered and peeled as the fire rocketed directly through her.

Her eyes snapped open as she shot up off the bed, the heat from the explosion still on her skin.

Max.

She had to get to Max.

She let out a startled scream when the dog appeared inside her camper. It paced from the bed to the door, and back again, barking all the while. It stopped at the door, barked, and ran back to her, only to bark again.

It barked one last time, then ran straight through the door to the outside. Rosie untied her wrist and threw on her jeans and a sweatshirt. She opened the door, the dog running from the camper to her bike, barking.

This was Max's spirit guide. It stayed with Max all the time. If it was here, trying to get her attention, it was only because there was something wrong with Max. The dog's appearance, in addition to her dream, instilled a sense of urgency that made her rush as if Max's life depended on it.

"Is it Max?" she asked. If anything, the dog went even more berserk and ran down the driveway toward the road. Rosie ran to her bike, flipped on the flashlight attached the handlebars, and followed.

The more the dog barked, the faster Rosie pedaled.

There were no cars on the road, and she made it to Max's, skidding into the driveway. She followed the dog up the porch steps, and it ran through the front door, then stood in the entryway barking at her through the glass. Pressing her face to the door, hands cupped around her eyes, Rosie searched for Max. The light from the TV lit the living room, and she could see his boots resting on the coffee table. She pounded on the door, hoping she could get his attention. What she would say to him when he answered the door, she didn't know.

The dog was barking at Max, then running back to bark at her. Max didn't move at all. She used the flat of her hand to bang on the glass, this time calling his name, making more of a racket and still, Max's boots were unmoving.

"Shit," she muttered, trying the doorknob.

Locked, of course. Panicked, she tried a few windows, but when she caught sight of Max, unresponsive in the living room, she went into full-on rescue mode. Using her elbow, she closed her eyes and broke the glass on the front door.

"Max!" she yelled as she ran straight to him.

The dog continued to bark and ran from her to the front door and back again, telling her to get out of the house. She pushed away all thoughts of the house going up in a fireball and concentrated on getting Max up and out.

"Max, can you hear me?" she yelled, shaking his shoulder. He looked as though he was peacefully sleeping, yet no amount of yelling would wake him.

That was when terror set in.

He couldn't die, she wouldn't let him.

He was too funny. Too caring and sexy to be on the other side, beyond her reach. There was no way she was letting him die, and if his damn dog wanted him out of the house, then she was going to get him out of the house.

She stood on the couch and put her arms under him from behind and pulled. She dragged him, one painful step at a time, out of that damn house.

Her breathing was ragged, and her legs were on fire but she got him, gently even, down the porch stairs and well away from the house in case it did explode.

She groped in Max's pocket and sucked in a breath when she found his cell phone. She swiped the screen and stared for a second.

It was a picture of her holding the lamb.

She'd deal with that later. Going into the contacts, she pulled up Dallas's number, but he didn't answer, so she hung up and dialed again. And then again. On the fourth try, he answered.

"Jesus, Max, I'm a little busy,"

"It's Rosie. There's something wrong with Max! Come quick! Help!"

She could hear the change in Dallas' voice immediately. "Where are you?"

"Max's. I followed the dog, and Max is here, but he won't wake up." Her rambling sounded panicked even to her own mind.

"I'll call for help and call you right back okay. I'm across town, so it'll take me a minute to get to you."

"You have to help him. He won't wake up."

"I'll call you right back, Rosie. Just stay with him."

"Okay," she whispered as he hung up. She sat on her butt and pulled Max's head into her lap.

"Wake up, Max. Please." She ran her shaking fingers through his hair and talked to him, hoping he'd wake up.

He was breathing well, she could see that easily enough, but he wasn't waking up. She kept her eyes glued to the phone in her hand, waiting for Dallas to call her back.

It was a few minutes before he finally did.

"He's still not awake," she said by way of answering.

"Shit," he said quietly. "I called it in. The fire department's worried about carbon monoxide. Do you hear any alarms going off?"

She shook her head and then realized he couldn't see her. "No."

"Everyone's on their way, Rosie. They shouldn't be long. Talk to me."

"I just want him to wake up." It came out on a sob.

"I know. Me too." His voice was calm and even. "Tell me what happened."

She took a deep breath. "He just looked like he was sleeping on the couch, but he didn't move when I knocked on the door."

"And you just stopped by at two in the morning?"

"Yes," she answered. "Max!" she called again.

That time, he let out a deep moan and winced at her voice.

"I think he's waking up," she told Dallas.

"Oh, thank God," Dallas breathed in her ear. "Keep trying to get him awake. I'll be there soon."

She hung up and concentrated on Max.

Still stroking his hair, she leaned her face close to his. "Max. Can you hear me?"

"Rosie?" he whispered. "What are you doing here?"

"What happened to you?"

"Huh?" He opened his eyes, then slammed them shut.

"I can see the lights, Max. They're coming to help you, okay. Just hang on for me."

She was surprised at the sheer number of people that poured out of the fire trucks and ambulances. Suddenly it went from she and Max and a ghost dog to the three of them plus twenty.

The EMTs ran over. "What've we got?" one asked.

"I don't know," she said desperately as she relayed the story about finding him unresponsive.

"Let's get him on one hundred percent oxygen."

They went to work while the fire department went into the house.

Rosie stood and took a few steps back, giving them room to work. She wrapped her arms around her upper body and didn't take her eyes off him. They poked and prodded him and checked his vitals numerous times. He started to come around after a few minutes, complaining of nausea and a headache.

When he finally opened his eyes to look at the medics, Rosie took an instinctive step further into the darkness.

"We've got seriously dangerous CO_2 levels here," a fireman told the EMTs when he came out of the house.

"We're going to transport to the hospital, then."

"We'll get the house taken care of and wait for the PD here."

Dallas' truck screeched into the driveway, and he ran to Max's side. Rosie took another step back, deeper into the shadows.

Dallas would ask questions. He'd want to know what she was doing here or why she was knocking on the door so late. She couldn't answer those questions. She could barely stand there while they wheeled Max to the ambulance. She wanted to go with him. She wanted to hold his hand and be there for him.

But she didn't know how.

"Max!" Dallas came running to the ambulance.

"He's going to have to get to the hospital, Hunter. Are you in or out?" the EMT asked.

"In." Dallas didn't hesitate.

They pushed Max's gurney into the ambulance and went to close the doors. Dallas' head shot up and he grabbed the door, stopping it.

"Rosie?" he yelled, looking around the yard. He looked right past the shadow she was standing in and yelled again. She stood stock still not daring to move. He shook his head and sat back down, the door closing on his face. As they drove away, Rosie skulked through the darkness all the way home.

She wished she had the courage to jump in that ambulance with Max. She liked him, she truly did. When she was with him she felt safe. Being with him made her feel normal.

She'd had acquaintances the last few years, but those relationships had all been on the surface. The way she felt about the people she'd met in Jacob's Beach was so much more than that. The way they made her feel was as close to whole as she'd been in her entire life, like maybe she belonged somewhere.

Wendy may have pestered her until she'd given in, but deep down, she'd never regret it. Wendy was strong and independent, yet fun and a bit brash.

Max had an inviting energy surrounding him. Everything he did and said had an underlying current behind it that made her feel welcome. She felt at home when he asked her to have lunch with him. She felt welcome to be herself, and even let go a little bit.

Even Dallas, who she didn't know well, seemed to be of the belief that they were friends by proxy, because she was friends with Wendy.

So why did she take the step back? Why didn't she step up and be the friend he needed?

It was easy to tell herself she hadn't needed to because Dallas was there, but that was a cop-out. She'd done it because she was a coward that was too afraid of opening herself up and getting to know people. In her life, when that happened, they all left her. She was terrified she'd open herself to someone and they'd leave her, too.

Max told her he'd believe her. When they'd been in the barn with the lamb, he'd all but told her he knew she could see something. It was easy to pretend his smiles didn't affect her at all, or that his kindness wasn't melting her carefully constructed defenses. Pretending and acting were what her whole life was built on. Those came much easier than being herself.

Rosie waited out the rest of the morning hours wide awake on her fake patio, running through the night's events before heading to town. She chained her bike to a bench and hopped a bus to town. She was tempted to call Wendy to ask how Max was, but she didn't want to intrude, and she was afraid Wendy would make a big deal out of her asking.

She showed up at The Third Eye as Jay came out of the alley to the storefront.

"Hey," he smiled in greeting. "You're here early."

She nodded, exhausted and distracted by constant thoughts of Max.

"You're like, vibrating." He unlocked the door and let her in but kept the store sign on closed and locked the door behind her.

She looked at the lock and then back to him.

"I thought you'd want privacy, but I can unlock it and open the store."

"No, that's okay. I'm sorry."

"No," he argued. "I don't want you to worry at all. I'll unlock it, and we'll just have coffee like yesterday."

After opening the door, he started the coffee, then went to the glass case where the cash register was and rooted around. She went through the aisle of books and sat at the little round table they'd sat at the day before. She angled her chair so she could see out the front window, and watched traffic pass by until Jay came in, juggling coffee and a tray.

"Shit. I'm sorry," she apologized and helped him set the things on the table. "I should have asked if you needed help."

He laughed. "Happy, you're so distracted, I don't think you would have heard me if I did ask."

A lump formed in her throat as she grabbed the table with one hand to steady herself. "Please don't call me that."

He sat down as though nothing had happened. "Well, if you want your energies cleansed, that's something you're going to have to deal with. You're root chakra is in need of some serious overhaul."

"I don't know what that means," she told him. "I've never seen a chakra."

He spent a little time explaining the seven charkas and how he saw them, like her with auras.

"Yesterday, when I told you that you blasted me with energy? It all came from here." He held his throat. "Bright blue. Super happy. Relief."

"Okay," she said slowly.

"That's the fifth charka, the throat. Symbolizes communication. Do you remember what happened yesterday?"

She tried to think back to the exact point in their conversation, but her mind was swirling with too many emotions to concentrate.

"You told me you'd never talked to anyone about the spirits

before. It blew your throat charka wide open. Huge deal, by the way." He leaned forward. "Now, we have to work on the rest."

"I don't know how to do that."

"We don't." When she opened her mouth, he interrupted. "Not today, at least. You're too distracted. Whatever's going on has you too worked up to be productive."

She took a deep breath. "It's been a long day."

"It's only ten," he laughed.

"Don't tell me that," she sighed.

"I was thinking we could get some crystals picked out for you. Cleanse them, dedicate them, that kind of stuff." When she looked lost, he rolled his eyes. "They correlate to your charkas and will help keep you grounded. I can teach you some meditation techniques, too. I think those'll do you some good."

"Are you sure you don't mind?"

He waved her off. "Are you kidding? This is why I opened the shop. If you're the only real psychic I ever help, then I'm happy with that."

She was about to argue with him about not being psychic when she saw Dallas' big blue truck screech up to the curb. Quickly jumping out of her chair, bag in hand, she hid behind a huge column of bookcases.

"What the hell are you doing?"

She pressed a finger to her lips and begged him with her eyes to not give her up.

The cheery bell over the door sounded. "Rosie!" Dallas voice boomed through the store. He sounded mad.

"Can I help you?" Jay made himself sound very proper and put out by Dallas' intrusion. She had to give him credit for turning on a dime just to protect her.

"No." She heard loud footsteps coming closer. "Rosie!"

"She's not here." Jay sounded exasperated, his voice getting closer as well.

"Yeah, right. You always drink two cups of coffee by yourself?"

He was so observant.

"My boyfriend was just here," Jay said with all the flair of a scandalized Scarlett O'Hara.

"No, he wasn't," Dallas argued. "Where the hell is she?"

His footsteps halted a few feet away her.

"Don't you think if she wanted to be found, she would be? Give her some space."

"Yeah, well, when she calls you in the middle of night crying for help and then disappears, let me know how much space you'd be giving her."

His angry footsteps started again, but this time heading away from her. The bells jingled, but the door didn't close.

"Just tell me she's alright." Dallas's voice was soft. "If you won't tell me where the hell she is, at least give me that much."

Jay heaved a sigh. "She's alright."

The door closed with a near silent click.

"What the hell was that?" Jay's annoyed voice came from across the room.

She leaned her head against the bookcase behind her and berated herself for being such an idiot.

"I don't know," she said quietly.

"Yes, you do. Now get out here and explain."

She came out from her hiding spot but didn't get any closer.

"I get a good vibe from him," Jay told her when she just stood there looking ashamed. "He's a doer, that one. Take charge. In control."

"Smart," she agreed. "Observant."

"Can you read him?" he asked.

She shrugged. "It's more of an echo now than a true read."

"Unlike you, his root chakra is very clean. Totally in sync."

"I don't know what that means," she told him again, rubbing her eyes with her fingers.

"Let's get you set up with some rocks of your own." He held out a hand to her. "Meditate a little. Then you can spill your pretty little guts to me about calling that handsome man in the middle of night."

13

S he spent nearly three hours in the Reiki room of The Third
Eye with Jay. He placed rocks around her and had her close
her eyes while they meditated for long minutes, concen-
trating their energies on healing her spirit and helping her move
forward with her life. Jay was good at what he did, and she left feeling
lighter, like she'd gained some insight lying on that bed. They
discussed her meditation and where she would place her crystals at
home. He made sure she knew she was welcome to come back
anytime, but they made an appointment for a few days down
the road.

It was strange that she felt so comfortable with him. She hadn't
told him anything about her past, but talking about what she could
see made her feel free. He was right when he reminded her she'd felt
relief and when he asked, she hadn't hesitated to tell him why Dallas
was seeking her out. She even told him about the dream she had with
the woman and the explosion.

She called the hospital. Max had been released, so she knew
Dallas wasn't delivering bad news, but hiding and avoiding him just
made him more suspicious. That's why he was trying to find her.

She walked toward the pier and away from her usual bus stop.

The beach was a part of town she avoided as it was usually crowded. With Thanksgiving quickly approaching and the cool weather, it was nearly deserted. She found a bench at the end of the pier and sat, letting the cool ocean breeze wash over her.

It was a beautiful place. Picturing what she remembered of where she grew up, it was no wonder she ended up somewhere like this. There were no burned-out, hulking shells of buildings. No whores on street corners or gunfire at night. Just blue ocean waves as far as her eyes could see. Seagulls floated above the water, dancing through the clouds above.

She couldn't stay on the pier forever. Eventually, she'd have to go back to the camper and then to work. Someone would ask questions she didn't have answers for. She sighed, desperately wanting to take Jay's unsolicited advice and just tell them the truth.

Her heart wanted that. She wanted someone to know who she was and accept her.

But her head remembered too much, and every time the urge struck, it reminded her why she couldn't.

"Butch, she has to go! I can't have her here when this baby's born, telling him about the dead people she sees!"

"She can't help it."

"Neither can we! We've tried everything to fix her and we can't. It's time to let her go."

"I know."

She pushed the memory from her mind. She hadn't realized at the time, most of the adults who visited were shrinks Butch and Erin had hired. She hadn't known they were trying to fix her.

She didn't know she was broken.

Rosie sat on the pier, huddled in her sweater, until the sun went down and it got too cold, even for a northerner, to sit there. She trudged to the bus stop and waited for her bus. The ride was uneventful, certainly a nice benefit of her ability being on the fritz. There were times when sitting with a bus load of strangers and the spirits that surrounded them was overwhelming, like the time she'd gone to the bar to meet Wendy.

She unlocked her bike from the bench when she got to her stop and rode home. The woman in the woods was quiet. She turned down her driveway but slowed as she reached her camper.

Max was sitting in one of the chairs outside, her string lights lit up cheerfully, the dog lazing at his feet.

Rosie slid off the seat and walked closer. Hearing her approach, Max turned, his expression unreadable as he stood. He looked good and was dressed in his usual jeans and long-sleeve shirt. His hair was finger combed, and there was a short stubble growth on his chin.

She tentatively leaned her bike in its spot against the tree and stood in front of him.

"Are you okay?" It was all she cared about. She'd told herself all day long that she knew he was fine, but telling herself and hearing him say it were two different things.

He nodded. "I'm alive. Thanks to you."

She shook her head and looked away.

"Where've you been all day? I've been looking for you."

She turned to look back at him. "Why?"

He let out a laugh. "Are you kidding? Christ, Rosie, you showed up at my house in the middle of the night, saved my life, and disappeared. Did you really think I wasn't going to come looking?"

She lifted her hands and then dropped them. "I don't know."

"Well, you should have."

He reached out one of his big, work-roughened hands and held it out to her. She looked from his face and then back to his hand, hesitating before extending her hand to his. He quickly wrapped his fingers around hers and pulled her to him, his arm wrapping around her shoulders and holding her close. At first, she wasn't sure how to react, her free hand bent against his chest, not sure if she should push him away. Max pulled her hand around his body, wordlessly instructing her to wrap her arms around him. Cautiously, she did and felt the firm press of his chest against her face as he held her close.

She felt him rest his cheek against her hair.

"Thank you, Rosie." There was no mistaking his lips against the top of her head. "Thank you."

He held her close, not squeezing her too tightly, but not giving her any room to move, either.

It had been a long time since she'd been held by anyone, and just about never since she'd been held by a man. Though it was a just a thank you hug, she felt something stir beneath her skin. Her heart sped up to match the rhythm she felt beating beneath her cheek. She closed her eyes and inhaled deeply, breathing in his fresh smell, soap, fresh air, and Max all rolled into one.

"How did you know?" he asked, his cheek still resting on top of her head.

She shook her head, not wanting to think about it. All she wanted to do was catalog the moment so she could remember it forever.

He leaned back and pressed his palms to her cheeks, holding her face in his hands. His thumbs brushed gently back and forth.

It was, by far, the most intimate moment of her entire life.

"How did you know, Rosie?"

She was caught in his golden gaze, her eyes unable to look away from his.

"I don't know." She shook her head, mumbling an excuse by rote.

"I'll believe you," he insisted.

She reached her hands to cover his, intending to pull them away. "I don't know."

"I'll believe you," he said again.

"I was just stopping by."

He never looked away from her, his eyes pinning her in place and demanding the truth.

She felt something inside crack at his insistence.

"I'll believe you, Rosie. I swear I will."

Her hands were still on top of his as he held her face. With every word, he got closer until their noses were nearly touching, his breath on her lips when he spoke.

"I can't," she whispered, her eyes begging him to understand.

"You can," he argued, the tip of his nose gently brushing the side of hers. "I'm going to believe you, Rosie. I swear. I just need to hear you say it."

"No," she argued, closing her eyes in a last-ditch effort to break his spell.

"Yes." His gentle statement was followed by the barest press of his lips against hers. She kept her eyes closed, her hands instinctively tightening on his.

"I'll believe you," he told her again.

"No, you won't," she said, opening her eyes to convey her desperation.

"I will," he continued without hesitation.

It was on the tip of her tongue to just blurt it out and let him have it, but she held back. If she was going to tell him the truth, then she wanted to enjoy having him touch her just this one time if it was all she was going to get.

"Rosie," he started to say.

"Just wait." Her voice came out wobbly. "I just..." She stopped before she truly embarrassed herself.

She was going to tell him.

Max's lips brushed one cheek, and then the other before he rested his forehead against hers.

That was it. The moment she'd remember when things inevitably went south.

"I saw it in a dream." Her voice was soft. "And your dog told me."

Rosie opened her eyes when his fingers fell from her face and his forehead lifted. He looked confused.

"My dog?" He moved his hands to her shoulders.

"It's big and has long droopy ears? Blondish color?" She described the dog that was lazing by the door to the camper.

"Hannah?" He sounded puzzled, but when he said the dog's name, her tail thumped loudly against the ground.

"Say it again," Rosie instructed, watching the dog.

"Hannah," he said. The dog responded with a happy woof.

"That's her," Rosie agreed, her solemn eyes meeting his, knowing this could very well be the end of Max showing up on her patio and inviting her over to feed tiny, baby farm animals.

"Hannah's here?" he asked haltingly.

"By my camper. She follows you everywhere."

Strangely, that brought a smile to his face. "But she's..." He shook his head. "I loved that dog. I was devastated when she died."

Rosie said nothing.

"So, she's like, a ghost. And you can see her?"

She swallowed nervously and nodded, ready to take a step back.

"Holy shit," he breathed. "I knew." His hands went back to her cheeks. "After the cove, I knew." Out of nowhere, he laid a kiss on her lips, surprising her. "That's crazy." When her eyes widened, he was quick to correct himself. "Not crazy, crazy. Amazing crazy. You're amazing."

"No," she said. "I'm not."

"You saved my life after my dog that's been dead for ten years...what? What did Hannah do?"

The dog's tail thumped again.

"Showed up here barking like crazy."

"And you just followed a ghost dog down the street in the middle of the night?"

"She was pretty insistent that I follow her."

"Where is she?" He looked around, as if he might be able to see her.

She pointed to the door of the trailer. "She's lying right below Gizmo." Her face screwed up in confusion as a thought hit her. "How did Gizmo get out?"

Max shrugged. "He was crying to come out when I got here, so I opened the door."

"Wasn't it locked?"

"I used the key I found under the fake rock."

"Great," she groused.

"Back to my ghost friend. She just hangs out with me?"

"Pretty much."

"And you can see her. Like she's really there?"

"Pretty much," she agreed, although there were times when it was more complicated than that. She was going to take what she could get in the fact that he wasn't running for the hills and let the technicalities go.

"Is she unhappy?" he asked. "Isn't she supposed to, I don't know, follow the light or something?"

She raised her eyebrows in surprise. "She doesn't seem unhappy," Rosie offered.

He was truly concerned. He hadn't shown any disbelief or wariness in her. Just like he said, he believed her.

"You really believe me?"

His head shifted back as he looked down at her, his brows drawn in confusion. "Of course I do. I told you I would."

His promise had meant nothing to her. People said things they didn't mean all the time. They made promises they either never kept or never meant to keep in the first place.

"Did you not believe me?" he asked, sounding confused.

She shook her head. "It's not that." She hadn't dared to believe him, and that seemed like a totally different thing. "I just don't tell anyone. Ever."

"But you told me." He sent her a half smile and reached his arm around her and pulled her into a hug. "I was hoping we could hang out. I could thank you every few seconds for saving my life."

"That seems like it would get awkward really fast," she joked, her cheek pressed against his chest, feeling his laugh rumble through her body.

"Now, we have something else to talk about.

MAX'S FURNACE was being replaced. It had been the cause of the carbon monoxide leak, and he wasn't in any hurry to get back there, so they decided to spend some time at the camper, hanging out.

She showed him in and went to her tiny kitchen area but Max just stood there, staring at her, before he closed the door behind him. Rosie looked at him in question.

"Should I hold the door open in case Hannah wants to come in?"

She rolled her eyes. "If Hannah wants to come in, she will. Believe me."

"Is that weird?"

"Every damn time," she answered without hesitating, then looked back to the kitchen. "Uh, one problem," she said. "I don't have much for food unless you don't mind eating granola bars and popcorn."

"Yeah, no." He shook his head and winced. "We'll go grab some takeout or something." Two seconds later, he followed that with, "We'll get it delivered."

She wondered if Max wasn't feeling as well as he was letting on.

"Do you like pizza?" he asked.

"How are you feeling? Really?" she asked, ignoring his question.

He made a pained face causing her level of concern jump about ten notches. "I've got a headache like you read about, but other than that, I'm good."

"Did you take something?"

"Not in a while," he admitted, then tapped his phone's screen a few times and held it to his ear. "I'll take something after we eat."

He ordered pizza and salad, then gave them specific directions to her camper.

She picked up some of the throw blankets and pillows from her little couch and put them off to the side. Then she set-up her laptop on the table, which was how she normally watched a movie or TV shows. Remembering her bag, she opened it up and placed her new crystals and stones around the camper. As instructed by Jay, she placed a piece of quartz in each corner of the camper, from the far end where her small living area was to the other end, where the bed was. One went in the kitchen, and one right across from that, where the little table was. She then put a stone on the first step heading out the door, tucked way in the back so she wouldn't kill herself tripping on it.

"What are you doing?" Max asked, looking on curiously.

She grabbed three more stones and turned around, kneeling at the side of her bed. She shoved the crystals between her mattress and box spring.

"I'm cleansing my energies." It sounded skeptical to her own ears. Even though she believed Jay and in what he did, it was hard to imagine anything helping her.

"Are your energies dirty?" Obviously, he didn't know any more about it than she did. "That sounded bad," he immediately corrected himself. "Are your energies in need of cleansing?"

She shrugged and smiled at him as she stood. "I'm all kinds of out of whack. This is supposed to help."

"What's that mean?"

"You want to watch a movie?"

"Sure." He followed her lead and began looking over her online movie list. "So, tell me more about your energy stuff."

"You don't want to hear that." She waved him off and threw some popcorn in the microwave.

He let out a laugh. "I'm doing my best from not sitting you down and grilling you about the whole thing. You just told me you see ghosts and, what? Dream the future? If you think I don't have a million questions, then you don't know me very well."

She knew better than to believe he'd just let it go. He was a determined type of guy, but also nurturing enough to not bulldoze her for information.

"Have you heard of The Third Eye?" she asked.

"Yeah, that hippie store downtown."

"That's the place. The owner, Jay, has been working with me, trying to get me back to normal."

He sat and gave her his full attention. "I didn't know you weren't normal."

She laughed. "Well, if you didn't before, you do now."

"That's not what I meant. I didn't know there was something wrong."

Without realizing she was doing it, she touched the side of her face where her scabs were nearly all gone.

"I've been having a few ongoing issues." She evaded his implied question.

"That have something to do with your bike accident?" At her

sharp look, he explained the obvious. "You touched your face when I asked about it. I figured that was why."

She took a deep breath and came to sit next to him, looking over the movies on the computer with him.

"I've been off since then," she agreed vaguely.

"What's that mean?"

She shrugged like it was no big deal. "Not being able to see some of the things I used to. Sleepwalking. Being stalked by a ghost in the woods."

He stilled her hand on the computer's touchpad.

"You're being stalked by a ghost?" He sounded alarmed.

With good reason, she thought.

She nodded. "That might be an exaggeration. I just see her in the woods sometimes."

"What does she want?"

Rosie couldn't remember the killer's face, but she remembered his eyes and the feeling of his hands pressing down on her throat. Her mind went to her mother, and she immediately wiped both memories from her mind.

Rosie took a deep breath, looked away from him, and let herself be honest with him, even if it was only a half truth.

"She wants to be found."

14

R osie woke to a strip of sunlight in her eyes. She lifted her hand to block the light and looked around.

"Good morning." Max's voice, deep and rough from sleep, came from behind her. His voice rumbled through her and she realized they were both still on her little couch.

"Oh God," she groaned as she tried to sit up, her back aching. "Why did we sleep on the couch?".

He laughed and wrapped an arm around the top of her chest, pulling her back to him. "You fell asleep watching some creepy zombie show. I was too scared to walk home."

"I didn't expect you to walk home," she argued. "But the bed would have been more comfortable."

"After you fell asleep, I put on a documentary. Guess I crashed, too."

She closed her eyes and reveled in the feel of his hard chest behind her, his breath puffing in her hair.

"Is she here?"

Rosie's eyes popped open and she looked around.

"Who?"

"Hannah," he said, like it was obvious.

"No." She sat up and looked back at him. "She's probably outside with Gizmo."

"He can see her, too."

"They like to chase each other around. Remember that day when you were here and Gizmo came flying out of the woods?" At his nod, she continued. "Hannah was right behind him."

"She always did like getting into trouble with other animals."

"Yeah, well, she's why your poor sheep has been hiding in that corner. Hannah just corrals her there and barks her fool head off."

He tilted his head and stared at her. "Is that who you were shooing that day?"

"The minute she ran off, the sheep did, too. I felt bad for her."

"That's crazy," he exclaimed, bewildered.

Rosie knew he didn't mean to say *she* was crazy. She was aware how unbelievable her talents could be, but the word struck a nerve. It put her right back in the Coleman Institute, where she never wanted to be again.

He pulled her back and kissed her hair.

"What you can do is crazy. Unbelievable." He sighed. "It sounds bad no matter how I say it. I believe you, Rosie, and I don't think you're crazy. Not even a little bit."

"I didn't say anything."

"Don't worry. Your eyes said it all."

"I'm sorry," she started.

"You have nothing to be sorry about." His stomach growled. "Other than trying to starve me."

She looked around. "Is there any leftover pizza?"

"Yeah, right," he scoffed. "I polished that off last night. Let's go get breakfast."

"Don't you have a job?" She sat up and pulled out of his arms, turning to face him.

"You're sexy in the morning." He had a smile on his face but his golden eyes seared her with heat.

She covered her face in embarrassment. "Don't do that."

He laughed again. "Do what? Tell you you're sexy?"

"Yes!" She squeaked with a giggle that made her feel ridiculous.

His hands wrapped around the sides of her head, and he pulled her closer, but she ducked her head.

"I'm not kissing you before I brush my teeth."

"You better get in the bathroom and get working then, because I'm not waiting much longer to kiss you," he warned.

Heart pounding, she fled to the bathroom to clean herself up. When she finished, Max was gone, so she took the opportunity to throw on a pair of her favorite ripped jeans, a sweater, and her well-loved flowered combat boots. She found Max waiting right outside the door, watching the woods.

When he saw her, he sent her that full-bodied, sexy smile.

"My turn," he said before he slipped past her and into the camper.

She didn't think he meant for his smile to be that sexy. Frankly, he'd sent it her way a few times, and she'd interpreted it as completely platonic. But this morning, it seemed different somehow, more poignant. It was strange to be so attracted to Max. Not that she'd never experienced attraction, but she'd never felt comfortable enough to act on it. She'd never cuddled on a couch before and had definitely never slept with a man, even if it was just sleeping and nothing more.

Rosie took a few steps forward and squatted down, scratching Gizmo behind his ears. She rubbed her hands back and forth through his thick fur as he stood and rubbed one side of his body against her palm and then the other. Hannah looked on in question, her tail thumping against the ground.

"Sorry, Hannah. I can't touch you," she told the shaggy dog.

The camper door opened behind her, and Rosie stood nervously, turning to find Max watching her. She resisted the urge to shove her hands in her pockets, which she was glad for, because he reached her in three quick strides. She needed her hands to balance when he grabbed her head and swiftly brought his lips to hers, her hands filled with the front of his shirt.

"I used your toothbrush," he said, right before his lips touched hers, soft and hot, insisting she reciprocate. She didn't hesitate to join in, opening her mouth and touching her tongue to his lips. He groaned, his hands sliding down to her shoulders and back, ending on her butt. He pulled her tighter against him, which made her squeak in surprise.

Suddenly her feet were off the ground and she was spun around, her back pressed to the outside of her camper. Their mouths moved hungrily against each other, and she instinctively threaded her fingers through his hair. His hips pressed against the apex of her thighs, sending tiny jolts of lightning through her core. The next time he pressed against her, she pressed back. Max made a deep growling sound.

The sound of a siren pierced the air. Rosie let out a strangled scream while Max dropped her legs and shielded her from the intrusion. He turned around, blocking her view.

"You're such an asshole," he said.

"Nothing going on my ass." It was Dallas. "I have a bone to pick with her."

"Yeah, well, she's busy."

Dallas laughed. "You can feel her up while I talk to her."

Max laughed, too, their banter casual. "Not gonna happen."

"Come on," Dallas complained. "He sent me looking for you all over goddamn town, you know."

He was talking to her. She peeked out from behind Max and looked at Dallas, rugged and imposing in his uniform.

"You didn't find me."

It was a lie and he knew it. "Whatever you need to tell yourself, honey. I want to know why you disappeared."

Max took a step away from her and faced her, silently telling her he'd like to know the answer, too.

She looked between them and stubbornly kept quiet, folding her arms over her chest.

"You called me in the middle of the night," Dallas said with a frustrated sigh. "Hysterical, begging me for help, and then you disappeared."

She shrugged. "You came. You went with Max. That's why I called you."

His head reared back, and he stared at her in confusion. "Did you think I'd forget you were there? Why didn't you come with us?"

"You didn't need me. You had it covered."

"That's not the point," Dallas argued and turned his frustrated gaze to Max. "Did you not talk to her about this?"

Max looked uncomfortable. "It hadn't come up yet."

Rosie realized whatever they were talking about was something they had discussed before. She took a step back, away from Max, which he immediately noticed. He grabbed her hand and didn't let her get any further.

"No," he told her firmly, then turned to Dallas. "Just go, man. I'll call you later."

She watched Dallas fight his desire to stay and argue, although she didn't know what he was so mad about. Max's grip was tight on her wrist, not giving her any room to wiggle away.

He finally threw up his hands and rolled his eyes. "This is nuts, you know. People don't call for help and disappear. That's some crazy shit, Rosie." He spun on his heel, got in his cruiser, and drove away.

"It's just hard to understand, that's all." Max's voice was gentle. "You weren't there when I woke up. I was confused. Dallas couldn't find you when he showed up at my house, and no one remembered you leaving. Then we couldn't find you."

She took a deep breath to calm her heart rate. It was the thing she hadn't even been able to explain even to herself. That inexplicable reason she stayed in the shadows. Her deep-rooted fear of living in the light and all it entailed. The shadows were where people like Rosie lived, where she could hide and no one noticed her.

Somehow, here, they'd noticed her.

"I don't know why I hid," she whispered. "I'm just used to hiding."

He cupped her shoulders and turned her to face him, not letting go. "Baby, you can hide from everyone else, but you can't hide from us. We're you're friends."

Frustrated, she told him the same thing she'd told Wendy. "I don't want any friends! I don't need friends!"

"But you have us," he said simply.

"I didn't ask for friends."

"I know."

"I'm better at hiding."

"Nah." He smiled down at her. "You just think that. We'll get it all figured out."

"Don't do that," she snapped.

"Do what?" He asked, unruffled despite her frustration and anger.

"Don't make promises you can't keep."

"What? That we'll get it all figured out? I believe that, Rosie."

"You don't even know what you're trying to figure out. I don't know what my problem is half the time." She held a hand to her forehead in frustration. "You have no idea what you're talking about."

He leaned in quickly and placed a kiss on her lips, catching her completely off guard.

"We'll figure it out." He slipped her hand inside his and tugged her toward her bike. "Come on. You can ride on the handlebars."

～

THEY ENDED up at Max's, where he whipped up some egg sandwiches. She hadn't said much since they arrived, just sat on the other side of the counter, watching as he worked in the kitchen. Max was comfortable in everything he did, from working on his farm to cooking in the kitchen. She wished she could be so at ease with everything. She wondered what it would be like to just enjoy being who you were and being comfortable in that.

He slid a hot sandwich across the counter to her and sat down.

"Are you working tonight?"

She nodded, her mouth full.

"Wendy said you've been mostly in the office but picked up new clients. How's that going?"

"I've never met them. They aren't home when I'm there."

135

"Do you like it so far?"

"It's alright," she admitted. "Not much different than before, other than the hours. How's the lamb?"

She'd thought about the baby sheep a few times over the last few days, wondering how it was faring with the big girls.

Max's face lit up with a smile. "She's great. We feed her and she spends all of her time with Cocoa."

"The bigger sheep?"

"The one you said Hannah was bugging."

Rosie nodded.

"Is she here?"

"Hannah?" He'd been looking around suspiciously since they walked through the door, like he expected her to pop up and beg for scraps at his feet.

"She ran out back when we got here."

"So, she came with us?"

"Ran beside the bike."

He shook his head in disbelief and muttered, "So crazy."

Max let her finish her sandwich before he started with more questions. "Okay." He pulled her plate aside and faced her. "Time to talk more about the bomb you dropped on me last night."

Warily, she leaned away from him. "I don't do parlor tricks."

"Parlor tricks?" he asked confused. "I don't need you to prove anything to me. I want to know about whatever's been going on since your bike accident."

"Oh," she said.

"You said there's someone stalking you. That she wants to be found."

She nodded and resisted the urge to look away.

"Can you find her?"

Her entire being shied away from that idea. Nothing good ever came from finding the dead.

When she was younger, she'd done her best to help the police by locating the remains of spirits that had come to her. Slogging through woods and swamps, and blindly following ghosts. Eventually, they moved on to the other side while she stayed behind and endured sidelong glances and whispered conversations.

Max changed tactics. "What about the sleepwalking? You said that's new?"

"It's all her," Rosie told him and finally looked away. "My accident..." she trailed off and tried again. "I came around the corner and she was right there, just standing in front of me." She turned her eyes back to him and felt the ridiculous sting of tears, remembering what she'd seen of the woman's death. It had been truly horrible. "I tried not to hit her. I dumped the bike, but I still slid right through her."

He lifted a hand to her face, his thumb stroking her cheek.

"I can't touch them," she whispered, her lower lip trembling. "I touched her and it was awful. Now she won't leave me alone. I see her in the woods and in my dreams. In my dreams, I'm following her, through the woods and into the water."

"And then you're in the water?" At her nod, he asked, "Is that where she is?"

"I don't know. He killed her in the woods"

"Who killed her?" He sat up, alarmed. "Rosie, someone killed this lady?"

She pressed her hands to her throat. "He squeezed so tight. So hard."

"How do you know that?"

"When we touched, I saw how she died. Now she won't leave me alone, and everything's been totally out of whack."

"When we went to Smith's Cove, you couldn't hear me. Was that her?"

"It's just water. All I can hear is water in my ears."

"How do we get her to go away?" His voice was firm.

She didn't miss that he said "we." "It's never happened to me like this before, so I don't know. I wish I did," she told him. "Jay's trying to help, with the crystals."

"Somehow I don't think crystals are going to solve the problem."

She agreed but was willing to try anything.

"What happens if we try to find her?"

At best, she got run out of town and became known as a lying charlatan, or at worst, a raving lunatic.

"How do I explain that?" she asked. "Finding a dead body? Are you ready to go out looking for a corpse?"

"Dallas-"

"Is a cop," she interrupted. "He'd have a million questions I wouldn't be able to answer."

"He'd believe the truth, baby."

"No, he wouldn't," she argued. "And even if he did, I'm not prepared to be the police department's go-to psychic bloodhound. I don't want to be used and then called a fraud if I'm wrong. I don't need to be talked about and laughed at behind my back."

His face held a trace of awareness. "You've worked with the police before."

"I tried. It didn't work and I won't go there again, Max. I won't. I don't want Dallas to know."

"Then we need to find another way, because you can't keep getting dragged to the cove. That's not safe."

She shrugged, not sure how to take his help.

"You said you had a dream about what happened here. Is that part of the ghost thing? The thing with the lady in the woods?"

She shook her head. "No, that's something else."

Rosie watched him carefully, knowing it was too much, too fast.

"We don't have to talk about that," she offered, giving him an out. "We don't have to talk about any of this."

"I don't know anything about ghosts. I don't know anything about whatever kids of dreams you're having. You're going to have to give me a learning curve here."

"It's okay," she assured him. "You don't have to worry about it. I have to get going to work soon anyway."

"Will you stop doing that?" He sounded put out. "Will you stop telling me everything's okay? Like that gives me permission to not worry about you. I worry about you, Rosie. I'm going to keep worrying about you. Probably even after we get this shit figured out, so you're going to have to get used to it."

She had no answer for that other than to argue that he was wrong, and doing that would get them nowhere.

"Sometimes I have dreams about things that haven't happened yet."

"Like seeing the future?" His eyebrows were nearly to his hairline.

"Something like that," she said, thinking about the woman from her dream.

"And you had a dream you needed to come here?"

She thought about the woman that looked exactly like her, and the exploding fireball.

"Yeah," she answered simply, leaving the rest out.

15

Since she wasn't working late hours anymore, Max offered to pick her up from the bus stop after work. She refused, but promised she'd swing by on her way home. She went to the office and worked on paperwork for a while before having a run-in with Wendy.

"Where the hell have you been? Max was in the hospital, and you didn't even show up." Wendy stormed into the office she'd given Rosie.

"Obviously, you haven't talked to your brother," Rosie answered.

"Not today, no," she admitted. "But he and Dallas were looking for you like crazy yesterday. Why didn't you stick around?"

"Sticking around isn't really my thing."

"You saved his life." Wendy's voice was soft. "I could have given my friend a hug for saving my little brother's life."

"It wasn't a big deal, Wendy."

"It was a huge deal."

Rosie waved her off. "It's fine. Did you need me for something?"

"Yeah." Wendy was giving her a look like she'd lost her mind. "I needed to give you a hug for saving my brother's life. I just told you that."

"Oh." She looked wary. "I thought that was just something people said."

"No, you lunkhead, it's something we're about to do. Come on." She held her arms open. "Bring it in."

"Can I file this as workplace harassment?"

"Only if you want me to bug the crap out of you for the rest of the day."

Rolling her eyes, Rosie stood and gave Wendy a loose hug while Wendy squeezed her tightly. "Thank you, Rosie. Thank you."

"Okay." She tried to pull away from the embrace. "I get it. You're welcome."

Being thanked for saving Max's life seemed crazy to her. It's not like she would have to let him die if she could do anything to help it.

When she pulled away, Wendy was smiling. "So. You've been hanging out with Max?"

"What?"

"You said, 'Obviously, you haven't talked to your brother' when I asked about not seeing him, which means you've seen him."

Spent the night in his arms, Rosie thought with a little zing in her chest. "I did. We had breakfast this morning."

Wendy did that ridiculous eyebrow bob. "And I assume he thanked you, too."

By holding her up against her camper and pressing his erection into her core. "He made me an egg sandwich."

She rolled her eyes. "What a loser. I thought he'd at least try to romance you. I'll have to talk to him."

"I'm all set on the romance." She was too afraid to tell Wendy what was really going on with Max. She'd never had a girlfriend before, and she didn't really know how that was supposed to work. Would she be embarrassed when Wendy asked a million questions? Would she feel silly for not being more experienced? Would Wendy tease her because Max was her younger brother and that was a strange dynamic? There were too many variables she wasn't sure how to navigate, so she just didn't do it at all.

Besides, what was going on with Max? It wasn't like she had any idea herself.

Wendy sat on the edge of Rosie's desk. "Someone hurt you really badly, didn't they?"

Rosie swallowed audibly and looked back at her paperwork. Yes, she thought in answer. They had. Just not in the way Wendy thought.

"I keep wondering why a woman like you doesn't go out at all and doesn't want any friends. You don't want to work near anyone or even work hours where you have to be near anyone. All I can think is someone must have really hurt you."

"We all get hurt at some point, don't we?" she answered vaguely.

"We do." Wendy considered with a nod of her head. "I haven't removed myself from social situations or society all together though."

"It's nothing that extreme, Wendy. I'm just not great with people, that's all."

"Somehow, I doubt that." She changed the subject. "The Martin's were very happy with your work last week. They asked about bumping their service up to twice a week."

"That's good." Rosie smiled.

"How's working days? Treating you okay?"

"It's been fine. I meant to ask you what the schedule will be next week with Thanksgiving."

"Everyone's got the day off, you know that. Most of our clients are closed through the weekend, so we'll all get a few days off. I'm thinking the beginning of the week, we're going to be running ragged."

"I was thinking the same thing. I'm going to put in a few extra shifts if you don't mind. I want to make sure we get everything done."

"You don't have to do that. It should be okay."

"It should be, but if they aren't and the girls need an extra hand, I want to be there."

Wendy sent her a smile. "That's why I put you in charge."

MAX WAS WAITING on his porch swing when she stopped by after work. It was eight and pitch black, the light on her handlebars lighting her way.

"I really hate you riding that road at night," he told her when she climbed the steps.

She sat next to him, enjoying the feel of his arm when he wrapped it around her shoulder.

"I really appreciate you not making a big deal about it even though you hate it." She knew it must have been hard for him. He would want to take care of her, it was his personality, and it spoke very much to his self-control to not take over and just come pick her up anyway.

"How was your day, dear?" he joked.

"Pushing papers and cleaning toilets. Yours?"

"Weeding the gardens and shoveling shit," he replied with a smile in his voice.

His foot pushed them gently back and forth.

"Your sister gave me an earful and then tried to hug the life out of me."

"She's an emotional rollercoaster, that one."

"How can she be so nice all the time? Even when she's mad, she's nice."

Max didn't answer, just kept swinging them back and forth.

"I'm just a maid, but she's still giving me a chance to grow based on who I am and what I can do, not where I went to college." Or didn't go, as the case may be.

Max squeezed her a little closer.

"She's just a great boss."

"She's your friend, baby. You're going to have to say the words eventually."

"What is this that we're doing here, Max?" she asked out of the blue. "You keep calling me baby."

He kissed the back of her head. "You want me to call you something else?"

That was not her point, and no, she absolutely didn't want him to call her something else. When he used that endearment, it twisted her up inside and made her feel unbelievably special.

"That's not what I asked."

"You want to know what we're doing," he mused as they looked out over the expanse of the front yard. "We're hanging out and getting to know each other."

"Sometimes, I feel like you're trying to save me."

"I am," he admitted. "Just like you're saving me."

She let out a small laugh. "What do you need saving from? Goats?"

"No. From being lonely. From not taking the time to see what's out there in the world. I went to sleep a few weeks ago thinking my sheep was skittish. Now I know that isn't the case. You're teaching me things, Rosie. You're saving me from being closed minded."

"Do you want to be saved?"

"By you? Hell yes."

Again, her growling stomach interrupted them.

"Are you always hungry?" he laughed.

"I haven't eaten dinner yet," she defended.

"What were you going to do? Go back to your camper and eat popcorn?" She looked vaguely guilty. "Jesus. Come on. Time to eat."

She took her usual seat at the counter as he pulled out leftover pasta and meatballs.

"Sauce or no sauce?" he asked.

"Sauce."

He fixed her a plate and set it in front of her. "You want a soda or something?"

"Water?"

She twirled the pasta around her fork and ate with gusto. The meatballs tasted homemade, and she swore, when she was done eating, she'd ask if he made them himself. She added some cheese and had more pasta, and then took a slice of the bread he'd put out.

"Did you eat lunch?" Max was watching her with wide eyes.

She shook her head no and covered her mouth with a napkin as she finished chewing.

"Sorry. I'm being a pig. I'm just starving."

He held out his hand in invitation. "Pig out all you want. I think it's sexy as hell."

She rolled her eyes. "There isn't much about spaghetti and meatballs that's sexy."

"Yeah, but we could work on that. I'm thinking about the trail of sauce a meatball might leave if I were to, say, roll one across the skin on your stomach."

She looked up sharply to see that hot look in his eyes again, his vague aura pulsing the red of passion, and she knew he was telling the truth.

"I never thought anyone could make the word meatball sound sexy," she told him with a smile. "Did you make these meatballs yourself, by the way?" She took a daintier bite of pasta this time.

"I did." His eyes watched her mouth as she put the fork in and slid the pasta off.

She covered her face. "Stop!"

"What?" He laughed.

"You know what!"

"I can't help it. You're sexy. I like a girl with an appetite."

"Well, I like to eat, but you can't watch me like that."

"I might have to turn around then."

"I'm done, anyway." She pushed her nearly clean plate away. "But no more of that."

"Meatballs?" he asked, his voice clearly indicating he wasn't talking about the meatballs.

She threw her napkin at him, but he caught it and put it on the counter. He then pulled her plate over to himself and finished it off.

"What are we watching tonight?" he asked as he polished off the last of her spaghetti.

"Oh, am I hanging out here tonight?" she asked, taking the now empty plate and bringing it to the sink.

Max followed and wrapped his arms around her from behind and nuzzled her neck as she washed the dish.

"I was hoping so," he said. "But if you're tired or just want to go home, I'll bring you."

"No." She was quick to answer. "I want to hang out. But I have to sleep in a bed tonight. My back is killing me from that couch last night."

He turned her around and brought his face close to hers, rubbing the tip of his nose along the length of hers. "I have a bed here." His voice was soft and tempting.

She closed her eyes and enjoyed the feel of him so close to her.

"I'm not having sex with you tonight, Max," she told him.

He pulled back just a tiny bit. "I didn't say anything about sex. Get your mind out of the gutter. I was talking about sleeping, like we did last night."

She rolled her eyes. "Do you really think sleeping in the same bed is a good idea?"

"I think it's the best idea I've had all day."

"Well, that makes one of us." She pressed her hands against his chest and pushed him back a few inches. "I mean it when I say I don't want to sleep with you, like that, tonight. I don't want to be pressured or have an 'oops, it just happened' kind of moment."

He leaned further back, giving her more space. "Do you think I'd do that?"

"I just don't want there to be confusion between us in this. I know a lot of girls-"

He pressed a finger to her lips, which she'd always thought was strange when she saw it happen on TV, but in real life, it was sweet because he followed it up with a kiss.

"You aren't a lot of girls. You're you. I don't expect anything from you other than your always interesting company. If you sleep here tonight, it will be totally PG." He screwed his face up. "PG-13. We'll cross those other bridges when we come to them." He planted a quick kiss on her lips. "You set up the TV. I'll make the popcorn."

IT WAS MUCH LATER when Max was pulling her off the couch.

"Come on, sleepy girl. Let's go to bed."

She trudged up the stairs. He showed her to his bedroom and the attached bathroom.

"You can go in here. My toothbrush is in the holder. I'll give you a couple minutes." He left the room, giving her privacy to use the facilities and brush her teeth. When she opened the door, she recognized the room from the last time she'd been there, after Max had found her wandering down the side of the road. She pushed the thought from her mind.

Max had left her a pair of gym shorts on the bed, and she slipped back into the bathroom to put them on. It was a big, spacious bathroom, and had obviously been remodeled recently. The fixtures were all new but the antique clawfoot tub remained, the centerpiece of the room. When she was changed, she went into his room and waited for Max to come back.

A minute or two later, the door pushed open and he came in, smiling when he saw her sitting on his bed. He leaned in and kissed her. "Let me brush my teeth and I'll be right back."

"Which side do you sleep on?" she asked, hoping to get into the bed.

"The middle," he laughed as he went into the bathroom.

"Uh-oh, me too," she answered, slipping under the covers right in the center of the bed.

He poked his head out of the bathroom, his hand still moving the toothbrush back and forth in his mouth. Then he mumbled something completely unintelligible and disappeared.

"That sounds like a great idea," she said, pretending she understood him. "I'll sleep here while you sleep on this tiny side. You're such a gentleman."

He mumbled something else, but louder from the bathroom.

"You want me to have your pillow, too? You are too kind. Really."

"You're feisty at night." Max smiled as he came out and switched the bathroom light off. He had on a t-shirt and gym shorts. He put a knee on the bed and eyed her for a second. "Ready to make out before we go to sleep?"

She let out a laugh. "Do we have it all planned out?"

"Yep." He lowered himself over her, covers between them. "First I lay here, kind of half on top."

"Check," she said quietly.

"Check," he agreed. "Then I kiss your neck, right here." His lips moved to where her shoulder met her neck, and he began to kiss her gently. "That's your favorite spot, so far."

She swallowed. "Check."

One of his hands slid from where it was resting on the bed to her hip.

His lips moved from her neck and across her chest, above her tank top, and to the other side.

His head pulled back slightly when his mouth passed a raised ridge, his fingers coming up to trace the pattern.

"What's this?"

He looked up at her face, but his eyes quickly shifted down to her lips, the moment forgotten.

"I think I might go in for the lips next. I'm not sure I can follow the rest of the plan."

"That works for me," she whispered, grabbing his head and pulling him to her, happy for his distraction.

His lips felt the same as they had the first time, hot and soft against hers. He was gentle with her, not forcing her or moving too fast, but was still able to convey how much he was enjoying himself. They explored each other's mouths, leisurely getting to know one another and the passion between them.

Max's hand slid slowly from her hip, up her stomach, and over her breast. She sucked in a breath.

"Oh God, yeah," he breathed against her lips and kissed her deeper.

His thumb and fingers played with her nipple as it pressed against the thin tank she was wearing. Her hips moved of their own volition, her legs spreading wider to accommodate him.

She explored his back and shoulders, threading her fingers through his dark hair while he toyed with her breasts, going from one to the other.

Eventually he stopped and rested his forehead against hers. "PG-13," he breathed. "Time to stop."

This was obviously the point in time where most people took a cold shower. Her body felt like there were sparks dancing under her skin, and she could barely keep herself from squirming under the covers.

"Good idea," she agreed. She wasn't ready for sex with Max. She knew in her mind that she needed to trust him completely before something so personal happened between the two of them. But, oh God, her body was disagreeing.

He backed off just a little and fixed the blankets around her, then slid in under the blanket but above the sheet.

"That okay?" he asked.

It was perfect, she thought. So close, but not too close.

"That's good," she told him.

She turned to her side and let him slide in behind her, wrapping her in his arms.

They both ended up in the middle, sharing the same space.

16

The woman was standing in the doorway of Max's bedroom when Rosie opened her eyes. She was more ethereal now than when Rosie had first run into her. Some spirits came dressed in what they wanted to be seen in, a favorite shirt or something similar. Some came in what they'd been buried in like Max and Wendy's grandmother. This spirit was obviously in the clothes she'd been killed in, a World War II era blouse and long skirt, the hem caked with mud. One of her shoes had been lost, and her bare foot was covered with dried blood.

"Please."

"Don't follow her," Toby said a she stood next to the door, leaning against the wall. Her arms were folded across her chest as she glared at the woman.

The voices were in her head, along with the sound of rushing water.

"Who are you?" Rosie said, not sure if she was asking the ghost or Toby.

"Please help me," the ghost repeated, desperation clinging to her every word.

"Help yourself, Happy. Don't keep worrying about everyone else," Toby insisted.

Rosie felt pulled, against her will, to stand and follow the spirit as she floated out of Max's bedroom. She led Rosie down the stairs and through the kitchen, right out the back door. She passed the chicken coop and the sheep pasture, blindly following as the woman floated over the tilled surface of Max's gardens.

"Help me," the woman's voice repeated, as though Rosie might forget.

They passed three separate garden areas until the woman stopped at the edge of the woodline, hesitating before going on. Rosie hurried through the dirt, her subconscious pushing her, concerned she might lose the woman. When she neared, the spirit continued through the woods, soundlessly veering around rocks and fallen branches. She came to a small stream and hovered above it, turning to Rosie. Her body heeded the woman's pull, and she stepped up to the stream. When her feet touched the water, she fell to her knees and groped around the rocky bed, feeling the grit and stones that lay there. Remembering something from her moment in the woman's mind, Rosie looked up in a daze and caught a glimpse of the same trees that had towered over her in those final moments.

This was where she died, Rosie knew.

But this was not where she lay.

～

DALLAS PULLED to the side of old route thirteen and shook his head. The girl was complicated with a capital C. Max was crazy for getting involved with someone like her. After their last run-in, he wasn't sure where they stood. So, instead of getting out of his car and having her run away for whatever reason, he picked up his phone.

"What's with your girl?" he asked outright when Max answered.

"Rosie?"

"No, the other one," he deadpanned. "Of course, Rosie! She's out here wandering around the woods."

"She's what?"

"She just crossed the road in front of me. Coming from the woods behind your place and heading-"

"To Smith's Cove. Shit." Max's breathing was loud in Dallas' ears. "I'm in town at the feed store. Follow her! Do not let her get in that water."

"Listen, if she's into skinny dipping-"

"She's asleep, Dallas!" He heard a car door slam and assumed Max was already on his way. "She'll go in through the woods but she's going to Smith's Cove, and if you don't get there and stop her, she's going in the water."

Dallas rolled his eyes. "Are you kidding?"

"Do I sound like I'm joking?" Max, who rarely got angry, yelled in his ear. "I'm on my way, but I won't get there in time."

He put his cruiser in gear and headed toward Smith's Cove, having lost sight of Rosie in the woods. "Is she nuts or what?" he asked. "This might be one even you can't save, buddy."

"Don't call her that."

"Come on. The bike accident, the hermit routine, the running away and now this? If it walks like a duck and quacks like a duck, Max. Rosie's crazy."

"We can argue about it later, just do me a favor and don't let her drown before I get there."

With another sigh, Dallas drove out to Smith's Cove and looked around. There was no sign of Rosie yet, so he got out of his car, leaned against the hood, and waited. He liked Rosie and all, she seemed like a sweet girl, but like he said before, complicated as hell. Who wanted to throw that kind of monkey wrench in their lives if they didn't have to? Max was a smart guy, had his shit together and his life working like a well-oiled machine. Why would he want to add someone like Rosie to the mix and run himself ragged trying to chase her all over God's creation? Made no sense to him.

It was at least five minutes before he heard a branch break in the woods. He turned to see Rosie barreling her way out of a thick growth of bushes, her eerie eyes glued to the water. He sat up a little straighter, watching her forward progress.

It was a cool day, a chill in the air, and Rosie was wearing nothing more than a tank top and what looked like a pair of Max's gym shorts. She made her way closer, moving around big rocks and driftwood piles, but her gaze never left the water. He waited as she closed in on him, walking through the parking lot and heading straight for him, but her stare never wavered. He saw it coming before it happened and winced as the ball of her foot crunched a shard of a broken glass, but she took no notice. She just kept walking, her dirty foot leaving a trail of blood in the sand behind her.

More curious than alarmed, wondering how far could she really take this, Dallas watched her approach. When she neared, he pushed his butt off the hood and stood in front of her, blocking her path.

She stepped around him like he was just another pile of debris in her way. With a roll of his eyes, he spun around and grabbed her wrist.

"Rosie. Come on," he said. Her hands were like ice, and when he looked down, her fingers were wrinkled, like they'd been soaking in water.

She never looked his way, so he walked in front of her again. He leaned down to look in her eyes and a chill ran down his spine. That clear, uncanny blue of her eyes was barely visible, her pupils so dilated, they took up nearly her whole eye.

"Rosie," he called again, hoping to get her attention.

She tugged against his hold, still trying to get to the water. Max had been right. She was going to get in that damn water.

The leaves around them rustled loudly and the trees around them began swaying wildly. It started small, but the wind quickly became a roar in his ears, whipping around his face as leaves flew by. When it started picking up sand, he put a hand up to cover his eyes, and Rosie broke free. She stepped around him, and in a few strides was knee-deep in the cove.

The wind swirled as he tried to follow her.

"Rosie!" In a flash, Max was behind Rosie, his arms around her waist, pulling her from the water.

Her feet continued to move, her hands reaching for something unseen as Max pulled her to solid ground.

"I said don't let her get in the water!" Max yelled as he wrapped his arms around her. "I'm here. Come back, Rosie."

"I didn't let her do anything!" Dallas argued. "I grabbed her, and then the wind kicked up and there was sand flying everywhere."

Max looked around skeptically. That was when Dallas noticed the air around them was still and serene.

He looked away as Max murmured to Rosie, uncomfortable with how intimate they were.

"Come on, baby. Come back. Wake up." He had his arms wrapped around her, her cheek pressed to his chest.

Dallas could see her eyes, and they hadn't changed at all, not one iota of recognition there.

"She's still out of it," he told Max, who looked at him in question. "Her eyes."

"She's freezing," Max said, rubbing his hands up and down her back. "Wake up, Rosie." He cupped her cheeks and kissed her. Not invasive kissing, but pecks on her forehead, her lips, her chin. His hands ran through her hair. "Wake up."

Dal watched as Rosie blinked rapidly, her hands rising to fist in Max's shirt.

"That's it," Max urged her. "Come back to me, baby."

She blinked a few more times and sagged into Max's arms.

"I can't hear anything," she whispered.

"Okay, we're gonna get you out of here." He turned her around and started leading her to his truck.

Dallas saw she was still leaving a watery trail of blood behind her. He took a few short steps and scooped Rosie up in his arms, completely ignoring Max's protest.

"What the hell?"

"Her foot. She stepped on a piece of glass," he answered simply. "Open the door of your truck."

With a growl, Max trotted off and opened the door. Dallas looked down to see Rosie, pale faced and shaking, staring up at him with a vaguely lost expression on her face. He could see the outline of her nipples through her tank top, which he studiously avoided looking at. The burn scar was a whole different story. It was about four inches long and shaped like a T.

"I've got you," he assured her.

"I can't hear you," she murmured and then closed her eyes.

"Why the hell can't she hear me?" His angry gaze turned to Max.

"Just get her in the truck," Max ordered. "It's this place. I've got to get her out of here."

Dallas slid her onto the seat. "What the hell is going on, Max? What the hell is wrong with her?"

Max slammed the door shut. "There's nothing wrong with her."

"What the hell is she on?"

Max shook his head. "She's not on anything. I don't have time for this, Dal. You want to follow us to my house, that's fine. I'll see you there."

Hands on hips, Dallas watched as Max got in the truck and drove away.

"What the hell was that?" he asked himself.

~

ROSIE FELT HEAVY, like her limbs were dead weight and she couldn't lift them. Her eyes were heavy, and it was so much easier to keep them closed. Things had gotten strange when the woman had led her to the water this time. Though her body had urged her closer, begged her to go in, something held her back. She didn't know what it was that wouldn't let her go any further, but she wondered if it had saved her life. How far into the water would she have gone?

She knew Max and Dallas had been there, though how or why they were there, she wasn't sure. She remembered nothing but the dream up to that point.

She opened her leaded eyes and was comforted to know she was on Max's couch, under the thick comforter he kept on his bed. It took herculean effort, but she forced herself to sit up and take stock.

"Max?" she called.

What sounded like more than one set of footsteps came down the hall from the kitchen.

"Hey." Max's voice held a deep note of concern. He sat down without hesitation and pulled her into his arms. "I'm so glad you're up. You scared the shit out of me."

"Sorry," she said softly.

Dallas appeared, in full police uniform and sat opposite her. He leaned forward, elbows on knees, and watched her carefully.

"Are you okay?" he asked, a note of gruffness in his voice.

"I'm fine," she answered automatically, having no idea if it was true or not.

"Yeah?" He rolled his eyes in annoyance. "How's your foot feel?

Her brows pulled down. She wiggled her toes and winced as a sting lanced through the bottom of her foot.

"Still fine?"

"I'll survive."

When he opened his mouth to say something else, Max interrupted. "Lay off, Dal."

He threw his hands up. "You want me to pretend this didn't happen, is that it? You know me better than that. I want to know what the hell is going on with her, and I want to know now." He turned back to Rosie. "Are you on drugs? Do you need help?"

She was completely caught off guard. He didn't know it, but drugs had been a huge part of her childhood. She'd been surrounded by junkies and dealers, had lived in crack houses and brothels. She'd never touched an illegal drug in her life, and she didn't plan to.

"No," she ground out.

"Erratic behavior, dilated pupils," he said, ticking off symptoms of drug use.

"I'm not on drugs!" she argued again.

"She's not on drugs," Max confirmed. "I left her here sleeping this morning." He turned to Rosie. "Dal said the wind picked up when he was down there, so strong he had to cover his face so sand didn't get in his eyes. But when I got there a second later, it there wasn't any wind at all. The air was totally still."

She'd experienced the same thing in the woods with the woman.

"Oh, come on." Dallas threw up his hands in frustration. "Who gives a shit about the wind?"

"Rosie," Max prompted. "Just tell him."

Her eyes widened. Hadn't it been just yesterday she'd told him how much she didn't want to tell Dallas. A stab of betrayal lanced through her sharply, and she wanted to kick herself. Why did she let herself get attached in the first place? She'd known from the very beginning something like this would happen. Wasn't it what happened every time she opened herself up to someone?

"Tell me what?" Dallas asked.

"Don't look at me like that," Max backtracked warily, putting his hand out and touching her leg. "We need help."

She didn't need help. She never asked for help.

"Can I use the bathroom?" she asked, looking away from Max and never even looking back in Dallas' direction.

Max stood when she did. "Babe," he started.

"I'll be out in a few minutes." She brushed past him and darted up the stairs quickly, grabbing her clothes. Suddenly, she felt uncomfortable changing in Max's bathroom, so she used the hall bath.

While she dressed, she berated herself for getting too invested. Why would she let herself trust someone? How could she let herself almost fall for Max when she knew he'd betray her in the end? Had she really thought he'd be there for her, that he'd stay true to his word? For her?

"A promise is no different than a lie, Happy," she reminded herself, wiping a ridiculous tear from her cheek as she looked in the mirror. She fixed her hair and gave herself a minute to breathe. Making sure she looked the best she could, she shored herself up, telling herself the same thing she always did when trusting someone felt tempting. "They're just things people think you want hear."

She threw Max's gym shorts in a laundry basket in the hallway and went back downstairs. They both stood this time when she walked in the room, but Max quickly moved toward her.

"Rosie."

She held up a hand and took a step back, Max's face taking on a confused expression.

"Rosie," he tried again.

She shifted her eyes to look at Dallas and laid everything on the line. If she didn't, Max would, and in the end what difference would it really make? That way, she'd have control when things went to shit, which they inevitably would.

"I see ghosts sometimes." Max sucked in a breath, but Rosie kept her eyes on Dallas. He was paying close attention but didn't look like he really believed her. "There's a spirit that keeps bringing me to that cove, and sometimes I end up in the water. I assume her remains are out there somewhere, but I know she wasn't killed there. I don't know who she is or when she was killed, although I suspect it was sometime in the late forties based on the clothes she's wearing."

Dallas stayed quiet for nearly a full minute, and then he spent nearly the same amount of time looking back and forth between she and Max.

Finally, he spoke. "And you expect me to buy that?"

"Dal," Max cut in.

"No," she said over him and gave Dallas a self-depreciating half smile. "I don't."

"Then tell me something I can believe, Rosie," he urged. "Tell me something that makes some sense other than what seems obvious to me."

"She's not on drugs," Max argued.

"I'm gonna go," she told them quietly as she headed for the door.

"Wait," Max said, making a grab for her arm but she pulled away. "Rosie, please."

"It was the only thing I asked for, Max," she said, her voice wobbling. "The only thing I told you I absolutely didn't want, and it was yesterday."

"It was the only way to get him to believe you. There's nothing wrong with the truth."

"You're right. There's nothing wrong with the truth, but it wasn't your truth to tell."

"Baby."

"Don't call me that." She took another step back when those awful tears filled her eyes again. "I told him, he didn't believe me, end of story. I have to go."

"Wait," Dallas interrupted. "That's all I get? One second to accept you're some kind of psychic, and if I don't then I'm the bad guy?"

She smiled at him. "No, Dal, you're not the bad guy. It's not your fault." She shrugged. "It's not anyone's fault."

She turned and opened the front door and went searching for her bike, Max right behind her.

"Rosie, please. Talk to me."

Her bike was leaned against the garage, and she got on, turning to face him. "I told you something really personal, Max. Something I don't tell anyone. Ever. I told you something that every single time I tell someone, something bad happens. And within a day, you sold me out."

"I didn't sell you out."

"I told you, flat out, I didn't want to tell Dallas. Within twenty-four hours, you put me on the spot and want me to tell him."

"Rosie, I'm worried for you!" he argued. "One of these times, you're gonna go in that water, and I don't know how deep you'll go!"

"So, your solution was to throw me under the bus and force my hand?"

"Dallas is my best friend. I trust him with everything I have. You can trust him with this."

"I don't even trust you!" His head reared back in shock, disbelief marring his handsome face. "What? You think a few kisses and movies is all it takes? I know you probably think I'm just some slacker that maybe doesn't like people. Maybe you think I'm alone because I like to be, but you couldn't be more wrong. I'm no one, Max. I came from nothing, I have nothing. Everything I've had has been taken away from me, and every time, it was by someone I trusted. I don't trust other people, and certainly not because they're nice."

She was on a roll, and though he looked ready to interrupt, she kept going.

"Maybe, especially when they're nice, because nice just means someone wants something from you, and when they want something from you, they're going to screw you over."

"I didn't screw you over," Max argued. "I'm trying to help you."

"Then don't," she told him flatly.

"Rosie, give me a chance to wrap my brain around this," Dallas urged from the front yard as he approached.

"I'll help you find her, because if I don't, she won't give me any peace. But after that? I can't do any more."

"You don't have to do anything you don't want to." Dallas's voice held a note of sincerity. "This is just all a little crazy."

"The first night we met, there was a man standing behind you. He was tall and had gray hair and a big belly. I assume he was your grandfather. He apologized to me on your behalf, told me he was sorry you were such a clod. Said you got it from him."

His face screwed up in confusion as she pushed off and headed off on her bike.

"Grandpa John?" Dallas muttered as Max yelled after her.

"Rosie!"

17

Rosie wasn't sure if she was happy no one came looking for her, or disappointed.

On one hand, she'd asked to be left alone and they'd respected her wishes.

On the other hand, if they cared, wouldn't they have come?

She chided herself for being so passive aggressive, but it didn't change the way she felt. So, she stewed away the rest of the morning and early afternoon in her camper with Gizmo. She busied herself, showering and then cleaning everything in sight. After that didn't clear her mind, she tried reading, but that was well beyond her mental state.

By late afternoon, she couldn't stand herself anymore. She rode her bike to the bus stop and went to work her old shift with the other maids. The methodic scrubbing of bathrooms and back and forth motion of the vacuum soothed a little. She worked in solitude through the night and well into the early morning hours, clearing her mind and trying not to dwell on what she'd done.

She was furious with herself for some of the things she'd said to Max. Telling him she'd come from nothing and that she had no one was stupid on her part. At the very least, he'd tell Wendy and she'd a have a million questions. The worst? Maybe Dallas, as a cop, got curious and tried looking into her past.

She sighed and wiped the hair off her forehead.

Rosie liked Max, she truly did. He was funny and sweet. He had a naturally calming energy that made her feel at home when they were together. His life was so together, he was so aware of himself and where he was going, he exuded confidence. He was handsome, with his messy brown hair and golden eyes, and he looked at her like she was something he'd care for and treasure.

The problem was, she hated herself for wanting that. She'd built her life around being alone and never needing to rely on anyone else. How could she suddenly meet a guy and let all that go? Was Max worth changing the life she'd made for herself?

She pondered that as she got out of work, and instead of riding back to the office with Marta, wandered her way to a diner. She sat with her cup of coffee, staring out a window at the ocean as the sun rose.

Where did that leave her? Going to the cove by herself was unwise, she knew that much. She was too out of control when she went there. She would need someone with her.

An hour later, she paid her coffee tab and walked to The Third Eye, hoping Jay might have some insight. Strangely, she realized, she trusted Jay. He was like her. He knew what it was like for her to live with her abilities. More than that, with just a touch, he knew more about her than she'd ever said out loud. She didn't have to tell him about her past, because he could already see plenty of it.

Would he betray her, too? Would he do what everyone else in her life had done?

Jay's voice called to her from above, and she looked up to see his head out the second story window. He was clearly shirtless. "You're killing me here, darlin'. Your waves are like crashing through my windows. Come up. Stairway's around the side."

He smiled and waved her in the right direction.

She found the old iron stairs on the side of the building and when she reached the top, the door opened. Jay stood there, shirt on, smiling.

"Come on in. Have breakfast. Unload the doubt."

She took a deep breath and stepped through the door.

Jay's apartment was just like she'd expect, eclectic but neat, new age but without the messy, immature feel one might expect. There was a purple velvet couch, with two white chairs all clustered around a wooden coffee table strewn with crystals. She spied a few dream catchers near the windows, but it wasn't kitschy.

"Sit anywhere," he instructed. "You want coffee?"

"No," she refused, knowing more coffee wouldn't do her any good.

He poured himself a fresh cup and sat on the purple couch. She took one of the white chairs and just sat there, not knowing what to say.

Jay patiently watched her, waiting. He blew across the top of his coffee cup, making tiny ripples before sipping. When she met his eyes, he smiled.

"I got in a fight with Max," she admitted.

"And?"

"And it knocked me for a loop, I guess."

He nodded at her answer but didn't respond.

"I almost trusted him," she admitted, looking away, afraid of what her eyes might tell him.

"You did trust him," he replied. "That's why you're so upset about whatever happened."

"No," she argued right away. "It's not that easy for me."

"And it can't be true because it was easy?"

"Are you a therapist now?"

"You're the one who showed up here," he laughed. "Not that you aren't welcome. I've already told you that, Rosie. But you came here for a reason, so let's get to it."

"He threw me under the bus."

"How?"

"I told him about what I see."

He whistled. "That's a big deal, considering how you feel about that."

"It was. But I've had a few run-ins with that woman in the woods when he's been around. I felt like he deserved an explanation."

"How'd he take it?"

"Like Max." She shrugged and couldn't help the small smile that came to her face. "In stride. He believed me right away. No demand for tricks I can't perform or explanations. He just...believed me."

"What an ogre," Jay deadpanned. "I can see why you got in a fight."

She tilted her head and glared at him. "I told him I didn't want him to tell anyone, then the next day, he sits me down in front of Dallas,"

"The hot cop?"

"The hot cop, and then insists I tell him the truth."

"Why?"

"Why what? Why did he insist that I tell Dallas?" At his nod, she continued. "I had another incident yesterday out at the cove. In the water."

"Yikes. Did you go in the water again?"

"Yeah, but Max pulled me out. Dallas was there."

"Naturally, he'd want an explanation."

"He accused me of being on drugs." Jay winced at that bit of information. "Which strikes a nerve with me, I admit, and I lashed out. Especially after Max said, 'tell him the truth' right in front of him."

"He kinda threw you under the bus," Jay agreed, which made her feel nominally better. "But he didn't do it intentionally."

"I know that, but it doesn't change what happened."

"I'm sure he was trying to help. You trusted him enough to tell him what was going on, and he tried to help you by bringing you the person he trusts."

She threw up her hands.

"And then you thought yourself to death and ended up here, on my doorstep, doubting everything that's ever happened to you." He laughed.

"Not everything that ever happened," she disagreed.

"Me then? Is that why it felt so localized?"

She looked sheepish.

"You were doubting me?" He seemed truly hurt. "Don't doubt me, Rosie. I'll be here when you need me. I promise."

"I have this thing I say to myself every time someone makes me a promise," she told him.

"I have a feeling it's not a good thing."

"Promises are like fog," she said quietly. "You can't see through them, but they don't amount to a whole lot."

~

SHE SPENT the rest of the morning with Jay, trying to work everything out. He made some good points about Max's intentions she'd been too mad to take seriously. He did another aura cleansing in the Reiki room, but it seemed to get her nowhere.

From there, she rode her bike to work, where she got started on making sure Thanksgiving week ran smoothly. It was Monday, and they had to make sure the next few days were perfect so everyone could enjoy a few days off. She went to the office Wendy had told her to use, and shut the door. It was easy to lose herself in schedules and supply orders. She made sure the orders were set for the next month, and then she went to the supply room to make sure all the carts and shelves were fully stocked.

"What are you doing in here?" Wendy asked with a smile as she appeared in the doorway.

Rosie smiled. "Just making sure we're all stocked up for tonight."

"I was thinking before we finish up for the holiday, we should make sure we've got an order in to restock."

"Already done," Rosie told her as she filled a shelf with paper towels.

Her boss smiled. "I love having you here."

"I love being here."

"Have you talked to Max?" She could hear the smile in Wendy's voice and chose to ignore it.

"Not today."

"Oh," Wendy's voice fell. "I'm hoping the girls get finished up this week so we can get a few days off."

"They will." Rosie assured her. "We got a ton done last night, and it went well. They deserve a nice little break."

Wendy stood from where she was leaning on the door frame. "Wait. We? You were here last night?"

"I worked downtown with the girls."

"You worked all night? What time did you get here?"

"About eleven?"

"What the hell are you doing here? Go home, Rosie."

She waved her hand carelessly. "I'm good. I'll grab some coffee in a while and keep going."

She hadn't eaten since the night Max fed her meatballs. She sighed, stupidly missing Max.

"Well, if you need to take off, go ahead. You've put in your time today."

"It's not a big deal. Like you said, I want to make sure it all gets done. That's all."

Wendy shook her head. "Stubborn. I'll be in my office if you need me."

~

ROSIE WORKED until six that night. She could have gone home much sooner. There truly wasn't much work to be done, but she was avoiding going home. Now that she'd cooled off a little, she wasn't quite so mad at Max. Yes, she'd clearly asked him not to tell Dallas, but she'd also boxed him into a corner, as Jay said. He had his own way of coping with problems, and clearly it was to ask for help if he needed it. She'd forced herself to outgrow that option, as it had never worked for her. He used the skills he had when a problem arose. He was just trying to help.

Granted, she hadn't asked for that, and he'd crossed a boundary that made her very uncomfortable, but she had to make a choice. She and Jay had discussed it at length.

She had to choose between stepping out of her comfort zone and letting Max help, or living in the past and letting that dictate where her future was going to take her. Maybe it was time to stop relying on her mistrust of other people and start relying on the trust she had in her own abilities. If nothing else, it was something to think about.

She rode the bus home and tiredly exited, hesitating on the last step off. Max was sitting on the bench next to where her bike was locked. She stepped down and waited until the hiss of brakes eased off and the bus was gone.

He sat there looking pained, his usually messy brown hair even more unruly than normal. His mouth was turned down in a frown and he looked worried.

"Hey," she greeted him quietly.

"Hey," he said back.

She went to the bench and sat next to him, looking out at the deserted road in front of them.

"I'm sorry," she told him.

She felt him shift on the seat. "No, Rosie. You have nothing to be sorry about. You were right. I promised you I wouldn't say anything, and then I practically made you tell Dallas. I'm sorry."

She nodded. "I wasn't ready to tell him."

"He believed you," he said. "When you told him about his grandfather, he believed you."

It didn't matter to her if Dallas believed her or not.

"I'm not ready to be the town sideshow. I don't want that here."

"It won't go any further than Dallas and I." He reached out and grabbed her hand. "I swear."

She turned her face and sent him a sad smile. "Don't say that. There's nothing I trust less than a promise."

"Shit," he muttered and pulled her hand up to kiss the back. "I'm so fucking sorry."

"Can we just let it go for now?" She leaned back and put her back to his side, his arms quickly wrapping around her. "I just want to close my eyes for a minute."

He kissed the top of her head. "At the bus stop?"

"I'm just so tired, and right now, just being with you is so quiet. There's no extra noise when you're here. I can't even think about the rest of that stuff right now."

"So, we're good for now?" He sounded leery.

"We can talk it to death tomorrow."

"Can I put your bike in my truck now or are you gonna insist on riding it home?"

She shook her head. "No, I'm gonna take the ride."

What felt like a minute later, Max was carrying her from his truck up his porch stairs.

"I can walk," she insisted tiredly.

"I know," he said. "I've got you, though."

"It's too early to go to sleep." She was so tired her words were slurred.

"We'll hang out upstairs. That way, when you want to go to sleep you can just close your eyes." His voice was soft, and she felt her eyes close again.

∾

HER MOTHER HAD LOCKED her in the closet again. The all-encompassing darkness surrounded her but didn't frighten her the way her mother probably meant it to. She found it comforting to know where all the walls were, to feel them around her. That way, she knew there would be no surprises coming out of the dark. Just her mother on the other side of the door.

"She's coming for you," Mama whispered through the door. "Better buckle up, Happy, because she's coming for you, and she's far more powerful than you."

∾

ROSIE'S EYES POPPED OPENED, and she found her head on Max's shirt-less chest, his arm wrapped around her. There was a TV on across the room, the volume barely reaching her ears. One of her hands was resting on his abs. Yeah, she didn't mind this. His skin was hot and smooth, a thin trail of hair leading straight down his waistband.

"You okay?" he asked.

She took a deep breath and groaned a little.

"I can feel your eyelashes blinking on my chest," he laughed, running his hand over her hair.

She sat up, hoping she hadn't been doing something ridiculously embarrassing, like snoring or drooling on him, or heaven forbid talking in her sleep.

"Hey." Her voice was scratchy from sleep, but she felt much better than she had before. Clearly, she had reached the age where staying up all night wasn't as easy as it used to be.

He smiled down at her and continued to run his hand down her hair. "You okay?"

"Yeah." She put her chin down on his chest and looked back at him. "Was tired, I guess."

"I guess," he agreed softly.

It was a peaceful moment, backlit by the flickering television. They stared at each other, enjoying each other's touch and company without trying to fill the void the silence created. He watched her eyes, going back and forth from one to the other. She catalogued the straight line of his nose and the arch of his top lip. His thumb brushed her lips, and he watched its path carefully. It was a serene connection between them, one she welcomed after the day's upheaval.

"I missed you," he broke into the quiet.

She smiled and hid her face in his chest. "It was only a day."

"I don't care." He gently lifted her face. "I missed you."

Without thought, she pressed a kiss to his chest. "I missed you, too."

"I need to tell you something." His voice had a serious tone to it.

One that made her push herself further up on her elbows and take notice.

"Okay." Her voice was wary.

"I hate when you disappear on me." He pressed his hand to her cheek. "I hate when I can't find you and I have no way to get a hold of you."

"I'm sorry,"

"I get it. I get why you took off, but when a whole day goes by and I don't know where you went or if you're okay, that drives me a little crazy."

She could see where he'd be frustrated. She'd never had a reason to get herself a fancy cell phone, but she had a pay as you go phone she carried in case she needed it.

"I can just give you my phone number, you know," she started.

Max sat up straighter, knocking her off his chest. She sat up then, too.

"You have a cell phone?" He sounded surprised.

"Well, it's nothing fancy." She shrugged.

"But you have one?"

"I do," she said.

Max grabbed her by the shoulders and pulled her in for a kiss. The second his lips touched hers, it was as if her pulse spiked. She felt herself heat from the inside out and opened her mouth to him, wanting him closer. She loved the feel of his hands on her back, his tongue rubbing against hers as though he couldn't get enough of her. She felt the same way, just as insistent as he was, her hands and mouth demanding just as much from him.

His fingers found the hem of her shirt and began tugging it upwards. She broke the kiss.

"No sex," he whispered through his ragged breath, his eyes hot on hers. "I remember. Totally clear."

"No sex," she agreed as she lifted her arms, letting him pull the shirt over her head.

He tossed it carelessly on the floor without taking his eyes off her. Her breasts were on the smaller side, though she'd never say she was flat chested. Her bra was purple, keeping her well contained in a shiny satin cup.

"Yeah," he muttered, pressing his nose to her chest and inhaling deeply, then rubbing lips across her chest. He reached the raised ridge of her scar again and stopped. "You never told me about this."

"Seriously?" She breathed in frustration. "You want to talk right now?"

"Baby, there's a lot I want to do right now. Most of them involve you being naked." His hands came up to cup each of her breasts.

"No naked," she said on a breathy sigh.

"What if you were naked and I wasn't? I can do a lot with you naked." He gently pulled down each of the straps of her bra, waiting for her to protest. When she didn't, he lowered the cups until her breasts were standing at attention right in front of his face.

She wondered briefly if she should feel embarrassed. She'd never been this naked with a guy before. The thought flitted from her mind when his tongue circled one of her nipples. His big hand held her while he continued to use his mouth on her. She kneaded his bare shoulders as she struggled to stay still under his onslaught.

Rosie hadn't realized her nipples had a direct connection to her core, but the more Max worked her breasts, the more desperate she felt. Her hips moved of their own volition, pressing against his lap and moving back and forth, searching for relief. In a quick motion, Max had her on her back, his mouth pressing kisses down her chest and stomach. Her fingers threaded through his hair as he dipped his tongue quickly into her belly button.

"Max," she whispered.

He kissed his way back up her body, stopping briefly to suck each of her nipples in mouth.

When he appeared above her, he spoke before she could. "You're so fucking beautiful." His cheeks were flushed and his hair was a mess.

She smiled up at him. "So are you."

"Did you want me to stop?"

No, she didn't. She wanted whatever the ache inside of her was to be sated.

"It would probably be a good idea," she told him.

He shrugged and smiled. "I have other ideas." He pressed a kiss to her lips and swiped his tongue across her bottom lip. "Still, no sex," he reiterated, "But there's something else I can do for you."

She knew exactly what he meant. She didn't live under a rock for heaven's sake, it was just something she'd never done. The more she thought about it, the more nervous and uncomfortable she became. First of all, she'd never been naked in front of someone else before, let alone exposed herself like that. Second, she also hadn't showered in longer than she could remember and was horrified to imagine him down there. Third, she was back to her first point. How could she ever let anyone do that?

Max laughed. "You're eyes just got as big as dinner plates."

She shook her head and stuttered, "I haven't...I've never..."

He shifted further back and looked at her, his smile fading. "You've never had oral sex?

She was a little jealous of Max and how comfortable he was just putting it all out there, like people talked about this stuff all the time. Without uttering a word, she shook her head and let him make of that what he would.

He slid to her side and laid partially on top of her, giving her plenty of space. Then he pulled the covers over them.

"What are you worried about?" he asked, settling them in the bed together. His hand came to rest on her breast under the covers, his fingers casually toying with her nipple.

She wasn't sure she could do this. She didn't think she could just talk about it like he could.

"Rosie," he laughed. "You told me you see ghosts for fuck's sake. I'd think that would be way harder than this."

She shook her head. "I have a lot more experience with that than this."

"Okay." He, as per usual, accepted it without issue. "So, let's lay it out there. What are you worried about? What makes you most nervous?"

She gave him a deadpan look. "You. Being down there."

"Mmm," he hummed, his eyes glowing with the same heat she'd seen before. "That's what I'm looking forward to most. Seeing you. Tasting you."

She brought a hand up to cover her face. "Stop it."

"What?" He laughed, pulling her hand away. "You want me to be honest, right?"

"A little less honesty wouldn't kill you."

"No," he argued. "I want you to trust me, Rosie. So, I'll tell you the truth even if you might not want to hear it. I want to go down on you. I want to see you naked. I want to taste every inch of you. That's just the way it is."

"Well, I'm not ready to be tasted," she said primly. "I haven't showered in I don't know how long."

"I don't care," he told her seriously.

"I do." Her voice was quiet.

He lowered his lips and kissed her again. "I can accept that."

"Well, that's gracious of you," she groused.

He kissed her, yet again, and popped himself out of bed. She sat up and watched him leave the room.

"Where are you going?" she called after him.

"Solving one of your problems."

She heard the water turn on in the bathroom and assumed he was filling the tub. He cluttered around a bit in the bathroom, the smell of perfume filling the air while she sat and waited for him to come back. After a moment, he came to the door of the bedroom.

"Come on." He held out his hand.

Still nervous, she held the blanket to her chest.

"I just had your nipples in my mouth," he said plainly. "No need to hide them now."

"Well, that's different than me just walking across the room with my boobs hanging out."

"Want me to turn around?"

That seemed dumb, she had to admit. He had just had his mouth all over her, and they'd just had a conversation while he fondled her breasts the entire time. Gathering her courage, she threw the comforter off and slid out of the bed, walking toward him as gracefully as possible. When she got close enough, he grabbed her hand and pulled her to him with a laugh.

He held her cheeks in his hands and kissed her, the smile still on his face, then he pointed her in the direction of the tub. The room was steamy, and the tub was nearly full of bubbles.

Max slid his arms around her from behind, his fingers going for the button of her jeans. When it was undone, he put his thumbs in her pants at the hips and began tugging them down. She quickly stepped out of his arms.

"Okay," he laughed, knowing she wasn't there yet. "I'll turn around."

He did, which made her feel a little better. She quickly stripped, keeping an eye on him the whole time, and got in the big tub. True to his word, he didn't peek. The water felt heavenly around her, hot and soothing.

"You in?"

"Yeah," she answered.

He turned around and hooked his own fingers in his shorts and pulled them down without giving her a second to brace herself. She felt her mouth drop open at the sight of him, his body naked and lean, his penis long and standing nearly straight out.

"You're staring," he said as he lowered himself in the tub across from her, and she lost sight of the part of him that had snagged her attention. Her eyes flew to his face, and she caught him laughing. "You're face." He leaned back and laughed some more.

"I...didn't..." She shook off the shock. "I didn't know you were joining me."

He shrugged. "I thought we could keep talking. Continue the conversation we were having."

She wished she could sink into the tub and put her head underwater.

"Come on," he urged. "Let's just get it all out there."

"I don't want it all out there," she told him, not able to hold in a laugh. She felt her face heat at the memory of seeing his penis.

"Uh-huh. You're blushing."

"You just flashed me." She splashed water at him.

"You flashed me first." He leaned forward and grabbed her hand.

She didn't have a response, because he was right, she had.

"Though, I kind of asked you too," he admitted.

He let go of her hand and leaned back, his feet coming to rest next to her hips.

"I can't believe I'm naked in a tub with you," she told him truthfully.

"Me neither." He sank down and closed his eyes.

She couldn't get that comfortable, moving to sit with a knee raised out of the water, arms hooked around it.

She watched him relax like this kind of thing happened all the time. He really was an amazing guy. Sure, he was good looking, and that helped, but his looks took a backseat compared to his better qualities. He was infinitely patient, honest, and funny. He had a comforting quality about him, something that made her feel at home and less lonely than she usually did. Inclusive was the word, she thought. He'd included her in everything, from farm chores to dinner at his home.

She took a deep breath and went back to something he'd said while they were in bed. "I trust you."

He slowly lifted his head and opened his eyes. He watched her for a few seconds.

"I could have sworn two days ago you practically laughed in my face at the idea that you could trust me."

She shrugged and looked down at her hand swirling in the bubbles. "When I really thought about why I was so pissed, I kind of realized it was because I did trust you and thought you'd screwed me over." She lifted her eyes to him. "Trust issues."

"Ya think?" He rolled his light brown eyes. "Why?"

"Experience?"

"Is this part of the 'I'm no one, I have no one, I come from nothing' speech you gave me?"

"Something like that," she agreed. "Although I was hoping you forgot about that."

"No such luck." He grabbed her foot and pulled it so it rested on his chest. Then he began massaging it. "Can I ask you about having no one?" She nodded but found it hard to meet his eyes. "You said your family was traveling for Thanksgiving. True or False?"

"False," she admitted without hesitating. When he went to talk again, she interrupted. "You have a picture of me on your phone. Why?"

"Because I like to look at you." If he was embarrassed, he didn't show it. "You lied. Why?"

"Truth?"

"Obviously."

"Because the truth sucks,' she admitted. "I don't like to tell it and don't like people to hear it."

He sat up and brought her foot to his mouth, kissing the bottom before putting it back in the water.

"I'm not just people anymore, you know. I think we're past that. If anything, I'm your people."

She agreed, although she wasn't sure how it happened. "I've, ah...." She swallowed past the lump in her throat. "I've never really had people before."

"You don't have any family? Parents?" He sat up and pulled her so they were face-to-face, both sitting cross legged.

"I never knew my father," she said. "I mean, I never even knew who he was."

He was holding her hand, playing with her fingers in the water. "Your mom?"

Her laugh came without her permission, sarcastic and humorless. "Yeah. No."

His head tilted while he listened. "No, what? What does that mean?" he asked.

"Do we have to talk about this now? Naked?" she asked, hoping to change the subject.

"I wish we would," he told her. "Just tell me about your mom, and then we'll go back to bed."

It was late and the skies out the bathroom window were black and cloudless.

"How about the abridged version?"

"I'll take that." He leaned in and placed a soft kiss on her nose.

She took a deep breath. "My mom went to jail when I was six. When she got out, she claimed she'd found God, and instead of thinking I was just a crazy kid, she thought I was a demon."

"Wait, like a demon, demon?"

"Eventually, she petitioned the court to have me committed, which they granted in a hearing after I was released from the hospital."

"She had you committed?" He sounded disbelieving

"In a nutshell." A very small nutshell, give or take a near-death experience and a life on the lam. He said nothing about her hospital comment and she made no more mention of it.

"She had you committed?" he repeated.

"I'm not crazy."

"I know that," he insisted. "How long were you..." He hesitated to even say it.

"A couple weeks. I didn't stay long."

"Didn't the court make you stay?"

"It wasn't like that."

"So, they let you do that? Just leave when you're ready to go?" He sounded skeptical, with good reason. In truth, she'd run like hell the second she had the chance and had been running ever since.

"Not exactly."

His head shifted back so he could get a good look at her. "So, you what? Ran away? And no one came looking for you?"

She faced him, tilted her head, and watched him.

"How old were you?"

"Sixteen. Can we be done now?"

"And you just ran away?"

"You said I just had to tell you about my mom. The rest isn't part of the abridged version."

"Then make it part of it," he insisted. "How did no one come looking? You aren't exactly hard to miss, Rosie."

"Who, exactly, do you think would be looking for me?"

"The court I guess?" Even he sounded unsure which gave her a small, unfounded, piece of hope. "Your mother."

"You think the court cares about some runaway kid from seven or eight years ago? I'm just another drop in the barrel to them."

"But your name must be in some kind of database or something. The minute Wendy hired you and filed your social security number with the IRS they would have come for you." Without waiting a beat, he answered his own question. "Oh my God, your name isn't Rosie Knight is it?"

18

"Julie."

Rosie woke to Max whispering in her ear.

"Heather. Kayla. Jill."

"Jesus," she mumbled and turned her face into the pillow. "Will you quit it?"

He'd spent half the night trying to guess her real name like it was a new game. Though telling some of the truth had made her feel lighter, especially when he didn't get upset and leave her, she was beginning to regret it.

"Margot, Kristin, Lauren, Alexis."

"Rosie." She tried to put a pillow over her head, but he held it away from her. "My name is Rosie."

"But it's not," he argued.

She rolled on her back and looked at him through half-opened eyes. "If I knew you were going to pursue it, I never would have told you."

He pulled back. "Seriously."

"Yeah, seriously. I've gone out of my way to not be that person. Why would I want to go into details about it?"

She noticed he was dressed in his work clothes and not in the gym shorts he'd been wearing when they'd gone to sleep. "You're dressed."

He chuckled. "I do that when I go to work. Otherwise, it gets weird."

"You're going to work?"

"I've been at work. For a couple hours."

She was startled when Gizmo jumped onto the bed and settled at her feet. She looked to Max.

"I figured you'd want to run right back to your place to let him out, so I just brought him here."

She tried to sit up and find a clock, feeling a little bewildered at his forethought and his brazenness. "What time is it?"

"Nine," he continued. "But I already talked to my sister, and she told me you're not working today."

"I'm not, huh?"

She covered her mouth with the comforter when he leaned in to kiss her. Was he nuts? He laughed and pressed his lips to her forehead instead.

"She said you worked enough yesterday and the night before. You're off until Monday."

She spoke to him through he covers. "I have to tell you something." When he just looked at her, waiting, she spoke again. "It's serious."

"I'm listening."

"I'm starving."

He laughed.

"Like, chew my own arm off, starving."

"That bad?"

"Like, stranded in the Andes after a plane crash and eating the flesh from my friend's asses starving."

He laughed louder and pulled the comforter off her, kissing her on the lips.

"You have problems, you know." He pulled her hands until she was sitting up. "Don't you ever feed yourself?"

She shook her head, her white hair falling in her eyes. "Not if I know you'll be around to do it for me."

His voice was further away when he spoke. "You're so goddamn sexy in the morning."

When she looked through her hair, he was standing in the doorframe.

"Then why are you all the way over there?"

"Because if I get any closer, you won't be eating anytime soon."

"Then stay far, far away." She held up both hands, warding him off.

"Do I even want to know when you ate last?"

She screwed up her face, thinking. He'd probably lecture her. "No. Probably not."

He turned on his heel with a sigh and called on his way down the hallway. "Get it together, babe. I can get breakfast together pretty quick."

Rosie hopped out of bed and went into the bathroom. She had no idea what Max was talking about or who he was looking at when he called her sexy. Leaning closer, she examined herself in the mirror above the sink. Her hair was a mess, like she'd gone through a wind tunnel, and her eyes were barely open. She leaned down and splashed some water in her face, then wrapped her hair into a bun.

When she went out into Max's room, she debated putting her jeans and sweater back on but decided to stick with the t-shirt she'd borrowed to sleep in and her undies. She practically skipped down the stairs, feeling young and lighthearted, something that had been foreign to her, until now. She skidded around the corner to the kitchen on a laugh.

"Now, that's what I'm talking about."

Rosie let out a squeak and grabbed her chest, her heart banging against her ribs. Dallas stood at the kitchen counter, holding a cup of coffee and wearing a huge smile. Max was behind him, cooking at the stove. He turned and saw her standing there, not quite as dressed as she normally might be, and Dallas leering at her.

"Why don't you sit?" He gestured with his chin to the spot at the counter she usually sat at.

"I didn't know you were here," she said to Dallas, who chuckled into his coffee mug as she sat.

"I got that, though I don't mind."

"Keep your eyes to yourself," Max warned, sliding a plate of eggs, toast, and bacon across the counter to Rosie.

"I'll keep my hands to myself, but my eyes? That's a tall order."

"Well, try," Max told him as he leaned his elbows on the counter across from her.

She hadn't been lying when she said she was starving. If she thought about it, she hadn't eaten at all the day before. She powered through breakfast quickly, piling the bacon and eggs onto the toast and folding it into a little sandwich. She took a few swigs of orange juice, then went back to eating. Max put more eggs on her plate and few more strips of bacon.

"Mmmhmm." She mumbled her thank you and kept eating.

The eggs were the brightest yellow she'd ever seen and they were cooked perfectly. It wasn't until she shoveled the last bite into her mouth that she even noticed, which she regretted. It would have been nice to enjoy the meal while she ate it. Embarrassed, she grabbed her napkin and wiped her mouth. When she looked up, Max was smiling and Dallas's mouth was gaping open.

"Sorry," she said with a wince. "I was hungry. Thank you, that was really good."

Dallas didn't move.

"You're welcome." Max's smile dimmed. "When'd you eat last?"

She sighed. "Meatballs."

She winced again at how stupid that sounded. In her defense, she had been upset. She wasn't one of those people that ate during times of stress, she was someone who didn't. It was just how she was built.

Max stood and threw up his hands. "Jesus."

"I was upset," she defended herself.

"What's meatballs?" Dallas butt in.

"Nothing." She waved him off.

"Rosie." Max's voice held a warning tone.

"I know," she admitted. "I was just upset." She turned to Dallas. "What are you doing here?"

He shrugged. "Just came to hang with Max. See what's up for tomorrow?"

She tilted her head. "What's tomorrow?"

His eyes got big. "Uh, Thanksgiving."

"Oh."

"I was gonna ask you last night if you wanted to come with us to my parent's house but then I took off your shirt and got distracted," Max told her plainly, grabbing her plate and bringing it to the sink.

"Tell me more," Dallas laughed

Her face heated. Had he really just said that in front of Dallas? She mentally rolled her eyes. Of course, he had.

And did she really want to go to Max's family's house for a major holiday? Her answer was an unequivocal no. She wasn't good with families. She'd spend the day like she normally spent holidays, watching parades on her computer and reading. She could remember having a real Thanksgiving twice. Once when she was eight with the Hardys and then again when she was nine.

"Rosie." Dallas waved a hand in front of her face.

She sat up straighter. "Huh?"

"Tomorrow? The Murphy's?"

She shook her head immediately and sent them a small smile. "No." She looked at Max. "Thank you. No."

Unfazed, he shrugged and sent her a smile. "Want to feed the lamb?"

Somewhat leery of his reaction, she nodded slowly. "Yeah."

"Go get dressed. I'll take you out there." He looked to Dallas with a slight scowl. "Turn around, at least."

She made a quick dash up the stairs, grabbing her bag from the floor of Max's bedroom and heading into the master bath. As she changed, she considered Max's reaction to her refusal of his invitation. It was suspect. Being the healer he was, it would go against everything he believed in to let her be alone on the holiday. He'd want to fix that for her.

She sighed, wondering what he might have in store for her. She threw on her jeans and a clean flannel and headed down the stairs, leaving her bag by the front door.

"Max?" she called, not hearing any noise in the house. When there was no answer, she headed through the empty kitchen and out the back door.

Knowing she was going to be feeding the lamb, she hurried to the sheep barn, assuming he'd be there, though that wasn't what she found. Dallas was sitting on the edge of a stack of hay bales, baby bottle in hand, waiting for her.

"Hi," she said hesitantly, stopping short in the doorway. She and Dallas had not had the best few weeks. It had been rocky and dramatic, all the things she generally avoided in her life, and she wasn't sure how to approach him.

"Hey," he greeted and held up the bottle. "Max left this for you. The little thing is in the pen over there." He pointed to the pallet playpen.

She walked over and looked in at the sleeping lump. "Little thing?" She laughed. "It's a lamb."

"Whatever." He shrugged. "You know what I meant."

She leaned in and picked up the lamb, then held out her hand for the bottle. When he gave it to her, she sat on the floor and began feeding it.

"How've you been?" she asked. Might as well just get it over with, she thought. She liked Dallas. She wanted him to like her, too. He was Max's best friend, it was the least she could do.

He slid down the wall across from her, looking casual and totally at home. "I've been good. You?"

"Hangin' in."

"Is that good or bad?"

She tilted her head from side to side. "A little of both."

"Been down to the cove again?"

"No," she said immediately. "No."

He nodded. "So, what all happens down there?"

"Swimming. Fishing. I suppose you could put in a small boat if you had one."

"Ha ha," he said dryly. "What happens for you?"

"Hard to explain."

"Try," he urged.

She took a deep breath. "I lose control. Like I'm not me anymore, and I have no control of what I'm doing anymore."

"And it's a ghost?" He didn't sound skeptical as much as curious.

She nodded. "A woman."

"From the forties."

She searched his face when he spoke. "Are you just humoring me, or do you really believe me?

"Did you really see my grandpa?"

She nodded.

"Did he really call me a clod?"

"After you told me my eyes were freaky."

"Ah." Realization dawned. "That was probably rude."

"Probably," she agreed.

The lamb finished its bottle, and Rosie lowered it to the ground, then snuggled the little animal for a minute before putting it back in the playpen. She wondered why Max had taken it out of the field with the other sheep.

She turned around and leaned on the wall opposite where Dallas was now standing.

"You know, I trust Max," Dallas told her. "If he believes you, then I believe you."

She couldn't blame him for not trusting her word. He didn't know her from a hole in the wall, though for reasons she couldn't explain, it still stung.

"Thanks," she said anyway.

"Is this something you really want to pursue?" he asked. "Because I have to be honest with you, Rosie, you don't seem all that excited at the prospect of even talking about this, let alone trying to solve the problem."

How could she explain this to him, to anyone? How could they ever understand that solving the problem would, in the end, do nothing for her? Once this ghost passed on, there would be another one. There would be no peace for her.

She was reminded of the woman at the cove who'd said the same thing to her about being in the water.

But there could be momentary peace, she thought. It didn't have to be as bad as it was right now, without her other senses.

"I'd like to just get back to my own twisted version of normal."

"Like seeing ghosts?" Dallas asked with a strange half smile, like he couldn't believe what he'd just said.

"More like not tying myself to my bed at night so I don't sleepwalk to my death," she admitted.

Max's voice came from the door of the small barn. "You've been what?"

Surprised, she turned to find him staring at her angrily. She held up her hands to pacify him. "A precaution."

"You've been tying yourself to the bed?" His hands were on his hips and his eyebrows were drawn.

"That sounds way sexier than it should," Dallas mused, making her laugh.

"Don't make light of it," Max argued. "If you were that worried, you should have said something."

She wanted to argue that she wouldn't even know how to ask for help, that something like that wasn't in her nature, but he wouldn't understand.

"Okay," she said plainly.

"Okay?" Max threw up his hands, which made Dallas laugh. "Don't just say things just to placate me."

"I-I-I..." she stuttered and looked from Max's furious expression to Dallas's humorous one. She'd never seen Max get this angry about anything. "I don't know what you want me to say."

"He doesn't either," Dallas laughed.

"Shut up," Max growled.

"What? I rarely get to see you this worked up! It's hilarious."

"It's not hilarious," Max argued.

She held up her hands in real apology. "I'm sorry." She didn't know what she was sorry for, other than making the otherwise even-keeled Max upset.

Max took the few steps to her, grabbed her shoulders, and pressed his lips to hers in a searing kiss.

"Okay, this just got weird," Dallas said.

When Max lifted his lips, he was breathing hard and still looked angry.

"I'm sorry," she said again.

He closed his eyes and moved his hands to her cheeks. "You can't say stuff like that, Rosie."

"Like what?" She was truly lost.

"Like you tie yourself to the bed at night because you're afraid, instead of just asking for some goddamn help once in a while."

"But I-"

"But you're so fucking stubborn," he growled. "When you need help, you call."

"But-"

"When you're terrified, you call!"

"Okay." Dallas's hand appeared between their faces, and he pressed his body between them. Then he turned his back on her and faced Max. "Dude. Get a grip."

She stared at Dallas's back and heard Max take a deep breath.

In a way, she knew he was right. It was time for her to at least try to put her trust in Max, which was a huge step for her. On the other hand, she hadn't had to tie herself to the bed in at least a week. Before that, she wouldn't have felt comfortable calling him for help.

"Next time, I'll call." She put a hand on Dallas's shoulder and tried to press him to the side so she could see Max. "I'll call."

Dallas moved from between them and stood to the side.

Max looked somewhere between relived and resigned. "You promise?" He asked.

That stunned her silent and she looked at Max, lost. How could she make him a promise when she didn't believe in promises?

"You have to promise. There's nothing I trust more than a promise," Max told her, twisting her own words and throwing them back at her.

Could she do it? Could she be the one to prove to herself that promises could be kept?

She took a deep breath and jumped off the ledge. "I promise."

~

AFTER THE SCENE in the barn, Dallas stopped them outside.

"Listen, you all have some seriously freaky shit going on here, and I don't want to intrude, but I was hoping we could talk about the dead lady."

"Jesus, Dallas," Max muttered.

"What? You guys want to play out *The Notebook* all over the place, that's cool. But I can't shake that shit from the cove the other day. So, let's get it all out on the table. Rosie sees dead people. There's a ghost following her around and driving her nuts. Seems like the bottom line is to try to get rid of it. Right?"

Rosie shook her head. "Seems simple, right?"

"I take it, it's not that easy," Max said.

"It could be." She shrugged. "It's not like I have conversations with her. I have no idea what she really wants. All I know is that she knows I can see her, and she's trying to get my attention."

"By dragging you down to the cove all the time," Max said.

"I guess." She pulled a face. "Sometimes she yells at me to help her. But a few times, she mentioned helping Jack."

"A husband? Son?" Dallas guessed. "Could be anyone."

She breathed deep. "I think her husband killed her."

Dallas's head reared back. "Wait, what?"

"When I saw..." She hesitated and shook her head. There was no easy way to describe what she'd seen. And there was definitely no easy way to forget how closely it had resembled her own experience with her mother. "When I saw her die, there was a man above her, squeezing her neck and holding her under the water."

Dallas stared at her.

Max moved to stand behind her, sliding an arm around her chest, and kissed the back of her head.

"Under the water." Dallas snapped out of his momentary stupor. "Under the water at the cove? Is that why she keeps bringing you there?"

"No." She knew with certainty. "I think she's at the cove, for sure, somewhere. But that isn't where she died. There's a stream that runs through the woods, and it has a few small places where it pools. It's in there."

"You saw that?" Max asked gently.

She swallowed and looked away, hating the memory burned into her mind. "I can see the trees behind his head while he's choking me and holding me down."

"Her," Max corrected immediately. "While he's holding her down."

She nodded, though it was hard to separate herself from the vision. "Yeah."

"I'm confused," Dallas said. "I thought you said you see her. Are you saying that you like, see through her eyes?"

She shook her head again. "Not usually. It's happened before though, when I touch them."

"You got close enough to this lady that you touched her?" Dallas's demeanor was intense, his aura that had been merely a wisp before was becoming darker and more vivid.

"That was the accident she had on her bike," Max told him, his arm still around her. She reached her hands up and held onto his forearm, glad for his support. "The woman was in the road, so Rosie dumped her bike to avoid her, but ended up sliding right through her."

Rosie did her best to not tear up. The woman's emotions mixed with her own memories affecting her more than she could have imagined.

"I take it that's bad," Dallas guessed, watching her closely.

"Very, very bad," Rosie agreed quietly.

"And you, what? Can see what happened to her?"

"No," Max corrected. "She lives what happened to her."

"So, she..." With what looked like startling realization, Dallas looked back at her. "That's why you had defensive scratches? Because you lived her death?"

She nodded. "Technically, I died her death."

19

Max squeezed her tightly. "God, don't say that."

"Holy shit," Dallas breathed. "This isn't like the Ghost Whisperer at all."

Rosie couldn't help but give a watery chuckle.

"When we were talking earlier, I got an idea," Dallas said. "About the cove, when I asked what all goes on there."

"Swimming and fishing?" she asked.

"And probably boating if you had a small one," he supplied.

"Okay?" She drew the word out.

"Say instead of you wandering into the water, we put you safely on a boat," Dallas said. "Do you think you'd be able to point us in the right direction?"

She shrugged. "I don't know. It might depend on me being awake or asleep."

She'd never gone in the water awake before. When she was awake at the cove the spirit called her but didn't direct her anywhere, though it might be worth a try.

"We could try," she said.

"Is this something you really want to do?" Max asked from behind her.

"I don't think I have much choice," she admitted.

"I'll back you on whatever you want to do," Max said with another squeeze. "You're my priority."

"Shit!" Dallas exclaimed. "That was fast."

She looked at him confused, but Max laughed. She assumed she'd missed something.

"So, the boat," Max steered them back to the conversation. "I've got my kayak that fits two."

"I have the same, so we can all go out there. I'm working tonight, so that's out, tomorrow's the holiday. How's Friday?"

"I'm ready whenever Rosie's ready," Max said.

"I'm off the rest of the weekend. Friday's fine."

It seemed strange and completely foreign that that conversation had just happened. It felt like she had a team of people behind her, ready to be there and support her.

When she'd tried to assist in police investigations as a child, it had been more of a sideshow than anything else. Butch was with her but he was always using her as a tool, nothing more.

In a way, she had put herself in that position when she'd led him to Lainey's body, but she hadn't known any better at that age. She hadn't learned to protect herself from people she'd put her trust in.

Her mother, for example, was another person she hadn't protected herself from. She knew the people her mom hung out with were bad. Some had tried to touch her, make her do things like sit on their laps and touch them. Some had burned her with cigarettes and pulled her hair. Them, she didn't trust.

But her mother, when she'd been in the room and mostly sober, had protected her, so Rosie thought she could count on her.

She'd thought the same of Butch until she realized he thought she was a freak, just like everyone else did.

"Babe?" Max spoke quietly in her ear.

"Yeah," she said automatically and looked around. "Sorry."

"It's okay," he told her. "We were just talking about tomorrow."

"Tomorrow?" she asked.

"Jesus, girl. Thanksgiving. " Dallas rolled his eyes.

"Oh." She remembered Max's invitation.

"He asked if you're coming with us to his parent's house," Dallas informed her with a smile.

Automatically, she shook her head. "No. Thanks."

"Well," Dallas said with a smile. "The cove on Friday, then."

He and Max fist bumped and he was gone.

"You okay?" Max asked, turning her around holding her in his arms.

She slid her arms around his waist, and it felt natural and wonderfully comforting, no matter how loud her inner voice screamed.

"I'm fine." Her answer was automatic, and from the crinkle in his brow, he knew it.

"You're fine. You're okay. I know. But seriously," he amended with a penetrating stare. "Between you and me. Are you okay?"

"Between you and me?" she asked. "Honestly?"

"Always." He leaned in and kissed her softly, making her melt just a little.

"I feel restless. Like, I need to keep busy because I'm scared to death of what might happen Friday and I'm not sure if I want it to come faster, or if I want to forget about it completely. I think if I can work and keep my mind off it, I'll be okay."

"You'll be okay either way, baby. I'll make sure of that. But if you need to keep busy, there's plenty of work to keep you busy here."

"Really?" Her face lit up. "You'd let me help?"

"I can use all the help I can get." He grabbed her hand and started pulling her toward the fields. "Come on, I'll show you how to weed."

~

THAT AFTERNOON, Max fed her lunch after she weeded an entire patch of cabbage. At her insistence, he showed her how to feed the animals, and she then took it upon herself to tidy up the work areas in the chicken coop and the goat barn.

By the end of the day, she had sufficiently kept herself busy enough that she'd barely thought about the impending boat trip on Friday.

If she let herself think too much about it, she'd freak herself out about the things that were beyond her control. Her options were severely limited when it came to ways to solve the problem of the woman in the woods. If she ignored it, she was the one who suffered. Other than the woman, she reminded herself. When she thought about doing nothing, she wondered if she'd even be able to stand living in her trailer anymore, or even living in Jacob's beach. She'd possibly have to move and find somewhere new to be.

Her main issue with moving used to be trying to pack her things and physically moving them. Now, she looked at Max sitting at the counter, and she knew he would be the hardest thing to let go when it came time to leave.

He had been so unexpected. She hadn't counted on trusting someone or finding someone who accepted her for who she was. She'd been blindsided by his casual humor and unyielding patience.

She was falling in love with him.

She sat up straighter at the realization. She was falling in love with him. She felt the sudden urge to slap herself on the forehead for her carelessness yet, at the same time, she could have hugged herself.

"You're kinda freakin' me out." Max interrupted her thoughts, motioning to her fork stopped between her plate and her mouth. "What's going on in that head?" he asked, still eating, completely relaxed.

She turned her chair to face him. "What if we don't find anything Friday? What if we get out there and she's not there?"

It was the best she could come up with in the moment. There was no way she'd tell him what she was really thinking.

"Then we try again."

She shook head. "You make it sound so simple."

He grabbed her hand. "It is simple. It doesn't work Friday, then we try something else another day. And if that doesn't work, then we try something else until we find the right thing."

"It just..." She huffed out a breath, unsure of how to say what she wanted to say to him. "Never mind."

He'd told her just a few hours earlier, if she was scared, she needed to tell him. She wanted to. She wanted to tell him she was scared of what might happen on Friday at the cove.

What if she went down there, completely lost it and Max got so freaked out, he bailed? What if they went down there and stumbled across the woman's remains.

"No, not never mind," he persisted. "Talk to me."

It had gotten dark as they'd eaten, and the house was quiet around them. Hannah and Gizmo were sleeping on the carpet near the back door, and she watched them lay quietly.

"I'm just tired," she lied. "Don't mind me."

"Yeah, okay." He pulled a face that said he didn't believe her. "Come on, Rosie. It's me. Talk to me."

"Remember last night?"

He sent her a smile and raised his eyebrows, letting her change the subject. "Which part?"

"Mostly the bathtub part."

"I liked that part," he offered.

"Can we do that again? I'm not used to all that hard work you made me do today. I could use a hot bath."

"Am I invited again?"

"You weren't invited the first time," she reminded him.

"I didn't hear you complain."

She felt her face redden at the memory of him, completely naked. "No, you didn't," she agreed.

"Ah, so you didn't mind." He stood and took both of their plates. "You go up and start the tub. I'll clean up down here. After that, I need to start some laundry. You want to throw some of your stuff in, too?" He turned to look at her from over his shoulder as he stood at the sink.

"Is that weird?" she asked, twisting her mouth in question.

He lifted and dropped his shoulders. "I don't know. It's just laundry."

She could wash the few things she'd used the last few days. "Okay, if you don't mind."

"No big deal. Maybe we'll play a couple video games or something later."

She'd never played video games before. "Okay."

~

UPSTAIRS, Rosie gathered her laundry into a small pile and started the tub. Gizmo followed her and settled himself on the plush rug outside of the shower. When the tub was half full, she stripped her remaining clothes off and got in. The bubbles covered most of her chest, and the water rose rapidly. She took her little travel shampoo and conditioner and got to work washing her hair.

"Now that's a good look for you."

Her hair was full of bubbles when she heard Max's voice. She turned to him with a laugh and motioned to her head with her hands. "This old thing?"

He walked closer, turning off the overhead light leaving just the dim fan light on, and knelt on the tile.

"Turn around." He reached over and grabbed the removable shower-head.

She gave him her back, letting him spray the water gently on her hair, the bubbles snaking down her skin. He was careful not to spray her face, using his other hand to keep the water from her forehead.

"Smells good," he said quietly.

"Mmm," she hummed, enjoying the feel of the water.

He rinsed her hair for probably longer than was necessary.

"All done," he told her.

She sat up and reached for the conditioner, but he took it out of her hand the second she touched it.

"I've got it," he told her.

The tub was filled, and he shut the water off before he started massaging the conditioner into her hair. His fingertips, rubbing along her scalp, sent a shiver up her spine.

"That feels good," she breathed.

Her eyes were closed, but she could feel the steam on the air surrounding her, the scent of the bubbles and shampoo permeating her senses. It was a heady feeling, intimate in a way she'd never experienced.

"Ready to rinse?" His voice was soft, matching the mood and lighting of the room.

"Sure," she said, though she wasn't sure she was ready for him to stop touching her.

He repeated the same motions he'd used to rinse the shampoo, and even started to towel off the top for her. She turned and took the towel, wrapping her long hair in it and pulling it to the side.

"Are you getting in?" she asked, her voice sounding strange and deep to her own ears.

"Is that an invitation?" At her nod, he leaned in and kissed her. "Are you going to watch like you did last night?"

"Not if you don't want me to," she told him, watching as he pulled his shirt over his head. His skin was smooth across his chest, hard and lean from farm work. A sexy trail of dark hair started below his bellybutton and disappeared under his pants.

"You do whatever you want to." His fingers quickly worked his button open, and then in a flash he had them over his hips.

She swallowed at the sight of him stripping his pant legs off one at a time, his hard penis bobbing up and down, pointing directly at her. Max showed not one ounce of modesty, not that he had anything to be ashamed about, there wasn't an imperfection on him.

He lowered himself across from her, his mouth pulled up into a sexy smile.

"I like when you watch me," he told her.

"I can tell," she said, sending him smile.

He barked a laugh. "I'm sure you can." His long arms were resting on the sides of the tub, extending in her direction.

"Do you usually take baths?" She hadn't taken one in years, though she also didn't have a tub, so that was a factor.

"Only if I've had a really hard day." She felt his foot reach out and rub her calf. "How was your first day on the farm?"

She felt good, not sore at all. "It was fun. I liked it."

"You're hired," he told her.

"I think Wendy would have something to say about that."

He waved his hand. "Wendy, Shemndy."

That brought her to something that had occurred to her earlier in the day.

"You know, I think if you and Dallas both know about the uh, ghost thing, I should tell Wendy. I wouldn't want her to feel like we're all keeping secrets from her."

Max watched her for a few seconds before answering. "I think that would be a good idea."

She knew he'd agree. She just wondered how much was too much when it came to pushing her luck. It seemed like things were going so well, she could practically feel the other shoe hovering above her, waiting to drop.

"It was your idea, but you don't look too excited about the whole thing."

Rosie felt her fingernails scratching her palm, an old nervous habit that reared its head sometimes.

"I'm waiting for this all to blow up in my face," she admitted.

"How so?"

"It's just what always happens."

"Nothing's gonna blow up in your face, baby."

Again, it was just that simple for him. He believed it to be true and that was that.

She envied his confidence in himself and the world around him. What she wouldn't give to believe in everything she did and the people she loved. Part of that belief had to rely on trust. Max trusted his friends and family. He trusted his own judgment and knew who he was. She'd told him she trusted him, but she hadn't been willing to tell him some of her truths.

She didn't know if she'd ever be ready to tell him those.

But there was something she was willing to admit that he needed to hear.

"I'm..." She hesitated, looking away.

"You're what?" She felt the water shift around her, and when she looked back, he was sitting up, watching her. "You're what?"

"I'm, ah...I'm terrified."

She had to choke the word out, emotional from admitting it to him and because she'd promised him just that afternoon she'd tell him what she was feeling.

He sucked in a breath and grabbed her hand. "Of what?"

"Everything," she admitted. "What might happen Friday. What might not happen Friday. Telling Wendy. Dallas changing his mind about believing me. You, changing your mind about being with me." There was more, but Max interrupted.

"First of all, I'm not changing my mind, Rosie. Not ever. So, you can throw that worry right out the window." His fingers intertwined with hers under the water. "I'm not going anywhere. I won't promise because you wouldn't believe me if I did, so I'll just say it and that's it. It's fact." He watched her closely. "Okay?"

God, she wanted to believe him so badly. Her heart was thumping in her chest, like it was trying to get out of her body and reach his, but her head kept getting in the way.

"Tell me what keeps holding you back, baby." His golden eyes searched her face. "I can see you, you know. You're right here with me most of the time. Right on the edge of this cliff, but every time I'm ready to jump in, you get spooked. Not enough to back out completely, but just enough to not let yourself go."

He was absolutely right.

"Tell me what's going on, Rosie. We'll figure it out so when the time's right, we can jump together."

"It's hard to explain," she hedged.

"No, it's probably not," he argued. "Someone broke your heart and you're scared to death to give it someone else. Is it about your mom? Or was there someone else?"

"No, not my mom." She shook her head, distractedly taking the towel from her hair and dropping it on the floor.

"Then who?"

"The abridged version?" she asked just as she had the night before.

"If that's all you want to tell." He squeezed her hand encouragingly.

"He was a cop."

"You dated a cop?" He sounded shocked.

She pulled a face. "He was my foster dad for a while."

"Oh. You had foster parents?"

"That's what they do with kids when their parents are in jail," she reminded him. "And yeah, I ended up having lots of foster parents."

"But this one..."

"Promised me a lot of things."

"And broke his promise," Max guessed.

She nodded. "Something like that."

"And now you don't trust anyone? Must have been one heck of a promise."

"It kind of was."

They were both quiet for a minute, Rosie looking down and toying with the bubbles and Max watching her.

"He promised to keep you, didn't he?" he asked softly, to which she eventually nodded. "Why did he break his promise?"

"They had a new baby," she told him with a careless shrug. "And thought I was too weird to be around him."

"You're not weird, Rosie, you're special. Gifted," he told her immediately.

She let out a humorless laugh. "That's the same thing he told me."

"Jesus," he muttered. "It's the truth. You're incredibly special." He pulled their entwined hands up and kissed hers. "I'm so glad I found you."

"If this doesn't end up coming back to bite me in the ass I think I'll be glad you found me, too."

His face turned up into a sexy smile.

"Why are you looking at me like that?"

"You just said bite me in the ass. It gave me a few ideas."

She rolled her eyes. "You're easily distracted."

"You're anything but easy, baby," he joked before he grabbed the soap and began washing up and down his arms. When he noticed she was staring, he held the bar out to her. "Wash my back?"

She took it from him and twirled her finger around in the air, telling him to turn around. His back was incredibly smooth, much like the rest of his body, with lean, ropy muscles. She pressed a thumb into his shoulder, massaging a knot she found just under the blade. He twisted and squirmed a bit, his breathing loud in the dark room, but he never pulled away. When that knot was gone, she moved on, pressing her fingers up and down the muscles surrounding his spine. He leaned way forward, giving her more access, groaning a little when she massaged a tight spot. When that was gone, she moved on.

After about twenty minutes, Max sat there, unmoving.

She pressed a hand to his back, wondering if maybe she'd hurt him. "Are you okay? Did I hurt you?"

He shook his head. "Hurt me? God, no, but I don't think I can move right now." His head turned to look behind him, and he startled a bit, staring at her breasts. "I was gonna ask if I could lay back on you but I can't look away."

She brought her hands up to cover her breasts with a laugh, and his eyes flipped up to hers. "You're so beautiful." Rosie felt her cheeks heat. "And you're blushing, which is adorable, by the way." He motioned to her chest. "Can I lay back for a second? You can be my pillow."

She knew, even naked, Max would take care to not cross any of her boundaries. So she slid down and opened her arms, while he leaned back on her. His head rested on her chest, between her breasts. He wrapped his arms around her legs, her knees up and out of the water, his hands latched onto her calves. It was between her legs that was giving her pause, where Max's back was pressed to her core.

"Am I crushing you?" he asked.

Deciding to ignore the inherent strangeness of having someone else naked and so close to her, she answered, "No," and slid her hands down his chest.

"Wendy's like me in a lot of ways," he said out of the blue. "She'll listen to what you have to say and just accept it. She might have a million questions, but she'll believe you."

He was back to her admission, which she appreciated. It made her realize he not only had been listening when she spoke, but felt it was important to address what she said.

"Dallas won't change his mind, and if he does, we'll vote him off the island. It'll be three against one."

"It's hard for some people to accept and understand," she told him, having too much experience with both scenarios in her life.

"Some people, maybe. But not us, baby. We're your friends."

"We just met."

"Seems like a lifetime ago doesn't it?" he asked. "As far as Friday goes, I can't tell you which way things will go. I can just tell you we'll deal with whatever gets thrown at us."

"I should call Jay," she realized. "He should be there, too."

"The crystals guy."

She laughed a little. Jay was so much more than that, but if that was as far as Max grasped right now, that was okay, too.

"He sees energy, too," she told him. "He reads chakras."

"What the hell is that?"

"He says they're the body's energy points. He can read feelings through them, see emotions, sickness, that kind of thing."

"Sickness? That's freaky."

"Remember when we met? At the restaurant?"

"Like I could forget." There was a smile in his voice, and he reached up to hold one of her hands.

"Our waiter was sick."

He shifted around, making waves in the bathwater, until he was hovering above her, his stomach now pressed between her legs.

"Sick how?"

She stared up at him. "I'm not sure. Something in his midsection."

"Something serious?"

"I don't know."

"How could you tell?"

She shrugged. "I could see his aura."

"Aura?" His face wrinkled in confusion. "Is that like chakras or something?"

"Or something," she agreed vaguely.

"Did you tell him? Whatever it was that you saw?"

"What? Like, 'Hey guy, sorry to interrupt, but I noticed a black aura around your guts, maybe you want to get checked out?' People don't really appreciate that kind of stuff. Besides, it could have been anything. Maybe he just had indigestion." She knew that wasn't true. There had been an inherent sadness that had followed him around that made her believe it was something far more serious than that.

He nodded. "I guess. It just seems sad to let him go on thinking he's alright if he's not."

"I can't fix everyone," she told him. "People, spirits...I can barely take care of myself, Max. I can't help everyone."

He leaned down and kissed her. "I think you've done a pretty good job so far." He leaned way back and inspected her face. "Krista."

"Oh my God," she laughed.

~

HE EVENTUALLY GOT out of the tub first and then gave her a few minutes to dry off and change. He'd set out a t-shirt and a pair of shorts for her to wear while they gathered a load of laundry. He showed her to the upstairs laundry room, where she measured the soap and he pressed the right buttons, setting their laundry washing.

From there, they went back to his bedroom, where he set up some video game system and handed her a controller.

"No, like this," he told her with a laugh and turned it around. She'd been holding it upside down. "You've really never played video games before?"

She shook her head, watching the TV screen flash with bright lights. "I'm not sure it will be any fun to play with me."

"Nah, it's Mario Party. You'll be fine."

For an hour, he did his best to teach her the ins and outs of Mario Party. She thought the little mushroom guy was adorable but insisted on being the guy with the purple sweater. Max said he was always Mario. There were all kinds of fun little mini-games built into the bigger game. All in all, it was fun, but she didn't see herself becoming a gamer. Books were still her thing.

For the first time, Max joined her in the bathroom while she brushed her teeth. He stood next to her, scrubbing his own teeth as if this kind of thing happened all the time. When they got into bed that night, he was still settled with the sheet between them. They bathed together but slept with a sheet between them. Again, she appreciated his respect for her boundaries.

"Hang on." He held her shoulder before she settled in. "I don't think you need this to sleep." He tugged her shirt.

He was in nothing but gym shorts.

"I'm not sleeping topless."

"Why not? I am." His hand slipped under her shirt, and his hot palm covered her breast. He played with her nipple between his thumb and the side of his hand.

"I don't sleep topless."

He added a little pressure and her eyes slid closed. She felt him tug at her nipple making her suck in a breath. Her shirt lifted and his mouth surrounded her, hot and insistent. His tongue laved the underside of her breast as he sucked at her skin. Her shirt shifted again and he moved to the other side.

He was right, she didn't need a shirt for this. Trying to help she struggled to get out of the top but couldn't quite manage, her arm tangled in the sleeve. He unlatched himself from her chest and, breathing heavily, helped her out of it.

"You're like, all these colors," he mumbled when he looked down at her.

"Huh?" She was confused.

His glazed, caramel eyes were taking in her naked breasts. "When we first met, it was the blue of your eyes and the black of that one spot. And your hair. All the white, you know." This was the closest she'd ever seen him come to rambling. Her eyebrows were drawn in confusion. "I thought..." He just shook his head.

"You thought what?"

"I thought your nipples would be pink," he admitted, looking at her chest and running his tongue along his bottom lip.

"Is pink better?" She didn't know what he was getting at.

Now he was looking at her in confusion. "Better? What? No! No. Your skin. Your hair, I don't know. The first time I saw you like this, I was surprised."

She looked down at her small breasts that were tipped with brown nipples.

"Oh," she murmured inanely.

He nodded, bringing his mouth back to her chest.

She was not having sex with him tonight, she repeated to herself. She was not one of those girls that said she wasn't ready but then did it anyway. Though she trusted Max to some extent, she wasn't ready to share her entire self with him, and she wasn't the kind of girl that went halfway either. She needed to know she was truly in love before she went that far.

Not only that, she wanted to know Max was in love with her, too.

She gasped when Max pressed his erection to her core and rocked. He was long and hard, his length rubbing her in a spot that sent a shiver up her spine.

He kept rubbing rhythmically at the same time he trailed kisses from breast to breast. It was thrilling and dizzying all at the same time. Back and forth he rubbed, her body tightening at every pass. Her fingers flexed as she held onto his shoulders, holding on.

"Max," she whispered, excited but still nervous.

"I've got you," he told her, pressing open mouth kisses to her throat. "You can let go, baby."

She didn't feel like she could let go. She felt edgy, even though she knew what was happening. It had just never happened with someone else.

Max persisted, kissing her gently, while rocking and teasing her nipples. He brought his lips to hers eventually and swiped his tongue across her lower lip.

"I've got you," he assured her again.

He kissed her fully then, completely investing himself in her, and she felt herself implode in a dazzling fireworks display. Sparks flew from her center to the ends of her fingertips and the tips of her toes. Her back was bowed and her breath was ragged.

It was a moment before she swallowed and lowered herself back to the bed, eyes still closed.

"Wow," she whispered. Flexing her fingers, she let go of his arms.

Max's hips were still pressed into her, but he had stopped rubbing. He was languidly pressing kisses to her cheeks and forehead.

She flipped her eyes open and looked up at him, finding his expression somewhere between cocky and pleased.

"You okay?" he asked, the smile plain on his face.

She let out a breathy laugh. "Yeah."

"Good." He leaned in to kiss her again, then laid himself on the bed next to her, turning quickly to turn the light on his nightstand off.

She just laid there, reveling in what just happened.

"You're quiet," he said, suddenly wary.

"I just had an orgasm," she said, spilling her thought out loud.

He barked out a laugh. "Yeah, you did."

She didn't say anything else and let that sink in.

For the first time in her life, she truly believed she might just be okay.

20

"You're sure you won't come to Thanksgiving with me?" Max asked for the hundredth time as he drove her back to the camper.

Apparently, he, his father, and Dallas were going out hunting for turkey for most of the day, as was their tradition. She didn't have any big plans, other than to call Jay, but she wasn't ready to spend a holiday with Max's family. Though she thought that maybe she was going to be just fine in life, there were still moments she just felt apart, like she wouldn't know how to act at a real family Thanksgiving.

"No, thank you," she answered again. "Do you actually eat the turkey you shoot?"

"No," he admitted. "Usually we don't shoot anything other than the breeze. I think the tradition mostly started just so we'd get out of my mom's hair while she was cooking."

"Oh."

He pulled up to the camper and put his truck in park.

"You're sure?" he asked again.

"I'm sure." She leaned over Gizmo, who was sitting in the middle seat between them, and pressed her lips to his. "We'll talk later."

"I'll call when we finish up."

She grabbed the cat and hopped out, waving as Max drove away.

Letting herself in the camper, she looked around. It seemed strange being there, two days at Max's, and she'd made herself at home there. It had to be something about his energy as a healer. Where she would normally feel uncomfortable being herself, she felt empowered because she knew he was listening.

First thing, she left a message for Jay, telling him basics about heading to Smith's Cove Friday.

Then she decided cleaning wouldn't be completely out of the question, so she began pulling out the stacks of books she kept under her bed, along with a few shoeboxes full of cash and began sweeping and dusting.

Before long, she was surrounded by piles of her old favorites, friends that kept her company when she had no one else. She picked up her well-worn copy of *The Return of the King* and flipped through the pages, remembering when she bought it back when she lived in Virginia. It had been her favorite of the trilogy, and she'd read it twice as many times as the other two books.

Putting it aside, she grabbed the broom and began sweeping under the bed. It wasn't dirty, but she kept at it anyway until all the corners were clean. Before she put the books back, she decided to make herself a snack and put a toaster pastry in to heat.

She got to work, washing the linoleum under the bed and rinsing the mop. While that was working, she inspected her face in the mirror and decided her eyebrows needed a touch-up.

Five minutes of tweezing later, she smelled smoke and remembered the toaster pastry.

"Shit," she swore and hurried to the living area, which was filled with smoke.

Quickly, she unplugged the toaster and put the small fire out by smothering it. She propped the door open to air the trailer out and stood watching smoke pour out of her camper.

When she went back in, she stared at the toaster, hands on hips, lamenting the lost pastry.

"Knock, knock! Oh, gross. Did you burn something?"

Rosie turned to see Wendy standing in the doorway.

"My breakfast." Rosie pulled a face. "It's still too hot to take out."

Wendy stepped into the camper, covering her mouth with the sleeve of her sweater, and stared at the still-smoking black rectangle.

"Bummer."

"Come outside." Rosie lead her out.

Wendy stepped around all the books again, but this time paid attention to them. "What are you doing in here? Having a yard sale?" She eyed the shoe boxes. "Holy shit, Rosie. What the hell are you doing with all that money?"

"Just cleaning up." She plopped herself into a chair and ignored the real question. "What brings you out here?"

"I came to get you for Thanksgiving," Wendy said, as if they'd made plans.

Rosie sent her a look. "I'm not going to Thanksgiving."

Wendy scoffed. "Yeah, you are."

"Wendy-"

"No." She held up a hand. "You're coming. End of story."

"I don't want to come," Rosie argued.

"Like you don't want to be my friend?"

Rosie rolled her eyes. "That's different."

"Okay." She shrugged. "You're still coming."

"You're bossy, you know that?"

"I've been told," Wendy admitted.

Telling her she was bossy reminded Rosie of Mrs. Murphy, Wendy's grandmother. She wondered where the spirit had gone, and in a strange, self-torturing way, even missed her a little. She told Max she wanted to tell Wendy the truth about herself, but now that the moment had arrived, she wasn't sure it was such a great idea. What if Wendy didn't believe her? What if she thought she was nuts and fired her?

She'll believe you, Max had said.

Rosie turned her head to find Wendy staring at her.

"You look like you have something to say. I'm waiting to argue."

Rosie shook her head. "No arguments. I just," she nearly hesitated but persisted. "I have something I need to tell you."

Wendy leaned back like she was settling in and had all the time in the world. "Okay."

Rosie went back and forth in her mind about how to tell Wendy the truth. Did she tell her about her grandmother first, or did she start with her abnormal senses?

"I don't know where to start," she admitted.

"The beginning's fine."

"That would be too much," she told her. "Do you want to hear the part that has to do with you, or the part that has to do with me?"

"Uh, me, obviously," Wendy laughed.

That helped. "There's a little more to the story about when I found out Lisa was stealing."

Wendy sat up.

"I didn't just find out through an invoice. I mean, I proved it that way, but there was someone else that knew. Someone else that told me."

"Someone else knew? One of the other girls?" Wendy fumed.

"No, no one else in the office knew. It was someone else. She kept coming to me and telling me every detail, even when I kept telling her to stop."

"Who-"

"I tried ignoring her but, my God, the woman is persistent. She wouldn't leave me alone."

"Who was it?"

Rosie took a deep breath and looked Wendy square in those eyes that were so much like Max's.

"Your grandmother."

Wendy's head reared back. "My-" She couldn't even finish the sentence.

"She used to walk around the jobs in this hideous pink skirt set with a clipboard, making sure everyone was doing their jobs."

"My grandmother's dead."

Rosie nodded. "I know."

"You saw her?"

"I did. A lot, actually."

"You see dead people?" Her voice was flat and Rosie worried she'd made a mistake.

"It's something I was born with. I've been doing it all my life. I don't mean to. I mean, I wish I didn't. Some people, like your grandmother, have no boundaries. She would show up here in the middle of the night and yell at me for not telling you. She'd follow me around the jobs, telling me I was an awful person for not being truthful with you."

"You see dead people," Wendy repeated. "You see my grandmother."

"To be fair, I haven't seen her since I told you about Lisa."

"Where'd she go? Did she, like, cross over?"

"I'm not really sure where she went."

Rosie didn't say anything else and just let Wendy sit and think on it for a while. Every now and then she'd raise her finger and open her mouth like she was going to say something, but then never did. Rosie looked out over the yard and saw Hannah, laying in a beam of sunlight in the clearing.

She pointed and turned to Wendy. "See those trees over there? And that ray of sunshine on the ground?"

"Yeah." She sat up and looked.

"Your brother's dog, Hannah, is sleeping there."

"Hannah?" Her head spun to stare at Rosie. "She's here."

Rosie nodded. "Hannah's one of the only spirits I can see right now." She looked back at the dog. "Actually, it's strange she's here. She usually stays close to Max."

"Does Max...know about this?"

Rosie nodded. "He's like your grandmother. Really persistent."

Wendy put her elbows on her knees and held her head in her hands. "This is crazy. You know that, right?"

"Yeah," Rosie agreed quietly. "I know. It's okay if you don't believe me."

Wendy shot her an angry look. "Of course I believe you, you idiot.

I just can't believe it, you know." Rosie was confused, and it must have showed on her face because Wendy continued. "I believe you. I do. It's just hard to take in."

"There's more."

Wendy sat, watchful and so much like Max, while Rosie explained her bike accident and the woman in the woods. She told her about the events at Smith's Cove and how she couldn't really see spirits other than the woman and Hannah. She didn't get into auras or psychic dreams, it seemed extraneous.

Wendy asked some good questions about trying to identify the woman and offered to go to the cove when they made the trip.

"I don't know what's going to happen tomorrow," she admitted. "I don't know what it's going to be like, so I can't say if you'd want to come or not."

"Well, if you're there, and Max and Dallas are there, then I want be there, too."

Rosie shook her head. "I don't know how I got so lucky to find you. You're one of a kind, you know that?"

"I do." Wendy stood. "Now get changed. You can't go to Thanksgiving smelling like burnt Pop Tarts."

~

"My parents moved into this place a few years ago," Wendy told her when they pulled up to a classic Florida ranch style home, nestled in a neatly groomed neighborhood.

"Are you sure they won't mind when I show up?"

Wendy laughed. "For the millionth time, they know you're coming." She pulled into the driveway and parked. "Come on."

She led the way to a side door and walked right in.

"Mom?" Wendy called into the house.

Rosie followed her through the door and into a kitchen. She could smell the food cooking, a sign of the impending holiday dinner.

"I'm in the dining room, setting the table." The voice came from another room.

Rosie took a few steps into the house and Wendy shut the door behind her. The kitchen was a good size, with dark cabinets and black granite countertops. It was obviously a kitchen built for someone who enjoyed cooking, fancy appliances and neat gadgets everywhere. There were vegetables on the counters, and other ingredients strewn about.

Wendy's mom bustled into the kitchen, a smile on her face. She was tall, like Wendy, but her hair was black and very short. She was wearing stylish skinny jeans and what looked like a designer, casual sweatshirt. Her face lit up when she saw her daughter.

"I'm so glad you're here!" She rushed over and pulled Wendy into a hug. "We have so much work to do."

Then she turned to Rosie. "You must be Rosie." Her smile was so genuine and real, like she was truly happy Rosie was there.

"Hi," Rosie said, quietly holding out her hand.

Mrs. Murphy stopped short, the smile freezing on her face as she looked between Rosie's face and hand.

Wendy interrupted and whispered loudly, "Mom's a hugger. You've stumped her."

Rosie kept her hand out, which Mrs. Murphy eventually took.

"Thank you for having me."

"Oh, please." The woman waved her off. "I love having company for the holidays. Thanks for coming." She grabbed Rosie by the shoulders and inspected her face, particularly her eyes. "My word, that's incredible."

"Mom," Wendy protested. "Let's not freak her out the first minute she's here."

She looked at her daughter. "What? What am I doing?"

"You're staring intensely in her eyes like a psycho. I already told you she likes to keep to herself."

She'd told her mother that?

"She's keeping to herself," the woman argued, but still let go of Rosie's shoulders and took a step back. "Sorry. I'm a people person."

Then she turned to the kitchen and pointed in all different directions. "Potatoes need peeling and boiling. Sweet potatoes need the same. The veggies for the stuffing need to be chopped..."

She went on and on, dish after dish, leaving Rosie's mouth hanging open. She didn't know how to do any of that stuff. Well, she could peel a potato, but the rest there was no way.

"You look lost," Mrs. Murphy laughed. She noticed Wendy was already tying on an apron.

"I don't know how to cook," she admitted.

"Rosie just about burned her place down today making a Pop Tart," Wendy laughed.

"Pop Tarts?" Mrs. Murphy made a disgusted face. "You shouldn't eat those things. Who knows what's in them."

"Brown sugar and cinnamon," Rosie told her. "S'mores."

"Ashes if Rosie's making it," Wendy joked even making Rosie laugh.

"I can help peel, I think."

"You think?" Wendy sounded dubious.

"If someone shows me how," she hedged.

"We'll find something for you," Mrs. Murphy promised. "We'll start with potatoes."

~

Two hours later, Rosie was charged with putting cookies on a platter for dessert. Also, filling the little cream holder and sugar for coffee. She had band-aids on her fingers from that stupid peeler, and one more one from a can of green beans. She felt like an idiot. Wendy and her mom had been kind, if not a little bewildered at her ineptitude, and had helped her find something to keep her busy.

She'd finished setting the table as instructed. She'd filled pickle dishes. And now, she was organizing cookies.

"I think our intrepid hunters have returned," *Mrs. Call-Me-Christine* said, leaning forward on her tiptoes to look out the window above the sink.

Rosie was nervous about what Max would say when he showed up. She'd refused him numerous times when he invited her to dinner, but yet, here she was. She hoped he wouldn't be upset she came.

Without turning around, she continued setting out dessert even as she heard the door open and what sounded like a herd of elephants pile through the door.

"Hi!" Christine chirped. "How'd it go?"

"It was great!" That was a voice she'd never heard, so she assumed it was Mr. Murphy. "Dallas shot at one,"

"But I missed," Dallas's voice cut in. He didn't sound upset that he hadn't hit his target.

"Hi!" Mrs. Murphy threw out greetings as the sound of rustling and shuffling filled the room.

"Well lookee here," Dallas sang.

"Yeah," Wendy growled, and a slapping noise sounded in the room. "Hands off, Hunter."

"Go wash up," Christine sang.

Finally, she heard Max's voice. "Now this is a nice surprise."

Then he was sliding his arms around her from behind and nuzzling her neck. Her cheeks heated, acutely aware of the silence in the room.

"I thought you weren't coming."

She shrugged, unable to hold in a sigh when he kissed behind her ear.

"I asked you a million times."

"You asked?" Wendy laughed. "I didn't ask her to come. I just went to her camper and told her she was coming."

"I'm glad you're here."

"She was about to burn the joint down when I showed up at her place, so we're saving her from starving to death anyway."

Max held up her hand, inspecting it. "What's going on here?"

She opened her mouth to explain, but Wendy cut her off. "The first three were peeling potatoes. The fourth is from opening a can of green beans. She literally cut herself opening a can. She's like an accident waiting to happen."

215

"I told you, I don't know how to cook," Rosie shot back, still held in Max's arms.

He laughed and kissed the back of her head.

"Time to go wash up, Max. I don't want any more mud in the house."

"I'll be right back." His hand pressed against her cheek and forced her to look his way so he could press a kiss to her lips, his tongue sweeping across her bottom lip.

He was smiling when he pulled back. "Rosie's been eating cookies."

Her mouth dropped open. "You tattletale!"

He kissed her one more time before he walked out of the room.

"Now you're the one feeling the feelings!" Wendy exclaimed. "I knew something was going on with you two!"

Christine waved her off with a laugh. "Where've you been? Max told me weeks ago."

Wendy released a put-out sigh. "I'm always the last to know. I should have known when you started acting like you didn't hate him. That's a sure sign of love."

"Wendy!" Christine sounded appalled.

"Okay," she conceded quickly. "But at least admit to feeling the feelings!"

Rosie lifted a shoulder and tried to hide a smile as she turned back around. "There may be some feelings," she hedged.

Wendy made a loud *pfft* sound, and Christine laughed under her breath. Okay, so they knew she was lying. She was most definitely, feeling the feelings. She was fighting the feelings at every turn, and frankly, she was worried if she didn't control herself, she'd fall head over heels for Max.

It seemed like it would be a good thing, but for her, it screamed impending disaster. For her, loving someone was a sure sign they were about to leave her.

Or betray her.

She knew it was crazy, but she couldn't help but feel that if she just didn't love Max, if she didn't let herself go that far, then things would be okay.

She went back to her cookie platter and coffee tray as Wendy and Christine plated dinner. Mr. Murphy came into the kitchen a moment later, a smile on his face.

"You must be Rosie!" His hair was the same shade of brown as Max's, and he had the exact same brown eyes. It was uncanny.

She held out her hand and smiled. The gesture had the same effect it had on Mrs. Murphy. He stopped, his smile wavering as he looked at her outstretched hand.

"Huggers. I told you," Wendy called from the other side of the room. "Dad, you can't hug everyone you meet."

He looked to Wendy. "She's not just anyone."

"I know that," she argued. "But not everyone's a hugger."

"But-" He seemed to want to argue, but when he looked back at her, he extended his hand to enclose hers. "I'm glad you ended up making it."

"Me too," Rosie told him, and she was pretty sure she even meant it.

⁓

IT WAS STRANGE, Rosie thought as they ate dinner, Thanksgiving was a fairly universal event. Though she'd only been to two of the holiday meals herself, she'd seen countless representations on television and in movies, and they were all similar. The table was set with the good china, candles were lit, and everyone was gathered around a meal that could feed an army.

"I always make too much!" Christine marveled as they all neared the point of being stuffed.

"Every year," Sam, Max and Wendy's father, agreed. "But it's always delicious."

She smiled prettily at him.

"Every year, Wendy does more and more. Hopefully soon, she'll take over and I can sit back and watch."

Wendy laughed. "Keep dreaming."

"I'll take next year," Dallas offered, and though everyone laughed like he was joking, Rosie suspected he was serious.

"I think I'll pass on anything you cooked," Wendy joked.

"Yeah, I'd like to live to see Christmas," Max added.

Rosie watched Dallas as they continued ribbing him, the color of his wispy aura shifting from deep blue to gray.

He was hurt, even if his face was still holding that flirty smile.

She didn't know what came over her. "I'll come," she told him quietly, interrupting Max. Her eyes never left Dallas's.

His aura changed from dark gray to more of a smoky color.

"Yeah?" he asked, sounding more vulnerable than she imagined he could.

If I'm here, she wanted to add. Instead, she nodded.

"Brave," Max laughed and held her hand under the table.

"Well, don't expect any help from Rosie." Wendy pointed her fork at Dallas. "She'll burn the place down."

Rosie rolled her eyes. "You burn one Pop Tart and suddenly, you're the town pyro."

"I didn't hear the fire department get called out, so it couldn't have been that bad," Dallas offered with a wink.

"See! Thank you."

"I'm sure Max can teach you to cook," Christine offered. "Or, if you'd like to come here sometime, I can show you a few things."

Rosie was stunned for second. It was incredibly generous of Max's mother to offer to teach her to cook. No wonder Max and Wendy were so inherently kind. They came from two warm, loving people who obviously had taught them well.

"You know, if you teach her to cook, I'll be useless to her," Max said to his mother.

"I doubt that," Dallas muttered under his breath.

"Not at the table, Dallas," Christine scolded.

"Yeah, no sex talk at the table," Wendy laughed.

"Wendy." her mother's voice held a warning tone.

"Mom. In case you haven't noticed, we're all grown-ups."

"Not at my table, you aren't."

Rosie leaned over to Max and whispered, "How did we get from cooking to sex?"

He tilted his head and looked down at her lips. "Say sex again."

She rolled her eyes and sat back up.

"Okay, kids." Sam knocked on the table. "No more of that talk. It's time to clean up and watch movies."

Everyone's chairs slid out and they began picking up.

"What movies?" she asked Max as she gathered plates.

"After we eat dinner, my parents like to dig out old home movies. We watch until we're all sufficiently embarrassed, then they switch to Christmas movies."

They cleaned the table as Christine packed three sets of leftovers and put them in grocery bags.

"For when you go home." She smiled.

Max and Dallas were stationed at the sink, dutifully washing dirty dishes and loading the dishwasher. Mr. Murphy was packing leftovers with Wendy. Mrs. Murphy roped Rosie into setting out dessert in the dining room.

"So, you said your family was traveling for the holidays?" Christine asked idly.

Actually, Rosie hadn't said anything about her family at all since she'd been here. Wendy or Max had shared that information.

"Yeah," she answered quietly, the lie tasting like ashes on her tongue, not as easy to tell as it used to be.

"Did they go somewhere special?" Christine was putting out napkins and arranging them neatly, glancing up with a curious smile.

"No," Rosie answered, making new lies as she went along. "Just didn't want to stay home, I guess."

"It's cold up north this time of year. I imagine it's a nice break to get away from that." She looked thoughtful for a minute. "I assumed they went somewhere warm. Maybe they went somewhere cold. Skiing or something like that? Have they been to visit you here?"

"I haven't been here that long."

"Oh." Her eyes widened. "How long have you been living in Jacob's Beach?"

She shrugged and set out some plates. "About nine months."

"And they haven't come to see you? There's so much to see here! Maybe I'm biased because I love it so much there."

"Why'd you move?" Rosie asked curiously.

"Once the kids moved out, the house was just too big. We were looking for something smaller and a new adventure."

"Do you like it out here?"

"We do. It's a nice little neighborhood."

They finished putting everything out, and Mrs. Murphy stood up and sent a serious look Rosie's way.

"Don't think I didn't notice just then how you changed the subject and tried to distract me."

"I…" Rosie stuttered, mouth open. Had she been that obvious?

Christine held up a hand. "It's okay. I was pushing and I made you uncomfortable."

"No-"

"Yes," she said, rolling right over Rosie. "That's okay, I'm nosy."

It must run in the family, Rosie thought.

"But do me a favor, honey." Rosie just stared at her. "I've been a mom a long time. I can smell a lie a mile away. I'd rather you just tell me you don't want to talk about it or to mind my own business before you lie to me. You understand?"

"Yes." Rosie nodded, feeling sufficiently chastised.

"Now. Max tells me your parents are traveling."

Rosie took a deep breath. "I'd rather not talk about it."

Christine smiled. "Good girl. That's better. Now let's call in the troops for dessert. You like pie?"

They carried on through dessert, as though Christine hadn't called Rosie out for lying. Max and Dallas piled their plates with pie and cookies, sampling a piece of everything.

Mr. Murphy wasn't far behind. "Grab a plate. ladies. Movie time."

Rosie got a coffee and joined Max in the living room along with everyone else. He was sitting on the couch while his father sat in a chair and Wendy sat on the loveseat. Dallas had settled himself on the floor in front if Wendy, his shoulders wedged between her knees. Mrs. Murphy sat on the end of the couch. next to her husband.

Rosie had to admit, she'd never experienced anything like it. Sitting down to watch family movies was something she'd never even imagined people did in real life, but sure enough, Mr. Murphy pressed a few buttons and a tiny Wendy danced her way across the television. Then a dirty, toddling Max built a sandcastle, smiling happily the whole time. The Murphy's kept a running commentary about each event. There were even movies of Dallas playing baseball with Max, the two of them looking sweaty and awkward in their pre-teen years.

She wondered what her home movies would look like if there were any. Coloring on the bathroom floor in the crack house where her mom turned tricks. Hiding in the closet so the mean man wouldn't put out his cigarette on her again. The differences in their lives were unfathomable.

When she thought about how she'd grown up, she hadn't turned out so bad. A little screwed up maybe, but she wasn't beyond help, she hoped.

After the family movies, they put on It's A Wonderful Life.

"You okay?" Max whispered, his lips against her hair. Partway through the family movies, he'd pulled her to his side and wrapped his arms around her. Now she found herself leaning on him completely, her legs up on the couch. "You're quiet."

"Just taking it all in," she admitted.

"Yeah?" He gave her a squeeze. "How is it?"

Magical, she wanted to say. "Nice."

Wendy was lounged in her chair, under a blanket, Dallas's head resting at her hip. Mrs. Murphy had moved to her husband's lap. As she watched the movie, she contemplated how quaint the whole scene was and how hard to believe it was that she was a part of it. It was something she'd never imagined for herself and would love to be a part of again.

Her heart stuttered. She never dared to hope for something like that. She should just be content with right now, because when she hoped for a future, it inevitably turned out a disaster. A cosmic joke that always got played on her. Maybe, if she didn't think about it, it would just happen for her.

Her eyes slid closed as the movie played. Maybe if she just ignored the happiness coursing through her, the universe wouldn't know she coveted it so much, and it wouldn't be so quick to take it away.

21

Max looked at the top of Rosie's head and smiled. Her body was heavy and he could feel her deep, even breaths against his chest.

There were so many things he didn't know about her. Like where she was from exactly, or where she went to school or what her favorite color was. Those were things she hadn't shared with him yet.

They'd get there. Every day, she trusted him a little more. It took time and persistence, but she'd finally started opening up. There was more she was hiding, but they'd get there.

The things he knew about her now were enough. She was thoughtful, and though distant at times, it wasn't from lack of feeling. It was because she felt too much. It had become clear to him that if Rosie was pulling back, it was because she was trying to separate herself from feeling. It was too much for her, too hard somehow. She was strong and incredibly brave for powering through hard situations and coming out on the other side in one piece.

Finding her in his parent's kitchen had been the highlight of his day. She'd told him no every time he'd asked, but it was fear that held her back, nothing more. Wendy was the perfect person to drag Rosie along, it was just what she did.

He looked at the kitchen longingly, dying for a cup of coffee. He could shift Rosie around and grab a cup. It would just be a few minutes.

Carefully, he snuck out from underneath her and tucked a blanket around her. She barely noticed, cuddling into the couch in his absence.

In the kitchen, he grabbed a mug and poured himself some coffee.

"I like her. She's sweet," his mother said as she joined him in the kitchen.

"She is," he agreed.

"Private."

"That, too."

"Though, she did lie to me." Her tone was offhand.

"You want a mug?" he asked, not overly surprised his mom had picked up on Rosie's fibs and evasions. At her nod, he turned and poured her a cup.

"Does she lie a lot?"

"She's not like that, Mom. She's not a liar."

"I got that impression." She stirred cream and sugar into her mug. "I did tell her I can smell a lie a mile away."

He rolled his eyes. "You know, I didn't bring her here to be interrogated."

"You didn't bring her here at all," she reminded him. "Your sister did."

"You'll see." It was all he could tell her. Things with Rosie took a little time.

"Despite the lie, I get a good feeling from her. She seems very genuine."

Max considered the fact that Rosie wasn't really Rosie's name at all and kept his mouth shut.

"This is like pulling teeth, Max. Tell me about her. Where is she from? What's she like? How are things going?"

He let out a chuckle and sipped his coffee. "All that?"

"Anything would be a start."

Max shook his head. "She's private, and she has some trust issues." He lifted his shoulder and dropped it, then looked away. "I, uh, already broke her trust once, and I don't want to do it again."

"You broke her trust?" His mother sounded shocked. "Max!"

"It wasn't on purpose," he defended. "Anyway, the stuff she tells me is private. That's how she needs it to be, so that's how it will stay until Rosie's ready to share more on her own."

Her lips pulled into a smile. "Why, Max, I think that's one of the most mature things I've ever heard you say. You sound like you're in love."

He opened his mouth to reply but was interrupted by a knock on the glass of the kitchen door.

"Oh, it's Janice!" His mother rushed to the door and opened it to her neighbor. "What are you doing here? Happy Thanksgiving."

She was an older retired lady his mother had made friends with over the last few years. She was a tall blonde who looked like she could have been on the Russian shot put team other than her accent, which was pure Southern belle.

"Well, I saw Max's truck and wondered if y'all were done eating if I couldn't steal him away for a few minutes. I took his advice about compost and had a bin made, but I was hoping he could make sure I was using it right. My Norman is just clueless when it comes to the outdoors."

Max thought longingly about Rosie on the couch. He hoped his annoyance didn't show in his pained smile. "Sure. No problem."

~

DALLAS SAT on the floor at Wendy's feet content. He hated this particular Christmas movie, but since it was a Murphy tradition, he didn't say anything. Besides, it was a relaxing few hours after a special family meal, and he couldn't complain about that.

Max had gone to the kitchen with his mother a while ago. Rosie slept soundly on the couch for the duration.

He had to admit, she wasn't as crazy as he'd first thought. He had given Max some shit about getting involved with complicated chicks, but the commentary had fallen on deaf ears. But now, he could see why. There was something special about Rosie, and he didn't just mean her ghostly gifts.

She'd offered to have Thanksgiving with him. Everyone else acted like he'd be serving bubonic plague on a platter, but Rosie, sweetheart that she was, still said she'd come.

Ghosts? Auras? He could barely figure out a basic relationship and keeping that shit together, let alone throwing all that other stuff in it. Still, Max seemed happy, and that was enough.

Spending Thanksgiving with the Murphy's had become his own holiday tradition. In the beginning, it felt strange that his own parents weren't around. The rest of his family celebrated together, without him or his younger brother Jackson. Some years, he wondered if they even noticed something was missing. He hated to admit it, but the fact that no one seemed to notice their absence stung. No one ever called to ask why he wasn't coming, or if he could find the time. They didn't Facetime or send silly pictures to one another saying, "I miss you". There was just radio silence.

He loved his family, he did. They were supportive, from a distance. Maybe it was a proximity thing, out of sight, out of mind.

He was happy with his life in Jacob's Beach and had no plans to follow any of them up north. That cold shit was not for him. He was meant to be a cop, and he was meant to do it in the place he'd always called home.

"It has to be here."

Rosie was sitting straight up, eyes open wide.

"What'd you say?" Wendy asked, turning her head.

"It has to be now." Rosie's voice was flat and deeper. Her face was expressionless, pale and strained, her eyes sightless.

"Where's Max?" he asked quietly, never taking his eyes of Rosie.

"I'm not sure. What's going on?" Wendy asked.

"It has to be here."

"Rosie? Is something wrong?" Sam asked thoughtfully from his chair.

"Rosie," Dallas said gently, squatting in front of her.

He shook his head, startled by the size of her pupils and her complete lack of awareness.

"Dal?" It was Sam.

"Can someone find Max? Now." He felt more than saw Sam leave the room.

"What's going on?" Wendy's voice was serious and concerned.

"She's asleep, I think." He focused on Rosie. "What's going on Rosie? What can I do?"

She stood, nearly knocking him over.

"It has to be now," she murmured.

"Where's she going? Rosie?" Wendy hurried after her friend, who was making a somewhat drunken beeline down the hallway.

Dallas followed as Rosie staggered into Sam's office. He met Wendy at the door, and they watched with concern.

"Are we supposed to let her do this?"

"I don't know what this is." He tried to sound calm, but he had no clue what to do. "Last time I saw her do this, Max woke her up. Where did he go?"

"It has to be here," Rosie said again as she stood with her nose against a shelf of books. Her head moved back and forth, from one side of the shelf to the other.

"What's she doing?" Wendy whispered.

"Speed reading?"

"Our family pictures?" she answered doubtfully.

Rosie reached up and began pulling photo albums down, one by one. They landed in a haphazard pile around her feet, some of them knocking her legs on their way down.

"No." Rosie's voice was lifeless and eerie. She reached for the higher shelf but was unable to reach. She put a foot on a low shelf and hoisted herself up, making the shelf wobble.

"Shit." Dallas made a quick few steps and held it against the wall so it wouldn't fall on her.

"It's here," Rosie murmured, still reaching.

More books flew past his head and landed on the floor before Rosie finally stepped off the shelf.

"Dallas." Wendy sounded panicked. "Shouldn't we wake her up?"

"I don't know," he admitted. "Max will know."

Rosie dropped to the floor and began flipping the pages of the last album. Dallas squatted next to her and watched.

"I'm here," she murmured. "I'm here."

"You're where?" Wendy asked gently.

Rosie's head popped up, and she turned to Dallas with blind eyes. "He's here now."

"Who's here?"

They heard a door slam, and then Max's voice. "Rosie?"

Her head tilted as though she was listening for something very far away.

"In here," Dallas called, never taking his eyes off her.

Max skidded into the doorway, his father close behind, and dropped to his knees in front of her. "You with me?"

Rosie blinked herself back into consciousness.

"There you are." Max smiled warmly. "Where'd you go?"

She shook her head, disoriented.

"It's okay. I've got you." He pulled her into his arms.

"What happened?" she whispered.

"I wasn't here. I ran next door to talk to a neighbor. I thought you were sleeping."

"She was." Wendy brimmed with distress.

"She was, but she got up and came in here. Then she did this." Dal held his arms out to encompass the mess.

"What's going on in here?" Sam asked bewildered.

"Can you just give us a minute, Dad?" Max turned and asked his father. "I'll explain everything, and we'll put everything back the way it was."

His father hesitated but left the room.

Max sat back and looked around. "What is all this?"

Rosie was just as surprised. "I have no idea. It wasn't like the other times I dreamt about her."

228

"You fell asleep," Max told her.

"Why would I do this?" Rosie looked around at the albums. "What are these?"

"They're my dad's old picture albums," Wendy explained. "You were pretty adamant about the one you have in your hands."

Rosie held it out and looked at it.

"Why?" she whispered.

Max stood and pulled Rosie along with him. "Why don't you flip through it while we pick up the rest of this stuff?"

"No," Rosie argued. "I made the mess-"

"We've got it," Wendy assured her. "Sit on the couch and see what you see."

Dallas, along with Wendy and Max, made short work shelving the books. If they'd been in a certain order, Sam would have to fix it himself. Before too long, they were assembled around the couch, silently watching as Rosie inspected each picture in the album.

Max watched Rosie intensely, and it became clearer than ever that his friend had already fallen in love with this girl. Dal had known Max for most of his life and had never seen him so invested in someone else before. Sure, he'd had a few girlfriends here and there over the years, but nothing serious. All his previous girlfriends had been casual for Max, something friendly and easygoing he could pick up and drop when it ran its course. He couldn't remember a single time one of Max's relationships contained an ounce of emotional upheaval. Saying that Max was thriving on Rosie's predicament wasn't the right word. Her pain clearly tortured him. It was more that Max's love for Rosie made him stronger and more sure of himself, if that was possible. He stood taller for her.

It made him wonder if that's what falling in love did for everyone, or if it was just Max.

Rosie flipped a page and sucked in a breath.

"It's her," she whispered, her eyes snapping to Max's.

"Wait." He leaned closer to examine the picture she was showing him. "Her?"

"Right there," Rosie said. "That's her."

She had described the woman right the first time, mid to late thirties with dark hair, World War II era clothing.

"Who is she?" Rosie asked.

Wendy shook her head. "These are my Dad's old family pictures. We'd have to ask him."

"Are you sure?" Max asked Rosie.

"One hundred percent," she nodded.

The picture was of a woman standing in front of a house, smiling prettily with a set of keys dangling from her finger.

"Want me to get Dad?" Wendy asked.

Max looked to Rosie. "It's your call."

There were times when Rosie was bold and spoke with authority, times she was almost sassy and sure of herself. But times like this, when she hesitated and backed away from people, he was reminded of how isolated she kept herself

"We should," she replied after a brief pause. "She wants us to know who she is."

Max leaned in and grabbed the back of her neck, pulling her in for a kiss.

"Okay, gross," Wendy complained.

Dallas chuckled.

Max never took his eyes off Rosie. "You're going to want to get used to that."

22

Mr. Murphy calmly ignored her insane outburst and perused the picture Max was showing him. Never in her wildest dreams did she imagine Max being the key to finding the spirit's identity. She wouldn't even be in the Murphy's home if it weren't for him. She and Wendy were friends, but if she weren't involved with Max, she would never have ever accepted a holiday invitation, and she wouldn't have found the picture.

She may have found the picture, but what led her to find it was a different story altogether. Unlike when the woman led her to the cove, this time was different. What she'd seen had been hazy, almost through a window, and she'd had no control whatsoever. It had been like being trapped inside her own body somehow.

"Do you know who that is?" Wendy was pointing to the picture.

"Sure," Sam nodded. "That was my great aunt. Helene." He looked at them all in turn. "Why?"

"Can you tell us about her?" Max asked, his hand squeezing Rosie's.

"What's going on here, guys?" Sam let out a frustrated breath. "Why the interest?"

"She's been haunting me," Rosie told him tiredly, her filter completely sapped along with her energy.

Sam's head reared back. "Haunting you?" He sounded as disbelieving as she assumed he would.

"Can you just tell us about her? We'll deal with the rest later," Max said, the tone of his voice conveying more than his words.

"She's haunting you?" Sam used the *yeah right* tone again.

"I know how it sounds." She sent him a small smile but looked away quickly. "Believe me, I know."

He watched her for a minute before looking back down at the picture. "Helene was the sister-in-law of my grandfather, married to his brother. She was gone long before I was born, but I remember my grandfather telling me about her."

"How did she die?" Dallas interrupted.

"She didn't die. She left her husband and ran off with another man."

"No," Rosie whispered.

Sam's brow crinkled. "Yes," he argued. "At least, that's the story as far as I remember it. It's not the kind of family story we told around the campfire. I just remember hearing the adults talking in whispers whenever she came up."

"And that was the story? That she ran off?"

"And left behind her husband and son," Sam finished.

"Do you have any pictures of them?" Dallas asked, making Rosie thankful he was there.

"Oh, sure," Sam answered, going back to the shelves. "Now where is that..." He muttered as he pawed through a few books.

She wanted to apologize for rearranging his books but couldn't bring herself to do it. Since announcing to him that she was a medium, she'd regained a small sense of her self-preservation instinct. She felt off, like she wasn't quite herself. The entire experience, added to the feelings she was having, led her to a conclusion she couldn't fathom. Despite being in the middle of something important with people she cared for deeply, her fight-or-flight response was screaming at her to flee. The situation had jumped into territory she'd never experienced before, and she wasn't sure she was equipped to handle it.

"You okay?" Dallas whispered in her direction.

Max was now standing with his father at the bookcase, and they were whispering, Sam's eyes cutting to her and then to Max. She was used to it, the sidelong glances and whispers.

She looked back to Dallas. "No."

He inspected her face and turned to the bookshelf. "Can we get to this sometime tonight? Not that I want to interrupt your pow-wow or anything."

"We're coming," Max said hurriedly and seated himself next to Rosie again. "You okay?"

Instead of answering, she watched Sam flip through the pages. "Here." He turned the book around on the tabletop and pushed it to her.

There was a photo of the woman she'd seen so many times but this time, she was standing with a man and a little boy. The man had a cigar out the side of his mouth, his arm slung around her shoulders. A little boy, blonder than blonde, held on to her leg. Rosie looked closely at the man's eyes and the shade of his hair. She inspected the shape and size of his hands.

She shook her head. "That's not him."

"That's my great uncle Jerry, Helene's husband. He was my grandfather's brother. That's their son John."

"That's not the man that killed her."

"Rosie," Sam said gently. "I'm not exactly sure what's going on here, but Helene ran off with another man. I'm not sure what it matters now. It's been more than sixty years."

They were all looking at her now and avoided looking directly at any of them. Let them wonder how crazy she really was, she thought. Let them whisper when she wasn't looking. Let them leave her hanging when she needed them the most.

Maybe they were all waiting for her to argue her point or a grand declaration about the truth.

She could easily tell Sam his mother followed her around for months at work in all her pink, skirt-set glory.

She could argue that she knew what she saw.

She knew how that woman had died, and no excuse in the world would change the truth.

"Maybe we can just take a few of these albums home and flip through them," Dallas suggested, his voice barely reaching how far she'd retreated.

Rosie nodded.

"Rosie," Sam began uneasily.

"It's okay," she assured him, saying the words by rote. "I don't expect you to believe me." It wasn't her first rodeo. She'd played this game before.

"I believe you," Dallas said, his voice unwavering.

She had expected Max to make that declaration, but he stood idly by, watching the interaction.

This time it was Dallas standing by her side. He was unexpected, his loyalty steadfast.

"Of course, we believe you," Max added, his voice just as firm. Wendy added her support as well, though they felt flat.

"I'm sorry to ruin your holiday," she told the room at large, knowing they had more movies they'd been planning to watch. "I'm going to head home, though."

Max rolled his eyes. "You aren't ruining anyone's holiday. I think we're all partied out anyway. We'll say our goodbyes and head out."

Max's mom and dad asked no questions as they all left. She got into Max's truck and began the half-hour drive home.

After a few minutes of silence, he spoke. "You want to tell me what happened here?"

She shrugged and kept her gaze out the window. "I need to get in touch with Jay."

"I'm not talking about Jay right now. I'm talking about the freeze you're giving me. You haven't looked at me since you woke up."

She wasn't about to tell him she was getting all girly and sad over the fact that he hadn't come to her rescue. Hadn't she spent her entire life making sure she was the one that came to her own rescue and suddenly, she's upset because he didn't put himself out there for her.

It was the reason she held back every time she was ready to jump off that ledge with Max. Because no matter how many ways he assured her that he was right there with her, he really wasn't.

She hefted her bag onto her lap and rifled through it, searching for her cell phone.

"Talk to me, Rosie. I'm not good at the silent treatment. I like to talk shit out. I can see you're upset, and I get it. I'm a little freaked out that this ghost is some distant relative of mine. I mean, what are the odds on that? It's got be astronomical. I thought you'd want to talk about it. I thought you'd want to talk about something. Anything."

She didn't want to think about the spirit. She'd done her damndest to not think about her, because every time she did, she freaked herself out.

"I can't talk about it right now. I need to get to Jay's. I-"

"Screw Jay's," Max growled. "I want to know what's bothering you. What did I do?"

Rosie flipped through her three contacts and pressed the call button.

"Damn it," he muttered.

"Hey there," Jay chirped after a few rings. "Happy Thanksgiving."

"Are you home?"

"Why yes, I am," he replied as though she hadn't been rude. "I had a great day, too, thanks for asking. What's up with you?"

"I need a reading."

"Now?" He laughed.

"Right now."

He lost all trace of humor. "Come up to my place. I'm here. What happened?"

Rosie took a breath and closed her eyes. "I think she possessed me."

Max and Jay each sucked in air. "Did you feel her?"

"She what?" Max was angry.

She held up a hand so she could talk to Jay. "I was asleep."

"Isn't that what usually happens?" Jay asked.

"She usually leads me when I'm asleep. This time, it was like I was there but watching through a window. I couldn't move or speak. I was trapped in my own body."

"Holy Christ," Max muttered.

"Come here," Jay told her. "We'll make sure she's gone and get you cleansed."

"Thank you," she told him.

"Don't thank me yet, sugar."

She hung up and never looked at Max. How could that pang of hurt still slice so deep? Shouldn't she be used to it by now?

"Why the hell didn't you say anything?" Max asked angrily.

"Why the hell didn't you say anything?" she countered. He looked at her, confused. "Your dad stood there and told me I was wrong, and instead of telling him I wasn't lying or insane, you just looked at me. Like I was supposed to come up with some kind of explanation."

"Baby, no-"

"Yes, Max. It was Dallas who backed me up."

"I wasn't waiting for you to explain. I was seeing what you were going to say."

"What the hell was I supposed to say?" she asked. "That I saw her die? That I think I know where her remains are?"

"You told him you saw ghosts. I thought you were coming clean."

"I only did that because I was out of sorts. Apparently being possessed scrambles your system."

"Why the hell didn't you say something?"

"We were a little busy trying to deal with the first scene I made. I wasn't ready to make another one." She sent him a glare. "Don't throw this back on me. We were talking about you."

"Yeah, and how you think I what? Didn't back you up?"

"You didn't."

"I did."

"After you left me swaying in the breeze." She shook her head. "Never mind. It doesn't matter."

"Like hell it doesn't," he argued. "You want to use this against me like some kind of excuse. I won't let you add me to that list of people who betrayed you."

His eyes were fierce, his face a mask of determination.

He was right. That was exactly what she was doing.

"If you tell me you have my back, then have my back. But if you aren't sure and can't be on my side, then I need you to tell me."

"I have your back, Rosie," he said immediately. "Every second of every day, I have your fucking back." He took a second to calm down. "I know you don't trust people. I get that, and when I think about it, you're right. I stumbled tonight. I didn't mean to, I swear. I thought we were just having a discussion. Like, my dad would say his side and you'd say yours and we'd talk it out. I didn't know you were just gonna fold up."

"I didn't fold up."

"You did, too."

"I just didn't argue. That's not folding. I don't agree with your dad, but I'm just someone he met five minutes ago. Why would I argue his own family history with him in his own home?"

"He would have listened to you."

"And thought I was nuts?" she asked. "And called you later, concerned you've gotten yourself tangled up with some kind of crazy person."

"He's not like that."

"Everyone's like that," she told him firmly. "Everyone gives side-long stares, and everyone whispers. Everyone talks. And you're right, I could have argued and given a little show. I could have told him about your grandmother and how she followed me around at work for months in her hideous pink skirt and blazer, but I didn't. I don't want that."

"She did?" Max asked surprised.

She turned her head and looked out the window.

They rode in silence for a few minutes.

"I have your back," Max said quietly. "I don't want you to question that."

"It's not that easy for me," she said.

"I know. I'll just have to keep telling you and proving it to you. That's all I can do."

She nodded but didn't say anything. How was she supposed to respond to that?

Not long after, they pulled up to the sidewalk in front of The Third Eye. She led Max up the stairs in the alley as Jay opened the door.

"Hey." It was the first time she'd seen him so sedate. He watched her, scanning as she came to the door.

She gestured behind her. "This is Max. Max, this is Jay."

He shut the door behind them and watched her again.

"She's still there, isn't she?" Rosie asked him.

Jay shook his head. "Not entirely. But she left almost like a residue. It's like a film over you. It's her, but it's you."

"I can feel it," she admitted. "It's like...heavy."

"What are you talking about?" Max asked, curious. His hand was resting on the small of her back.

"I feel like she's still in me," Rosie told them. "Like she left part of herself in there."

"What?" Max breathed.

"From what I've read, possession is no easy feat for a spirit. Or the vessel, for that matter. It would take just about everything she's got unless she has some super-power you haven't told me about."

She opened her mouth to speak, but Max interrupted. "I'm sorry, am I the only one that doesn't give a shit what possession does to Helene or whatever her name is? I want to make sure Rosie's okay."

"Helene?" Jay asked.

"Long story," Rosie said. "Can you get her out?"

"I think so," he told her.

23

Through all the craziness, Max still sat by her side. Through Jay dusting salt on her, flicking holy water at her, and waving crystals over her, Max hadn't let go of her hand.

Somewhere, in all of that, Helene's weight had lifted, and Rosie felt like herself again.

"If it were me," Jay told her seriously, "I'd make a border around your windows and doors with salt. It's well known that spirits aren't able to cross that line."

"Seriously?" Max asked.

Jay shrugged. "I mean, there's no textbook or anything."

Rosie pulled her feet up, curling into Max a little, and listened to them talk. When her head leaned on Max's shoulder he automatically took the mug from her hand and held it in his own.

"Rosie says you have your own way of reading people."

Jay hummed his agreement. "It's like hers, only different."

"Chakras, she said."

Jay smiled. "She told you. That's sweet."

"Then she tried to explain chakras and I got lost."

"Energies and the paranormal are easy subjects to get lost in. The lack of actual scientific data makes people skeptics, and they're not willing to think outside the box."

Jay looked from Max to Rosie, a smile stretching across his face.

"She's sleeping," he said quietly.

~

MAX COULD ONLY SEE the top of Rosie's head as she rested on his shoulder. Being with her was unlike anything he'd ever experienced. His entire life, he'd been the guy everyone turned to for help. When Wendy needed someone for anything, from a quick chat to hanging a shelf, she called him. When Dallas was missing his family or needed a beer, he called Max. His parents called. His neighbor called. He was the guy everyone counted on.

The look on Rosie's face when she accused him of not backing her up hurt. He'd never been accused of something like that before, and in reality, the solution probably sat somewhere between both of their points of view.

Hers that he hadn't done anything, and his that he'd been listening and waiting. It would take more for him to get past the walls Rosie had built up around herself. He'd have to truly be there, time and again, before she believed him.

"Long day?" Jay asked, breaking Max's musings.

"Nah." He waved Jay off. "Tell me more about the salt."

So, Max sat there and learned about salt lines, Tibetan spirit blockers, and cleansing rituals. Jay steered clear of specifics regarding his own abilities and spoke mostly in generalities.

When Jay circled back around and started talking about crystals, Max asked, "Is there something I should have at my house? For Rosie."

Jay tilted his head. "Has she been spending time at your house?"

Max weighed his words carefully, not wanting to tell Jay more than Rosie would be comfortable with.

"Some."

"I would say if she's spending any significant amount of time in your house, then yes, we should dedicate a few specifically to your home."

"Do you do that, or is there something I have to do?" He wasn't sure they would work if he did it. What the hell did he know about dedicating crystals? Driving a tractor, yes. Crystals, no.

"We can work on it together. Not too much voodoo involved," Jay laughed. "To tell you the truth, I'm surprised you're this calm."

"What other choice do I have?" Max asked. "I'm calm because Rosie needs me to be."

"You think she'd freak out if you were freaking out?"

"No," Max admitted. "I think she'd disappear."

∽

WHEN ROSIE FINALLY STIRRED, they left Jay's and drove back to Rosie's camper. She was less distant than she had been on the way to The Third Eye, but not nearly as comfortable as she'd been that morning.

They pulled up, and Rosie went right to the camper to let the cat out. Max sat on the little patio and she joined him, settling in the other chair.

"I told Jay we weren't going to the cove tomorrow." Her voice was quiet, almost shy.

"I heard. I'll let Dal and Wendy know."

She'd put on a pair of sunglasses, hiding her striking eyes and any thoughts he could read there.

"Thanks."

Her quiet politeness was killing him. Since she'd woken up, she'd been distant, making him wonder if he'd done irreparable damage to their relationship in one single moment.

"Do you really think I'd just disappear?" Her cheek was resting on the knee she had pulled up to her chest.

He shrugged. "Maybe. I don't know."

"That's what you told Jay. That you thought I'd disappear."

"It's a concern," he admitted. "That I'll make some boneheaded mistake, like I did today, and you'll take off."

She nodded and propped her chin on her knee, looking out at the trees.

"Were you awake the whole time?"

"No. Just in and out, mostly. I couldn't keep my eyes open."

"You want to talk about it?"

"Not yet."

He didn't want to accept that. He wanted to demand she talk to him and tell him what the hell was going on, but that wouldn't help, so he kept his mouth shut.

"If you need to freak out, it's okay," she told him.

"Why would I need to freak out?" He laughed.

"You told Jay you keep calm because you think that's what I need."

"No-"

"But I don't want you to be something you aren't, Max. If you need to freak out or yell or whatever, then you should do it."

He shook his head. "Jesus, this is ridiculous. Rosie, I'm calm because that's just who I am. I'm not holding anything back from you."

"Not from me-"

"I'm not holding back!" he yelled. "I'm just fucking calm!"

She let out a laugh and covered her mouth with her hand, trying to hold in her mirth.

He ran both hands roughly through his hair and grunted in frustration. "I'm fucking calm," he said in a normal tone.

"I can see that," she replied, fighting laughter.

He narrowed his eyes, which only made her laugh harder. Honestly, if him acting frazzled made her laugh, he was willing to take it, even at his own expense. The distance between them shrank with each giggle she let out.

Max stood from his chair. "I'm glad you think it's funny," he huffed.

She stood, too, holding her hands to her cheeks and smiling. "I'm sorry."

He took a small step forward. "You don't seem very sorry."

Her smile stayed in place, but she took a step back. "I am. I swear."

She stepped around her chair when he continued to advance.

"You're still laughing at me."

"Not at you."

Another step.

"Not with me."

"But not at you. Just at what you said."

Another step.

"That I was calm?"

"That you were fucking calm," she corrected.

She took another step back until she hit the camper with a gasp. He took one more step until his body was pressed against hers. He reached around and pressed her hips closer to him, squeezing her ass at the same time.

"I'm feeling pretty fucking calm right now," he told her quietly.

"I'm not," she whispered as his lips crashed onto hers.

It amazed him that every time their lips touched, everything seemed right. Even if they were fighting. Even if things in their world were crazy or intense. Above all of that, every time they touched, he knew they were right for each other. She was the one for him.

She wasn't the most experienced woman, but she always gave him everything she had. Her tongue explored his with a boldness that made him press his length closer, lifting her off the ground. Her legs wrapped around his hips and he squeezed the round cheeks beneath his hands again.

Rosie's arms wound around his neck when he kissed his way down her neck. He slid a hand under her top, his fingertips tingling at the feel of her hot, silky skin.

A horn sounded around them.

"Gross!" Wendy's voice rang out.

"Second time I've caught them there." Dallas laughed. "I think it's their thing."

"Oh my god." Rosie laughed out a breath.

"Tell me they aren't here," Max begged. "Tell me it's just a bad dream and I'm still about to take your shirt off."

"You were going to take off my shirt?"

He leveled a look at her and squeezed her closer. "You bet your ass I was."

"Okay, cowboy." Dallas clapped a few times. "Hands off."

"We thought you guys would be all business, going through all the albums by now. We gave you plenty of time to get this stuff out of the way." Wendy sat in one of the patio chairs like she lived there.

With a sigh, Max let Rosie down. He took a second to adjust her top and make sure she was decent before adjusting his pants and turning around.

Dallas's eyes dropped to Max's crotch for a nanosecond before a laugh rumbled from his chest. Max adjusted himself again in hopes that at least his sister wouldn't see his predicament.

"I think it's safe to say they haven't been looking at old picture books, Wend." Dallas leaned to the side and looked at Rosie behind Max. "How're you doing?"

She opened her mouth to say something, then snapped it shut. She did it again, a blush coloring her cheeks. Max hooked an arm around her neck and pulled her close, kissing the top of her head.

"We're good."

Dallas scoffed. "I wasn't talking to you, Romeo."

"What are you guys doing out here, anyway?" Max changed the subject, pulling Rosie from the spotlight.

"We've been waiting at your house, but you never showed. Figured we'd check here," Wendy offered. "I wanted to look through those albums with you."

"We haven't looked at them yet," Rosie said.

They both looked surprised. "We figured you'd have gone through them all. Just what the hell have you guys been doing?"

"Nothing," Rosie answered quickly. "I want to check them out, too. Here's not great, though, I don't have room for everyone."

"Yeah, and it probably still smells like burnt Pop Tarts," Wendy reminded her, then continued talking.

He wasn't sure why, but it was clear that Rosie didn't want to tell Wendy and Dallas about their little side trip to The Third Eye, or the reason behind it. He watched her, hiding behind her sunglasses, evade Wendy's line of questioning about what they'd been doing.

"So, what really happened?" Dallas asked, sidling up next to him.

"Nothing," he replied, not willing to say anything until he knew why Rosie was keeping it a secret.

"You know, we've known each other a long ass time," Dallas said casually. "Been through a lot of shit."

Max pulled in a deep breath and looked at his best friend. Dallas wasn't wrong. There had been a time in his life he'd been going off the rails and Dallas had been the one to set him straight again. He didn't deserve to be lied to.

"I know." Max put a hand on Dal's shoulder and squeezed.

"You really want to start lying to me now? Tell me it's nothing when it's not?"

Max shook his head. "It's just not that easy anymore."

"Because you're in love with Rosie?"

The answer was a flat out yes, but that wasn't the right answer to the question.

"Because it's not my story to tell, and I can't force her to tell it."

Dallas sighed and looked back at the girls. Wendy sitting in her chair, chatting away while Rosie looked on, mostly quiet.

"And will she ever do that?" Dallas asked.

Max shrugged. He didn't know if she'd ever be able to open up and tell them everything. She'd been hiding for so long, he wondered if not sharing what was going on with her was just her natural reaction to life.

"Give her time," Max told him, hoping patience would win out eventually.

"Are we going back to your place?" Wendy turned around and asked.

Max shook his head. "Rosie wanted to be here."

"No." Rosie stood and wiped her palms on her jeans. "We can go to your house. We'll look through the albums together. Let me just grab Gizmo and lock up." She turned and disappeared into her camper, leaving his sister and his best friend both staring, like he might have answers for them.

Without a word, he walked into the camper with Rosie.

"Need a hand?" he asked, seeing her down the little hallway throwing a few things in her bag.

"No, thanks," she told him.

"Are you sure you want to go back to my place?"

She nodded, still packing her bag. "It's fine."

"You were pretty insistent before that you be here."

She looked up at him and sent him a small smile, making the nerves he'd been holding on to dissipate a little.

"I was in my head a little," she admitted. "Thinking you needed to freak out."

"Even if I did, what would it matter?" He closed the distance between them, sat on the bed next to her bag and books. He noticed the shoeboxes and looked up at her.

"Is that a shoebox full of money?"

"Maybe," she hedged.

"Seriously, you can't keep that here. It belongs at a bank."

"Okay," she said, her eyes never meeting his. "Weren't we leaving?"

"No, we were talking about you thinking I needed to freak out or something."

"I don't know," she huffed. "I just...thought maybe you..."

"You were what? Giving me an out?"

"If you needed one."

"Shit, Rosie." He growled, grabbing behind her thighs and pulling her to stand between his legs. "I don't need a goddamn out. I'm not going anywhere."

"I just don't want you to be stuck with me."

The lost look in her eyes told him what it cost her to admit that. Like she was embarrassed but expected it all the same.

"Don't you get it, baby?" he told her softly. "I do want to be stuck with you." He interrupted when she was going to argue. "I'm here,

Rosie. I'm not going anywhere, and you can't get rid of me that easily."

"As easily as getting possessed by the ghost of your boyfriend's dead great-great-aunt?"

His lips twitched as he fought a smile.

"It's not funny," she told him.

"You called me your boyfriend."

She rolled her eyes. "You missed the point."

He shook his head and smiled up at her. "No, baby. You missed the point."

24

Rosie sat in the corner of Max's oversized sectional, surrounded by Max, Wendy, and Dallas. They passed the albums back and forth, all of them trying not to overlook anything.

Max, expert in the kitchen that he was, had put out some food to munch on while Dallas had grabbed everyone a bottle of beer. Not surprisingly, Max had been right there handing her a bottle of water when she declined Dallas's offer.

The television was on in the background, playing some football game she had no interest in. Once in a while, one of the guys would make some noise about it and they'd discuss whatever was going on.

Rosie opened the next album that was passed to her and inspected each picture. The idea that people went to so much trouble to chronicle their family's lives in pictures was so foreign to her. Her mother hadn't even fed her half the time, let alone paid actual money to have pictures taken of her. Someone in Max's family had taken a lot of care to put the photos together. Someone really loved these people.

Every page was filled with things Rosie thought only happened in movies. First days of school and first dates. Dances and wedding photos filled with women dressed in gorgeous vintage dresses.

When she flipped a page over, she stopped at a picture of a teenage boy. He looked to be about sixteen, and though his mouth was smiling, his eyes weren't. His eyes were dark, even in the black and white photograph, making him look tired and older than his age. His blonde hair was combed neatly to one side as he stood in front of an old-fashioned car.

"My Jack." The whisper feathered through her mind, the quiet rush of water close behind.

She snapped her head up to look at the others, to see if they'd heard, but none of them noticed as they watched the game.

Rosie looked at the picture again. This was Helene's Jack. She thought back to what Sam, Max's father, had told them about Helene's family.

"John," Rosie remembered out loud. "Jerry and John."

"Babe?" Max leaned in and put his hand on her back. "Find something?"

"My Jack," the voice whispered again. Rosie shook off the irritation of Helene's intrusion, the feeling of someone else in her mind an unwelcome invasion.

"John." Rosie pointed to the picture.

"Are you sure?" Max asked.

"Jack," Helene whispered again.

"Get the hell out of my head, lady!" Rosie growled through her teeth. "I get it."

Max leaned back. "Is she here?"

Rosie pointed to her head. "In here, and she won't shut up. She keeps saying *my Jack*."

"So, this is him," Max said.

"Not that it gets us anywhere." Rosie shrugged but marked the page anyway.

"Should we be worried you're hearing voices?" Wendy asked jokingly.

Rosie couldn't help but remember her mother's testimony in

court, sitting there telling people her daughter was crazy and heard voices. She remembered the hospital and the drugs that followed her commitment. Mostly, she remembered Butch's back as he walked away from her that last time in the courtroom.

"Shut up Wendy," Max told his sister.

"Okay," Dallas said, keeping the conversation moving. "So, this is Jack, but Rosie's right, that alone doesn't get us anywhere. I'm sure if we really needed to get in touch with this guy, your dad could take care of that."

Rosie took a breath, calming herself and ridding herself of Helene's energy. "Right," she agreed. "Let's take a break for a while. I can look at this stuff later."

"Are you sure?" Wendy asked, though she didn't argue.

"Yeah." She closed the book and set it on the coffee table with the others. "Let's talk about something else for a while."

And that's just what they did. Rosie gave herself a chance to laugh with her friends and be normal. Max stayed by her side, sometimes taking her hand in his or slinging an arm around her shoulder. It was easy to see how much they cared for each other, their relationship effortless and comfortable. It was easy for her to imagine herself fitting in with them, but only because they made it look so easy.

"So, we're really not going tomorrow?" Dallas asked after a brief silence.

"No," Rosie said firmly.

"Do you think it won't work?"

"Dal," Max tried to interrupt.

"I might work, but I'm not strong enough. I'll have to try another day."

"From what happened today?" Wendy asked curiously.

Rosie nodded, though not from the incident at the Murphy's like Wendy assumed but from Helene's intrusion.

"I need to get some balance back first. Then we'll go."

∽

WENDY AND DALLAS LEFT, claiming they were tired. Rosie had a feeling they were trying to give her and Max time alone, which she didn't mind. Time alone with Max grounded her in a way and gave her clarity. When she wasn't ruining things with worry and doubt, time alone with Max was unbelievably soothing.

He sent her upstairs to get ready for bed while he locked up. She headed straight for Max's bedroom and wasted no time, throwing her pajamas on. At some point, Max had put a toothbrush in there for her. With a smile, she picked it up and used it. Halfway through, Max appeared, shirtless and smiling, in the mirror behind her.

"Hey," he smiled, reaching around her to grab his toothbrush.

She didn't dare speak with a mouthful of toothpaste, but she smiled back, lifting the toothbrush a little, making a few mumbles that sounded like a thank you.

He laughed. "You're welcome."

She was slowly getting used to sharing a space with Max. She hadn't stayed there every night but enough that they'd started a routine, and it was one she enjoyed. She finished brushing and moved back so he'd be able to use the sink. When he was in front of her, she slid her arms around his waist and rested her cheek on his back. She held him through the rest of his routine until he was finished, and he put his hands on top of hers.

"You ready for bed?" he asked.

She nodded against his back but didn't loosen her arms.

"Not that I mind, but are you going to let me go?"

She loosened her grip and, with a smile, he turned and placed a gentle kiss on her lips. As usual, he tucked her under the sheet and then slid between the sheet and the comforter. When she was finally wrapped in his arms, in the quiet of the night, she finally felt the tension slide away. She relaxed into him and the cocoon he'd made for her.

"Night, baby," he whispered, kissing the back of her head.

~

THE DAYS after Thanksgiving passed quickly and much the same for Rosie. She and Gizmo stayed with Max and learned how to work the farm. Max temporarily put her in charge of the chickens and lamb while he worked the fields with his interns. It was mind-blowing how much work went into keeping the farm running. Max, of course, made everything look easy, though she learned quickly that just because Max could sling a fifty-pound bag of feed over his shoulder, did not mean she could.

Friday after Thanksgiving had dawned and Max had given her a pair of muck boots and sent her off to work. He played it off as though it was not a big deal, but he'd bought her boots. She couldn't remember the last time someone bought her something. The dinner at Wendy's came to mind, but she shoved the memory away.

The weekend passed quickly, and before she knew it, the sun was setting on Sunday night and her real job loomed on the horizon. Max had made them a nice dinner and they were relaxing on the porch swing, watching the sunset.

"I'll miss you here tomorrow," Max told her with a smile.

"I'll miss being here. Not so much lifting hay bales, but some of the other stuff."

"I told you not to lift those," Max scolded. "You're so stubborn."

"You said they needed to be moved to the barn," she argued.

"I meant I needed to move them to the barn, not you."

"Now you don't have to move them, because I did. See, I helped."

He rolled his eyes. "Thank you. Next time, let me do it."

"Okay," she agreed. "Those suckers were heavy."

They rocked for a few minutes until Max looked at her. "There's something I've been wanting to ask you."

She watched him, waiting.

"Will you go to dinner with me?"

That was it, she thought. They ate together all the time.

He must have seen her confusion because he continued. "We've kind of gone at this thing a little sideways, which is fine, but we skipped some of the good stuff. Like going on a date or two."

Rosie hoped she didn't look as petrified as she felt. She'd never been on a date. She didn't know anything about going on dates.

"Will you let me take you to dinner Friday night?" he asked.

There was no way she could say no, not that she wanted to. In her heart, she was already there, dressed and waiting, but her mind was dragging behind. Where would he take her? Would there be a lot of people there? Would she be able to handle that? What would they talk about? Would he ask her personal questions she didn't want to answer?

"Nothing to worry about, babe. Just me and you, having dinner."

She nodded automatically. "Yes."

His smile was wide, and he let out a relieved breath. "Friday it is."

~

THE NEXT MORNING Rosie stormed into Wendy's office without knocking.

It was so unlike her, Wendy shot up from behind her desk. "Are you okay?"

"Your brother wants to go on a date with me!"

Wendy let out a laugh. "I thought something bad happened! You've been sleeping at his house all weekend. What's the big deal with a date?"

"I've never been on a date!" Rosie told her, panicked. "I don't know what to do on a date!"

"Okay." Wendy laughed. "Don't have a melt down. We'll work it out."

"How?"

"Okay." Wendy came around her desk and grabbed Rosie by the shoulders. "Calm down."

Rosie looked at her friend wide eyed. "I can't."

"You're done at four tonight, right?" Rosie nodded. "After that, we'll go to my place and find you an outfit. Then we'll go from there."

Rosie didn't know what *go from there* meant, but Wendy seemed calm, like she knew what she was doing. That didn't keep her from

JENNI M ROSE

thinking about her impending date all day. While she cleaned her
client's house, she imagined where Max might take her and the questions he might ask. What did people talk about on dates? Was he
planning to ask her questions she didn't want to answer?

She should have been excited, but she was terrified.

In a moment of sudden clarity, she thought of her promise to
Max, to call him when she needed to. Then she talked herself out of
it. How could she call him and tell him she was scared to go out to
dinner with him? Wendy was right, she'd been sleeping at his house
for days on end, how scary could dinner really be?

That night after work, she went back to Wendy's condo, a place
she hadn't been since the night she came clean about Lisa's stealing.
Wendy led Rosie to her bedroom and opened the closet doors. The
amount of clothing she had was something Rosie never fathomed
possible, and she wondered how many hundreds of pieces of clothes
Wendy had.

"Holy crap," she whispered.

"I know," Wendy boasted. "I'm kind of a clothes hoarder." She
turned around and started pulling pieces out one by one, some of
them buried so deep Rosie didn't know where they came from.
"Casual, I think. Maybe not jeans, but I have these black pants."

She held up a pair of black skinny jeans with leather striping
down the side.

"With a cute top. Hang on." She dove back into the closet. When
she turned around, she had a turquoise tank top in her hands. "Start
with that."

Rosie just held them in her hand and looked at Wendy.

"Thank you."

As usual, Wendy brushed her off. "No big. Let's see what
you've got."

Rosie went into the bathroom and changed. The jeans were a
little long but otherwise didn't fit too bad. The shirt though was not
her favorite. Too bright. Too sparkly.

She went back to the bedroom and found Wendy, pulling out
more outfits.

"What do you think?" Wendy asked.

"I'm a no on the shirt."

"Agreed. Too much. Try this."

Forgoing the bathroom trip, Rosie pulled the shirt off and put the new one on. This one was a light gray with wide black stripes. It was loose on the top but fitted at the waist.

"Better," Rosie hedged as she looked at herself in the mirror.

"Eh." Wendy waved it off. "Not that one, either. Try this."

She must have swapped shirts a dozen times before she found a lacy, coral tank top that worked. Wendy sat her down at the vanity and started working on her hair.

"So, spill it. Why the big date freak-out?"

Rosie met her eyes in the mirror as Wendy pulled her hair this way and that. "I told you. I've never been on a date before."

"Like, ever?"

"Like ever," she confirmed.

"But it's just Max. Imagine how us poor shmoes feel when we go on blind dates."

"That sounds horrifying," Rosie agreed. "I'd probably die of a heart attack."

Wendy laughed. "It's not quite that bad, but it's no picnic. At least you and Max are already together, so there's no pressure."

"Max and I aren't really together," she hedged.

Wendy laughed. "Yeah you are. You might not know every detail about each other, but you're together, and you like him enough to spend all your time with him already, so it shouldn't be a big deal."

"It shouldn't be," Rosie agreed. "But it feels like it is."

"Why haven't you ever been on a date?" Wendy asked.

Rosie shrugged. "I'm not really a people person."

Wendy rolled her eyes and waved her off. "Honey, ugly people go on dates all the time. Mean people go on dates. Shy people go on dates. You aren't any of those things."

"Well, I appreciate that pick me up," Rosie deadpanned.

"I'm just saying, you're gorgeous. You're sweet and funny and interesting. You're mysterious, which men love, though I never got the hang of it. You're totally date material. So, spill it. Why no dates?"

"Who would I go on dates with?" Rosie asked.

"Co-workers. Friends. Friends of friends. Brothers of your boss."

"Yeah, no." She shook her head. "I haven't had any of those things until you guys."

Wendy's eyes met hers in the mirror, the scope of Rosie's loneliness making a dent in her usually bright gaze.

"No one at all?"

Rosie shook her head.

"Jesus, Rosie. It sounds so lonely."

"I don't mind lonely," Rosie admitted.

"I don't think lonely is supposed to be a good thing."

"Not lonely, I guess," she corrected. "Alone."

"I don't think alone is any better." Wendy took in her handiwork with Rosie's hair and spun her in the chair to start her makeup.

Rosie held up a hand. "Are we doing like a full trial run here or what?"

"Or what," Wendy nodded and got to work. "I don't like thinking about you lonely or alone. It makes me sad, mostly because I feel like you have so much to offer. You're so smart, Rosie. From a boss's perspective, you're the best employee. You're efficient and born management, but you're like that as a friend, too. I know you have secrets. I get that. Heck, we're women, we all have secrets. Mine are more like gel inserts in my bra sometimes, while I have a feeling yours are a little darker, but I still get it. Open." Rosie opened her eyes while Wendy worked on her eye makeup. "It's time to come out of the closet, honey."

Rosie's brow furrowed.

"Not that closet," Wendy laughed. "Whichever closet you're hiding in. Whatever secrets you're keeping, whatever truth you're hiding, it's time to let it out. I'm here, Rosie. I'm not going anywhere, and I suspect Max isn't either. Time to let us catch you if you need to fall."

Rosie pulled her head out of Wendy's grip. "It's not that simple."

"I know." Wendy smiled and spun the chair around. "What do you think?"

Rosie looked at herself in the mirror and smiled. She still looked like herself with a little more polish. Her hair hung in a cool side braid a-la-Katniss Everdeen, and her eyes popped, surrounded by smoky makeup.

"I think this will be good," she told Wendy, who stood smiling behind her. "You really are the best."

"I know," Wendy said, no hint of doubt in her voice. "And like I said, I'm here when you want to talk."

"I want to," Rosie said. "I really do. I'm just not good at it."

"Lucky for you, I am. I'll help you." Her smile stretched wide. "But not tonight."

Wendy's finality gave her pause.

"What do you mean, not tonight?"

"Well..."

Rosie covered her face with her hands. "What did you do?"

Wendy laughed. "I have no idea what you're talking about."

"You're a terrible liar," Rosie told her. "What did you do?"

"Anyone home?" The voice came from the area of Wendy's front door.

It was Max.

"Come on back," Wendy yelled. To Rosie, she stage-whispered. "I might have moved your date up to tonight."

Rosie's eyes widened. "You did what?"

"Just helping you rip off the band aid."

25

"Hey." Max appeared in the doorway of Wendy's bedroom. Dressed in jeans and a casual, collared dress shirt, he looked handsome and relaxed, like he didn't have a care in the world.

"Hey," she greeted, trying not to let her nerves show.

"Want to go grab some dinner?"

"Of course she does." Wendy pushed Rosie out of the chair and propelled her forward.

He took her hand and led her to his truck, helping her in before calmly walking around the hood and getting in.

"Have a good day?" he asked as he backed out of his parking space and started driving towards town.

She nodded. "Fine. You?"

He shrugged. "It could have been better."

Rosie forgot about being nervous and concentrated on Max. "What happened?"

He glanced at her and then back at the road. "Everything was going really good. Great actually. Then my sister called and told me you were freaking out."

She wanted to deny it but couldn't. She shrugged. "I'm nervous."

His brow furrowed. "What are you so nervous about? We already spend all our time together. We'll just be doing it somewhere else."

It sounded so easy when he said it like that, but the pressure was immense. "It doesn't feel that easy," she told him. "What if we don't have anything to talk about? What if you think I'm boring?"

He barked out a laugh. "I'm not going to think you're boring."

"Well, what if you do? What if it's the worst date you've ever been on."

"It's not going to be the worst date I've ever been on." He rolled his eyes. "It's going to be just like when we hang out at my house, only somewhere else. We're going to laugh and joke and talk and have an all-around good time."

"But-"

"No buts. That's it. End of story." He reached over and held her hand. "You've got to trust me, Rosie. One of these days, you've got to trust me."

"I do," she argued.

He just shook his head in response and squeezed her fingers. They continued driving through downtown until Max pulled up and parked against a curb. She followed his lead and got out, looking around. There were no restaurants on this block. A few shops, but they were all closed.

"Come on." He grabbed a basket from the back of truck led her into a park.

"Where are we going?" The park was lit up with string lights, and the weather had taken a warm turn, reminding her that Florida winters were better than New England winters.

Around a small bend in the sidewalk, they came to a small grassy area, lit up with tall street lamps that overlooked the ocean.

"This spot okay?" he asked.

She nodded. She'd been worried he was going to take her to a restaurant where she'd get overwhelmed and make a scene. She should have given him more credit than that. He had to know a setting like that wouldn't work for her.

"I thought you might like this. It's private and quiet, but still a date."

"Do you bring all your dates here?" she asked, mostly in jest as she sat on the blanket he set out.

"I don't," he said. "I've never dated a woman like you."

"A crazy woman?"

"No. I meant, I've never dated anyone that felt so special. Someone that I'd want to go out of my way for."

She looked at the picnic he was setting out. It was a huge spread of gourmet food, certainly neither of them would go home hungry. He'd most certainly gone out of his way. "I like this park. It's cute," she said.

"There might be a tale or two regarding a rowdy group of boys roaming this area," he chuckled.

"Rowdy?" She laughed at the idea of clean-cut, by-the-rules Max being rowdy. She thought back to her childhood surrounded by drugs, hookers, and bikers. She'd seen rowdy, Max and his teenage friends did not fit that mold. "Somehow I doubt that."

He looked offended. "Believe me. Put a handful of teenage boys together and let them loose. They'll be rowdy."

She rolled her eyes. "Whatever you have to tell yourself, tough guy." When he still looked sour over it, she leaned in and pressed a kiss against his lips. "I don't think I'd be into rowdy. I like you the way you are."

Max threaded his fingers through her hair and pulled her back to his lips, cutting off all playful chat. He was warm and soft, just like always, but insistent. He kissed her with so much feeling, so much desire, she could do nothing but kiss him back and hope she conveyed the same message.

Being surrounded by Max's energy made her feel silly for being nervous in the first place. He was right, one day she was going to have to trust him. She was going to have to believe he wasn't going to put her in uncomfortable positions, that he wasn't going to bring her places she really didn't want to be. He was going to do what was best for her.

Telling herself those things and believing them were two different things. She believed he meant well, but relying on him to follow through was her real problem.

For now, she let that go, knowing that he got it right that night. She was safe and happy in his arms.

They ate in companionable silence, watching the water below as the seagulls swooped down to eat their own dinner.

When they were through and still silent, she bumped his shoulder with her own. "Can I ask you something?"

"Of course," he answered, throwing his arm around her shoulder, watching the moonlight flicker over the ocean.

"You said you were having a great day earlier."

"I did," he confirmed with a smile.

"Well? Are you going to share what was so great?"

He looked at her. "You want me to?"

She rolled her eyes. "Of course I do."

"It's going to involve another date," he warned. "I got a call from the Jacob's Beach Business Association. They voted me, well, the farm really, the best new business of the year."

She couldn't hold back the smile that spread across her face. She'd only known Max a short time, and she'd seen how hard he worked. Not just on the crops, but with the animals and their well-being as well. He was constantly working on making things healthier, from the soil to his end product, be it eggs or kale. He'd talked to her about how he'd implemented a garden for the kids at the local school to learn about biology, ecology, and nutrition, and she'd only known him in what he called his off-season. She couldn't imagine how busy he was when he was in his peak season.

She wrapped her arms around him and pulled him in for a hug. "Congratulations Max! That's incredible."

"Thanks."

"You deserve it. You work so hard."

"Well, I've kind of been slacking lately, but I have worked hard," he admitted. "Here's the thing." He leaned back so she could see his face. "There's an award ceremony. A whole banquet thing I have to go to."

"Oh."

"Black tie. Very formal."

"Oh."

"January first."

"New Year's day?"

"Night," he confirmed. "New Year's day night." Even he looked confused. "That's why I said January first. Anyway..."

"You're going to need a date," she said.

"One with whitish hair," he confirmed with a smile. "Intensely, gorgeous blue eyes." She rolled said eyes. "Smoking hot body." He held out his hands like he was grabbing something. "Boobs about this big."

She smacked him and laughed. "Okay. I get it."

"Will you be my date?"

She felt her face heat. "I feel like I just got asked to the prom."

He looked thoughtful. "I never mentioned breast size in any of my other prom proposals. Is that how it works in Massachusetts?" She could see the laughter in his eyes.

"You're asking me? What would I know about it? But yes," she said quickly. "I'll go with you."

He looked thoroughly pleased with himself. Somehow, a happy Max lifted some of the weight she carried on her shoulders. The thought of trying to prep for a black-tie event left her with an excitement she'd never felt before, but she knew, with Wendy, she'd be in good hands.

26

The three weeks after Thanksgiving passed quickly. Max worked his ass off on the farm while Rosie continued working for Wendy and helping him on her days off. She swore she didn't mind, and he knew she was telling the truth the day he found that she'd hung curtains in the chicken coop. He'd stood there, kind of stunned, the hens almost preening as they inspected them.

He and Rosie had developed a nice, if not frustrating, routine. She came to his house after work, although once in a while, they'd grab the cat and head to her place. They ate and watched movies, some days they played games or read. At night, they'd often bathe together, letting the quiet settle around them. He had yet to talk Rosie into letting him go down on her, though he'd mentioned it a few times. He could see she was curious, and there were times, when they were really fooling around, that he'd probably be able to sneak it in there. But that wasn't what he wanted, and he knew it wasn't what she wanted either. As much as she trusted him now, and as much as she'd opened up, he wasn't willing to take that decision out of her hands. He was waiting for her go ahead.

She had little to no experience with sex, so it wasn't surprising that she was hesitant. And even though it was possible that he was the most sexually frustrated guy in the world, he was still going to sleep with that fucking sheet between them, because it was what she needed.

Mostly, the ghost hunt had been quiet as well. Rosie had quietly investigated the story of Helene leaving Jerry but hadn't invited him into her search.

She'd been to see Jay a few times in the weeks since the incident at Thanksgiving. He still got goose bumps when he remembered hearing her tell Jay that Helene had possessed her. Never, in all his life, did he think something like that could happen. Rosie wore a metal charm on now that Jay swore would stop a possession from happening again.

His father, as Rosie predicted, called a few days after the holiday, concerned with who he was involved with. Despite his assurances that Rosie could do what she said she could, his father didn't believe him. No amount of talking was going to change his father's mind.

He couldn't say he missed the upheaval Helene's spirit brought into their lives, but her absence unnerved Rosie. She'd told him more than once that even though she hated some of the gifts, she felt naked without them. Of course, that always distracted him, which she found funny, and they always ended up offtrack.

Max had put in a full day and was fixing a broken water line in the tomato beds. Mentally, he was planning dinner and picturing Rosie sitting across from him eating. Some nights it happened like that, they would sit together and laugh, learning about each other. Other nights, it was harder to draw Rosie out of her head. She did a lot of internalizing, which he found equal parts fascinating and maddening. He told himself, many times, to be patient. He couldn't imagine what it would be like to have a normal relationship after years of having nothing and trusting no one.

Instead of focusing on normal, he focused on happy. Eventually, they would find their own version of normal, their own happiness.

Max tilted his head back and inspected the sky and shook his head. Too dark, too deep of a blue. He'd check again tomorrow.

~

Rosie was sure there was steam coming out of her ears.

How could anyone in the history of everyone be so incredibly incompetent?

The man standing in front of her was the ineptest moron she had ever come across. She watched him strut around, proud as a peacock, as if he'd done something wonderful.

Nothing she'd said to him had penetrated the thick veil of stupidity surrounding him. He was right and not one word she said would change his mind. It wasn't until another person came in the room that hope finally bloomed.

"Excuse me?" she called.

The man looked at her, disinterest written on his face, although the second he caught sight of her, his interest grew.

"Aren't I supposed to get a phone call or something?" Rosie asked.

"That's only on TV, sweetheart."

"Really? Can someone call Dallas for me?"

That got his attention. She'd asked the other one a dozen times to call Dallas, but he hadn't listened. This guy though, he took notice.

"Dallas Hunter," she tried again. "He works here. Can you call him? Or let me call him? This is all a huge misunderstanding." She adjusted her handcuffed wrists behind her back.

"It's always a misunderstanding," the man laughed. He was tall and looked to be nearing forty. One thing she remembered from living with Butch was how exhausting being a cop was. This man looked as though he'd seen enough in his day, maybe too tired to hear any more excuses.

"I'm sure that's true." She sent him her most pleading look. "Please."

The man rolled his eyes and then looked at the little shit that had arrested her.

"What's she in for?"

"Open container. DUI."

"I'm not drunk!" she insisted. "I was picking up empty cans in the park. I was putting them in the trash!"

The older man rolled his eyes again.

"Please call Dallas. He'll tell you. I don't even drink!"

"I'll call him, but only because you're going to need someone to bail you out at some point."

She'd been riding her bike through the park and hated to see the beer cans littering a spot that was special to her. It was where she'd had her fist date, and it deserved respect. She'd picked up the empty cans and bottles and the next thing she knew, she was being arrested for open container and operating her bike while under the influence.

The older one talked into his phone and after a moment asked, "What's your name again?"

"Rosie Knight."

"Name's Rosie Knight." He held the phone away from his ear, and she felt a modicum of satisfaction. "Jonah pulled her in for DUI and a few other charges." Silence. "We'll wait for you." He hung up and looked at her. "Hunter says you don't drink."

"I don't," she confirmed. "I was honestly picking up empties on my way through the park. I was trying to help."

He shook his head and opened the cell she was in. "Come on, Jonah. Get her the breathalyzer and let her go if need be."

"I've already put her in the system," he whined.

"Without doing due diligence? You know better," Murdoch scolded. "Stand up and turn around," he instructed.

He fiddled with the cuffs before the lock released. She turned, rubbing her sore wrists and staring at the ink on her fingers.

"Some departments have digital fingerprint systems. They don't use ink anymore." His tone was conversational. "We're too small. The district won't approve it."

"Wonderful," she snarled.

Never in her life did she plan to see the inside of a jail cell. Sure, she'd done some questionable things when she'd run away. Shit, she'd even stolen from Butch, but she'd paid him back, so it didn't count as stealing. But to be put in jail? She was furious. Embarrassed and furious.

"Come on now. I let you out of there." He smiled at her, and she narrowed her eyes. "I can't take a glare from you seriously. You're like an angry fairy." He waved her off. "Come sit." He brought her to a desk, where he promptly shoved her in a seat.

Jonah came back with a little machine and handed it to Murdoch. He gave her instructions, and she blew her breath into it for an eternity. When it beeped, he took it back and looked at it.

"Clean as a whistle." He smiled. "We'll get your paperwork squared away and get you out of here."

If he smiled at her again, she was going to punch him.

This was what people got when they tried to help. She had just been trying to do something good. She should have known. Trying to help had always come back to bite her.

"How do you know Hunter?"

She ignored him.

"He your boyfriend?" She stared at a wall. "Nice kid. Good cop. You could do worse, I suppose. I like your shirt. Is that some kind of band or something?" After an extended silence, he whistled. "Tough crowd."

Minutes later, Dallas stormed in. A rush of relief hit her, and without her permission hot tears filled her eyes.

"Hey now, it wasn't that bad," Murdoch said.

Dallas let himself through the secure door and made a beeline for her.

"What the hell happened?" Dallas asked as he approached. He quickly pulled her from the chair and into a hug.

It was so unnatural to her that people wanted to hug or touch her. She'd nearly gotten used to Max, but being hugged by Wendy and Dallas was alien. Still, she hesitantly wrapped her arms around him and let him comfort her, if only to get some of her strength back.

Jonah sounded like he was going to pee his pants, his voice shaky and quiet, making Rosie wonder what kind of glare Dallas was sending him. He mumbled about finding her with a basket of empty cans and acting drunk.

She had not been acting drunk.

"Get her discharged," Dallas ordered. "Like she was never here."

When Jonah began to argue, Dal interrupted. "Like this cluster-fuck didn't happen, Jonah. You hear me?"

"Yes, Hunter."

"She's free to leave," Murdoch said. "With our sincerest apologies."

Rosie looked to Dallas, who now stood, hand on hips, furious.

"I can't leave you alone for a second, can I?" he joked, though his tone was anything but humorous.

They'd had a few rocky moments, but Dallas had become a fixture in her life. He was a rock, always there, always helping. Not that Max wasn't, but the end payoff was different for Dallas. He wasn't hoping for a happily ever after with her. He was just looking to make sure she was happy. He was just being a friend.

There had been moments when she'd let her guard down, sure no one was looking, only to find that Dallas was. He was, in every sense of the word, loyal. Times like this, when her faith in others shook, Dallas restored it with a few words.

She shrugged in response to his question.

"I tried to tell her it wasn't that bad," Murdoch put in offhand.

"Let's get you home," Dallas said.

Murdoch stuck his hand out in apology. "Sorry about the mix -up."

She looked down at it, knowing he was the one that had helped her out of the mess. It wasn't his fault she'd been brought in, it was Jonah's. But when she looked up into his eyes, she flew back in time, nearly twenty years, to another police station, with another policeman looking down at her.

She took a step back and crossed her arms. His face fell and she looked away.

He wasn't sorry.

"Let's go," Dallas repeated. Without another look at Murdoch, she followed Dallas out of the station. Outside she easily spotted his truck and got in, her nails digging a path across her palms.

He slid into his seat and started the truck but just sat there, looking at her. She stared straight ahead

"I did not see that coming," he murmured.

"Sorry," Rosie said, unable to look him in the eye.

She could not believe she'd been in jail a few minutes ago. Literally, her whole existence revolved around not becoming her mother. Not doing drugs. Not drinking. Not getting into trouble. Avoiding the wrong crowd. Still, she'd ended up just where she didn't want to be.

Maybe there is no outrunning your destiny.

Dallas reached across the seat and put his hand over hers. "Stop. You'll scratch through the skin."

She flexed her fingers a few times, hoping to quell the urge.

"It's not a big deal, Rosie," Dallas said. "Max's been in that same cell."

She looked up at him. "He has?"

"He didn't tell you?" Dallas asked.

"No."

"Huh," he said, then shrugged. "You'll have to ask him about it." He leaned over and opened the glove box. "Grab one of those alcohol wipes. It'll take that ink right off."

She nodded, wondering what Max could have possibly done to end up there, and then looked back at Dallas.

"Thanks."

He shrugged. "What good would I be if I couldn't pull a few strings?"

"I didn't do anything wrong."

"No, you didn't," he agreed. "Glad we could get it straightened out."

"I tried to tell him,"

He must have known she meant the younger cop. "He's really gung-ho about the whole cop thing. He's new."

"Well, he should listen to the people he's talking to," she argued. "I told him a million times I wasn't drinking. I told him to call you."

He held a hand to his chest. "I'm so flattered." She rolled her eyes. "Murdoch would have listened to you eventually. He's a good guy."

"Sure," she responded, Butch's face swimming in front of her.

They drove the winding roads to the far side of town where she lived, an easy silence surrounding them. Dallas turned off the main road, the bumps of the road as familiar to her as the feeling that enveloped her when Dallas took the next turn.

"Stop," she murmured, sitting up straight. Helene was out there somewhere, Rosie could feel it, her senses on high alert.

"Stop where?" Dallas scoffed.

Rosie looked from the side of the road to the woods. "Stop," she said again, catching a glimpse of the spirit in the deep woods. "Stop!" she yelled louder.

Dallas muttered, but the truck slowed.

"Stop," she told him again, a cloud of urgent desperation surrounding her. Her hands fumbled for the handle, opening the door while the truck was still moving.

"Wait!" Dallas shouted, slamming on the brakes.

The second the car stopped, she jumped out and waded toward the trees.

There was something about not having seen Helene for weeks that had made Rosie's skin crawl. She knew she didn't, but there was a sense that she owed this to Helene, possession aside. Helene was Max's family, part of his legacy and where he came from. Helene had become a smudge in an otherwise happy existence for the Murphy family because no one knew the awful truth of what had really happened to her.

Mr. Murphy could argue all he wanted, but that woman had not left her family voluntarily. She hadn't not run off with another man, heedless of the people around her. She had been stolen from them. It was no wonder Helene's spirit had never rested.

Rosie heard Dallas crashing through the trees behind her but kept her focus on Helene. The closer Rosie got, the farther the apparition drifted.

"Stop, Rosie!" Dallas was shouting.

"I can't," she whispered, something beyond her control driving her.

It wasn't like the time Helene had possessed her, though. This was different. She was conscious, and her faculties were completely intact, but there was something compelling her to keep following.

"You have to!" Dallas said, sounding like he was right on her heels.

"She needs me to follow her."

"This is crazy," he huffed. "It's fucking dark out here!"

"We're almost there," Rosie said, knowing they were rapidly approaching Smith's cove.

"You shouldn't be out here," Dallas persisted. "We talked about this."

"I can't stop. She's pulling me." The sense of desperation and resolve coursing through her, making her feet move even faster, was like nothing she'd ever felt.

She broke through the trees, and Helene was waiting for her. Had she been human and corporeal, her feet would have been in the water. She still looked as she had when she was killed, her dress torn and her shirt filthy. What was probably at one time a neat and tidy head of long chestnut pin curls was wildly askew and matted.

Rosie felt Dallas bump into her back, his hands landing on her shoulders to steady her. Rosie stood there, unmoving, watching Helene while Dallas quietly looked around.

"Is she here?" he whispered.

She nodded. "By the water."

His head swiveled, but he wouldn't see her.

"You can't just drag her anywhere you want, you know," Dallas called, his voice filled with annoyance.

Rosie wanted to laugh. Leave it to Dallas to tell a spirit what was what, whether he could see it or not.

Instead, she reached up and patted his hand. "It's okay."

"No, it's not," he disagreed. "I'm calling Max."

"Please, no," Helene's voice whispered.

Rosie lifted a hand, hoping for silence to hear the spirit better.

"Wait," she told Dallas.

"For what?"

"He can't come," her quivering voice whispered through Rosie.

"Max can't come?" she clarified.

Helene's head shook back and forth. "When he's here, you're not."

"Like, you can't find me?"

"She's talking to you?" Dallas whispered, like he just realized what was going on. Rosie held up a hand to silence him.

"When you're with him, you're lost to me."

To some extent, Max's energy must shield her. She knew his energy calmed her and evened hers out, and when she was with him, her senses were quieter.

Was it being with Max that kept the spirits away? She thought back to the first time they'd met and remembered she'd seen other spirits when she was with him, so that couldn't be right. What did it all mean?

"No," Rosie told Helene. "I've seen other spirits when I'm with him. Maybe it's just you he's blocking. Is there something I need to be protected from?"

The spirit seemed to watch her. "I mean you no harm."

Rosie remembered being possessed and disagreed. "Well, you aren't welcome in my body."

"What the fuck?" Dallas muttered.

"I need to show you."

"Show me what?"

"I need you to see."

"Is that why you keep dragging me here? To show me?"

The spirit drifted closer, making Rosie back up a step until she felt Dallas pressed against her back.

"Let's go," he told her. "This is spooky as hell."

"Wait."

"I just want you to see."

"To see what? Where you are?" Rosie asked.

"No way. We're outta here," Dallas insisted, grabbing her arm and pulling her away.

"I'm here." The spirit's presence held a tinge of desperation that ate at Rosie as Dallas pulled her away.

She had already gathered that Helene was in the cove some-where, but to be flat-out told was a little unnerving. She wondered how many families had visited and played at the cove, not knowing there were human remains there. Not knowing there was a spirit walking among them.

"Is that what you're after? Me finding your remains?"

"He needs to know. My Jack."

Dallas pulled her closer to his truck and even though she wasn't fighting him, she wasn't exactly ready to leave.

"Know you didn't leave him?" Rosie asked as Helene faded the farther away she got.

"Never." The voice was a whisper as Dallas shoved her in the passenger side of his truck.

He crossed the hood and jumped in the driver's seat, cranking the engine and driving away. Helene faded until she was barely a silhouette in the dark, and then she was gone. Rosie watched as the cove disappeared and Dallas drove like a maniac down the darkened back roads.

"You can slow down," Rosie murmured, her mind still on the conversation with Helene.

"I'm getting as far away from that fucking place as fast as I can," he told her, not slowing down at all.

"You must think I'm nuts," she said, trying to picture what had just happened as someone looking on.

He turned his head to look at her and said nothing, then went back to looking at the road.

"It's always been there." She shook her head, wondering how to explain. "That link to the other side. They've always just been there. Sitting on the bus next to me. Waiting in the hall in my apartment building." She took a deep breath and looked out the window. "Playing in the grass across the street."

"Did it ever freak you out?" Dallas asked. "Because I'm totally freaked out."

She shook her head. "No. But like I said, it's always been there."

"Always."

"As far back as I can remember."

"Must have freaked your parents out." He was watching her out of the corner of his eye, like he was waiting to see if she'd tell the truth. He had to know by now, the story she'd told in the bar about having a family was a lie.

He turned the corner into Max's driveway and parked behind a car Rosie didn't recognize. How much honesty did a friend deserve when they bailed you out of jail and followed that up with an encounter of the ghostly kind? Just about all she could muster, she figured. Dallas deserved more than the lies she usually told.

"Yeah, they weren't crazy about it," she lied quietly, shame making her look away to hide her face.

"Huh. Did they believe you?"

The thing about Dallas was, as she had already readily discovered, he was very intuitive. Maybe not in the same sense she was, but he could read people in a very insightful way. So even though she told him a half-truth, basically a lie, he'd picked up that something wasn't quite right. It wasn't what she said to him that piqued his radar, it was something in the way she said it.

She lifted a shoulder in response to his question. Did her mother believe her? Depended which day you asked her. Depended where they were living and which drugs her mom chose to do that day. Depended on what mood her mother was in or which friends were there at the time.

"We've got company." He interrupted her musing, his finger pointed to the front porch.

Max was there, a look of concern marring his face, his mother next to him.

"Shit," Rosie muttered as she grabbed her bag from the floor of the truck. "Can we just not mention anything that happened tonight? Until later?"

"Yeah," Dallas agreed as they both got out.

Rosie mustered up the best fake smile she could as she climbed the stairs to the porch.

"Where's your bike?" Max asked.

She wanted to smack her own forehead. She'd never even gotten the thing from the damn police station. It was probably still shoved in the back of that idiot's cruiser.

"I saw Rosie on her way to the bus stop and noticed she had a flat. We dropped it at the bike shop," Dallas cut in. The lie was so smooth and came out so easily, she nearly raised her eyebrow at him. "Hi Mom," he continued easily as he squeezed Mrs. Murphy in a hug.

"Oh, it's always so good to see you, Dallas." She hugged him back.

Max sidled to her side and pulled her to him, his arm over her shoulder as he kissed her head.

"Everything okay?" he asked.

She shrugged and sent him a half smile. "Getting better." When he looked like he was going to ask more questions, she told him, "We can talk about it later."

For now, she had to brave a conversation with the human lie detector, Mrs. Murphy.

27

Mrs. Murphy hadn't stayed long. She'd been picking a few things up from the farm and was headed out when she and Dallas got there. Normally, Rosie would pick up on some of the things the other woman was thinking, but the complete absence of information struck her.

She thought back to what the spirit had said down at the cove and wondered if it was Max's doing. Not just the sense of peace she got when he was around, but the silence. Give or take one or two pushes from Helene, maybe Max was shielding her from the other side.

"Babe?" Max's voice cut in.

The three of them were sitting at the counter, eating a late dinner, but she hadn't touched hers.

"Sorry," she apologized automatically.

"What's wrong?" He cut it before she could make any excuses.

Dallas had been quiet about the events of the evening up to that point. She met his eyes across the counter, and he just watched her, waiting.

Max caught the exchange and looked between them. "What's going on?"

"Dallas and I had a run-in at the cove on our way here. With Helene."

His shoulders dropped. "And you're just telling me now?"

"I didn't think your mom would be super interested," Rosie shot back. "Not after what happened that Thanksgiving."

"It's a lot to process," Dallas said, putting a hand on Max's shoulder. "And I only heard one side of the conversation."

Max grabbed his plate and walked to the sink. "Well, you guys process away. Don't mind me, I'll just leave you to it."

"Dude," Dallas argued.

Rosie put a hand on his arm. "How about we catch up with you tomorrow?"

He watched her for a second before nodding his head. "Yeah. Okay."

When she heard the front door close, she walked to the sink.

Max was standing, hands braced on the countertop. She slid her arms around his waist, her cheek resting against his strong back. She held him like that for a good two minutes before speaking.

"Please, don't be mad at me."

She felt him take a deep breath. "I'm not mad." The words came from behind clenched teeth.

"Yes, you are," she said, her voice quiet. "I can feel it."

And she could. Max's usually green aura was now an angry maroon with gray static floating inside of it. The static pelted her arms in a way that made the hair stand up when it shocked her.

When she closed her eyes, she could finally get a read on what he was thinking.

"I'm not sleeping with Dallas," she told him after getting a particularly vivid vision.

"I know that," he said angrily.

"Then why are you thinking I am?" She let him go and took a step back.

When he turned around, he was more upset than angry. Hurt, she supposed.

277

"I am not," he argued.

"You're worried that I call him when I need help and not you. You think I'm going to realize he's better at helping people than you are."

"Are you reading my mind?" He sounded appalled, like she'd violated him in some way, which she kind of had.

"I don't mean to," she argued. "You're like, yelling it at me!"

"Well, stop it," he told her.

She let out a laugh, as if it was that easy. "I can't! Don't you get it. I can't shut it off!"

"You said you couldn't read me."

"I usually can't. Your guard must be down because you're mad."

He took a few deep breaths, hands on hips.

People didn't like to have their minds read. They didn't want other people in their head. This was when people left. When it became clear that she was just too different.

Like a bubble popping, the silence returned.

"You can't see it anymore," he said, like he knew it was true.

She shook her head. "No."

"I know. If you could, you'd be blushing." He leaned back and reached his hands out. When she put her hands in his, he pulled her into his arms. "I want to be the one you call when you need something. Thinking about you running to Dallas drives me a little nuts."

She shook her head and leaned back to look at him. "I didn't run to Dallas."

He shrugged. "Even so. It's tough talking jealousy down from a ledge. It doesn't always make sense."

She shook her head again. "It's not what you think."

"I know that," he told her. "In my head, I know that. But..." He shrugged again.

"I didn't peg you as the jealous type."

"I never have been before." He leaned down and kissed her quickly. "I think it's just you."

Rosie rolled her eyes. "All that aside, I do have a lot to tell you."

He held out his arms. "Tell me."

She took a few steps backwards. "Not here. Upstairs."

～

TWENTY MINUTES LATER, Rosie and Max sat across from each other in the big master bathroom tub. It was funny, something that had been so foreign to her before, like being naked around a man, had become such a comfort. She and Max had yet to do anything sexually that required no clothes, but bathing wasn't so strange anymore. It had become a calming ritual. The dim, steamy bathroom, the hushed conversations, the intimacy of being together without having to be together in a way she wasn't yet comfortable. She knew they'd come at their relationship from a strange angle, but it worked for them.

For now, at least.

"So. Let's hear it," Max said as he pulled her foot to his chest and massaged the sole. "Why'd you call Dallas?"

"Well, I didn't call Dallas, first of all."

"So, the 'bike flat-tire story' was true?" he asked skeptically.

"No. That was a lie. More for your mom's benefit than yours."

"So, your bike isn't at the shop," he clarified.

"No. It's at the police station."

His fingers stopped moving. "The what now?"

"The police station."

"What the hell is it doing there?"

"They impounded it when I got arrested."

He quickly let go of her foot and sat up. "What?"

"It was a total misunderstanding,"

"For what?"

It sounded so stupid when she said it out loud. She sheepishly recounted the story of riding her bike through the park, picking up empty beer bottles and cans.

"By the time I finally got someone to listen to me, I just asked for Dallas. I was trying to name drop so they'd let me go!"

"And it worked."

"That guy called Dallas, and when he got there, they threw the whole thing out. I wasn't drinking." She didn't know why she felt like she needed to tell him that. She was of legal drinking age, and she was an adult. Drinking wouldn't be doing anything wrong. But drinking also wasn't her, and it wasn't something she did. With the life she'd lived, she felt it was important for her to stay drug and alcohol free. "I was just trying to help."

Max was still sitting up and watching her closely. "I know," he said simply.

"I didn't mean to call Dallas and not you. It wasn't like that."

"It's okay." He reached out and stroked her shoulder. "I get it."

"And then, on the way home, we ended up at the cove."

"How did that happen?"

Rosie sat up, so they were sitting face-to-face. "That was my fault. I made Dallas go."

"I thought you were waiting to go back."

"I was planning to. I guess Helene had other plans."

"She made you go there?" At her nod, he asked, "How?"

"Just pulled me, I guess. Anyway, she said something that makes a lot of sense to me now that I think about it."

"About how she was killed?"

"No, about my abilities not working."

"You said it was her. Is it? Did she say that?"

"No." She shook her head. "It's you."

His head reared back. "Me?"

Rosie nodded. "It makes more sense."

"How am I doing it?"

"I'm not sure, really. But she said she can't get to me when you're around. She said you protect me."

"How?" he asked perplexed. "I don't think I'm doing it."

"I think you are," Rosie disagreed. "You might not know you're doing it, but it makes sense. I told you, when I'm with you, everything's quiet. The spirits, the dreams, they're not there. Even the little things I usually learn about people from sitting with them for a while, that's gone too."

"But you've heard her when we've been together. Down at the cove and here."

"I think that's all she can do when you're doing it."

"I don't even know what I'm doing. And even if I did? What, I'm supposed to stop protecting you so you can go running off after ghosts into the ocean?"

"Okay, well, I don't think we have to go that far. But, if we can get you to ease up a little and see where it leads us."

"Last time, it led you neck deep in Smith's Cove. I'm all set with that happening anymore."

"Maybe we can practice you letting your guard down a little. Like before, when I could read you."

He let out a laugh. "Babe, I swear, I don't have my guard up."

"Well, you have something going on, because I could read you loud and clear downstairs."

"When I lost my temper. I don't think that means I'm the one walking around with my guard up all the time."

He eyed her somewhat accusingly.

"I'm just saying, maybe we could work on you trying to be less protective." She ignored his not-so-subtle dig.

"Okay, so you want me to meditate or something? Visualize myself not protecting you?" He shook his head. "So dumb. Why are we taking her word for it again?"

"It makes the most sense, that's all. It's not like we have to do it right now. Maybe we should talk to Jay about it. See if he has any ideas."

"I can go whenever you need me to. Tomorrow?"

"Can't. I'm supposed to go dress shopping with your sister."

He smiled. Not the happy smile she was used to seeing but that cat-that-ate-the-canary, cocky smile he saved for special occasions, like this one.

"Is it gonna be short?" He eyed her chest. "Low-cut?"

"That's what you want me to wear to the business association dinner? Something short and low-cut?"

"Works for me."

"With that jealous streak you showed tonight? Seems like a bad idea. I might get a burlap sack instead."

"Would it be a short burlap sack?"

She laughed. "You have a way of turning crappy situations into something not so crappy."

"They always say that about me. You know that Max, always making the crappy just a little less crappy."

28

"That's the one," Wendy said with a confident nod.

Problem was, she'd said the same thing about four other dresses.

"You said that about the red one and the purple one."

"I know, but I hadn't seen this one yet," she argued. "This is it. We aren't leaving without that dress."

"Oh my," Pamela, the saleslady, said as she came into the mirrored area of the changing room. "That looks lovely on you, dear."

"Thank you," Rosie mumbled, eyeing herself critically.

The dress was gorgeous, there was no doubt about that. Stark white and form-fitting, it covered her from neck to toes. Looking over her shoulder, she inspected her back, the entire thing exposed.

"Are you sure it isn't too much?" she asked Wendy. "I don't want to show up and be overdressed."

"You did see the dress I bought, right?"

Wendy purchased an incredible floor-length dress with a delicate lace overlay. If Wendy wore that, Rosie knew she wouldn't be overdressed.

"I'm telling you. It's the one."

The dinner was two weeks away, and if she didn't find a dress soon, she was going to run out of time.

She took a step back and looked at herself again. Wendy was right. This was the dress.

"I'll take it," Rosie said.

"How could you not?" The saleswoman smiled. "It fits like it was made for you."

"Now shoes," Wendy insisted.

"I think I have the perfect pair. Would you like to try them on?" Pamela asked.

Rosie told the woman her shoe size, and she disappeared behind a curtain.

"I shouldn't be this excited about a dinner," Wendy said conversationally. "I mean, really, it's just a dinner, but I love a good dress up."

"I've never done anything like this." She considered the process so far. "It's been kind of fun."

"Kind of?" Wendy scoffed. "Finding the dress is half the fun. I think I spent months finding the perfect prom dresses. This was too fast."

"Months? Really?"

"Uh, yeah," Wendy said plainly. "If I ever get married, I better give myself a good year to find the right dress. Conservatively."

Rosie turned around to look at her friend. "If you ever get married? You don't think you will?"

Wendy shrugged as if it didn't matter. "We'll see. I have yet to find Mr. Not a Complete Douchenozzle."

"Oh dear," Pamela muttered as she returned.

"Sorry," Wendy winced.

The woman waved her off. "Plenty of fish in the sea."

Rosie held back a laugh as Wendy rolled her eyes at the placation. She inspected the silver strappy sandals on top of a sky-high heel.

Wendy must have seen the terrified look on her face.

"No?"

"They're so high," she murmured.

"Okay, so something not too tall." Wendy eyed them from her seat. "They're not you anyway. I think I know a place."

"Why am I not surprised?"

~

AFTER HER SHOPPING EXCURSION, Wendy brought her back to the camper. It'd been a while since she'd spent any length of time there, and she wanted to make sure everything was okay. She texted Max to let him know where she was, then she took out her supplies and started cleaning. From top to bottom, she cleaned the bathroom and the living room. She changed the sheets, even though they weren't dirty. She dusted her books and refolded some of her clothes. It felt good to be in her own space. She enjoyed staying at Max's, but it felt good being with her own things again.

They'd talked with Jay about Max being the one blocking her abilities, and he agreed, it was a possibility. At Jay's recommendation, they often worked on trying to connect with each other on a deeper level, attempting to make Max more comfortable with letting Rosie protect herself. They tried connecting without speaking or touching, pushing thoughts at each other, sending feelings across a metaphysical divide.

So far, it was a no-go. Things were just as quiet as they'd been before, and their connection was nothing more than a fuzzy feeling she felt bumping against her once in a while.

It was an interesting theory, that Max blanketed her without knowing he was doing it. In some ways, it annoyed her. She'd been taking care of herself for so long, it was almost insulting. On the other hand, in the exact same vein, the idea that Max wanted to protect her so thoroughly was sweet and kind of flattering.

She'd been circling a terrifying thought for weeks, and the more days she and Max spent together, the clearer it became.

She was falling for him.

Scratch that. She had fallen for him.

Not that she was going to tell him. There was still too much he didn't know about her. She still, no matter how many times she tried to tell herself otherwise, didn't quite trust that he was going to be there when she needed him. She couldn't see a future where he found out who and what she really was and stuck around.

But, she'd at least talked herself into enjoying it while it lasted. Someday, she'd move on from Jacob's Beach, but she'd finally know what falling in love felt like.

She was finishing some of the laundry when a car drove up and a flash of headlights lit the camper. Rosie tilted her head, surprised to get a flash of Max's thoughts. He was trying to calculate space on the farm, not for next year's garden, but the following year. Was he distracted enough that the thought slipped through, or was he working on letting up a little?

"Knock, knock?" He rapped on the camper door as he opened it.

"Come in," she called.

He stepped in and smiled at her. "Hey."

"Hey yourself."

"How'd the shopping go?" He took the few steps into the tiny bedroom area and sat on the bed, next to her laundry piles.

"Pretty good, I think." She added a folded shirt to the pile. "Your sister's a good shopping buddy."

"She's got enough experience."

"She's got good taste," Rosie corrected. "It was nice to have someone with such a good eye with me."

"I'll take your word for it," he laughed. "Find something to wear?"

She tried not to smile from ear to ear. She loved the dress and couldn't wait, not just to wear it, but for Max to see her in it.

"Ah, that's a yes," he deduced. "Let's see it."

"No way!" She laughed. "You'll have to wait."

"Nope. I'm looking now."

He didn't even have to get off the bed to check her closet. She wasn't worried, the dress was at the store being pressed.

"Good luck." She lifted a shoulder.

His face fell. "It's not here?"

"No. Nice try, though." She handed him a stack of shirts. "Make yourself useful and put this on the shelf."

With a sigh, he did as she asked.

"You know," he said, casually looking over his shoulder. "We could save you the trouble of doing this and just bring this stuff to my house."

Without missing a beat, she said, "You put laundry away at your house, too, don't you?"

He sent her a dry look. "You know what I meant."

"Yes."

When she didn't elaborate, he stood and began rummaging around her tiny closet. He casually threw a box on the bed in front of her, knocking the lid off.

Even he looked surprised.

"Holy Shit, Rosie, I thought it was a couple hundred bucks. You can't keep cash like that lying around."

She hastily leaned over, put the cover back on, and moved it further away from him.

"It wasn't lying around!" she argued. "You went looking for it."

"Because I knew it was there," he shot back. "You can't keep thousands of dollars of cash around. People don't actually keep shoeboxes full of money under their beds these days."

She did her best to go back to folding laundry and not look guilty. Max watched, cataloging her every move.

"It's not a big deal," she insisted.

"You can't look me in the eye right now," he pointed out, studying her. After a second, his eyes widened. "Oh my..." He jumped off the bed and dropped to the floor.

"Max," she shouted. "Stop it." She tried to pull him up by the back of his shirt, but it was too late.

He knelt in front of her, another small box in his hand.

"Babe." He wrapped his other hand around the back of her knee. "This is dangerous for you to have here. If someone out there thought you had a bunch of cash in here..." He let the thought trail off.

"It's not like people look at me and immediately think, *money*. Why would anyone ever think I have cash here?"

"I don't think that part really matters. It's not safe to have this here unlocked and easy to find."

He wasn't necessarily wrong, but neither was she. Jacob's beach wasn't exactly a crime haven, and she lived so far outside of town, it would be hard for someone to sneak up on her. On the other hand, if someone did sneak up on her, it would take a long time for the cops to show up if she called them.

"You need to put this in a bank," he said.

She held out her hand and waited. When he finally gave her the box back, she silently placed it with the other one on the bed and went back to folding laundry. Max stood and squeezed himself in front of her and sat down.

On her laundry.

"Talk to me," he said, looking up at her.

"You're sitting on my clean clothes."

"I'll rewash them." He put his hands on her hips and gave a squeeze.

"I don't want to rewash them."

"Talk to me, Rosie."

"I don't want to talk to you. I don't want to talk about it."

"I know," he admitted. "Try it anyway."

"Why? What's the big deal."

"Because that's what people who care about each other do. They talk to each other. Do you care about me?"

She let out a huff. "Yes."

"I care about you, too. Talk to me."

"Will you tell me later why you're worried about corn?"

His face stretched into a small smile. "You're reading me again."

She nodded.

"I'll bore you to death with all the details of sixty-day corn and making corn silage. I promise." He pulled her closer until she had no choice but to put her knees on the bed and straddle his lap. "Now, why won't you put it in the bank?"

She wondered how he couldn't see what was so obvious. "Max, I'm barely scraping by with the identity I have. Why would I push it and put it under bank scrutiny? They'd catch on in a heartbeat."

He thought on that for a second. "Can't you just use your real name? Just at the bank? Or even in a safe at my house?"

"Even if I wanted to, I don't have an ID with that name, don't have my social security number. And really, I don't want to put my money in a bank or anywhere else. I want it close."

"Where you can take it and run?" His voice was flat.

Yes, so she could take it and run.

"Just say it," he urged, anger written all over his face. "Just put it out there. Don't lie to me or lead me on, just say it like is. You're always going to have one foot out the door, aren't you?"

She shrugged. She wasn't going to apologize for who and what she was. She wasn't living on the run, but she wasn't a permanent fixture, either.

"Probably," she admitted.

"Do you really think after all these years someone's going to come looking for you? And what? Throw you in some institution? It's been years, Rosie. You even said it yourself, you're like a drop in the barrel to them."

"You have no idea what you're talking about." She tried to get off his lap, but he wouldn't let her go. "Let me up."

"I care about you, Rosie," he told her.

"Then let me go."

"I can't. I care too goddamn much to let you go. Stay with me. Talk to me. Tell me whatever it is that has you so stuck in the past."

"I'm not stuck in the past." She still struggled to stand, and he finally let her go. "I'm trying to move on with my life."

"No, you aren't."

"Yes, I am," she shouted. "I had to start a whole new life. I had to change my name and leave my home, and I did it anyway. What does it tell you that someone would prefer to buy the identity of a dead person and live with the fear of being found out every single day, rather than be who they were?"

"You can-"

"I don't want to." She flung out her arms. "Don't you see that? I don't want to be her. I want her dead and buried and gone forever. I hate her. Her life was shit. Absolute and complete shit."

"Babe." His voice softened and he held out a hand for her.

"You have no idea who she was or what she had to do to get out of that life. Just let her stay gone."

"But she's not gone. She's right here."

No," she said, dropping her hands down in defeat. He'd never see. He'd never understand. "Never mind."

"Talk to me," he said again. "This is the most honest you've ever been with me. This is the most you've ever said. If you're honesty comes with a fight or yelling, I don't care. I'd rather hear that than nothing at all."

"You want to fight?" she asked, confused.

"No, not really. But I want to hear you be you. I'd rather you yell out your truth than walk away. So, let's hear it. Her life was shit. You think living on the run or hiding out all the time is better?"

"You mean, would I rather be here with you fighting or living in a place I hated, surrounded by people that hated me? Hmm, tough call."

"I'm sure no one hated you."

"The last time I saw my foster dad." She shook her head, unable to continue.

"The one who said he'd keep you," Max remembered.

She wasn't surprised he did.

"He walked away, okay." Her voice was quiet. No matter how many times she replayed the scene in her head, Butch turning his back on her still made her insides quiver, like they were shriveling and dying. "He literally turned his back on me and walked away."

"I won't do that, you know," he told her. "Whatever happened that made him do that to you, won't happen to me."

"That's not the point, Max. I just don't want to be her. I want to leave her in the past and forget all about her. Just let me be Rosie."

"I wish it was easier for you to see that Rosie's future is clouded by that other girl's past. Every day, you're living both lives, whether you see it or not. If you could figure out a way to be both, I think you'd be a lot happier."

"I wish it was easier for you to see some things are just better left alone."

They were at a stalemate.

Max leaned forward, far enough that he could wrap his hands around her butt, and pulled her forward.

"Come back now," he said softly as he pulled her back to straddle him.

Rosie put her hands down on his shoulders, settling herself on his lap. She watched him carefully, wondering if he was still mad at her or if she was supposed to still be mad at him.

Max reached a hand up and rubbed the spot on her forehead, right between her eyes.

"No worries," he told her.

"You're not mad at me?"

He let out a soft laugh. "Not mad."

"Are we still fighting?"

He shook his head. "I don't think so."

"Okay," she said, confusion swamping her.

"Do you want me to be mad?"

"No," she argued. "Is that how this works? It just goes away."

"The fight?" His brow furrowed as he leaned back to look at her. When she nodded, he watched her for another moment. "You've never done this before, have you?"

"Not really, no."

"It's still there, but you said what you needed to say, and so did I. I'm good for now. You?"

"I think so."

"Then it goes away for now. When you want to talk about it again, or I do, we will."

She wondered if it would end up being a vicious cycle of them having the same fight over and over again.

"What if-"

"We cross the bridge when we get to it," he interrupted. "For now, let's talk about something else."

"Like corn?" she asked.

Max smiled, his big, joyful smile. "Yeah, like corn."

~

THIS TIME, when Rosie found herself at the water, it wasn't because she'd slogged through mud to get there, she'd just appeared. It gave her more confidence that she was dreaming.

She saw the same Smith's Cove she'd seen numerous times over the past few months. There were no cars or swimmers, it was as deserted as ever. Yet, Rosie knew she wasn't alone.

"Where are you?" she called.

The wind swirled, warm and gentle against her face. The menace she'd felt on previous, real-life visits was gone. At least for now.

"Thank you for coming back."

Rosie turned and Helene stood in the same place Rosie always saw her, visible but transparent.

"I wish you'd come to me like this instead of the other way."

"I can't. When they're protecting you, it's all I can do to even get a word to you."

"You can get to me now," Rosie concluded.

"Now. They're letting me. Barely."

"They?"

"It's Jack you must find. He needs you now."

"Needs me?" Rosie asked confused. "For what?"

"You must make him see."

"That you didn't leave him?"

"Never."

Helene blasted the wind in Rosie's direction. "Okay, no more of that." The heavy breeze slowed to a whisper. "If I find your remains, he'll know you never left. I can do that." Even though she absolutely, no questions asked, did not want to.

"He must know. You must find him." Rosie felt the relief coming off the spirit in waves.

Helene's figure turned darker then, more opaque than before.

"I must go now, but you need to know..." She looked over her shoulder, as if someone might be standing behind her.

Rosie's hair stood on end.

"You aren't alone anymore." Her voice dropped to a whisper. And her bony finger extended, pointing to something behind Rosie. "She's coming for you."

She turned to look, feeling someone at her back.

～

ROSIE STARTLED awake with a gasp and jolted up.

"She's coming for me," Rosie whispered in dark. "She's coming."

Not expecting it, she screamed when Max put his hand on her back.

"It's just me." His voice was soft as he put his arms around her. "It's just me."

She nodded. "I'm okay."

"Okay," he said simply.

He held her, sitting up in bed for a few minutes, letting the cadence of their breathing calm her back down.

"That's new," he said.

"Sorry."

He shook his head and pulled her back so they were laying together again. When he had her sufficiently cocooned in his arms, he asked, "Who's coming for you? Helene?"

Rosie tried to recall every detail of the dream that she could. "No. That was Helene's warning to me. She's coming for you. That's what she said. 'You're not alone anymore. She's coming for you.'"

"She didn't happen to tell you who it was, did she? Like, watch out for the lady at the grocery store–she's gonna put the bananas on top of your bread?"

He was trying to make light of it, which she appreciated. Sometimes, a little levity went a long way.

"She said she's coming for me. Not she's bagging my groceries wrong."

He shrugged. "It was worth a shot. So, no idea who the mysterious *she* is?"

She shook her head. "No, but..." Her voice trailed off remembering a few previous nights, haunted with the same warning.

"But what?"

On a sigh, she turned over to face him. Max wasn't into sleeping in the total darkness, he liked natural light. It wasn't uncommon for her to wake in the middle of the night and watch him sleep with the aid of the moonlight. Most nights, the moon poured enough light into the bedroom that she could see his handsome face.

"It's not the first time I've heard that."

His eyes widened a bit. "That someone's coming for you."

"Yeah."

He leaned up now, resting on his elbow. "Recently?"

She lifted a shoulder, twisting to rest on her back, looking up at him. "Somewhat."

"Enough runaround, Rosie," he said, frustrated. "Who told you that and when?"

"My mom. She's come to me a few times in my dreams. Leo. He's someone I used to know. That was the first time I woke up here. I remember not knowing where I was."

"Babe, that was like, months ago!"

"I didn't know what they meant. I still don't know what they mean."

He rested his big hand on her stomach and caressed her gently with his thumb. "If you see your mom, does that mean..."

"That she's dead," Rosie finished for him. "I assume so."

"So, you don't really know."

"I guess I could be just dreaming about her and it's not really her coming to me."

"But it could be."

"It could be," she agreed.

"Does that make you…" He struggled to find a word. "Sad?"

She hadn't told him much about her mother other than the barest of basics. He knew she wasn't into talking about it, so he didn't ask and she didn't tell. It wasn't the first time she'd seen her mother in her dreams, though it had been the first time she'd spoken.

Did it make her sad that her mother was most likely dead?

"No," she finally answered. "It doesn't make me sad. I feel relieved."

His head tilted. "Why relieved?"

"Because my mother wasn't a good person," she told him simply. "There wasn't anyone in this world she used more than me. No one she hated more than me, and she made sure I knew it. So, no. Sad isn't the word I think of when I think she might be dead. I feel relief, because I know she can't make me feel like that again."

Max leaned down and laid his lips to her forehead. It was a few seconds before he lifted them and looked down at her again.

"I'll never let anyone make you feel like that, you know. You have me now."

She knew he thought so, and that was sweet. In the long run, who knew if Max would still be there, but the thought was touching.

"Thank you," she said.

He watched her for a second before smiling again. "You'll believe me someday," he promised. "We'll get there."

29

C hristmas came quickly, and with it some things Rosie was unfamiliar with.

First was the day Max took her out to get a real Christmas tree. Like, real life, alive, out of the ground, chop it down Christmas tree. That had been just about the coolest thing she'd ever seen. Max out there, chopping down a tree she picked.

Then there had been the buying of the gifts. It had taken her what seemed like forever to find the right things for everyone. Having never bought gifts before, that came as a surprise. She'd thought she'd just walk in somewhere and pick something up. It wasn't nearly that simple.

There was Christmas Eve dinner at the Murphy's house. It had gone infinitely better than Thanksgiving and was straight out of a movie. It had eggnog in a punchbowl, a family decorating a tree together, and a roaring fire. If anyone noticed that her parents were absent for another holiday, they didn't mention it.

One Christmas was all she'd had with the Hardys. They'd played up the whole Santa thing, even though her mom had blown that for her when she was a little girl. She hadn't wanted to ruin it for them, so she'd played along.

At night, after she and Max both finished working, they'd meet back at his house, her camper all but forgotten. They ate dinner and laughed, talking about their day. From there, they turned off the lights and cuddled on the couch, watching the Christmas tree.

It felt like magic.

It felt like home.

There were some things she was completely familiar with, though, like the resurgence of her dreams. Since Helene's last visit and Max's effort to be less protective, Rosie had relived the same dream nearly every night.

In the dream, she was cooking dinner, a big roast with potatoes and carrots. There was homemade bread and cookies that she took time to dust with powdered sugar. She hummed as she cooked and set the table, no fear or anxiety. She dreamed of a normal life, but one that wasn't her own. The clothes she wore were long out of style, and the song she hummed was now considered an old time classic.

After a time, Max would come in laughing, carrying a basket full of flowers.

"Fresh for you, love," he'd say with a smile. Then he'd lean in and kiss her cheek and wink. "But, they're not from me."

She'd feign surprise.

"Not from you? Do I have a secret admirer?" Her smile would be sly, and Rosie felt joy coursing through her. No matter how many times they played the scene, it made her heart swell.

"Not so secret," Max would say.

Rosie would lean around him to catch sight of a little blond-haired boy hiding behind his father.

Max was not this boy's father, and Rosie was not his mother. They were stand-ins for the people that really lived the scene, but her mind kept putting her and Max in that kitchen.

"Are these from you?" she'd ask the boy.

He'd shyly smile up at her.

"Well, I have something for you, too." Rosie would hand him a cookie, and he'd snatch it quickly.

"You'll spoil his dinner."

"Sometimes a mother needs to spoil her son."

"How about her husband?" He'd lean in and kiss her cheek, then whisper in her ear. "Can she spoil him?"

A rattling growl then would fill the air and they'd all turn to look. The little boy smiled and lit up, as did Max. Rosie was more reserved but greeted the rabid black rabid dog with a cordial hello. It growled and snapped as it stalked toward them. Max and the boy welcomed it with open arms, but it only had eyes for her. It pushed her further into the kitchen, her backwards steps pressing her against the counter. The dog bent its front legs and Rosie knew it was going to pounce.

She looked at Max again, but he smiled at the dog, almost indulgently.

She looked back at the dog and it leapt, teeth bared, ready for the kill.

~

NEW YEAR'S came out of nowhere, and with it, the business association dinner.

It was just a dinner. That's what she kept telling herself, but her nerves wouldn't listen.

She checked herself in the mirror again. Her hair was up in a loose knot, her makeup heavier than normal but not overly done. Wendy had tried to persuade her to go with a heavy, smoky eye, but she'd passed, opting for her normal look, just with a touch more.

Her lips were the touch more. She'd chosen a deep red, and with her white hair and dress, it was the only pop of color she had on.

Other than her eyes.

Her dress was still as gorgeous as she remembered, long and white, pressed to perfection. She didn't feel one sliver of doubt, and for her, that was saying something.

The flash of headlights splashed across her tiny living room. Rosie took a deep breath and waited for him to knock.

"Be out in a second," she yelled when he finally got the door. She smiled to herself. He didn't need to know she'd been ready for twenty minutes.

Max waited about ten seconds before he got impatient. "You're killing me here. You come out or I'm coming in."

"Okay, okay," she laughed, as she made it to the door.

When it swung open, the smile died on her face. For some reason, she'd thought this was going to be her big reveal. She hadn't expected him to completely stun her.

He was spectacular. There was no other way to say it. He looked beyond gorgeous in his fitted tuxedo, black on black. She literally had no words.

He seemed to be in the same position, because his face turned stony and he inspected her head to toe. Then he did it again.

"I...I..." He stuttered.

She shook her head, feeling blindsided. "You're..."

"No, you." He leaned in and pressed his lips hard against hers.

That brought a sense of normalcy, and when they broke apart, she laughed at the lipstick on his mouth.

"You have lipstick on your mouth, now."

"Who cares?" he murmured and kissed her again, his hands squeezing her hips. It was another minute before he pulled away.

"You're so fucking beautiful."

"You look great."

They spoke at the same time.

He rested his forehead to hers as she wiped lipstick from his mouth.

"Is there any way you could just wear that every day?" she asked jokingly.

He leaned back. "This old thing?"

He was striking, his dark brown hair slicked to the side, his face clean-shaven. She would miss his messy hair and five o'clock shadow if he dressed up every day.

She shook her head. "I like you no matter what you're wearing."

He kissed her again, getting more lipstick on his mouth.

"You love me," he scoffed, as though it were nothing. "And I'll wear whatever you want me to wear." He shrugged and tacked on with a wink, "Or not wear."

Rosie wiped the red off his lips again. "You better stop doing that. I won't have any lipstick left."

"I can't. It's like a magnet." He let her go. "Let's get this all locked up so we can get going. If we don't leave now, I can't be held responsible for what I might do."

∿

WHEN THEY GOT to the dinner Max drove around front for valet parking.

The young man, he must have been a couple years younger than she was, stuttered as he helped her out of the truck. "W-w-w-elcome, M—M-Miss."

"Thank you." She smiled at him.

Max came around the front of the car and held out his arm. When she took it, he leaned down and whispered in her ear. "I think you just made his life."

She turned to see what Max was talking about and caught the young man looking at her butt.

"Oh my God." She whipped her head back around and stared straight ahead as they walked away.

Max just laughed.

∿

MAX KNEW everyone in the room, and from the second they arrived, he was shaking hands and making introductions. He introduced Rosie to the board of the business association, which she seemed to enjoy. She hadn't lost the smile from her face since they entered the room.

He tried to see it through her eyes and imagined it would all be pretty dazzling. The big, golden ballroom with enormous, vintage crystal chandeliers, filled with people dressed in fancy clothes. There was a string quartet and waiters walking around with drinks and food. Max could take or leave any of this stuff. Sure, the honor was flattering, but accolades weren't why he did what he did. So this? This big dinner? He could do without it.

The look on Rosie's face? That, he'd remember forever. She was enjoying herself. No bloody noses, no overwhelming spirits–just them. Just tonight.

He stood at the bar, waiting for Rosie's soda, and watched her talking with Wendy and his mother. Her white dress was like nothing anyone else was wearing tonight. She was stunning.

"Hey, Max."

When he turned, he found Caroline Humphreys standing there with a smile on her face. She was a nice girl. They'd dated briefly a few years ago, but it had ended when she'd switched to a medical school in Atlanta and he'd started his business.

"Hey." He smiled warmly at her and gave her a short hug. "How are you?"

"I'm good."

She was on the taller side, and now that he noticed, looked a lot like his sister with her brown hair and brown eyes.

"Still in Atlanta?"

She nodded. "I am. And I guess I don't need to ask about that farm you wanted to start."

"Ginger ale, sir," the bartender cut in.

"Thanks," he said offhand.

"Ooh, really hitting the hard stuff tonight, huh?" Caroline joked.

He held out his elbow to her, being a gentleman, which she took. "It's for my girlfriend, actually." When her step faltered, he pulled her along. "Come meet her."

He and Caroline joined Rosie and Wendy, his mother having moved on.

"Caroline, this is Rosie, my girlfriend. Rosie, this is Caroline."

They shook hands, Rosie carefully inspecting Caroline's face. He wondered if she got some kind of read off of her, or if his guard was up.

"Caroline's parent's run the marina," Wendy told Rosie.

"Are they here, too?" Rosie asked.

Caroline laughed. "Oh, they wouldn't miss it. They invited me, and I came back from Atlanta for it. It's like, their favorite night of the year."

"Really?" Rosie asked.

Caroline shrugged. "They love this town. It's a pride thing, I guess."

"That's nice." Rosie sounded like she genuinely meant it.

"I'm sorry, I don't want to be rude. But your eyes." Caroline leaned closer. "Is that natural?"

Max felt Rosie lean away from Caroline and knew she was uncomfortable.

"Yes," Max answered.

"It's very rare," Caroline said conversationally after giving Rosie her space. "Segmental heterochromia."

She then went on to catalogue a number of syndromes the condition was related to.

But not necessarily. She kept saying the last part.

By the time Caroline left, Rosie looked at them both. "Am I dying?"

Wendy laughed. "Yeah, I'm not sure where that was going."

"Seriously," Rosie joked. "I think she has me convinced."

When they sat down for dinner and the awards, he was sure Rosie had met everyone in the room. Even if it was someone he wasn't friendly with, they all seemed to want to talk to him tonight. He wondered how much of it had to do with the award and how much of it had to do with having Rosie on his arm.

30

Rosie nearly floated to the bathroom. She was so happy and was having a wonderful time. Max was amazing and was so dedicated to the farm. His acceptance speech nearly made her cry. She knew he had no idea how close to home it hit for her, but it was moving to say the least. He had dreams of community gardens feeding the hungry and making sure kids never went without a meal.

As happens in all bathrooms, a few women came in as she was finishing using the facilities and she immediately recognized Caroline's voice. Rosie finished quietly as she spoke.

"I'd heard he was with someone. I had no idea he was in so deep," Caroline said.

Her companion spoke in a voice that said she was super close to the mirror with her mouth open. "Did she have to be so fucking gorgeous?"

"Right," Caroline scoffed. "Or sweet? I want to hate her and be a bitch and steal Max away." The other woman laughed. "Just for a night, and then I'd give him back."

Another laugh. "He's not going anywhere, honey. He's stuck to that like glue."

Now Caroline spoke like she was super close to the mirror. "Right. Believe me, he never looked at me like that. If he did, I'd still be here."

"Oh, please. You laughed in his face when he talked about living on a farm. You told me you didn't want to smell shit all the time."

Caroline laughed. "Okay, so I thought it was silly."

"Max was definitely not smelling like shit tonight."

Rosie considered it, and there were times Max smelled not so fresh. The guy busted his ass on a farm all day, it was to be expected.

"I was hoping at least Dal would be here," Caroline's friend said.

"Haven't you already been there and done that?"

"Eh." Her friend let out a laugh. "I still like to visit once in a while."

Rosie flushed and casually exited her stall. Caroline and her friend, a stunning redhead, stopped what they were doing and stood stock still, watching her.

"Hi," Rosie greeted as she moved to the sink to wash her hands.

"Were you..." The friend pointed.

"In there the whole time?" Rosie finished.

"Oh my God, did I say anything awful?" Caroline pulled a face and seemed to play the conversation back to herself.

"Nothing awful," Rosie confirmed as she finished washing her hands and dried them.

As she was doing that, she felt a sudden wave of...she wasn't sure what, coming from outside the bathroom.

Tension? Not quite.

Impatience? No.

It was Max, she knew that much. A smile stretched across her lips. He was getting good at sending her messages.

She started to the door.

"He's crazy about you, you know," Caroline said behind her.

Anticipation. That's what it was.

She turned and looked at the other women and smiled. "I know." He'd shown her in a million different ways how much he cared. Hell, he was trying to tell her from the other side of the door.

She opened that last barrier and, like she knew he would be, Max was there, leaning on the wall across from the bathroom door. Hands in pockets, one foot resting in front of the other.

His face stretched into a sly smile. "I was waiting for you."

"I know," she told him, stepping into his body and wrapping her arms around his neck. She pressed her lips against his, his hands sliding up her bare back, firm and hot. He kissed her like her trip to the restroom had taken ten years instead of ten minutes.

Rosie went into that bathroom a girl on a date, but she came out a woman with a man that loved her. A man who was waiting for her.

She came out a woman who loved that man back, and she was done waiting. She knew how she felt about Max, and she knew how he felt about her. He'd made it clear to her and to everyone around them.

He broke the kiss and quickly looked around them, making sure they didn't have an audience.

"I like that," he told her.

"Me too." She felt a little breathless, not from the kiss but the realization that she loved him. She, the girl that no one had ever wanted, had fallen in love and it felt good.

"Are you almost ready to go?" he asked.

She looked around. "Is it over?"

He shrugged. "All the important stuff. Most of the board already left."

"If that's what you want," she told him. This was his night. She wasn't going to rush him out of it for her sake.

"Can I tell you what I want?"

Rosie let out a laugh. "Is it safe to say in public?"

He shook his head, no.

She looked up at him and let her smile drop. "Does it involve going home?"

He nodded and lifted a brow.

She fiddled with his bow tie for a second before asking. "Will we be wearing less clothes?"

Max shrugged. "I'll wear whatever you want me to wear, I already told you that."

She took a breath and smiled at him. "I think nothing is in the cards."

He stilled, his face turning serious. "Me wearing nothing, or you wearing nothing?"

"I was thinking both."

He was off the wall in a flash, her hand in his as he dragged her behind him.

"Max, wait," she laughed.

He stopped in his tracks, lifted his face to the ceiling, and breathed deep.

"I'm sorry. Too fast. I know."

"No, I was thinking we didn't say goodbye."

He let out a *pfft* sound and started walking again.

"And you never danced with me."

He turned around, still holding her hand.

"I didn't." His shoulders dropped a little. "Can I make it up to you later?"

She nodded, about to tell him it wasn't a big deal when he pressed a kiss to her mouth, cutting off what she was going to say. She ran her hands up the lapels of his jacket.

He lifted his head. "We have to leave now or I might embarrass myself."

She agreed, but she had no idea how Max could ever embarrass himself. He was so cool and calm, gorgeous and magnetic and, by the grace of fate, he was hers.

For now.

~

MAX WAS MOSTLY QUIET the entire ride back to his house. Like the first time he'd ridden in the car with Rosie, he was afraid he'd say something stupid and spook her. She'd all but told him at the hotel that she was ready to have sex.

It was so cheesy, but thinking of it as sex made him cringe. Sure, he'd had sex with women, it was no big deal but that was what made this so different. This was a huge deal.

He loved Rosie. There was no doubt in his mind, he loved her and wanted to spend the rest of his life with her.

For her to decide she was ready to take that step with him, had to mean she loved him, too. He already knew that, though. She'd told him so many times with her eyes. With the things she did for him, the things she said.

He'd always heard his mother talk about love being found in gestures. She'd say, *Your father cleaned my car today. That's how I know he loves me*. At the time, he'd thought, that's just what people say, but it really wasn't. It was all about what Rosie did for him that showed him how she felt.

Like helping him on the farm. She didn't have to. The farm wouldn't go under without her, but she wanted to help. She let him eat the last chocolate donut. She'd found an old picture of Hannah and had put it on the dresser in their bedroom. She'd started carrying her cell phone and was actually using it. It was all in the gestures.

When they got to his house, he parked close to the porch steps. He didn't want Rosie getting her dress dirty walking up the pathway.

"Wait for me," he told her as he jumped out of the driver's seat.

He trotted around the hood and opened her door, easily scooping her out of her seat. She let out a little squeak, and then a laugh.

It tickled him to hear her laugh like that.

"What are you doing?" she said, a smile on her voice as she rested her head against his shoulder.

"I don't want you to get your dress dirty." He climbed the stairs of the porch and opened the door.

When she moved like she was going to get down, he pulled her closer. "I've got you."

He kicked the door shut behind them and carried her straight upstairs to the bedroom. Rosie pulled his head closer and placed a few hot, open-mouthed kisses to the underside of his jaw. He wasn't sure if he'd ever made it up those stairs faster.

They made it to the bedroom, and he set her on her feet. Her wearing that white dress, plus the moonlight streaming into his bedroom, was a heady combination. He felt like every fate had aligned for he and Rosie to meet, and be together. This one night, he was sure, would be perfect. Some of her hair had fallen out of its clip and looked a little wild. He watched her eyes, knowing if she truly had reservations, that's how he'd know, she'd tell him with her eyes. All he saw there was hot need and desire.

"I've been wanting to slide that dress off you all night." He leaned his back against the closed bedroom door.

Rosie brazenly held her arms out to the side. "I'm ready for that."

"Are you sure?"

Without another word, she reached a hand up and began pulling the shoulder of the dress down and he took a hasty step forward.

"Let me," he said, his voice soft.

With both hands, he grasped the fabric of the dress and peeled the top down, revealing nothing but Rosie's skin underneath. Her small breasts swelled as she breathed, but she stayed still as a statue. He dropped the material of the dress, letting it hang at her waist, and reached to caress her breasts with both hands. They were warm and soft, and he knew, touching them affected Rosie in a major way. This time was no different, her breaths deepening and her eyes sliding closed.

He found the clip in her hair and let it tumble down, loose around her shoulders.

"There you are." He smiled down at her.

She sent him a small smile and began unbuttoning his shirt. "I'd like to see you, too."

He stood still as she removed his bow tie and slipped opened the buttons of his shirt. She slid his jacket off right along with the shirt, but he stopped her when she went for his pants.

"Not yet. You first."

He took the material bunched at her waist and, getting to his knees, pulled it over her hips and down her legs.

"My God," he whispered as he looked up at her. She was like a magical fairy, ethereal and delicate, yet proud and unashamed.

He slid his hands up the outsides of her legs and to her hips. Grasping the sides of her panties, he pulled those off, too.

Knowing she was apprehensive, he made sure to take things slow. He caressed her legs and her backside, rubbing his nose against her stomach and inhaling her sweet scent. When he finally brought one of his fingers around to tease her, her knees wobbled.

He backed her up to the bed.

"Lay down." He held out a hand and helped her scoot back.

Even though she was nervous, she didn't resist when he settled his shoulders between her legs. He'd waited months to taste her, to pleasure her, and he wanted to take his time. He reveled in her scent on his lips and the way she moved underneath his mouth. It wasn't long before Rosie was completely lost, and he let her go. He didn't need her to wait for him, not this time at least. He wanted this night to be about her and how she felt. He wanted to her to feel absolutely loved.

So, he let her fly when she needed to fly. Hips off the bed, grabbing the sheets in her fists, screaming his name, she flew.

While she came back to earth, he ditched his pants and grabbed protection.

"Why did I tell you no when you asked to do that?" she asked, her voice thick and low.

He kissed her then, long and deep, until she was clinging to him. Her legs wrapped around his hips, and he slowly sank into her. He'd intended to go slow, but Rosie shifted her hips and he was in all the way, filling her completely. His head dropped to her shoulder.

It was too good. He wasn't going to last. At all.

Rosie's lips moved against his ear and she wrapped her arms around him. "Are you okay?"

She was out of breath, squeezing him in a way she probably had no idea she was doing, and she was asking how he was doing.

He propped himself up on his hands and began to move inside her.

I love you, he wanted to tell her. He tried to remember the tricks he'd learned about energy and sending the thought to her instead.

He thought about the love he felt and how full it made him feel. He thought about building a life with her and the future he saw for them together. He wanted her to see it, to feel what he felt.

Rosie's eyes closed as she held on, her mouth open as she started letting out a series of breathy moans. He pushed harder, wanting her to go off the edge before he did.

When her fingers dug into his shoulders, he knew she was close, so he kept on until she let go. He finished shortly after, Rosie holding him in the circle of her arms.

He rested for a minute before quickly discarding the condom and settling Rosie under the covers.

When they were facing each other, he pressed a kiss to her lips.

"I love you," he told her, not bothering with any of the excuses he'd given himself over the last few weeks.

She might not want to hear it and it might make her skittish, but he needed to say it to her.

He shook his head as he watched her. "I know you probably don't want to hear that, and that's okay, but I need to say it. I've wanted to say it all night, and it didn't feel right, doing what we just did, without telling you."

He could see her eyes getting wet, tears gathering at the corner of her eyes.

"I know," she whispered.

He smiled. "Good. Now come here."

He opened his arms, and Rosie slid closer, her head on his shoulder.

She hadn't disappeared the second he'd made his confession.

It was a start.

31

Max woke the next morning to a bright bedroom and a naked woman. He took a moment to catalogue Rosie's features so he'd remember everything about that morning for the rest of his life.

He slipped out of bed, headed to the kitchen for a cup of coffee, and settled himself on the couch to watch the news, Gizmo next to him, begging for scratches.

When Dallas's cruiser unexpectedly pulled into his driveway, he checked the time. It wasn't early, but it was too early for one of their regular visits.

Mug in hand, Max stepped onto the porch and waited for Dallas to get out of the car as Wendy's little electric car pulled up behind him. There was a man exiting Dallas's passenger seat that looked to be in his mid-forties. He was tall and lean, his face showing signs of wear, like maybe he was too tired to take what life threw at him next.

Max turned his eyes to Dallas, who was walking toward the porch, a sheaf of papers in his hand, Wendy right behind him, practically wringing her hands

"What's going on?" Max asked.

The other man stayed close to the cruiser, arms crossed as he looked up at Max's house.

"We've got a problem." Dallas climbed the steps. "It's about Rosie."

Max's defense went up. "What about her?"

"First of all, she isn't who she says she is." He held out the papers.

Max didn't even look at them. "Who's he?" The man by the car sent him a hard look and took a few steps closer.

"He's Rosie's father," Wendy said quietly.

Max scoffed. "No, he's not."

"Yeah, he is," Dallas argued, a hard scowl on his face.

"Yeah?" Max crossed his arms. "Did you match his name to her birth certificate or something? Do a DNA test?"

Dallas was quiet for a second. "No," he admitted. "Just look at the papers."

"No. Get out of here." He directed the furious statement at the man by the car.

"I need to see her," he said, his face pinched.

"Dude," Dallas said, trying to get his attention.

"Her name isn't even Rosie," Wendy told him.

Max sent them both a deadpan look.

"You already knew," Wendy whispered.

"Did she tell you she's a missing kid?" Dallas took the top sheet of paper. "Did she tell you she's registered with the National Center for Missing and Exploited Children?" He pushed the two papers against Max's chest. "Did she tell you she's a runaway?" Dallas held his hands up in frustration. "Did she tell you she had a family out there looking for her?"

"Is that what he told you?" Max asked, narrowing his eyes at his best friend and sister. He sent a glare to the man by the car. "You're the foster dad, right?" He was the only person from her past, other than her mother, Rosie had ever spoken about.

The man's expression turned from desperate to hopeful in a heartbeat. "Does she talk about me?"

Max felt his blood pressure rise. He'd scarred Rosie for life, and he was the one that needing coddling?

"No. She doesn't." His voice was cold. "In fact, she doesn't talk about anything. Ever. She's too goddamn afraid that once we really know her, we'll all leave her." He sent a red-hot look at the guy. "Where do you think she got that idea?"

"I fucked up." He took a few more steps up and ended up on the middle stair of the porch. "I know that. I went back for her, but by the time I got there, she was gone."

"I'm not doing this to her." Max slashed his hand through the air. "I'm not ambushing her with this." He sent a scathing look at his sister. "And you shouldn't have come here to do it, either. She thinks you're her friend."

"And I thought she was who she said she was. She lied." Dallas stepped in front of and unsure-looking Wendy.

"She wasn't trying to lie to you. She was trying to hide," Max corrected. He cut his eyes to the foster father. "That's what she does. She hides."

"I know," the man admitted. "I've been looking for almost eight years."

"For what?"

They all turned to find Rosie standing in the doorway. She was dressed in her regular clothes, an oversized, fuzzy white sweater and leggings, her hair fixed like it might be any other day.

Max went to her, his back to everyone else, and put a hand on her cheek. "We don't have to do this. They can all leave right now and we'll go back to bed."

She lifted a shoulder. "Guess it was bound to blow up sometime."

"I'm right here. I'm not going anywhere." When her eyes fell, he lifted her chin. "And neither are you."

"Happy?" Max turned to see the man, a hopeful look on his face, but this time he was trying to get a glimpse of Rosie.

"Want me to move or tell them to get lost?"

She shook her head. "It's okay. You can move."

He stood next to her and took her ice-cold hand in his.

"You look so different," the man said quietly. "So grown up." When she didn't say anything, he kept going. "Your hair." He shook his head, rethinking his tack. "I'm sorry, Happy. I fucked everything up from that first time I let you go. I should have fought harder for you." He put his thumb and forefinger in his eyes. "We all should have fought harder for you."

"I'm sorry I stole your money," Rosie said. "I needed something to get me started, and I didn't have anywhere else to go."

"That was your money. I always told you that."

She shrugged. "That's all I've ever had left to say to you. I've always felt bad about it, and for a long time, I wondered if you'd charge me for it. I can pay you back now."

"Happy," the man pleaded.

Max looked at Rosie and wondered if it was a cosmic joke that the woman he loved, the one who lived in a state of constant fight or flight, was named Happy.

"Rosie, there's nothing for you to run from." Dallas's voice was kind, but Max could see Rosie was beyond his kindness, her walls firmly back in place.

"I'm not running," she told them, straightening from the door-frame. She looked at Dallas and Wendy, hurt radiating off her in waves, and then back to the foster father. "I just didn't want to be found. I don't want to be Happy anymore. I don't want to be reminded of her or what she was. I just want to be left alone. Is that too much to ask?"

"I love you, honey," the man said. "I'd never stop looking."

Rosie scoffed and threw her arms out. "For what? So you could pick me up off the street again just to throw me back?"

He looked disappointed. "That's not what happened."

Dallas was looking at the man suspiciously. Max wanted to throttle him for not being suspicious before he brought him to confront Rosie.

"You led me to believe that Rosie had been an endangered runaway."

"She was," the man argued. "When I caught up to her in Virginia, she was eating out of a goddamned dumpster."

Max's head quickly swiveled in her direction and from the furious

314

expression on her face, he knew the guy was telling the truth. His heart sank at the thought of her being hungry. Not just hungry, but alone and desperate. It must have been terrifying.

And she'd never said a word to him about it.

"Did you find whatever it was you came for?" Rosie asked, her voice rough as she pulled her hand from Max's and crossed her arms.

He shook his head. "Happy, I came for you."

"Don't call me that. Happy died a long time ago. You can go and write that in some report somewhere and let her be."

"But-"

"I'm never going back there, Butch! There's nothing for me there, and I don't want you here. I just.." she shook her head, fighting tears. "I just want to be left alone."

"Well, hey there, buddy." Gizmo meowed eagerly and trotted to Butch, rubbing himself along his shins, happy to see his old friend. "It's been a long time, Gizmo. You're getting old, huh?" He picked the cat up in his arms and looked up at Rosie. "I can't believe you still have him."

"This is my fault," Dallas said under his breath. "I should have called."

"I just wanted to help," Wendy said as she looked to Rosie. "I thought you were on some list of missing kids."

Dallas shook his head. "That's what I saw when I looked at that report. I saw missing kids. Kidnapped kids or runaways, and then, here's this guy who's desperate to find you. I thought I was helping. He said you ran from a home," Dallas said, his eyes questioning.

Rosie sighed. She didn't want to tell them this shit. She wanted to let it go.

"Is that what he said?" She glared at Butch. "That I was in a home? That's a new spin on it."

"Like a group home," Dal nodded.

"It was a mental institution," she told him, her voice heated. "They dumped me in there and pumped me full of drugs and left me to rot."

"No." Wendy's voice shook and tears filled her eyes.

"I came back for you..." Butch stood, his hands out pleading.

Rosie took a step back. Not just away from Butch, but away from them all. "I ran the second I could."

"How did you end up there? There has to be more," Dal insisted.

Max looked on wordlessly, and she knew he wanted to know the truth, no matter what it cost them.

"You have my back?" she asked him, her voice shaking, cornered. "Is that what this is? Every second of every day, you said. Trust you. Trust this, you said."

"It's time to tell the truth, Rosie. Just tell us. Get it over with so we know what we're dealing with."

She shook her head. "There's no we, Max. It's not our story you want to hear. It's mine. When Dallas told me you got arrested, I never asked you about it." His head popped up in surprise. "Because I knew if you wanted me to know, you'd tell me." She turned to Dallas and Wendy. "I've never asked you about the abandonment you feel from your family moving away or about your cheating ex boyfriends-"

"Rosie," Max interrupted.

"Butch and his wife took me in. When I got too weird for them, which I always do, they threw me back where I belonged."

"That's not true," Butch argued. "You never belonged in any of those shitholes, Happy, and we never should have let you go. I've regretted it every day since." He climbed one stair closer and shoved his hands in his pockets. "I've never been sorrier about anything in my life. I promised you a lot of things, and I never came through."

"Don't be sorry. I trusted you," Rosie choked out. "My mistake, not yours."

"Happy,"

"Goddammit!" she yelled. "Stop calling me that!"

"I love your name," he argued. "We did have some happy times, didn't we?"

Rosie sucked in a breath through her nose.

"Like the time you sat on the witness stand and told a courtroom full of people you thought I was crazy?"

He paled. "That isn't how it happened."

"Like the time you told me I wouldn't be able to be a big sister after all because it was just too hard for you to have me around the baby." She took another step back.

"Michael talks about you all the time. He remembers you. Erin and I, we got divorced five years ago. I couldn't stop looking for you." He hung his head. "I couldn't forgive myself for letting you go, and I couldn't forgive her for making me do it."

For years, she'd assumed Butch and Erin had gone about their lives, one little, happy family. She couldn't fathom that she'd had that kind of impact on them.

"Your mom..." He looked away but didn't need to finish. She already knew.

"She's dead."

"What?" Wendy whispered.

His head turned back to her quickly. "How'd you find out?"

This time, Rosie was the one to look away. "She comes to me sometimes."

"Even now?" Butch's eyes narrowed.

Rosie looked out at the yard, trying to remember one day ago when this place had brought her so much peace.

"I know she lied, Happy–Rosie," he corrected. "I tried to come see you at Coleman to tell you but..."

When he didn't finish, Max prodded him along.

"But what?"

"But they had her pumped so full of drugs she couldn't even lift her head." He rubbed his eyes again. "Just a kid for Christ sake, and they had her restrained and totally gorked."

Rosie let out a humorless laugh as she took another step away, embarrassment and anger burning through her like wildfire. "And there, folks, is my life story."

She turned to make a hasty exit. There was no way she could stay here, she needed to be anywhere but here.

"I pressed charges against her. For what she did to you." Butch called after her, but she kept walking almost to the end of the porch.

Dallas grabbed her arm, and she pulled out of his grip, sending him a glare.

"She went to jail for attempted murder. That's where she died."

Rosie stilled. No one had believed her when she'd told them her mother had gone berserk. She'd locked Rosie in a closet, only to pull her out later to brand her with a crucifix and choke the devil out of her. That's what her mother had said. She needed to choke the demon out of Rosie's body.

"Wait? Murder? Your mother?" Dallas asked.

"Her mother tried to kill her." She heard them all take in a shocked breath. "Her mother did kill her."

"Rosie," Max took a step toward her, a look of pity on his face that made her heart crack in half.

She held her hands up, warding him off. "Please, don't."

He held out a hand to her, but she just shook her head.

"This is what you all wanted to hear, right? Why I ran. Who I really am. Well, there it is." She looked at all three of them. "Are you happy now?"

"No." Wendy was crying, tears slowly sliding down her cheeks.

"Killed her?" Dallas muttered, looking between Rosie and Butch.

"A neighbor came forward after the fact. Confirmed he'd helped revive Happy–Rosie, after he heard the commotion but ran due to an outstanding warrant." He looked to Rosie. "I booked her myself. I owed you that much."

Rosie took another step back and slashed her hand through the air. "I don't want anyone to owe me anything. I don't-" She shook her head, completely overwhelmed with them all. "I don't want any of this." Her eyes cut to Max. He was looking at her like he had no idea who she was. "I never wanted any of this."

She turned around, quickly scooped up Gizmo, who had been lounging on the porch, and took off.

None of them tried to come after her.

32

Rosie walked home through the woods, slogging through the dense forest. Stupidly, in her haste, she'd made her exit through the backyard even though her bike was in the front.

Once she got back to the trailer and locked the door behind her, she finally felt safe enough to let go. Her shoulders dropped and the tears came. At first, she wasn't even sure why she was crying, an emotional release more than anything else.

The first wave of tears came hard and fast, like a hurricane that descended and leveled everything in its wake. Her eyes leaked hot tears that streamed down her cheeks. She held in great big sobs, afraid if she let them out, she might not ever stop. She spent hours in that first torrent of emotion, feeling completely separate from the rest of the world.

The second wave was fueled by anger and came hot on the heels of the first. When the wracking of her sobs stopped, the growling of her rage began. Furiously, she stomped to her bedroom and dug out her old suitcase and flung it on the bed. In her frenzy, she cried while she packed her belongings. Jacob's Beach was ruined for her now. Her past caught up to her and had spoiled whatever life she'd been trying to build. It wasn't just about Butch. He'd been the trigger, but she kept going back to Max, letting her bleed in front of him because he wanted to know what color her blood was. Her pain was no different than anyone else's, and she resented being forced to share things she didn't want to. It wasn't the first time he'd done that to her, but it would certainly be the last.

The third wave came after she'd packed all the things she cared about. Her money and a few of her books, along with her clothes stashed in her suitcase, Gizmo in his carrying case stacked on top. She turned around to get one last view of the camper she loved so much, and then she broke. Her back hit the door, and she slid to the floor, holding her knees to her chest. How could everything go so wrong, so fast? How could the people that claimed to be her friends back her into that kind of corner? Max, who said he loved her, had pushed her further down when she was already on the ground.

It was dark by the time she dusted herself off and collected herself. She went to the bathroom and avoided glancing in the mirror. She knew, without looking, it wouldn't be pretty.

Cold washcloth pressed to her face, Rosie wavered between leaving right that very moment and waiting until the morning. She considered the bus stop a mile away and the advantage of leaving at night. She was honest with herself and knew she was being a coward by considering it. Leaving without saying goodbye or giving Wendy two-weeks' notice at work was a shitty thing to do. But when she thought about what had happened at Max's, she decided that had been shittier. So, leaving at night was a good option.

The con was, it was the middle of the night and she had nowhere to go, no real way to get there, and no bus schedule to find a new place to go.

She consulted her watch and made a face. It really wasn't that late. Chances were, she could get to the bus station while it was still open and hop on a bus to somewhere.

Anywhere.

ROSIE MADE it to her usual bus stop bench in good time, even pulling a suitcase behind her with Gizmo in his cat carrier. She painstakingly avoided thinking about everything that had transpired at Max's. At first, she told herself, it was because it was easier than breaking down in tears at any given moment. Later on, she admitted it was mostly because she didn't want to think about what she was doing or what the consequences were. Was it really that big of a deal that Max knew about her past? Would it really affect the way he saw her?

But she knew it was more than that. It was about her privacy and her desperate need to keep those things close to her heart. That was on her, but Max had violated that a few times, and as much as she thought she'd overcome the hurdle, she didn't trust him. Maybe even less now, even after the night they'd spent together.

She hunkered further into her hoodie at the sound of a vehicle approaching and turned her head, her face out of sight. It passed by her slowly but drove on without incident.

It was another twenty minutes before her bus came, and another thirty after that when she arrived at the main terminal.

She stood at the departures sign and contemplated. North, heading to Georgia, leaving in six hours. South, heading to Key West, via Miami, forty minutes. Seemed like an easy choice. She quickly bought her ticket and boarded her bus early after stowing her suitcase and poor Gizmo underneath.

It wasn't full, but seats were limited. Some people had clearly been on the bus for a while, camped out for the long haul. She found a window seat next to an elderly man.

He smiled when he saw her eyeing the seat and stood. "It's free," he said with a smile.

"Thanks," she murmured.

Like she had at the bus stop, she kept her hood up and, for good measure, slid her sunglasses on. The international sign for *leave me alone*. She crossed her arms over her chest and slid down in her seat.

Ten hours after stops, the ticket agent had said.

Ten hours until she started over somewhere new.

Again.

GIVE HER SPACE.

That's what they'd told him all day long.

Just give her some space.

It was strange, Max thought, he could go back and pinpoint the moment Rosie had piqued his interest. It had been months ago, way back that first night, at Tedesco's. He'd offered to give her a ride and she'd refused. It was her refusal that stuck with him. He could picture her, that look in her eye like an animal caught in a cage with her hands up. As if she could hold him back with a gesture alone, and she had.

She'd done it again, on his porch, when Butch had revealed more in five minutes than Rosie had in the last three months. Not only had her mother tried to hurt Rosie, but she'd succeeded.

Max could barely go there.

He'd taken a step toward her, and she'd taken a step back and held her hands up again. A plea for him to stay away that he'd stupidly obeyed.

Let her cool off, he'd thought.

An hour ago, his mother had shown up at his house to deliver some left-over cake from the business association dinner. She'd come in and casually talked for what seemed like forever before saying, "Where's Rosie headed at this time of night?"

Max had leaned back, his brows drawn. "What do you mean?"

"She was sitting at the bus stop when I drove by."

With a sigh, he put his hands on his hips and took in Rosie's empty trailer. Her clothes were gone. Some of her books were gone. A few of her personal items were gone.

Most important to Rosie, Gizmo and her money were gone.

He scrubbed a hand down his face and took a painful breath.

She ran.

He'd thought they'd come further than that. He'd thought they were in a place she'd at least trust him enough to work it out together. He didn't actually think she'd up and leave without a word.

Was this what Butch Hardy had felt when she'd run on out on him? Had he felt the same pain in his chest? The crushing sensation that seemed to center right where his heart was?

Was this his fault? Was Rosie right to feel betrayed by his need to know her past? What he'd learned hadn't changed the way he felt about her, but it had certainly pushed her away.

With one last look, Max exited the camper and headed to his truck.

He'd find her. He had to.

∼

THE WOMAN WORKING at the bus station recognized Rosie's picture and told Dallas she'd bought a ticket for a bus departing to Miami.

She was gone.

Dallas and Wendy had been with him all night as he searched every place he could think of to look. They'd gone to Jay's and the diner she liked. They'd gone to the park and the beach. The bus stop had been a last-ditch effort. It was the last place he wanted to look for her.

When his mother told him Rosie was sitting at the bus stop, his first thought was that she'd finally disappeared. Wasn't that what he'd always thought? That he'd get too close and she'd be gone before he knew it? He'd always thought it might happen, but the reality struck like a physical blow.

He squinted as the headlights from Dallas' truck hit his rear-view mirror and flashed in his eyes. Wendy was back there, too, riding with Dal, and the last thing he wanted to hear was their platitudes.

Those same lines they kept giving him.

She'll come back.

She wouldn't do that.

But she would, wouldn't she? She had. Not just tonight, but her whole life, that's what she did. And he'd forced her hand. Again.

He pulled up to his garage, threw the truck in park and sighed.

There was a good chance he'd never see Rosie again.

Bone-tired and dangerously close to losing his shit, he climbed out of his truck, hoping Dal and Wendy would take a hint and just leave him alone. They didn't seem to be faring much better than he was, both of them quiet and sullen. Silently, but together, they headed toward the porch.

Dal slapped his arm. "Hey,"

Max looked at him and then at the porch when Dal pointed.

Rosie rose from the porch swing, stepping out of the shadows and into the moonlight. He slowed to a stop at the bottom of the stairs and looked up at her.

Haggard, arms wrapped around herself, bundled in a hoodie covered by a denim jacket, she looked lost.

Leave it to Dal to not mince words. "Where the hell have you been? We thought you left."

"I did," she told them quietly.

"Bought a ticket to Miami?" Max asked.

Rosie shrugged and sat on the top step.

"I didn't know what else to do."

Dal huffed. "That's the stupidest shit I've ever heard."

"Dallas!" Wendy scolded. "She's here."

Rosie looked at Max and ignored the other two. He felt her despair all the way down to his bones. Her eyes pleaded with him to understand.

"I don't know how to fix things when they break. I don't know how to solve problems. I know how to run." She shrugged, her eyes unable to hold his as she darted her eyes away and then back. "Happy runs." She shook her head. "I don't want Rosie to run."

"So, you came back," Wendy murmured with a smile.

Rosie kept looking at Max but was unable to move, somewhere between afraid to spook her and afraid he was dreaming.

"Everything Butch said about me was true. He found me on the floor of a whorehouse when I was seven. I grew up mostly in the foster care system. I lived with Butch and his wife for a while until they didn't want me anymore."

She took a deep breath and looked down at her feet.

"He promised he'd keep me, and he lied."

She looked back up at them all.

"I have a hard time trusting people, letting people in. I was in over a dozen homes before my mom got out of jail. There were four homes before Butch brought me to his house. The one with the older kids I remember the most because it was the scariest, but there was one where I wasn't allowed to touch the refrigerator because they didn't want me eating their food, and one where the father wanted to watch me take a bath"

Max noticed Dal and Wendy had quietly seated themselves on the lower steps to listen, but he stayed where he was.

"Then there was Butch's. He bought me my own bike. I had a bed with sheets." She threw up her hands and angrily swiped at a tear that threatened to fall. "I'd never had a bed with sheets before, let alone my own room. They bought me clothes and brought me to school. They let me take a bath every day. By myself." She took a shuddering breath. "And they remembered to feed me, which my mother never did.

"Eventually, when Erin was ready to have her baby, they got rid of me." She shrugged, like she could shake the hurt off but it wasn't that easy. "When my mom got out of jail, I had just turned sixteen. She told everyone she found God in jail, and they all believed her."

She trailed off then, looking away and absently scratching her palms.

"But she didn't?" Dal asked quietly.

She turned back to him with a questioning look. Like she was contemplating something.

"I'd been shuffled from home to home at that point. The social worker thought I'd do better with a family member but after a while, she started locking me in a closet." Wendy sucked in a breath but Rosie let out a dry chuckle. "I didn't mind it so much. I was used to being alone. I liked knowing where all the walls were around me. There were no surprises in there. After a while, when I kept seeing ghosts, she tried to exorcise me, like I was possessed or something."

Rosie looked up at him and spoke directly to him.

"One night, when the closet wasn't doing what she wanted it to do, she dragged me out and branded her crucifix into my chest."

"Oh, my God," Wendy whispered.

He'd seen the scar. No wonder why she always blew off telling him how she got it.

"When I fought against her, she wrapped her hands around my throat and choked me. I uh..." She struggled then. For the first time in her retelling, she hesitated.

Max climbed the steps and sat next to her, without a word pulling her hand into his. Rosie followed his every move with her eyes and squeezed his hand when he held hers.

She took another breath and looked away. For a while, she just looked out at the barn and he wondered if she was even going to continue.

"I remember the edges all turning fuzzy," she said quietly, still looking away. "I thought it would be different there. I thought I'd see the other side, but there was nothing for me there, no one waiting. Next thing I knew, I was waking up in the hospital and everything was different. I was different. I could see things. I knew things."

"I thought you always could see things," Max asked when she stopped talking.

When she turned to look at him, her eyebrows furrowed and she tilted her head, watching him.

"I could," she answered distractedly. She shook her head and then turned her head to look at Dallas and Wendy. "I used to see like colored mists around people. They were all different, but everyone had one. When I woke up, it wasn't misty anymore. It was like thick fog. Dense and almost heavy." She shook her head. "I can't explain it. And I could hear things. Grocery lists, school pickup plans." She shrugged. "Things I didn't want to hear."

"What happened to your mom?" Dallas asked.

"She told the police I attacked her. That I'd gone crazy and she was defending herself. She petitioned to have me committed. Butch was at my hearing." She shook her head and angrily wiped at her eyes. Max squeezed her hand but didn't interrupt. "He testified that he'd sent me to numerous therapists, but none of them were able to help me. They couldn't fix me."

She looked up at him, and her lip wobbled.

"I didn't know I was broken. Until then, at least. Anyway, he testified and walked out of the courtroom and never looked back. They approved the petition, and I went to Coleman."

"A mental hospital," Dallas clarified.

She nodded. "It's not a hospital. It's a prison. It's torture. They didn't care for any of us. They drugged us and mistreated us. They were cruel. Hateful. After the first week, they stopped giving me injections and started giving me pills. I stopped swallowing them. One night I snuck out."

"Is it really that easy to break out of a place like that?" Dal asked.

"Not really," she answered vaguely. "I broke into Butch's house that night. I knew he had cash in his office. I took it and left town, bought a new identity. I never had to do much to hide, because my hair changed on its own, like it knew I needed to look different."

"But he found you," Max said, hating to think about it. "In Virginia."

"Listen, guys." She looked at them all. "I'm not like you. I've lived on the street. Like, literally, on the street. I've eaten out of dumpsters. I stole food when I needed to. I did what I had to do to get by. I'm not proud of everything I did." She held up her hands in a helpless gesture. "Butch caught up to me in one of my lower moments. That was the last time I saw him before the other day."

"Rosie," Dal started.

She shook her head and held her hand out to him. Max held in the urge to smack Dal's hand away when he grabbed hers back.

"No. That's on me. You did exactly what I thought you'd do if you found out. You're a cop, he's a cop."

"You're my friend. I should have come to you first."

She quirked her lips a little. "Doesn't matter." She let his hand go. "The point is, I don't want to be Happy anymore. I really want to leave her behind."

Max slid his arm around her shoulder and pulled her close to him. "I think Happy was really brave and smart despite being dealt a shit hand in life."

"I want Rosie to learn to fix things." She looked at them all. "I don't want to be afraid all the time. I want to learn how to be normal. Although, I admit that's going to be difficult given the things I can see."

∾

ROSIE LOOKED behind Wendy to see Grandma Murphy standing there, a pleased smile on her face.

The big Santa dude stood near Dallas looking impressed.

They were back.

Wendy's aura was pulsing with a melancholy gray.

Dallas's a bright royal blue.

It was all back.

When the telling of her story was complete, she noticed things changing. She still felt the encompassing peace she felt around Max, but she was herself again.

Knowing that she'd missed her gifts and hated being without them made her smile. The relief was overwhelming. She was herself again, and she was okay with that.

She laughed and felt a shift in the air. They were all looking at her like she'd lost her mind.

God, they were so perfect for her. Their auras were colorful and complex, complete and full-bodied. She had friends and someone to love.

She kept laughing, hands over her face.

Being herself had never felt so good.

She was free for the first time in her life. Absolutely and completely free.

"What did we miss?" Max asked, a small smile on his face.

Without care, she leaned over and pressed a kiss to his mouth. He didn't hesitate to kiss her back.

She was still smiling when she pulled back, and finally Max was, too.

"It's back," she told them. "It's all back."

"The..." Dallas waved his hands without finishing the sentence.

She looked back at the ghost of his grandfather. The spirit rolled his eyes at Dallas and turned to Grandma Murphy. The older woman looked at her grandchildren, and then back to Rosie.

"Congratulations, dear." With a sage nod of her head, she said, "It's good to see you again. Come, John."

They both blinked out and were gone. Rosie smiled.

"Does this mean I'm not blocking you anymore?" Max asked, confused.

He was exactly who she needed in her life, supportive yet challenging, intelligent and interesting, willing to step outside his comfort zone, but still there no matter what.

The change hadn't come from Max. The auras had come back when she'd laid herself bare to them. When she'd lifted that burden by sharing it, everything had come back.

"It was never you," she muttered, stunned by the realization.

All the time, she'd thought it was Max blocking her. After all, it had all started after her run-in with the woman, and when she and Max had gotten close. But that hadn't been what shut her down.

She'd built walls so thick, even she couldn't penetrate them.

"It was me," she admitted. "I was blocking myself."

"Yourself?" Max sounded just as bewildered as she did.

"Is that a thing?" Wendy asked. "Blocking yourself?"

They all exchanged confused looks, which made Rosie laugh again.

Max pulled her closer, his arm around her shoulders and kissed her on the head.

"I could get used to hearing you do that."

Dallas stood up and held a hand out to Wendy. "I think we'll leave you guys alone for the night."

She took his hand and stood. Rosie and Max followed suit.

Dallas climbed the few steps and wrapped his arms around her.

He was bigger than Max, and Rosie noted that his body was fuller as she slipped her arms around his waist.

"Don't be an idiot." His voice was gruff. "No more running."

Happy, she squeezed him around the middle. "No more running."

"Okay, break it up. My turn," Wendy said, annoyed.

When he let her go, Wendy wasted no time wrapping Rosie in her arms.

"Chicks before dicks, honey. If you ever need me..."

They separated, and within minutes, they were driving away in Dallas's truck.

~

ROSIE TURNED to Max and found him watching her with a small smile. It had been him that ultimately made her get off the bus.

She'd been sitting on that bus feeling sorry for herself when she'd replayed the night they'd made love. Not just the sex but the intimacy, the love they shared. That was real. That was her reality. She was stupid for running from it. She should have been running toward it. That love was what would save her from herself.

"What are you smiling about?" he asked.

She looked at his bright, caramel eyes and permanent five o'clock shadow, and she just knew. Now was the time.

"I came back for you." She shook her head, knowing that wasn't quite right. "I came back because I was sitting on the bus, watching Jacob's beach pass me by, and I thought to myself, who runs from love? Where are you going? When someone loves you the way you love me, you don't run. And I don't want to run anymore. I want to be loved." She thought for a second. "This isn't coming out right."

"Sounds right to me." Max lifted a hand and held her cheek. "It sounds perfect to me."

"I want to be loved by you," she told him softly. "I want to love you back."

"Do you? Love me back?"

Without having to think about it, she nodded. "I do."

"I knew it," he said softly before lowering his lips to hers.

Always so easy, she thought as she let herself be loved by Max.

Maybe Jay was right. Just because it's easy, doesn't mean it can't be true.

∼

"TELL ME AGAIN."

Rosie felt Max's hand, rough and hot, slide up her back. The smile that came to her face as she woke up reminded her of how they'd spent their night. In bed, laughing and loving each other until the sun rose.

She told him, without opening her eyes or lifting her head from the pillow, the truth she'd been telling him all night.

"I love you, Max."

The blankets shifted, and his body went from lying next to her to covering her, his hard length resting on her backside.

"I love you, too," he whispered, nipping at the back of her ear. "But I'm hungry. I need sustenance."

His hips pressed forward, and she felt him hard against her.

"You don't feel like you need sustenance." Rosie smiled and buried her face in the pillow.

She had never, in her life, felt so complete. This had to be what happiness felt like. She had nothing to compare it to, but this had to be it. Right?

Max laughed, and she felt the vibration through her whole body.

"Let's go eat, woman. It's almost noon and I'm hungry." He kissed his way down her spine and stopped at the small of her back. "Then we'll come back to bed."

It took them ten minutes to make it downstairs between getting dressed and getting distracted with each other. Max carried her down the stairs on his back, his hands holding her thighs, chatting all the while. He'd barely said anything about the events of the day before, seemingly letting all the bad things go and only taking in the end result.

Rosie contemplated how easy it had all been while Max plopped her butt on the counter and made them coffee.

"Why so quiet all of a sudden?" he asked as he brought two mugs to where she was sitting and stood between her legs.

She took her mug and blew across the top. "You haven't said much about yesterday."

"Weird day," was all he said, never taking his eyes off her.

Max was like that, casual yet direct. She loved that about him, it made him easier for her to understand.

"I just..." She tried to find the right words.

"I'm gonna screw it up again," he told her. "Probably a bunch of times, I'm gonna screw up."

"Me too," she admitted. That's what she'd done when she ran and hopped on a bus. "I've never done this before."

"I don't want to harp on stuff we already talked about yesterday. I'm sure it'll come up again, but I can leave it behind us." He watched her carefully. "Can you?"

She shrugged. "I want to. It's just been who I am for so long."

He nodded. "I get that. When you screw up, just come back to me."

Rosie put her mug down and slid her arms around his shoulders and let him hold her. She closed her eyes and let his aura, green like fresh grass, surround her. She couldn't see her own aura, but she hoped it was something that complimented his.

She opened her eyes, planning to tell him she could feel his aura, but she never got the chance, her spine stiffening.

"What?" Max asked, his voice sounding muffled.

Rosie pulled back, staring into the backyard. Helene was there, standing beside Max's tool shed. The woman raised her hand and made a motion that Rosie didn't understand at first, but then it hit her.

She was being carried. Someone's shoulder was digging into her stomach, every step torture. Her hands were dangling below her head, and there was a wet sucking sound every time the person carrying her took a step.

"So stupid," he muttered. "So stupid, Helene."

The wet sucking sounds continued.

Step. Step. Step.

The air was hot, sticky, and humid. Her hair swung back and forth, wet and clumped together.

Then she was falling, farther down than she could have imagined. Her back hit the cold mud, and it seeped through the back of her shirt. Her lungs were empty, there was no wind to knock out of them, and her sightless eyes stared up at the sky above.

She was in a shallow grave, and above her, trees shadowed her killer as he crouched above. She got a good look at his face then. Not through the water as he held her down, and not as he came to her in the form of a dog, but the man. Large in stature with a thick beard, he looked almost like a lumberjack. Dark eyes, stared moodily down at her.

"God, dammit," he said pained. "Why couldn't you just love me?"

Was he crying? Rosie blinked, surprised she was still alive.

He shot up and stared into the hole, horror on his face.

"You're alive?" He hurriedly took his coat off and threw it in at her, covering her face. Before it landed, as if in slow motion, she saw the letters EML embroidered on the lapel. "Stop looking at me!"

It was dark then, and she knew it was the end. Dirt quickly rained down on her.

"It wasn't supposed to be like this. You were supposed to leave him. This is all your fault."

The dirt kept coming. She'd known all along that he wanted her, that he'd stop at nothing to get to her. She'd known he was crazy.

And now, he was burying her alive.

~

Rosie startled, shaking her head and looking around. How had she not seen that part before? Had she not witnessed Helene's death the first time? Had that only been a part of what had happened?

"What happened?" Max's voice was serious and concerned. "Where'd you go?"

"He buried her alive." She met his eyes. "Out on one of those islands."

She was so certain. Something about the way the trees stood above her, the way the water seeped into the hole she was in. Somehow, she just knew, Helene was out there, somewhere.

"Who did?"

"The man. The one that killed her." She realized then how much she hadn't told Max and how much she'd held back. "I see him in my dreams sometimes. You and I..." She shook her head not sure how to explain it. "In my dreams, we're a family. There's a little boy-"

"Jack," Max filled in.

She looked at him, confused.

He quirked a smile. "I'm starting to get how all this works. Keep going."

"We're in the kitchen. Jack gives me flowers. Then he comes in, but he's not him, sometimes he's him, but sometimes-"

"The man," Max clarified.

"He's a dog."

"A dog?"

"Baring his teeth and growling. It's almost like he stalks me for a few minutes and then he jumps at me." She shrugged. "Then I wake up."

"What do you think it means?"

"I think he wanted her. I think he came into her life and was a companion of sorts." That had to be how the dog-centric dreams came into play. He placed himself at her side, or the family's side, as a caring partner. In the end, he was none of those things. "Like a dog would, he stayed by their side. He became their companion, but, he wanted Helene, and when she didn't want him back, he killed her."

Max ran his hands through his hair and blew out a breath. "This is way more than I think we can handle. What are we supposed to do? Go dig random holes on those islands? There must be fifteen of them."

"I think I'd know it if I saw it," she told him. "I think we need to call in the troops and go out there on those kayaks like we originally planned to do."

"Are you sure?" He asked. "Last time..."

She shrugged and leaned in, kissing him and leaving him speechless. "Last time, I wasn't sure about anything. This time is different."

"Well, I'm exactly where I was last time. I'm with you, no matter what you want to do."

She smiled and hopped off the counter. "I know."

33

R osie looked at the people assembled on the beach at Smith's Cove. Quite a crew she'd amassed for herself. Dallas stood talking logistics with Max and Jay, while Wendy stood by her side overlooking the cove.

It really was a beautiful place. She imagined, when she wasn't being haunted, it would be a lovely place for a picnic or a relaxing afternoon.

Max sent her a smile and wink.

"You know, I'm not sure what would have happened if you hadn't come back."

Rosie bumped her shoulder against Wendy's. "Thanks for not giving up on me. I know I'm not easy."

Wendy bumped her back. "You were right, you know. I expected you to tell me about your skeletons, and I kept mine in the closet. It wasn't exactly fair."

"You'll tell me when you're ready."

Sometimes, baring your soul is easier said than done. Some scars ran too deep, and exposing them was no mean feat. So, she'd wait until Wendy was ready. For the first time, she'd make sure she was there when her friend needed a shoulder.

"You're like, Zen now," Wendy remarked. "It's freaking me out."

"Me too, kind of," Rosie admitted. "Clarity comes in the strangest of places."

"Like, my brother's bed?" Wendy sang with a laugh.

Rosie slapped her friend's arm. "Like the fifty-six south bus was what I meant, you perv."

"But, my brother's bed, right?"

Uh-oh, the eyebrow bob was back.

"Like your brother's bed," she agreed.

"I knew it!" Wendy yelled loud enough to make the men all turn to look at them.

Rosie hid her face while Wendy laughed.

"I can't take you anywhere," Rosie told her.

"Yeah, thanks, by the way. I've never hunted for a dead body before."

Rosie was saved from answering when Max, Dallas, and Jay joined them. She was still a little awestruck they'd all showed up just because she'd called and asked. No questions, no problems. They'd just shown up.

Max stopped next to her and slid his hand inside of hers.

"So, we're thinking we'll go in there." Dallas, all business, pointed to the far end of the cove. "Seems like that's the most likely place to put a boat in, and we'll see which of the islands gives you a hit."

"I'm going to stay back here," Wendy put in, a little more sedate than she'd just been. "You can call if you need anything, but really, I don't want to find a skeleton."

"Not high on my list either," Rosie agreed.

Max squeezed her hand. "Let's drag the kayaks over." He gestured to the two kayaks in the sand.

Okay, so he did most of the work. She tried to help, but clearly it was just for show, because he didn't need her at all to drag the boat. They got it to the edge of the water, and Max began checking the oars.

He looked up at her. "Do you want a life vest?"

She lifted her brows. "That's probably a good idea since I can't swim."

Max was upright in a flash. "Are you shitting me?"

She shook her head and held out her hand.

"You never told me that. All those times you got pulled down here into the water and you can't even swim?"

She shrugged. She may have left that part out.

"You should have said something," he told her.

She just met his stare in response. He was right, she probably should have said something. There were a lot of things she should have told him, but hadn't. It would take time to remember she could trust him with everything. Even then, like she told him, she might screw it up.

"Hey Max, I can't swim," she said.

He shook his head and grabbed the life vest, helping her slip her arms into it.

"Can't cook. Can't drive. Can't swim." He laid a kiss on her lips. "What am I going to do with you?"

There were a lot of things she couldn't do, Rosie thought, but she was getting there.

She looked up at him, her heart in her eyes.

"Teach me."

~

NO MORE THAN forty minutes later, Rosie felt a stirring beneath her skin. It started as a small niggle at first, the feeling that maybe they were getting close but as they neared one of the islands something lit up inside of her.

"That one." She pointed. "Right there."

It wasn't far from there they were paddling and it would have been the next one they went by. It had to be the one. Something inside her body was urging her to get there, now.

She gripped the sides of the kayak as they slowly made their way over there.

"Baby? You okay?" Max asked from behind her.

She shook her head no but answered yes anyway. "Yeah, but..."

"But what?"

She looked back at him. "I feel like I need to jump."

"Jump? Out of the boat?"

She held the sides of the kayak tightly.

"I can't explain it. It's like I need to get there, now. My body is telling me to jump."

"Don't jump!" he exploded, and she felt the boat move a little faster.

She huffed out a laugh. "I don't want to. I'm just telling you what's going on."

"Don't you let go of the boat!" he ordered. "We're almost there."

She had no plans to let go, and she held on until both boats beached.

She took off the life vest and left it with the kayak and just stood, staring at the rest of the island.

It was small in the grand scheme of land masses. No bigger than your average grocery store might be, it was covered with a dense growth of trees and underbrush.

She felt a hand slip into hers and expected to see Max, but it was Jay.

"Two crazies are better than one," he laughed.

She smiled, thankful he'd come. He'd shown up at Max's along with everyone else, had taken one look at her and had known everything was different. He'd seen her energies and knew she wasn't blocked anymore. His gift was so interesting, she reminded herself to sit with him and compare notes when this whole thing ended.

"Do you see anything?" she asked him. "Feel anything?"

She looked to the woods and scanned the surrounding areas. The trees held no interest to her. She could still hear the sucking sounds of Helene's killer's boots in the water. They had to look closer to the water.

"Why isn't she here?" she heard Max ask. "You'd think if she was so determined to get you here she'd show up and show you right where she is."

She was saved from answering when Jay spoke.

"Yeah, spirits and energies don't usually work in that kind of logical way."

"It's somewhere over there." Rosie pointed to the left-hand side.

Even though she couldn't see anything, she just knew it was somewhere over there.

"I agree," Jay added.

Dallas ended up leading them, with Max bringing up the rear. Jay kept hold of her hand as they traversed a narrow beach area and climbed over small rocky outcroppings.

Still none of the places felt right.

"So weird," she commented. "It has to be here."

Dallas stopped short and turned around. "It has to be now." His voice was low, and she looked at him in confusion.

"What do you mean?"

"That's what you said when we were at the Murphy's for Thanksgiving. When you..." he trailed off.

"When Helene," Max corrected.

"When she–you know."

Rosie did know, so she nodded.

"What did I say?"

"It has to be here. It has to be now," Dallas repeated, and then looked at the beach that butted up to the woods. "Even I feel it. It has to be here."

"It is," she told them. "She's here."

She could feel Helene's presence, even if she couldn't see her. The spirit was with them on the island, somewhere.

"Keep going," she urged them.

She was still holding Jay's hand, and she turned, holding her other hand out to Max, who took it without question.

Jay looked back at the chain, and then turned to Dallas with a smile.

"Not a chance," Dallas ground out.

Rosie felt some of her tension seep away.

She never would have been able to do this alone. She wouldn't have been able to center herself enough to figure out what she was supposed to do, and it wasn't just Max that grounded her, it was all of them.

It was Wendy, back on the shore, being the anchor for all of them.

It was Dallas, leading the charge without question.

It was Jay, answering the call and being by her side when she needed him.

It was Max, having her back, literally and physically.

They walked on, the rocky shores turning to softer sand as they reached the back side of the small island. At first, the sand was hard and packed under their feet, but soon it gave way to a softer muddier silt.

It wasn't two more steps when she heard the sand make a suction noise when Dallas pulled his foot up.

"Wait," she told them. She had to think, had to try to remember her dream and how many steps the killer had taken before he'd thrown the body down. "I need to think for a second."

Rosie closed her eyes, trying to remember.

"I might have missed some," she said vaguely. "But he took twelve steps that I counted."

"From where?" Max asked.

She shrugged, not having a definite answer. "From when that sound started." She pointed at Dallas's foot.

"Then we go twelve more steps and look around," Jay urged.

They did, making that noise all the while. Rosie didn't think she'd ever hear that noise again and not remember what happened to Helene, being thrown in that hole like garbage.

Those twelve steps seemed like an eternity, but by the eleventh, she knew they were in the right place.

"That's twelve," Dallas said when he stopped.

"Oh," Jay whispered, his head tilted as he looked toward the woods.

Rosie followed his gaze. She had no idea what Jay saw, his gifts being different than hers. She only knew what she saw.

"Oh," she agreed on her own whisper.

She'd done this kind of thing before. Granted, she'd been younger and less attuned to the other side, but she still had some experience. She'd been led to graves by ghosts or loved ones that had already crossed over. They tended to just stand there, waiting.

"It's glowing," she noted, dumbstruck.

Jay let out a harsh breath. "I'm so glad it's not just me that's seeing that."

Max stood behind her and put his hands gently on her shoulders. "What is it?"

She pointed to an area just fifteen feet from them at the base of a tree and grown over with moss.

"It's glowing," she told him. "From under the ground."

"What color do you see?" Jay asked, still staring.

Rosie gauged what she was seeing, like sunbeams coming from underground. "Yellow. Pale yellow."

"This is the weirdest fucking thing," Dallas murmured.

"Come on," Rosie said, heading the few feet up off the sand and into the shallow underbrush, grabbing Max's hand and pulling him along.

She crested a tiny hill and looked around at the area before turning her eyes up to the sky. She may not recognize the ground she was walking on, but she might recognize the trees that loomed above her. Looking up at the trees, she closed her eyes, imagining what Helene had showed her, lying in the bottom of her grave.

Dirt walls rose around her, towering and closing in. Rosie flexed her fingers and felt the damp earth between them, loose and gritty. The tall pines loomed overhead, her killer crouching over the hole.

"I never wanted this for us, Helene. I wanted to make a life with you. Why couldn't you just listen?"

Rosie flexed her hands in the earth again, but this time it was soft and mossy.

She opened her eyes and saw her hands, full of moss, as she knelt over the place she was sure Helene was buried.

She sat up a little and looked to see Max, kneeling next to her, watchful and concerned.

"What did you see?"

"She's here." She looked down at her hand and the ground below it. "She's always been here."

～

THOUGH ROSIE WAS willing to go out onto that island and help determine where Helene's remains might be, she did not have it in her stay and watch.

Even hours later, as police swarmed the cove and a forensics specialist came in from Jacksonville, she waited on the shore by Max's truck.

Three feet.

That's how deep she'd been buried out there.

It had taken Max and Dallas less than an hour to find her. She and Jay had paddled back to where Wendy was waiting and told her everything. They'd sat there, nearly silent, until they saw the two men headed their way.

Max had given her a solemn nod of his head, and she knew, it was over.

Helene would go now, to wherever it was spirits went.

It almost seemed anti-climactic in the wake of everything Helene had put Rosie through. No big fight scene to resolve the story. No psychic showdown to bring closure to all those involved.

Just one very sad, unmarked grave belonging to a woman that hadn't deserved to die.

"He'll see now."

Rosie looked to her right to find Helene leaning against the truck bed.

"He'll see that I never left."

Rosie agreed. Her son, no matter how old, could come to terms that his mother had never left him, she'd been taken away.

"I lived for him"

"I know," Rosie told her. "I dreamt he brought you flowers sometimes. Your son," she clarified.

Helene smiled, and Rosie took note that she wasn't nearly as disheveled as when she'd first appeared. Her skirt wasn't torn anymore, and every hair was in place. Like finding her remains had put her back together again.

"My husband used to bring me flowers every Sunday. When he first came to court me, I refused. I wanted to be a modern woman and have a career, so I turned him down flat. Every Sunday, rain or shine, he'd bring me flowers. If I wasn't home, he'd wait until I got there just so he could hand them to me himself. Oh, he wore me down eventually. Took more than a year, but he did it. After we had Jack, Jerry started having him bring me the flowers."

She looked at Rosie. "I would have never left my husband. Not for all the money in the world, and certainly not for that man."

"Who was he?"

"Who are you talking to?"

Helene blinked out.

Officer Murdoch casually leaned on his forearms against the hood of the truck, watching her.

"Myself," she lied.

Some habits died hard. Self-preservation wasn't something she'd probably ever give up.

"It wasn't a he," he continued at her blank stare. "Out there. It was a woman. Forensics already confirmed that." When she still said nothing, he kept going. "I heard you ask who he was, I just thought I'd clear that up."

Rosie had no reply for him, unsure of what he wanted from her.

"So, I'm still sorry about what happened a few months back down at the station. I really took what you said into consideration, and I've tried to listen more."

Rosie's brow furrowed, wondering where he was taking the conversation.

"Not that you say much." He gestured to his face. "But you're very expressive, and I know what happened left a bad taste in your mouth."

"What do you want?" she finally asked, hoping he'd stop talking and leave her alone.

She wasn't sure if it was the lingering memory of sitting in the jail cell that made her burn with embarrassment, or the tears she'd shed when he'd been standing right there. Either way, she had no desire to carry on any more conversations with him.

"I happened to see some of the reports Deputy Hardy brought by for Hunter. The ones that say your name isn't really Rosie Knight."

She narrowed her eyes at him. "Why do you care?"

He shrugged. "I don't. Not really." He waved his hand carelessly. "I mean, if you had a warrant out or were wanted for a crime, that would be one thing. Running from your past? I can see that. Plus, Hardy made it clear you weren't in any trouble."

With her walls down, she could see his aura, very similar to Dallas's, with its blue hue and pure motives, and she wondered what he wanted from her.

He scratched the back of his neck, looking suddenly sheepish.

"Here's the thing. I know, from reading those reports, you haven't exactly lived the high life, that it hasn't been easy for you. But I wanted to tell you, you can overcome that." He pulled a face. "You don't have to be who you used to be." With a sigh, he rubbed his face and began again. "My father was a drunk, and my mother loved him too much to leave him. He hit her, and when she was too beat up, he hit me. It took me a while to realize it, but I'm more than what he tried to make me. He wanted me to feel like I was nothing. That I'd never be anything to anyone. Do you know what I mean?"

He sent her a look that was more vulnerable than she'd ever imagined he could be.

She nodded, because yes, she knew exactly what he meant.

"My dad wasn't a model citizen, and in turn, I made it my life to be exactly the opposite. When I read your file and where you came from, the look on your face when you were sitting in that cell made a lot more sense."

He squinted and looked off into the distance, where Max and Dallas were finally being brought back to shore by a Police boat.

"They'll never fully understand where people like us come from," he told her. "To them, being poor or beaten or neglected is just an idea. Something that happens to other people. Me and you? We're the other people. But we can be more than they made us think." He looked at her and pushed off the hood of the truck. "I guess that's what I've been trying to get at here. That every second we spend dwelling on the past is just another second of the future we're missing. Don't miss out because of them." He slapped a hand on the hood. "Let your future be what you want it to be. Not what they told you it would be."

With that, he waked away, leaving Rosie completely and utterly flummoxed. He was right, of course. She couldn't let her past dictate her future for one more second, but she never expected such wise words from someone she'd written off.

That was on her. He'd never done anything to wrong her personally. He'd done his job. She'd been the one that had been jaded about him from the get-go.

She looked out at Max, who was now reaching the shore. He was the real push she'd needed to not live in the past anymore, to somehow merge Happy and Rosie and figure out who she wanted to be and what she wanted to do with her life.

But it was up to her to stand on her own two feet and decide her future. If that included Max, she'd be happy. Scared and completely inexperienced, but happy. He'd be the icing on top of the cake. The main course would be taking her life back. Though her mother was dead and Rosie had run well and far from her past, Max was right when he said she was still living in Happy's shadow.

It was time for her to step out of that shadow she was so used to hiding in.

34

Rosie scratched her nails across her palm.

She'd spent so long hiding from life, the fact that she'd sought out another person was enough to make her quake a bit on the inside.

But sitting on Max's porch swing, surrounded by all the Murphy's, she knew she was doing the right thing. The discovery of the remains in Smith's Cove had been huge news in Jacob's Beach. It had even made the national news in the weeks since forensics had dated the body to be more than sixty years old.

Rosie had thought the discovery of the remains would have given Helene the peace she so craved, but it hadn't. She remained on the edges of Rosie's existence. She followed, fairly unobtrusive, but still present, as if she needed more.

And she did.

She needed her son to know the truth.

It had taken some doing, but Max had finally convinced his father to call Jack, Helene's son, and let him know the remains that had been found were his mother's. Mr. Murphy worried about not having proof to back up his claims, with good reason. He didn't want to cause his cousin any more pain than necessary, but Max was insistent, and

Rosie was positive she could prove it to Jack if she could just get him face-to-face. And it had to be today. If they were going to do this, Rosie insisted, this was the day they had to do it.

"Are you sure about this?"

Mr. Murphy had been convinced of her talents when Rosie had told him about his mother following her around at work. Since then, he'd shown nothing but respect and concern for her. The feeling was foreign, and it reminded her of how hard it was getting used to Max's natural calming effect.

Rosie nodded in answer to Mr. Murphy's question.

"He needs to know."

Max's fingers toyed with her hair, his arm stretched out along the back of the porch swing behind her. Despite what had happened at the cove and the morbid reality surrounding them, they'd had a lovely few weeks together.

With her barriers finally down, Rosie was able to enjoy what it was to be in love with Max. The ins and outs of living every day and learning how he ticked. She knew he laughed a lot when he talked on the phone to his father. He had a pair of slippers, but he never wore them. He also had a pair of reading glasses, and he never wore those, either. He didn't like ketchup or chewy candy or jalapeños.

Max asked her nearly every day, in that casually passive way of his, if she was ready to move her things over to his house from her camper. She wasn't. Not yet. She couldn't pinpoint what it was, but the thought of losing her space made her very uncomfortable.

She loved Max. There was no more doubt swirling inside her. She'd fallen. End of story.

But losing the place that kept her safe wasn't something she felt she could give up. So, she paid her rent and kept it clean, even if she wasn't actively staying there all the time.

Rosie turned her head at the sound of a car pulling up to Max's house.

This had to be Jack.

Helene stood at the bottom of the porch steps, wringing her hands.

Since being found, the ghost had lost the look of a woman that had been murdered. Her hair was neat and tidy, her clothes a beautiful representation of the era.

She turned nervous eyes up to Rosie as the man got out of his car.

Rosie was nervous but hopeful that they'd all be able to close this chapter of their lives and find some peace.

Jack slowly made his way around the car. Rosie stood, watching as he unknowingly stopped right next to his mother.

He looked up at them, his face a blank mask, but his aura pulsing with the dark gray waves of doubt as he stood imposingly in a dark suit. Of course, he was doubtful, she reminded herself. He had no reason to believe.

"He looks just like his father," Helene whispered.

"Jack." Sam greeted him with a hand shake.

Christine followed, and Max pulled her along to do the same. Social graces were not her strong suit, her instincts urging her to stay on the porch and keep her distance. When he told her he didn't believe her, she would be far enough away that the sting might not hurt so bad.

Old habits die hard, she thought as she put her hand in Jack's at their introduction.

"I know you don't believe," she told him, wasting no time. His unemotional mask faltered, and she knew he wasn't someone used to hiding what he felt. "That's okay," she assured him.

"I came because I trust Sam, and if he says I need to hear what you have to say, then I believe him."

He believed Sam, but not her. He was making the difference clear.

"I understand," she assured him because she did. This was old hat to her.

"Why don't we sit down?" Christine motioned to the porch, where she had a spread of sweet tea and cookies set out like they were having a party.

Max led her to sit back on the porch swing while the others sat in chairs across from them.

Helene hovered behind Jack, just looking down at him with watery eyes.

"I always thought he'd grow up to be a carpenter," the spirit said, her eyes never leaving her son. "He loved to build things. Bird houses and little derby cars." She looked up at Rosie for a second, and then back to Jack. "I never imagined him behind a desk."

"So, you think that was my mother out there?" Jack asked.

She liked that he wasn't beating around the bush or walking on eggshells. The least she could do was respond in kind.

"I do," she told him. "I know it is."

"And how do you know?"

"Because she led me there."

Jack watched her then. Maybe looking for the lie in her eyes or a motive for her to tell such a tall tale. He wouldn't find any of those things.

"Is she here?" The doubt still clung to him, and Rosie knew he wasn't asking because he believed her.

He was testing her.

"She is." She pointed her finger over his shoulder. "She's right behind you."

His face fell and he paled.

"It's been very important to her that you know that she never left you. I think that's why she's still here."

"There were witnesses that saw her leaving town with another man," he argued. "Her clothes were gone. Her things, packed and gone when we got home. She left us."

"Never!" Helene blasted an angry wind around them, swirling around their heads, and they all lifted their hands to block their faces.

Rosie sent him a look when it died down a second later.

"That's your mother. Disagreeing." She shot her eyes to Helene, who still looked angry. "Stop it. Let him tell us what happened from his side."

Max's hand slipped inside of hers, and she was immediately grateful for the support.

"I'm supposed to believe my dead mother did that?" Jack asked skeptically.

Rosie waved him off with her free hand. "You'll believe what you believe. I can only tell you the truth as I know it, through your mother. What you do from there is up to you."

"And she's disagreeing. That she didn't pack her things and leave us."

"I'm curious about this witness that saw her leaving with a man. To be honest, I really don't know much of anything about this situation other than what I've learned from Mr. Murphy,"

"Sam," Max's father corrected.

"Sam," she parroted, the name still feeling awkwardly informal on her tongue.

"A family friend saw my mother embrace another man, put a suitcase in his car, and drive away with him. She never came back."

Rosie could see that talking about this was emotional for Jack. Though his story was void of what his personal experience was, it clearly affected him very deeply. His voice was rough with emotion, and his cheeks flushed the more they spoke.

Rosie narrowed her eyes, suspiciously. "And who was this family friend?"

"His name was Edwin. He was a friend of my father's."

"Were his initials EML?" she asked, remembering the jacket that was thrown over Helene's face when she was thrown into her grave.

Jack sat up, leaning back and away from her.

"They were," his voice was quiet.

"The police found a piece of clothing covering your mother's remains. It was a jacket. A suit jacket. The initials EML were embroidered on the lapel," she told him.

"I didn't hear that in the news. Did the police tell you that?" He looked to Max. "I know you have a friend on the department. Has he been sharing details with you two?"

Max shook his head. "Dallas isn't allowed to be involved with the investigation because he was one of the people that found the body."

Jack flicked his eyes back to Rosie. "Then how do you know?"

"Because I saw when he threw the jacket over her face. He thought she was looking at him."

He sucked in a breath and, if anything, tried to sit further away.

"What do you mean you saw it?"

"I know what Mr. Murphy told you. I know he told you about the things I see. They aren't always nice. They aren't pleasant. But your mother showed me that for a reason. The witness that told everyone she left town was the same man that killed her."

Helene nodded. "He was a monster."

"Your mother never liked him," Rosie continued. "She felt like he was a wolf in sheep's clothing. That he insinuated himself into your lives for some reason. He made her nervous. She showed me a time when you would bring her flowers."

Jack put a hand to his mouth.

"I can see the kitchen. I can smell the cookies, fresh from baking. She dusted them with powdered sugar because she knew you liked them that way. The walls were yellow, and there was an old wooden ice box instead of a refrigerator. Her apron was robin's egg blue, and there was a hole in the bottom left corner from where she snagged it on the nail-"

"-in the old wood shed," Jack finished quietly.

"He came home with you one of those days that you and your father brought her flowers. She sensed it then, the danger in him. But your father, he was so kind."

"So kind," Helene repeated.

"He couldn't see the bad in people. And so, he came around more and more. Sometimes, without your father. No matter how many times or how many ways she refused him, he persisted."

Rosie looked at Helene then, finally seeing everything the spirit had been trying to show her. "It was a day you were at work with your father. He came and told me there'd been an accident, in the woods. That you were hurt. I didn't understand why you weren't at work with Jerry, but I was blinded by instinct."

"Rosie?" Max's hand squeezed hers.

She was beyond him, now. Helene, while not possessing her in the traditional sense was driving the car. Rosie, like the rest of them, was just a bystander.

"We ran, headlong into the woods. I knew we were heading to the old tree house." Her eyes met Jack's. "I'd told you hundreds of times not to play there, but you always did anyway. When I got there, you were nowhere to be found. It was just Edwin and I alone." Rosie's head shook back and forth. "I said no. Just like every other time he expressed interest in me, I said no."

Rosie felt Max get up and walk away.

"He wouldn't listen," she continued. "I said no, and when he tried to force himself on me, I pushed him off. He-" She paused then and just stared at Jack. "I never would have left you. The only thing I ever wanted more than your father in this life, was you. I wanted to watch you laugh and love. I wanted to watch you grow into a young man. I wanted to sit in the front row at church and watch you get married while holding your father's hand. All I've ever wanted was you, Jackie."

Rosie blinked back into herself and looked around. Nothing had changed. Helene was still looking on expectantly from behind Jack while Sam and Christine looked on.

It was Max, kneeling at her feet, that was new.

She looked down at him.

"What are you doing?" she asked, feeling like she'd missed something.

He held up her hand to show her a big, ugly ring on her index finger.

"Jay gave it to me," he told her quietly. "A spirit blocker."

"Oh," she said stupidly.

"No more of that." His voice was firm. "Can she hear me?"

Helene nodded, and so did Rosie, passing the message along.

"No more, Helene."

"That was her." Jack sounded like he was somewhere between awe and questioning.

"She has a tendency to invite herself into Rosie's body," Max complained. "And she isn't welcome to do it."

"It's okay," Rosie assured him. Completely different than last time, she hadn't felt the eeriness of watching from the inside. It had been different somehow. She didn't feel like she'd been invaded or violated, as she had before.

"I'm sorry," Helene said softly, "I don't know how that happened."

Rosie looked up to Jack. "He wanted her, and when she said no, he dragged her through the woods, and he killed her. Telling you all that she left with another man was just him covering his tracks. That coat will turn out to be his, and that body will turn out to be your mother." Rosie shook her head at the injustice of it all. "She never left you. Not willingly, at least."

Jack was quiet for a moment.

"And you're saying it was Edwin that did this? That all this time, the man who was like an uncle to me, murdered my mother?"

Rosie held her hand out to Max and helped him back into the seat next to her.

"Edwin LaClaire," Helene spat.

Rosie repeated the name back to Jack, and some of the dark gray in his aura dissipated. It lingered, his doubt still present, but she was making headway.

"He was my father's best friend," Jack reasoned. "He sat with me at my father's funeral."

"Jerry's gone?" Helene's whisper held a note of pain Rosie knew could only be grief. Isolated as she must have been, Helene would never have known Jerry had passed.

"How long ago did your father die?" Rosie asked.

"Oh, going on fifteen years," Jack said. "Edwin died about five years after dad."

Max sat back. "So, the killer died?" He sounded mystified. "If this wasn't about getting justice for Helene, what was it for?"

Rosie pointed at the man in front of them. "It's for him. So he knows the truth."

"But," Max argued, "didn't she want justice? I thought this whole time, we were trying to find out what happened to her. You know, make things right."

Rosie shrugged. "I don't think she cares much about that. She just wants her son to know she loves him. That she'd never leave him."

A warm breeze crossed her face, her hair shifting and blowing. She closed her eyes, and with the wind came a wave of relief so great it made Rosie sag in her seat.

"Thank you," a voice whispered across her skin.

Rosie opened her eyes and Helene was gone.

35

By the time spring rolled around, things at the farm were bustling from sun-up to sun down, including Max.

Rosie spent most of her free time there, sometimes trying to help and sometimes just watching.

Hannah still followed Max everywhere, and even though she'd told him it wouldn't make difference, Max set up a dog bed in the corner of his bedroom.

Her own job kept her busy as well. Working for Wendy was as therapeutic as it had always been. Grandma Murphy still made an occasional appearance, but she'd toned down the Henry VIII routine.

She still rode her bike to the bus stop every day and rode the bus to work. She still went to her camper to clean and trade outfits every few days. There was something about having her own space that she couldn't give up. Deep down, she knew it was because it was something she worked so hard for, something all her own.

In theory, she wanted to say yes when Max asked her to move in. She wanted to be the kind of person who could make a quick change on the fly, but that wasn't her and Max knew it. He accepted her quietly placating rejections with ease and grace.

In fact, he had a knack for knowing when she needed a little space. She'd go to leave for work one morning, and he'd say, "Why don't you call me from the trailer when you're ready to be picked up tonight?"

There were no questions about why she might want to go to the trailer.

There was no pressure that she should invite him.

There wasn't even any assumption she'd go back to his house when it was all said and done.

Once in a while, when she was out there, Dallas would swing by unannounced.

"Sometimes I drive by. Just to make sure everything's secure," he explained once.

Some nights, he'd sit on the patio and watch the woods with her. Some nights, he'd talk about missing his family a little. He wasn't the most talkative guy when it came to his feelings. She knew how he felt, so she didn't push. Some nights, he asked about her past.

There were times she told him some things.

But there were still times it hurt too much.

Rosie finished making Max's bed and gathered their laundry. After putting it in the machine, she grabbed a half a mug full of coffee and headed for the porch.

It was fun, watching the interns working the farm. Max was in his big spring planting rush and had all hands on deck. She could watch from the porch swing as they drove tractors to the fields and pushed wheelbarrows around.

Last week, she'd seen Denny, an intern, with a love seat on a pallet, headed out to the field. That had stumped her, but she knew she'd see it, eventually. Max would tell her when he was ready.

A love seat, she wondered with a snort. What was he up to now?

~

"ARE YOUR EYES CLOSED?" Max asked, the smile in his voice loud and clear.

357

"Your hands are covering my eyes," she deadpanned. "What difference does it make?"

He kissed the back of her head. "Humor me,"

She did, and it wasn't hard at all. "My eyes are closed."

He was walking her through the back field, now grown up with corn. The ground was uneven under her feet, but she trusted Max to not let her fall and eat dirt.

"Where are you taking me?" she asked with a smile of her own.

"It's a surprise," he said.

"Is it a good one?"

He laughed. "Why would I get you a bad surprise?"

She shrugged.

"It's a good one," he assured her. "Just keep your eyes closed and keep walking until I tell you to stop."

He led her through the fields until she felt grass under her feet again. Even then, they walked for a ways before he stopped, never taking his hands off her eyes.

"Can I look now?" she asked.

"Now, I'm nervous," he admitted. "Maybe I overstepped."

"Now you're making me nervous," she told him, reaching up and pulling his hands down.

"Oh," she breathed.

If there was anything she had dared to imagine, this would not have ever made the list. Not even close.

"Oh," she said again.

"Is it–" he broke off. "Is it too much?"

It was her trailer.

Not her trailer. A trailer. Happy string lights, patio chairs outside and all. She turned back around and still saw the lights of Max's house in the distance.

She looked back at the trailer.

There were lights on inside, and she could see books beyond the curtains and pictures on the walls.

She looked at Max.

"Is this-" She barely dared to ask on the off chance it wasn't real. What if it wasn't for her? What if this was something else?

"It's for you," he said, not making her ask. "It's yours. If you want it."

"Why would you do this?" she breathed.

"Because I want you here with me. On the farm. Forever."

Rosie turned her head to look at him.

"But I know you like space, and that's okay, too. I just was hoping you'd be okay with having a space here."

He'd recreated her safe place in his safe place.

Maybe, together, it could be their space.

"You did this for me?"

It sounded so ridiculous to ask. Of course he'd done it for her.

"Baby, I'd do anything for you," he told her, pulling her into a hug. "If you hate it, we'll get rid of it. I just wanted you to have somewhere you could go if you needed it."

"Without having to keep my trailer," she said, understanding.

"If you want to keep the other place, we can. Shit, I'll buy the whole damn thing if you want, and you can go there any time." He shook his head. "This is not coming out the way I want it to." He held her out by her shoulders and spoke directly to her. "I made you this. I've asked you dozens of times to move in with me, and you always tell me no. I know part of the reason is you like to have your own space. I wanted you to see I'm fine with you having your own space. I want you to have your own space, here."

"I love it," she admitted, letting him and his nerves off the hook.

Having her own place but still on the farm solved one of her hang-ups.

"Are you sure?"

She smiled and lifted onto her toes, pressing a kiss to his lips.

"I'm sure." Rosie grabbed his hand and led him to the camper. "Come show me!"

He followed with a laugh. "It's just like your other one."

She did the ridiculous eyebrow bob. "So, there's a bed?"

Max's pace quickened until he reached her and scooped her up. "There's a bed."

～

APRIL DAWNED, and so did the warm weather. Rosie rolled over and looked at Max, taking a rare Sunday morning to sleep in. He'd gotten a haircut and was back to looking like the clean-cut boy next door.

She tried to imagine him, drunk in a jail cell, but couldn't. That's what he'd been arrested for. Drunk and disorderly. He'd been twenty-two and dumb, he'd told her.

She just couldn't see it.

She'd seen drunk and disorderly. Heck, she'd lived with drunk and disorderly.

He'd been so ashamed when he'd told her, like somehow, his one mistake had tarnished his whole life.

But it hadn't. Wasn't his life more than the mistakes he'd made? Hadn't he worked hard enough to overcome those? Wasn't he a better person than that?

He'd looked at her and asked if she was the pot or the kettle.

Maybe he was right. Maybe officer Murdoch was right.

She was worth more than her past. Hadn't she done enough to be a good person, to overcome what her mother had done?

She was trying. That was all she could say for herself. Trying was something she could get up and do every single day.

And she got to do it next to the man lying next to her.

Rosie reached out and poked his shoulder.

He mumbled something and rolled over to face her.

"Hmmm," he hummed.

"It's my birthday," she whispered.

His eyes popped open. "Seriously?"

She smiled at his expression and nodded.

"Why didn't you tell me? I would have gotten you something. Done something. Taken you out to dinner."

"You've given me plenty," she told him. "More than I would have ever thought to ask for."

Max grabbed the cover over his shoulder and pulled it while he moved on top of her.

"Well, I would have gotten you more." He laid a series of kisses on her neck. "Now, you'll have to get by with what I've got on me."

Rosie laughed and looked down. "You've got nothing on you."

"We'll make do."

~

"You should be ready for me now," the woman said.

Rosie was lying in Max's bed, his arms around her.

The woman she'd seen in her dreams a few times was sitting in the chair across from Max's bed.

"Am I asleep?" Rosie asked.

"For now. But I'm coming for you."

"Why?"

"It's been long enough." She shrugged. "I've been looking for you for a long time."

"For me? Why?"

"I didn't know about you until after you ran. Once in a while, I get a good read on you and we connect, but other times, you go dark. You're good at building your walls up. Don't you remember me?"

"Should I?" Rosie asked, sitting up, holding the sheet to her chest.

"We've met before, in dreams. Sometimes, you push me out. Sometimes, you recognize me right away."

"I don't understand."

"You will." The woman smiled and blinked out of Max's room. "Time to wake up now," she said, her voice thundering in Rosie's head.

~

ROSIE'S BODY jackknifed off the bed. A sense of urgency filled her as she flung the covers off and jumped out of bed.

"What's the matter?" Max asked, concerned but sluggish.

"She's coming for me," Rosie told him. She could feel a desperate clawing inside of her pushing her to go.

Rosie didn't know where she needed to go or what she needed to do, she just knew she had to do something, right now.

Max followed suit and got dressed.

"What do you mean she's coming? Who's coming?"

"I don't know." Rosie pulled her skirt on. "She came to me again and said I need to wake up. That she's coming for me."

Max's head popped through the neckhole of his t-shirt. "Who came to you? The lady that stands on the side all creepy and not saying anything?"

She'd tried to explain the dreams to Max, but it always sounded convoluted and hard to convey.

"Yes," Rosie said. "And she said, *I'm coming for you.*"

"Wait." He grabbed her arm when she tried to leave the bedroom. "Baby, can we not go running headlong into a stranger?"

She shook her head. "I have to go."

"Where are we going?"

"I don't know."

He followed her down the stairs and straight out the front door.

Rosie stopped short.

The woman was leaning against a car, arms crossed as she waited. Her hair was deep brown, hanging around her shoulders and cascading down her back. There was a small smile on her face, familiar in a way that made a tingle race up Rosie's spine.

Her eyes were the same shade as Rosie's, minus the spot.

Rosie grabbed for the rail to steady herself.

"It's you," Rosie said.

The woman nodded. "I'm Toby."

"Wait," Max started.

"Mom wasn't great with names," Toby said, her eyes boring into Rosie's. "Toby is far better than October."

362

"Try living with Happy for a while," Rosie murmured. "You're..."

"Your sister," Toby confirmed.

"Holy. Shit," Max breathed. "How?"

"The usual way, I'd imagine," Toby mused.

"She's my sister." Rosie stood rooted in place.

She had a sister? A real, blood-related family member.

"I was in foster care by the time you were born," Toby said, pushing off the car and walking to the porch. "In fact, it wasn't until Butch Hardy started digging around that anyone brought up the fact that our mother had already lost custody of one child."

"How does that happen?" Max asked, slipping a hand in Rosie's.

She was glad for his support. Without it, she'd be floating into a void untethered.

"It's a complicated system with complicated problems. In his search for Happy, Butch stumbled across me. His face was about the same as yours is now, I'd say. He's a good guy that made some shitty mistakes and paid for them. His guilt helped me get through school and land my first job."

"You're my..."

"Sister," Toby repeated, again. "I thought you'd have figured it out by now. We look enough alike."

~

"You okay?" Max asked quietly.

Was she okay? There was a quivering rooted in her heart. Something emanating from deep in her soul at the thought of having a sister. Someone that somehow belonged to her, and that she might belong to someone else.

She looked up at Max and let out a watery laugh.

"You know. I think I finally am."

Jenni M Rose is a sometimes writer with an all the time imagination.

Jenni can usually be found at the grocery store or driving her kids from place to place. More often than not, she can be seen typing away in the waiting rooms of local gymnastics gyms or dance studios.

Married mom, business owner, writer, taxi driver, accidental chicken lady.

Made in the USA
Las Vegas, NV
13 January 2025